4/21

DUSTBORN

DUSTBORN

ERIN BOWMAN

HOUGHTON MIFFLIN HARCOURT

BOSTON   NEW YORK

hmhbooks.com

The text was set in Janson MT Std.
Map illustration © 2021 by Virginia Allyn
Interior illustrations © 2021 by Matt Griffin
Cover and interior design by Mary Claire Cruz

The Library of Congress Cataloging-in-Publication data is on file.

ISBN: 978-0-358-24443-1

Manufactured in the United States of America
DOC 10 9 8 7 6 5 4 3 2 1
4500820610

For anyone currently navigating a dust storm —
may there be clear skies ahead.

. . . all come from dust,
and to dust all return.

— ECCLESIASTES 3:20

NORTH

BLUE STAR

GODS' STAR

GREEN STAR

BACKBONE

DAM

BEDROCK

IRON MINES

TUNNEL

HARLIE'S HOPE

NORTH TOWER

THE BARREL

MESA

POWDER TOWN

BURNING GROUND

EAST TOWER

DAM

WEST TOWER

ALKALI LAKE

THE SERPENT RIVER

DEAD RIVER

SOUTH TOWER

DAM

ZULY'S WATCHTOWER

THE ARK

THE OLD COAST

OCEAN RIG

THE WASTES

I

THE
WASTES

CHAPTER ONE

There's a storm coming.

I can see it out across the plains, a cloud of haze along the horizon that's bearing down on Dead River like a blanket of shadow. It's a good four clicks off, maybe more, but dust storms move fast. Already the threadbare flags on the huts flap wildly.

I hurry on to the lake. "Big storm to the west," I call out to Old Fang. The wrinkled trapper is kneeling on the dock beside the dam, checking my traps for frogs or fish, not that we get many of either anymore. Dead River's been slowly dying for years, the lake drying up and the banks growing wider. I've had to extend the dock several times just so the traps can still sit in water.

Old Fang searches out the storm. The churning clouds crackle and glint with lightning. "That's the second one in ten days. We can't get a break."

It's not untrue. "Any catch?"

He shakes his head. We should have moved in the winter, but now the endless stink of summer is ahead of us. There's no chance of a pilgrimage for at least four moons, not unless we want to die in the heat, and even the damn frogs have had the sense to move on. Of course, frogs can't read the stars, and I know we need to have faith. The night skies warn of dangers ahead, of dry land and dust-caked tongues, but if we just sit tight, they also promise a bounty. Flowing rivers. Green land. There's to be a rebirth. I've seen it with my own eyes, and even before I could see it, there was Indie pointing it out to me in her sisterly way, and before she could read the stars, there was Ma, pointing it out to both of us. Still, it's hard to keep believing the sky when every sign here, on the land, shows nothing but death and decay.

Old Fang squints at the empty buckets I'm carrying, secured to the piece of driftwood I've got propped on my shoulders. "You grab the haul," he grunts. "I'll rally the pack."

From back near camp, Ma's voice is audible on the wind. She's already shouting orders to our people. I also catch the twinkle of my bone chimes, and once those start singing, it means a hell of a storm. Ma'll need all the help she can get.

I give Old Fang a quick nod, and he hobbles off. I pull my scarf over my mouth and nose, looping the loose end over my head to protect some of my hair. Then I scamper down the bank and sprint across the cracked, parched lakebed, the buckets clipping my hips as I run. Used to be I could grab a haul right from the bank. The river might have always been "dead," flowing only in the spring or after a rare rain, but the lake was a beauty when we first arrived. Now I have to go out a ways to reach water. Not even the dam helps much anymore.

The hard earth becomes damp dirt underfoot, then sticky mud, then shallows. I trudge out to my shins and throw down the buckets, listening to the glorious sound of water gurgling into their depths before I heave them back out. The flags along the dam are whipping like mad now, and the hazy cloud to the west is looking more like a wall of dust.

"Rot," I mutter. I can't run with the buckets full, but I've perfected a straight-legged scuttle over the years, and I start back as fast as I can.

Once I'm up the bank, I can see the huts clearly. Our pack is scrambling—pulling scrub-woven blankets over the struggling crop, yanking clean clothes from the lines, ushering our four goats and lone mule into the stable, and tying down sheets of scrap metal to shield the animals from the worst of the dust. Flint was supposed to bring fresh meat soon—jackrabbit, he'd promised—but the trader's not going to make it in this storm.

The wind picks up, pushing at my back. Instinctively I angle my head down, wishing for my goggles. They go everywhere with me and are a prime good pair. Real Old World tech, nothing like the cheap, slapdash ones the traders carry that are made of glass and fraying binds. Mine fit true, practically adhering to my face and blocking out all debris, and though the eyepiece can fog like glass, it won't crack or break like the ones the traders peddle. I'm not sure what sort of magic they're carved from. The leather head strap's failing for the first time in all the years I've owned my pair, and I started patching it this morning. Should have waited until sundown and repaired them from my bed mat. It's not worth going anywhere without them during the day. You never know when a storm might hit, and here I am without them, having dropped them on the table, half mended, as I raced for the buckets when the wind kicked up.

Squinting through the dust, I can tell most of our pack has

retreated to the safety of their huts. Old Fang is barking orders at his granddaughter, Pewter. "Just leave it," he shouts from the mouth of his home. At barely thirteen, Pewter's no match for the heavy sheet of scrap metal she's trying to use to smother the central bonfire. "The dust'll see to it."

True, but there's always a chance the wind will knock embers into a hut first, and then the scrub and straw-packed roof would be ablaze in minutes.

Pewter's eyes cut across the camp to me, my buckets. Water would kill the flames instantly, but it's too precious to waste. I give her a curt nod, telling her I agree with Old Fang. She leaves the scrap metal flopped over the bonfire and runs for her grandfather. I watch her long braid duck past him, and then he's inside too, lowering the blanket across the hut's doorway and cinching it tight.

"Delta!" Ma is waiting in the mouth of the place we call home, waving her arms feverishly.

Water sloshes down my side as the strengthening wind batters my frame and rubble pelts my back. I'm nearly to the hut when a crack of lightning strikes the scrap metal Pewter had been struggling with. Sparks fly. I flinch with shock, lose my footing. My knees hit earth, and I reach out instinctively to stop my fall. That's all it takes. With the weight of the buckets off kilter, one of them plummets and hits the ground. I lose the other trying to save the first.

The greedy soil soaks up the water.

"No." My hands fly over the damp dirt, patting, slapping, as if I can will the water back into the bucket.

"Delta!" my mother yells again.

I scramble to my feet, grab the empty buckets, and stagger the last few strides to our hut. Ma grabs my arm and hauls me inside.

"Right foolish of you," she scolds. "What good would water do when we can't even boil it under the hold?"

"The lake's cleanish. Some water sounded better than none."

"We've got plenty of purified water stored."

"Last I checked, we had four jars."

"It's enough."

"Not if the storm lasts more than a day, and with Indie being pregnant, I fig—"

"Delta!" There's a crease in her brow, an edge of fire in her tone. I suck my bottom lip to keep myself from saying any more, and I taste dirt. "Just get under with your sister."

I leave her to securing the door and head into the cellar, which isn't much more than a crawlspace. We'll spend the next few hours —maybe even days—hunched to half-height beneath the hut, old sheets pinned overhead to keep rubble and dust from falling on us. Only thing this cellar is good for is storage and sleeping. It's cool, this far into the earth. I especially don't mind it on summer evenings. But being stuck down here when you're not sure when you can go back up is a kind of torture.

At the bottom of the wooden steps, I find Indie reclining on her mat, the curve of her belly heaving as she breathes. "Thanks for trying with the water," she says. "It was kind of you."

"It was foolish," Ma repeats, coming down the steps behind me and yanking the door shut. The cellar is swallowed in darkness until Indie gets a candle going with the flint.

Overhead, the storm front crashes into the hut with a howl. Dust filters through the door, and pebbles gather in the hanging ceiling sheets with soft *pfffits*. Someday, one of these storms is going to cause the hut to collapse on us, or maybe just last so long that we suffocate in the cramped, clouded air.

Rotten place. Rotten weather. Rotten land.

We need to move.

We *can't* move.

Like always, there's no good answer.

Ma pulls our jars of water from the shelves—bottled just yesterday after boiling—and passes them out. One for me, one for her, and two for Indie. Skies damn her for getting pregnant. It's one thing to want a romp and another to do it when the window's not right. And with Clay, of all people. That trader couldn't keep his mouth shut if his life depended on it, and half of what he says is a farce. I bet he jawed her ear off even during the act.

Curse him *and* Indie. The pack doesn't need another mouth to feed. A fresh set of hands, sure, but the babe won't be any real help for at least five years, probably more.

I take a tiny swig of water—just enough to clean the dust from my lips—then screw the lid on, marveling at how it fits perfectly, even after all these years. I spend a bit of time hobbling together inventions for our pack—like the lake trap or bone chimes—and I can't even guess at how you'd make these jars and their locking lids. I could say that about all Old World tech, though.

"Did you talk to Astra yet?" I ask as Ma settles onto her mat.

She breathes out a tired sigh. "It won't help."

"If anyone can change Old Fang's mind, it's her. She's his niece."

Our pack is mostly female, but Old Fang still has the final say on all decisions because he's the oldest.

Indie raises a brow, then says, "Old Fang won't move us unless the Gods' Star fell into his hands and instructed him where to travel, and even then, he'd probably be suspicious." I snort, and Ma shoots us a look. Indie smoothes her skirt. "Besides, nothing good comes of leaving."

"Yes," Ma agrees. "Think of Alkali Lake."

I don't need to think about it. It haunts my dreams, and my back prickles at its mention even now, the brand on my skin seeming to burn. But nothing good comes of staying, either.

I was a kid when we left to settle at Dead River—just nine years old—and the half of the pack that stayed behind didn't live longer than another week. According to a trader, it was a raid. He trudged into our camp with his rickshaw and the gruesome news, and Old Fang's been spooked ever since.

I used to think it was cowardly, giving in to fear like that. But lately, every time traders come through, they bring stories of grisly deaths and broken homes. There are bands of raiders roaming the wastes. The only safe place is one you can defend. We can barely do that, but no one wants our dying chunk of land. There's no future here.

"We won't have enough water to make it through another summer," I argue. "This one, maybe, but not next. The well's practically dry, and the lake will follow. Maybe if we knew how to read the map . . ."

"No one knows how to read it."

"Then if we just tried Powder Town, found someone there who can."

"We show that map to no one, Delta. Not unless——"

"We trust them with our lives," I finish. "I know."

I don't add that it's been ages since I believed the map led anywhere. If it did, our pack would have found it long before the markings were branded onto my skin. But at this point I'm willing to say anything—propose anything—that might spring us to action.

"Besides," Ma goes on, "Powder Town is a good fifty clicks north, and there's no guarantee we'd even make it there alive."

"The traders make it," I point out.

"The traders are young. Healthy. One lone man, with nothing to defend but himself and his goods, and even then, think of how many times Clay has shown up here telling us that his most valuable wares had been robbed."

"Because he's a rusted idiot," I mutter.

Indie shoots me a wounded glance, and I fall quiet.

"We are fourteen people, mostly women," Ma continues. "Old Fang is nearing seventy. Brooke's girl is just four, and Indie will have a newborn in a matter of weeks. That is no herd fit for moving. We'd be easy prey."

"We'll be easy prey here, too, once we're dehydrated and starved. We've gotta go someplace better. *Anywhere* but Dead River. The crops are struggling. Potatoes and turnips smaller than we've seen in years. And the corn should be taller by now, right Indie?"

She opens her mouth to answer, but Ma cuts her off. "We're not leaving, and that's the end of it. The stars say a bounty is coming. The earth will be fertile again soon."

"They've said *soon* for years and could say it for decades more."

"Where is your faith?" Her eyes bore into me, sharp and vicious. "This is why the gods deserted us. This is why we're stuck on this dying earth. We are being tested, Delta. If we prove we are worthy, they will return, as will the riches of water and crop."

The wind howls outside, as if to agree. Rubble plinks above, joining what's already gathered on the blankets.

"I'll have no more talk of this." Ma turns to the shelves. "Here. Eat." She passes a strip of jerky to each of us.

"Delta only wants what's best for us, Marin." Ever since Indie got with child she's been calling Ma by her given name, as if it proves she's not a kid herself anymore. I don't think we've been kids for a very long time. Certainly not since Alkali Lake.

Ma just *humphs* and lies down on her mat. I gnaw on my jerky and take another small sip from my jar. Smack dust from my limbs. Unbelt my boots by their leather straps and kick them off so they can dry.

When Ma falls asleep, Indie says, "I grabbed your goggles. Thought you'd want to work on them while we're stuck down here." She passes them over, along with the tools.

"Thanks," I say, and immediately go to work, punching holes through the leather head strap with the awl. Indie watches me in silence.

"Think if we polished a piece of quartz real good, we could

convince Old Fang it's a fallen star?" she says finally. "Argue it's a sign from the gods that we need to move?"

"He won't buy that."

"You're right. We should polish a turd instead."

I snort again, and she giggles, one hand on her belly.

"So, are you going to do the honors of gathering patties from the stable, or is it on me?" she asks.

We snicker together until Ma mutters in her sleep. Indie pats the mat beside her, and I scoot nearer.

We sit shoulder to shoulder, our backs against the dirt wall. I set the awl aside and move on to stitching. I can still remember when I was smaller than her, my head only coming up to her shoulder. She'd tell me stories passed down through the pack, or on clear nights, when we weren't stuck underground from a storm, she'd point at the glinting sky and marvel at its beauty.

It still amazes me, how it can be so beautiful while everything down here dies.

As though she can hear my thoughts, Indie whispers, "In all seriousness, Delta, we shouldn't talk about the stars that way. The gods might hear."

"In the cellar? When we're half buried in dirt?" I raise an eyebrow, and she smiles. It's not a real smile, just an I'll-humor-you one. She's been doing that a lot since she got pregnant, still making jokes but then seeming to regret it, forcing herself to be the parent between us. Her green eyes glimmer, and I'm struck by how unalike we are. We share a mother, but our pas are different, and in the candlelight it's obvious. Her with green eyes, me with brown. Her nose broad and mine a narrow bridge. Her hair a shade of straw and mine as dark as the night. We've never met our fathers, though, and in this way, we're the same. Tied to Ma. Tied to the pack. Tied to Dead River.

"They'll come back for us—the gods. You have to believe that."

"I believe it, Indie." I tighten a stitch. "At least I'm trying to."

Her eyes go wide.

"Blasphemous, I know," I tease, but she's not laughing. She's looking only at her lap, her mouth twisted in concern. "It's just hard to accept that they'll return before it's too late. I know what happened last time we lost faith. I'll never forget what happened to Asher, or all the others we left behind at Alkali Lake, but if we—"

Indie's hand clasps over my wrist, stopping my work on the goggles.

"Delta?" she says, her voice small against the raging wind. "I think my waters just broke."

CHAPTER TWO

No. That can't be right. Indie's got another moon still, maybe a bit less. Either way, it's too early. But then she's on her feet and shaking Ma awake, muttering adamantly, "Marin. It's the baby. The baby's coming."

I stand there useless as Ma inspects Indie's skirt and underthings. "There's not enough for it to be your bag of waters."

"It's something," she insists.

"Could also be nothing to worry about. Especially if contractions don't come."

But deep into the night, when the storm is still howling around the hut, Indie starts complaining of pressure in her stomach. There's not an ounce of sarcasm in her tone, and she hasn't cracked a joke since before we sat shoulder to shoulder against the wall. That's an unnaturally long time for her to remain serious. She's begun to sweat too, and Ma worries aloud because Indie's pain waves aren't coming in any predictable increment.

"Should I get Astra?" I ask. Ma's best friend has delivered every baby in our pack.

"Not in this weather," Ma answers. "Just soak a rag in water for Indie's head." She holds my sister's hand while she lies panting on the mat.

I do as I'm told, hating to watch some of the water bead to the dirt floor, wasted. Indie grimaces when I set the damp cloth on her brow.

"Easy breaths, Indie," Ma tells her. "Low and long." She coaches her through the night. I help when I'm needed, finish the work on my goggles when I'm not, and somehow manage to sleep a bit in between.

When dawn breaks, the storm's gone, taking the dust with it, but Indie's deteriorated. She's a sweaty mess, and when Astra comes to check on her, I hear her and Ma discussing a fever.

"Flint's due soon," I offer. "Maybe he'll stop in today and we can send him to Zuly's for a tonic."

"Indie doesn't have that long," Astra says, crouched beside Indie's mat.

"How can she not have a day and a night? She's perfectly healthy. She was in the fields working just yesterday."

"Something's wrong. Something beyond my means. She needs to see Zuly. Someone needs to take her today."

I suck in a breath. Needing a tonic from Zuly is bad enough as it is, but to have to go straight to the Ark, to venture out into the wastes to get to her tanker . . . Only the desperate do that, the souls already on death's doorstep.

"Delta . . ." Ma begins, but I don't need to see the agony in her eyes or even hear her plead. I nod. This is my sister. What other choice do I have?

Ma rushes to our storage shelves, gathering anything of value that we might be able to trade. Three of her glass jars, one filled with salt, another flour, and the third baking soda. Then a loaf of bread for good measure and a handful of our pathetic potatoes. She wraps it all in a towel and tucks it into my rucksack.

"What if there's another storm?" Astra asks as I shoulder the bag.

"They rarely strike back to back, and if I move fast, I can be to Zuly's by nightfall."

"Indie is in no state to walk."

"I'll tow her. There's a dragger in the stable. I used it to move driftwood around while extending the dock. I can use it to move Indie, too."

"Be careful," Ma says, and presses a kiss into my forehead. "Trust—"

"—no one," I finish.

Trust no one. The rule of the wastes, the law of the land, our guiding order since Alkali Lake.

I slip upstairs and run to retrieve the dragger. Our camp has been transformed by the storm. The bonfire is a heaping mound of sand, and the huts all look lopsided now, sand and dirt piled up on their western sides, where the wind blew in.

Pewter's at the stable, checking the animals. "Delta," she gasps, startled by my sudden appearance. She meets my eyes, then frowns. "What's wrong?"

"It's Indie. I'm taking her to Zuly's." I pull ropes and harnesses from the hooks until I reach the dragger.

"But that's . . . You can't. It's not safe."

"No. But someone has to take her." I throw the dragger down, use a broom to clear it off.

"Let me help." Pewter shakes the braided handle, sending

dust scattering, then reaches for the broom. I let her take it. She's been helping me patch a leak in the dam lately, and I've seen what an efficient worker she is. As she cleans, I return the other ropes to their hooks, and by the time we get the dragger outside, a small crowd has gathered, wide-eyed and worried. Zuly's care comes to us by traders carrying meds. We never go to her. They know as much as I do that this is bad.

Ma and Astra help me load Indie onto the dragger, and Pewter brings two jars of fresh water from Old Fang's stores, then pours them into my waterskin. I race through goodbyes, hugging everyone in turn, even Astra's boy, Cobel, who's fifteen and declared himself too big for hugs five years ago. Then I slip the dragger's braided handle over my shoulder and across my torso and trudge off. It's hardest for the first few steps, but once I get moving, the sledge skids over the ground with a bit less fight.

When I reach the last hut of our camp, I can't help it — I pause and look over my shoulder. The whole pack's watching. They'll wait eagerly for our return, and as they do, they'll miss Indie most. I might build tools and extend docks and design traps, but I don't make people laugh the way Indie does. I can't tell a good story or distract from the drought or light up a hut when I enter.

I raise a hand in farewell.

Old Fang mirrors the gesture.

The rest of them follow suit.

Even Vee, nearing Old Fang's age and typically too stoic to get sentimental. The only person who doesn't wave is Ma. She clutches both hands to her chest, eyes pained as she watches us — the only blood she has left in the world — venture into the wastes.

There's nothing this way but dirt and sand and the dry beds of Dead River. I've never been far beyond camp except to check traps for jackrabbits and quail, but I know if I follow the river south, it will eventually open onto the parched ocean bed. If I carry on from there, I'll run into Zuly.

Flint told me the way once, with precise directions. I had to give him some moonblitz to even get him talking, but I trust his word more than Clay's. Not every trader is reliable.

If Indie were with it enough to talk, she'd say that's because I rolled with Flint once over the winter and now I have a bias. I wonder if that's what makes her oblivious to Clay's faults, if sharing something so intimate makes you drop your guard, grow blind to the things that matter. I hope not. I can't have Flint's directions steer me wrong.

By midday, I'm tiring. The dragger strap has managed to rub me raw near my neck, even with the collar of my leather jacket protecting my skin. My muscles are racked with exhaustion, my lips cracked. I've sweated through most of my clothes, but I know better than to take off layers. It would only be a brief escape from the heat, and if I stripped enough to give my skin a chance to breathe, I'd be sunburned within an hour. Besides, old habits don't die. The more layers, the better. The more hidden my back, the safer.

I trudge on until a small dust squall hits without warning. Once my goggles are pulled into place, I throw a blanket over Indie to protect her from any debris. I don't trust myself to move during the squall, so I stay crouched beside her, breathing through my nose, with my scarf wrapped up over most of my face. I clench Indie's palm beneath the blanket. There's nothing to worry about —it's only the storms you can see coming, bearing down like a wall, that tend to last any length of time—but it's impossible to keep my mind from wandering. What if this squall strengthens? What if we're stuck out here without shelter, breathing in dust while we're buried, one grain of sand at a time?

If Indie is concerned, she doesn't show it. Her hand remains limp in mine, clammy. I worry about her face. She's not wearing goggles, and sand is surely finding its way through the woven blanket. It's a good thing she's barely conscious. Her eyes are probably closed.

To my relief, the wind suddenly lets up and the squall dies as quickly as it hit. Dust settles in delicate swirls.

I yank the blanket off Indie. "You all right?"

She nods weakly. It's not like her to be so quiet. Any other day, she'd at least give me a sarcastic *Scorched skies, no*. But to only nod . . . I need to move faster.

I shove to my feet. My tracks are gone, and the sun hangs high overhead. I turn in circles, trying to find the wide, flat marks of the dragger. There's nothing. The brief flurry of dust has hidden everything.

Grumbling, I fiddle with the neck of my jacket. The zipper's been broken since I bartered it from Flint a few years back, but I've patched it up good, putting reinforcements over the elbows and a lone button near the throat so I can hold my scarf in place and keep the collar flipped up to protect the back of my neck. I unbutton it now and reach between my scarf and woven undershirt until my fingers find a leather cord. With a tug, I pull my necklace into view and hold it out before me. Hanging from the cord is a black lodestone, shaped like two pyramids stacked together, one summit pointing to the sky, the other to my feet. A small indentation is carved into one of the faces.

The lodestone spins freely for a moment, its metallic luster glinting in the sun. Then it quivers to a standstill. The indentation points at my left collarbone, meaning due north is over that shoulder. I angle myself until north is directly behind me and south straight ahead, then I tuck the lodestone away.

I wouldn't want to be traveling these wastes without it, but I also know it's the type of tech someone would kill for. It finds north no matter the weather, pointing true even in the worst of the gods-sent silent storms. Not even the Old World tech does that.

I button my jacket at my throat, wrap my scarf over my nose. Then I'm trudging south again.

✦ ✦ ✦

We come upon the Old Coast as the sun begins to sink behind the horizon. I slow to a standstill, taking it in for the first time. Flint's descriptions are accurate. It's like the wastes — just as endless, just as desolate — but witnessing it with my own eyes is harrowing.

The ground dips before me — the remnants of a shoreline — and I have to run to keep from getting clipped in the back of my ankles by the dragger. Once I'm on the dried ocean bed itself, things are easy for the first time since we left Dead River. No scrub to slow me down. No ruts to claw at the dragger. The ocean bed is hard-packed rock, a cobweb of cracked dirt. I'll make good time.

I confirm my heading with the lodestone again, then check on Indie. Her usually bronze skin is sallow, and despite the sweat on her brow, she feels cold.

"Hey, can you drink?" I ask.

She mutters something in response, which I take to be a *yes*. I tip the waterskin toward her mouth, and half the liquid dribbles uselessly down her chin.

"How much . . ." Her eyes flutter.

"Farther?" I glance out across the ocean bed. If I squint, I can make out a lump the height of my thumb in the distance. That'll be the oil rig Flint spoke of, Zuly's watch-pack. "Little over three clicks? Four at most."

Indie's head lolls, and her eyes fall shut.

"Just hang on. We're almost there."

I take off at a jog, the dragger strap burning my chest and torso. My feet are chapped now too, sweat having put blisters on my heels. I press on, ignoring the sting, my eyes pinned to the lump on the horizon. Soon it's not so much of a lump, but a small grave marker, a large boulder, then a hut on wide stilts. I pull a pale flag from my rucksack and hold it overhead. Flint said a white flag announces that you mean no harm, but with each step I can't help but feel that I'm waving a target and shouting, *Aim here!*

As twilight falls, my destination morphs into the behemoth rig Flint described. I've never seen something so large. The stilts are rusted and reddened from the elements, and slightly crooked too, as though the wind has tried to blow them over. Rungs are built into each of the stilts, turning them into ladders. They extend up to the hutlike portion of the rig, which is four times as large as our huts back home and encircled by a deck with a railing. It towers above me like an impossible island.

A figure appears on the deck, the unmistakable shape of a rifle aimed my way. I freeze, and the dragger slides to a halt.

"Name and business?" the figure calls down.

"I'm Delta of Dead River. My sister is sick. Pregnant, but something's gone wrong. I need to see Zuly."

His rifle lowers slightly, and if I squint, I can make out a weathered face, dark and wrinkled. "Patients outside of Zuly's pack aren't allowed on the Ark. If you need meds, you should have sent a trader."

"She's seen one of ours before. Years ago, when we still called Alkali Lake home. My friend Asher was sick with an endless fever. His ma brought him, and Zuly treated him."

"You must've had good payment."

I don't know what Silla paid Zuly that day, but I nod anyway. "I have payment again now. Please. My sister is dying."

It's only when I speak the words that I realize they're true. If Indie was fine, Astra would have delivered the baby at home. Ma never would have sent me into the wastes.

"The tanker is a half click that way," the watchman says, pointing southeast. "You better be quick. The skies paint warnings."

I glance over my shoulder. The northern sky is alight with ribbons of green and white, dancing and twining above the darkening horizon.

A silent storm is coming.

I curse, remembering the flare yesterday as I helped Indie in the cornfields. We had to take shelter among the stalks for a few minutes, shielding our eyes until the brightness passed. Was that really only a day ago? It feels like a lifetime. Doesn't matter. Flares always come before the auroras, and the auroras always come before the silent storms. The gods may send them to punish us, but at least they warn us, too.

I touch the lodestone beneath my shirt. I'll be able to find my way, but I worry about Indie. Some silent storms merely disrupt Old World compasses and stir up more dust. Others are so strong, you can feel your heart racing, your blood boiling. They've killed the elderly on rare occasions, caused their hearts to stop cold. And in Indie's weakened state . . .

Silent storms. Silent killers.

The watchman tugs at something behind him, and a faded red flag unfurls on the rig. "So they know you're coming," he explains.

"Thank you."

"Now go. Before the dust hits." The flag flaps gently above him, teased by a breeze that hasn't existed all day.

I turn southeast and run.

CHAPTER THREE

I thought the oil rig was large, but the tanker makes me feel no bigger than a beetle.

It waits ahead, partially swallowed by the earth and leaning to the side, as if it sank into the ocean's drying floor off kilter before the mud hardened. Sand has gathered at the tanker's base, a big rounded hull that extends up toward the deck. Like Zuly's watchtower rig, a railing surrounds it, but here, mounted torches flicker in the strengthening wind.

"Hello?" I call.

There's a creak, and something descends from the shadows. A miniature version of the tanker, lowered to the ocean bed by a series of pulleys. The mini-tanker has no deck or railings, and its curved hull is actually hollow. I'm supposed to sit in it, I realize.

I heave Indie from the dragger and into our ride. Completely limp, she seems to weigh a ton, and sweat beads her brow. Her eyes are closed, but moving behind her lids.

"Indie?" I ask her as the ropes creak and we're lifted into the air.

She murmurs something, but her eyes stay shut.

I hate this damn baby. I've hated it since I learned of it, and it must know, because now it's trying to punish me.

When the pulleys creak to a halt, the mini-tanker is level with the deck of the tanker itself. Hands grab me and pull me over the railing. My feet hit the pitched deck. It's massive. Floors are a rarity in the wastes, and the sheer size of what stretches before me is confounding. In the flickering torchlight I can make out rows of boxed plant beds and lattices filled with vines, all growing beneath cloth canopies. Basins for collecting water. Looms filled with wool. This high off the ocean bed, the wind is stronger, and several pack-members pull linens over the goods to protect them from the incoming storm.

I move toward Indie, only to find that two women are already hauling my sister onto the deck.

"You have payment?" a voice says.

I turn and find an old woman before me. Her skin is scored with wrinkles, her matted hair a white knot atop her head. Instead of goggles, she wears the remnants of a vulture's skull like a mask, and it covers her forehead and nose, making her appear birdlike herself. The hem of her long, dark wool robe is adorned with feathers.

This is Zuly of the Ark.

Asher had told me about her when he returned to Alkali Lake after his fever. Flint has described her to me also, but Asher's description was more accurate. I thought he was being dramatic. We were just six at that time. It made sense that he might have exaggerated things or hallucinated in the heat of his sickness, but Zuly is as he said: a doctor with the eyes of a fox, the face of a vulture, and the body of a witch.

I fumble for my rucksack, pull out the goods Ma packed.

Zuly turns over the jars and inspects the bread. She passes the potatoes to a young woman at her rear. "Plant these. They will grow better fare than these surely taste." She turns back to me. "What else?"

"Nothing," I manage. "That was it."

Zuly's eyes flick to Indie's prone form on the deck, then back to me. "To deal with this costs more. You have nothing else of value?"

Beneath my shirt and hidden from view, the lodestone seems to burn on my breastbone. Indie would be worth it, but I can't give it up. If I do, we'll never find our way home, and then all of this will be for nothing.

A shout across the deck draws my attention. The pack-members are struggling with one of the linens. Their tether has snapped. It is now too short to properly bind the cover in place.

"Rope," I say. "I can give you rope." I grab the tie that holds my hair in a knot and pull it loose. My dark hair tumbles to my waist. The pieces not already matted or braided are caught by the wind and blow across my eyes. I grab one of the long sections of braid. "How many?"

"Three."

I draw my Old World knife, gather the braids high near my scalp, and saw through them.

"I will do my best despite the meager payment," Zuly says as I hand the braids over. She nods to her pack-members and they scoop Indie up and lug her away, passing through a door that must lead to the inside of the tanker.

"Wait— I want to come. I need to stay with—"

"You will stay at a distance," Zuly says. "Your energy is too tight, young . . ."

"Delta," I tell her. "Of Dead River."

"You will bring disaster upon this healing. Keep back. Someone will get you when there is news." Zuly turns, her robe fanning out near her feet, and disappears after her women.

I look helplessly around the deck. Torches are whipping in the wind. Dust stings my cheeks. Glancing back across the ocean bed, I can no longer make out the watchtower rig.

"Come inside," says a young girl who is roughly Pewter's age.

I follow her through the door and into the belly of the tanker, where it smells of metal and rust and falseness. The air is stale. I can't hear the wind.

It's worse than our cellar during storms.

We climb down a series of ladders and snake through halls where I have to duck at each doorway to keep from hitting my head. The girl takes me to a small room where beds jut from the wall. They remind me of our mats back home, but, they're suspended by metal brackets.

"We don't have water to spare," the girl says to me.

"I didn't think you would."

I've been careful on the way in. My waterskin is still half full and will last me until I return home.

The girl sets a candle on the floor, and the walls seem to come to life beneath the flame, glinting and flashing. It's unnatural. Asher once said that the tanker felt like freedom, that he felt safe during his visit, but I just feel trapped.

"Do you like living here?" I ask the girl.

27

She shrugs. "It is all I know. But traders bring word of raids in the wastes, of men taking all they want, from goods to homes to women, and I know I'd rather be here. The Ark is impenetrable. We are above the lawless land. Protected. Zuly watches over us."

I sit on the lower of the two mats, my head nearly knocking the bed above, and try to keep my knees from bouncing.

"I will find you when there is news," the girl says.

✦ ✦ ✦

I sleep, my exhausted body succumbing to dreams, and when I wake, it's to my shoulder being jostled. "Come." The girl motions toward the hall.

When we emerge onto the deck, the aurora still dances low on the northern horizon, a sickly green mist that is so bright it disguises the true time of day. The girl says it's nearly dawn, sunrise just moments off. Zuly has been with Indie all night.

We pass the dust-covered linens the pack was stringing up when I arrived. A few pack-members are awake already, pulling the sheets down and shaking them out while others right a section of the canopy that collapsed in the wind. Chickens scatter, startled by the snapping fabric. A goat bleats from somewhere out of view.

The girl stops suddenly and points. Zuly is standing at the nose of the tanker, a baby in her arms. I rush forward. The baby has dark hair and paper-thin eyelids, and is far smaller than Brooke's girl was when she joined our pack. "She ate earlier and is sleeping now," Zuly says.

A sigh of relief escapes me. "Is Indie sleeping too? I want to see her."

Zuly frowns. "You misunderstand. The baby was fed goat's milk. Your sister died during the labor."

"What?"

"There was nothing I could do. She responded poorly to all tonics. I could barely keep her conscious. Her pulse had fled by the time I cut the baby from her."

"Cut? You cut the . . . Where is Indie? I want to see her!"

"There's nothing to see. We've burned her remains. She's at peace now."

I stagger back, certain I've heard her wrong.

"We stripped the body before the burning. You can have her clothes, of course."

"I don't want her damn clothes! I want my sister. How could you burn her body without letting me see her first?"

"She'd already sat cold while I worked to save the baby," Zuly says calmly. "Would you have risked your sister's soul being damned merely so I could fetch you for a pyre?"

Folks say that the sooner a body is burned after death, the more likely the gods are to accept that soul among the stars, but I don't care about superstitions at the moment. "I paid you to save her!" I erupt.

"You paid me to do what I could. I saved her child. A life for a life. It could have ended worse, but the baby is strong." The newborn starts in Zuly's arms, little fists flailing as a wail escapes her. It is an awful sound, shrill and angry. "You should feed her again," the woman adds.

"I don't want to feed it," I say, backing away. "I don't want to even look at it."

Zuly tries to hand me the child, but I turn and flee. My boots pound on the pitched deck. The gardens are a blur in my vision. Suddenly I'm at the other end of the ship, my hands grabbing the railing as my body comes up against the metal.

This wasn't how it was supposed to happen. If anyone was to die, it was the baby. A stillbirth, maybe, because it came too soon. But Indie was supposed to be fine. We should be heading home together, everything returning to normal. But now she's gone. My sister, who told jokes and pointed out stars and laughed freely, gone forever.

I don't realize I'm crying until Zuly reappears at my side and hands me a rag for my eyes. The baby's missing, off for another feeding probably.

"Do you see that, Delta of Dead River?" Zuly nods toward the horizon. It glistens like a river of metallic liquid.

"A mirage."

"Yes, but it used to be water. According to our ancestors, there was even a time when this tanker floated on the ocean itself. My pack severed the anchor when we made it our home. The water was long gone, and I didn't want mischief scaling the chain in the night." She angles her face to me, and her eyes seem to burn behind the mask. "But there was water here once. Now there is not. Change. Death. Both are a constant in life. So is rebirth. Your sister is gone, but her spirit lives on in her child. Someday you too will die, and a new soul will take your place. The cycle continues. Even in these wastelands, where our gods have abandoned us, life will not cease. I have faith in that, and the stars show it to be true."

I'm so sick of the stars and blind faith. "What is your point?"

"My point is, you must take the child."

"I don't want it. I have no means to feed it."

"I will give you a goat."

"I have nothing to pay in exchange," I point out.

"Consider it a gift, as we do not need the burden of a new child at the moment."

"Neither does my pack. Indie was foolish, getting herself pregnant. I can't take the baby back. The journey alone might kill it."

"*It* will need a name," Zuly says. "Pick a good one. And know that she will die if you leave her here. I will turn her out for the vultures."

"You save her only to let her die?"

"Life is cruel, Delta. It is a cruel, ceaseless cycle, but it is the way of things." Zuly lifts the mask from her face and pushes it onto her forehead. The formidable healer is gone, replaced with a wrinkled, kind woman. Her eyes no longer seem rimmed with fire, but with pain. She has witnessed things she wishes to forget.

She touches my check softly, and I'm so shocked, I freeze. No one has touched me like this, not even Flint. "Have you not come to me for care before?" she asks, staring intently.

"No. I've never left my pack. Not before yesterday."

"And your blood?"

"No." I tell her what I told the watchman last night, how before our pack splintered, Asher and his mother had come to the Ark, but never me. Never my blood.

Zuly frowns. "I see in you someone I once knew. Someone who passed through here many years ago. They were stubborn also, defiant. Wanted the world to make sense and for life to be easy."

"You know nothing about me," I say, stepping away.

Her hand hangs in the air a moment. "Never mind that," she says with a sigh. "Your things are in the lifeboat, along with the goat and your sister's kin. It is up to you if her blood lives on. It shouldn't be a hard question. Don't make it one." She lowers her mask and walks off. After just a few paces, she pauses to look over her shoulder. "How did your friend Asher fare after I treated him?"

"He's dead," I say. "Everyone who stayed at Alkali Lake is dead."

Zuly's mouth morphs into a frown. "That's too bad. I thought he'd be the key to our salvation."

Everyone who met Asher thought he was special. His faith was enormous; optimism radiated from him. But to think he might save us . . .

I wonder briefly if Zuly caught a glimpse of his back when she treated him. If she said something to the wrong person. If *she's* the reason why those men attacked Alkali Lake.

"Another soul gone too soon," she muses sadly.

"Life's cruel, right? Isn't that your story?"

"It is, Delta. But that doesn't mean we can't grieve our losses. You should grieve yours before they fester. I can see they've already taken root."

CHAPTER FOUR

f Asher was still alive, he'd be seventeen, like me. His mother, Silla, would be thirty-nine, like Ma, and our pack would be close to thirty strong, not a meager fourteen.

But they stayed behind.

Silla said it was too dangerous to move. Ma argued it was more dangerous to stay. People picked sides, and that's how the pack split. Roughly half of us went to Dead River. The rest learned that Ma had been right.

Asher and I were two halves of a whole back then. Always together, until we weren't.

I wonder sometimes if it would have turned out differently if he'd followed the rules that day when we were nine. We'd been about a click from camp, gathering snow-white alkali from the northeastern rim of the lake. A trader was due soon, and once the alkali was pulverized, the baking soda would look neat and clean, an easy good to peddle. Nothing raised bread quite like the soda from Alkali Lake, and our pack never had to want for much; traders made special trips to us just to restock their jars.

The swampy, stagnant air was thick that day, the sun blistering, and Asher had stripped off his shirt in the heat.

"Put it back on," I hissed.

The only place our shirts were to come off was in the safety of our huts, for a sponge bath while a roof and walls surrounded us. Ma beat me with a switch just a summer earlier when I'd lifted my hem to wipe sweat from my face. Only a sliver of my back had been revealed, but she went off. "How many times do I have to tell you not to take risks? Show it to no one. Unless you trust them with your own life, keep it hidden. Always." She brought the switch down again for good measure.

"Aw, come on, Delta," Asher said with a knowing look. "No one's here to see. Besides, you can't imagine how good the sun feels on your skin." He eyed my thin woven top. I'd already ditched my wool overshirt and was down to my final layer.

"I'm not taking it off."

"Stubborn devout," he teased.

"Rusted rule breaker!"

He trudged deeper into the alkali beds and bent to harvest the soda, giving me a clear view of his back and the brand that had been put there when we were five. It practically glistened in the sun, the pale scars standing out against his light brown skin. Lines and dashes and circles and curves. Like mine, it was a map, if you knew how to read it, though no one did.

Across the lake, something glinted—an unnatural flash of light. I ran for the binos. They were our pack's only pair, and as valuable as the Old World tech is, we were allowed to take them when harvesting in case a flag went up at camp to signal us back.

I brought the binos to my eyes and scanned across the way. On the western edge of the lake, nestled behind a knot of thick scrub, was a group of men. Four of them, dressed in black, scarves pulled over their mouths and long rifles in hand. One held binos up to his face, like me. But he wasn't looking my way. He was looking at the bank, where Asher was bent over the alkali beds, his back facing the strange men.

"Put your shirt back on," I snapped.

"Will you drop it?"

"Asher, I'm not kidding. Do it now."

Something about my tone got to him because he scrambled for his wool top and pulled it over his sun-bleached hair. "What's got you all raw?"

The men on the other side of the lake were slipping back into the scrub. I thought I could make out a mustang or two as they descended the slope and disappeared from view. Rare animals in these parts, and near impossible to break.

"Delta, are you even listening?"

"We have to go," I said, lowering the binos. "Now."

Back at camp, Silla said I was overreacting, that it could have been traders. One was due, after all. But traders don't move in groups, and they come towing rickshaws or wagons. Folks started to get worried. Asher was just soured that I'd tattled.

"Remember that trader who came through a few months ago?" Ma said around the bonfire that night. "Strange guy. Had a pet falcon with him." A few people nodded. "He would only trade for maps. Odd, no? Who turns down jars of the wastes' best baking soda to demand maps? He thought we had one. Maybe even *knew* we did. Word could've gotten around, and now more folks are looking for it."

"People have searched for the Verdant for as long as they've prayed to the gods," Silla argued.

"Maybe someone heard we branded the kids." Ma's gaze cut to me and Asher. He was sitting beside me—even in his anger he wouldn't leave—but he hadn't spoken a word to me since I told our mas about the men. "We should move, just to be safe," she added.

"We're safer here, together," Silla insisted. "A move would leave us exposed. And Delta's not even sure what she saw."

"I said I wasn't sure who they *were*," I squeaked out. "But I saw them. Four of them. They were working together."

The pack dissolved into bickering and arguing. Two days later, Ma rounded up a group that wanted to move. Silla had her people wanting to stay. The pack splintered, and I never saw Asher again.

A week after settling in Dead River, a trader brought word of the massacre at Alkali Lake. Dead bodies everywhere. Blood and smoke.

If we'd just stayed, maybe it would have been different. We could have held our ground as a group, fought them off. Maybe, if we'd valued the gods over the security of the map, the raiders never would have come. It was our punishment for leaving, losing so many we loved.

I look across Zuly's tanker now. The deck is crowded with pack-members seeing to chores. Someone waters the crops. A woman works at the loom. Laughing children knock stones across the deck with brooms, sending the chickens scattering.

I can see what Asher meant when he said this place felt free. At least on the deck, beneath the open sky, it has a sense of possibility

I've never felt on the desert wastes or in Dead River. Not even at Alkali Lake. It feels truly secure, lifted above.

It's how folks speak of the Verdant, too. It's why they search for it, even if it's been lost for centuries, just like our gods. The branded map on my back is no different from the one Asher had. Scrambled lines and curves. Impossible to read. Maybe we all knew how to read it once, but when the gods abandoned us, that knowledge vanished, too.

Still, we keep hoping, keep trying to understand it. It's why those men came for Asher at Alkali Lake, praying his markings would somehow lead them to salvation. It's why our pack continues to pass down the brand, even now. Because only the most worthy among us can find the Verdant, and once they do, they will have divine power over it. They will be blessed by the gods, granted the ability to control who can enter that green paradise and who should be locked out.

That person will reshape our world.

Supposedly.

I'm not sure what I believe anymore.

My back prickling, I stalk for the lifeboat. The goat stares up at me, perplexed. The baby rests in a sling Zuly has provided, twitching in a light sleep. I step in reluctantly, and two pack-members begin to lower the boat.

"You've chosen well, Delta of Dead River," Zuly calls from above. "Safe travels."

I ignore her, staring instead at the northern horizon. I've chosen this only because I know Ma will skin me if I leave the baby behind. I put on the sling not because I want the baby nestled into my chest, but because Indie would. I do it for her. And for our pack. I do it because I can't bear what they'll think of me otherwise.

"Gods damn you," I whisper to the baby.

It's only when the boat hits the earth that I realize these are the first words I've spoken to the cretin. Well, at least they aren't lies.

"Life *is* cruel," I tell her as I set out across the dry ocean bed. The goat tows the dragger, which is loaded with Indie's clothes instead of Indie. "It's cruel, and everything's dying, and no one wants you, because you're a drain and a burden."

She looks up at me, her eyes almost fogged, as if she's staring through me, not at me. But I see Indie in them. Everything else reminds me of Clay, but those green eyes are my sister's. The little thing's lids fall shut, and she turns into me, lulled by the rhythm of my march.

"Go ahead and try, Baby. You're not winning me over."

But she's already asleep.

CHAPTER FIVE

It takes longer to return to Dead River than it did to get to Zuly's tanker. In part, because I'm going steadily uphill, climbing out of the ocean ever so slowly, but also because Baby is a rotten pain. I have to stop constantly to feed the wailing beast, and what do I get? No thanks. No gratitude. No patience. I know she's a baby, and this is to be expected, but gods, I'm glad she's not my kid. I don't know how new mothers put up with it.

Zuly left a ceramic pot tucked within Indie's clothes, and that's helped with the feedings some. So narrow it's almost pitcher shaped, the pot is open on one end and has a spout on the side for Baby to drink from. I milk the goat into the pot, then have to hold it just so for Baby because she doesn't seem capable of controlling how quickly she swallows. I used to watch Brooke burp Wren over her shoulder, but when I do the same thing with Baby, she spits up on me.

After the first feeding, the process gets a bit easier, but her wrappings are another issue. She soils them nearly as often as she needs to be fed, and I'm not about to waste water washing them. Zuly tucked some clean rags among Indie's things, and I change Baby as needed, putting a fresh wrapping on and leaving the other behind.

By the time Dead River appears on the horizon, it's well past sun-fall. Twilight hangs heavy, and only a faint glow lingers. Camp is quiet as I close in. I can't make out our torches or even the bonfire, which should be easily recognizable by now, but the scent of smoke fills the night. Soon I can see it too. Great clouds billowing from the huts.

Did the bonfire spread embers in the storm last night? Was there not enough water to put out the flames?

I break into a jog, and Baby startles awake, crying into my chest.

"Not now," I hiss, but she goes on wailing.

No one hears her. In any case, no one runs to greet me.

I step into camp and know instantly that this wasn't an accident. The wind didn't blow a stray ember. No one knocked over a torch. Every hut is smoking. Every last one.

I reach for my waist, tugging my knife from its leather sheath. One arm around Baby, the other holding out the blade, I edge forward.

Some of the huts are nothing but ash. Others, like the one I called home, still stand but are smoldering. I brush through the curtained door, coughing on smoke. "Ma?" I call. I pull up the driftwood on the floor and tramp into the cellar. "Marin?" Her real name feels clumsy on my tongue. "Ma?"

Smoke has infiltrated even down here. Our jarred reserves are caked with ash.

Baby starts hacking into my chest, and I race back up the steps, breaking outside where we can breathe. "Astra? Pewter? Fang?"

Their names fall from my mouth, each one more urgent, until my fear eventually betrays me and I can't keep my voice calm.

There's no one here.

I turn in circles beneath the night sky, my throat tight. That's when I notice an extra plume of smoke coming from the lake. I run the hundred paces from memory, gagging as I get nearer. Three bodies lay prone on the dry bank.

I kneel beside them. I don't want to look, but I have to.

The first body is Astra. The second Cobel, her son. They've both been shot in the chest, the front of their skulls smashed open. I turn away and heave. I've had little to eat but goat's milk, jerky, and water, and I vomit it all up immediately.

"Delta?" the third body croaks. "Indie?"

I roll Astra and Cobel aside, finding Old Fang beneath them. He's been shot too—once in the shoulder and again below his arm. Dried blood marks his brow, as though he's been struck with a rock. Both of his legs are broken.

"A raid," he manages before I can ask. "Came from the north. A dozen of them. Wearing black and riding stallions."

I haven't seen a stallion on the plains in more than a year. They're wild beasts, far more trouble than the mares. How a raiding party managed to rope and break a dozen of them is beyond me.

"Where are the others? What happened?"

"They were looking for something. Don't think they found it. Killed anyone who fought back"—his eyes dart to Astra and her son—"and took everyone else."

"Took them where?"

His eyes roll, his breath coming in shallow bursts.

"Where, Fang?"

"I don't know."

"What did they say? Did you hear *anything?*"

He coughs up a spattering of blood. I help him sit and let him drink all that remains in my waterskin.

"They spoke of a general, that he'd be disappointed."

I've never heard of such a man. Not even Flint has mentioned him, and he's spoken of the raiding parties often in his recent visits. I don't know what would be worse—for the raids to be random, or for them to be orchestrated by this general.

"Anything else? Please, Fang."

"They checked our dead to see if they were gods touched. That's why they . . ." Again his gaze trails to poor Astra and her boy. *Gods touched.* I have never heard the term before. "I'd've been next, but another storm was coming. They didn't realize I was still breathing. They left with the pack."

Meaning this all happened last night, when I arrived at the Ark. I barely missed it.

"They're alive, though? Marin? Pewter? Our pack?"

"Were when they were taken."

The raiders couldn't have stayed here, not after setting the huts ablaze. But to leave *while* last night's storm approached . . . They must know something we don't. Another settlement nearby. Somewhere with shelter.

Old Fang's eyes roll, and he leans heavily into my arms. "I want to lie down, Delta. I want to see the stars."

I pull my hand from behind him, lower him softly to the ground. He smiles up at the stars, those indifferent bastards, the gods who abandoned us. He looks at them as though they mean the world, when really they mean nothing. They have brought us loss and misfortune. They have sat idly by my whole life, watching our earth die, refusing to help us.

They're not coming back. I realize this with a certainty I've never experienced before. It's undeniable. The gods abandoned us eons ago, and they have no intention of returning. Curse what the stars say. Damn those stories of rebirth. It's not coming.

"Where's . . . Indie?" Old Fang manages.

"Dead."

His brow wrinkles, and a tear breaks down his cheek.

I shake my head, worried that if I cry too, I'll never stop. "Her girl lived, though. Here." I lift Baby from the sling and lower her onto Old Fang's chest.

Baby squirms and fusses.

Old Fang manages a smile.

I think about what Zuly said, about one life leaving and another taking its place. But that's not what happened here. Three people are dead, four if I count Indie. Everything is dying, even the cursed cycle of life. Death outweighs birth.

"I don't know what to do," I tell Old Fang. "What am I supposed to do?"

He wheezes, struggling to raise his arm. He puts a pinkie beside Baby's flailing fists. Lets her fingers curl around his.

"Fang, where am I supposed to go? There's nothing here. I can't take care of Baby. I need to know what to —"

His hand falls away, hitting the lakebed with a muted *thump*.

"Fang?"

His blank eyes still stare at the stars.

"Fang!"

Baby starts crying. This time I cry with her, and the stars watch.

✦ ✦ ✦

I make a pyre for the deceased and send them back to the sky.

Even after everything, I can't bring myself to surrender our traditions. Rotting beneath the sun feels incredibly cruel — more suffering after a life of it — so I send their souls to the stars.

Standing upwind to avoid the worst of the smell, I watch the flames devour the corpses. When they are nothing but ash, I finally speak.

"Rest easy."

It is what we say to all our deceased. One final prayer that, in the afterlife, they will suffer less than they did in the wastes.

The only structure the raiders didn't bother to set ablaze is the now-empty stable. They've taken my pack *and* our livestock. I know I need to move. I won't last more than a handful of days here on my own, but I can't travel at night. Even with the lodestone directing me, I wouldn't be able to see the ground beneath my feet. The moon is currently weak, and a torch will only alert raiders of my presence. They're out there somewhere — the party that attacked Dead River. All serving some man known as the General.

I'll have to salvage what I can and move in the morning, follow the river to Powder Town. I can leave Baby with someone there and set out after Ma and the others. Try to find where they've been taken.

If only we'd moved to Powder Town in the winter, none of this would have happened. According to Flint, they have defenses there. He's never heard of a raiding party coming within even a stone's throw of the place.

I sleep in one of the stable's empty stalls with Baby — or I try to. She wakes constantly, wailing and crying for milk. Each time I have to milk the goat, fill the feeding pot, hold it while Baby guzzles.

She's a damn drain, a nuisance, a leech.

I hate her.

I hate that she lived while Indie died.

I hate that I had to trek to the Ark instead of being here with my pack. If I were here, maybe it would have turned out differently.

You'd be dead, like Astra, for fighting back, or you'd be in chains along-side the others, wherever they are now.

I know it's true, but logic doesn't make the pain or guilt lessen.

✦ ✦ ✦

Come first light, I gather what I can save from the huts. Any fresh food's been ruined, but there's a decent number of jarred dry goods I can take. Of course, those are heavy, so I only put five into my pack. One salt, two flour, and two baking soda. Astra's home yields a metal box she must have picked up from a trader. Inside is a piece of flint rock and Old World steel, along with an Old World knife. The handle is perfectly contoured to the shape of my palm, complete with grooves for each finger, but it's not made of wood or bone. The strange material is an unnatural color — bright orange, like a hot flame. There's a small sheath with it, and I add it to my belt. I can carry the Old World knife on one hip and my trusty bone blade and wood-handle knife on the other. I snap the tin shut and pocket that too.

I get really lucky in Old Fang's hut, where flames never made it into his cellar. There I find preserved jerky and three empty waterskins. The skins will kill my back at the beginning, but I'll be draining them during the trek, and I know better than to venture out for any type of extended travel without a fair amount of water on hand.

I plod out into the lake and gather a haul, letting the water boil over the central bonfire while I feed Baby. Again. Because the rusted child does nothing but eat and sleep and cry. The clean water goes into my waterskins. I use the smallest amount to bathe, wiping sweat and dust from my limbs with a rag before loading everything into my pack.

I consider burning Indie's clothes on the coals from the burial pyre, but they might come in handy if I need to trade with anyone, and I'll need more wrappings for Baby when the rags from Zuly run out. So I just stand there a moment, looking over Dead River for the final time while Baby hiccups against my chest.

A knot scratches my throat.

I feel like I should say something, but don't know what. I head north and don't look back.

CHAPTER SIX

The heat is driving me mad. It's even making Baby crankier than she typically is, which doesn't seem possible. Carrying her in the sling is like wearing a hot waterskin, and I'm sweating horribly within a half click of leaving home.

I glance over my shoulder to check on the goat. She's pulling the dragger, which is loaded with all my gear. If I'm jumped by raiders, my rucksack will be the first thing they snatch, but it seems a better fate than collapsing from exhaustion. To keep my mind off the heat, I think about what Old Fang said.

Raiders . . . the General . . . They were looking for something.

The lodestone weighs heavily on my chest. Anyone in their right mind would want it, but it can't be what they're after. I've told no one about it, not even Ma or Indie. It stays hidden beneath my shirts, and when I bathe, I make sure to bunch it up in my clothes so no one sees it lying about. The trader who gave it to me is the only person who knows I have it.

I'd been ten, checking for quail beyond the camp perimeter. The man startled me so thoroughly, I tripped on my own trap. He was lean and tall, as silent as a breeze, and when he stepped from behind a crop of boulders with a mare's rein in his hand, I thought maybe he was a god.

Then I noticed the wares slung over his steed, the state of his attire. Fancy Old World goggles like mine, but threadbare, fingerless gloves. Pale wool shirt, scarf, and leather vest, all beaten and patched. Old World rifle, but modified to shoot black powder because the Old World ammunition is long gone. If he was a god, he wouldn't need to modify anything.

"Is the trap full?" he asked.

I pulled my knife and held the blade in his direction.

He smiled. "I take it that means *yes*."

"You can't have any," I managed, shocked that I sounded somewhat brave. He was grown, towering over me. Forty years or so, maybe older. It was hard to tell with his goggles and scarf obscuring most of his face, but I didn't doubt that he could gut me in the blink of an eye. "It's been two weeks since this trap's been full, and the catch is mine."

"I know. I've been watching."

"It's my catch," I repeated sternly, even though my skin was crawling.

"Perhaps it can be mine, for a trade." He pulled the lodestone from the breast pocket of his vest and showed me the indentation, telling me how it worked.

"That's worth more than a quail. More than twenty," I said, eyeing the stone suspiciously.

"It will point north always," he insisted. "Even in the silent storms."

"No one in their right mind would want to trade a thing like that."

He shrugged. "Don't need it where I'm going."

"You're lying," I said. "It doesn't work, or you wouldn't give it up."

"It works, trust me."

"Why should I trust a mangy old trader who's been spying on my traps?"

"Because I know your destiny, Delta." I went rigid. Maybe he'd overheard my name as I left camp—he'd been spying, after all—but I gripped my knife harder. "I know your destiny, and I know mine. The stars tell it. You are meant to have this lodestone, and I am meant to find another."

"The stars don't say things like that. They don't speak of individual people, just the earth's greater fate."

"They speak of everything, if you know how to read them properly. If you have the right map." His eyes cut into me, deep and piercing and gray. My back felt as hot as coals.

Suddenly I wanted him gone.

"Toss over the stone," I instructed. He did. I squeezed it in the palm of my hand. It felt icy cold despite having been in his vest pocket, and when I held it out, the indentation pointed north, as he promised it would. If it continued to do so during silent storms, I'd be making out like a bandit. If it didn't, it was no loss. I'd catch another quail in time, and at least he'd have moved on.

I kicked the trap toward him. "I never want to see you here again," I said firmly.

And I didn't.

It's possible that he found himself in a bad place recently and spoke of the lodestone to a raider, but I doubt it. He hadn't lied about its capabilities, and he hadn't lied about making sure

I wouldn't see him again. Which meant he probably wasn't lying about destinies either. Maybe he has his own lodestone by now. Raiders would have slit his throat for it before he even had the chance to mention me *or* Dead River.

I've kept the thing well hidden, just to be safe, but the truth is, they weren't after the lodestone. No, they came seeking something else. Something that trader somehow knew about too.

My back prickles, the scars itching.

Show it to no one. Unless you trust them with your own life, keep it hidden. Always.

And I have.

Every map-bearer has kept it hidden since the very first one generations ago, when our pack's ancestors found an Old World rover half buried in sand. The vehicle's chassis was rusted, the paper remnants inside so parched and brittle that moving them would have sent the map disintegrating. That's why they coded it onto a pair of youngster's backs, one brand for each of the pack's bloodlines. The number of bloodlines grew in the years that followed, but two brands were kept for tradition, and in time, Asher and I were selected to receive it. When the first of our map-bearers died, Silla copied the brand from his back to Asher's. When the second passed, Ma did the same with me. The dead were burned, and no more than two people ever possessed the map at a time. More copies meant more chances of it falling into the wrong hands, of someone else finding the Verdant before we did and then sealing it off.

Our pack kept only two copies, with the understanding that

when we learned how to read it, we'd all travel together. We'd earn entry to paradise *together.*

And here we are, still unable to read the thing, still forcing our marked children to stay covered, hidden, cautious. And yet, trouble still keeps finding us.

After Asher was killed, along with half the pack, no one bothered copying my brand to ensure that there was a second bearer. It was the first time there was a break in the tradition, and maybe that's just as well. No one needs this burden, this curse, this map of a place that probably doesn't exist. The gods aren't returning, and the Verdant is an empty promise.

Something juts out of the earth ahead, and I pause. An Old World graveyard, left over from a time when the dead were buried in the ground. I can make out several rows of wooden crosses rippling in the heat. When I'm upon the site, I find each grave overturned, dirt flung about, long-dead bodies disrupted.

The bones are as white as ash, threadbare rags clinging to some of the remains. Anything of use that was buried with the dead has been claimed by scavengers. Most Old World tech comes from graves. Or sometimes from abandoned rovers with their rusted-out bodies, or the rare skeleton half buried in sand while a fraying noose sways from a tree overhead. I've never seen a tree, just heard about them from Flint. You have to head far north before the scrub gets any taller than your knee, and even there, the trees are sickly and weak.

I didn't know there was a graveyard so close to Dead River. I wonder when the scavengers found it. Sometimes the sands shift, covering or revealing. Could've been fifty years ago. Could've been five days. Only thing that's certain is the plot is old.

I'm about to move on when I notice the skeleton in the grave before me has a crushed skull. I peer into the next shallow grave, a third, a fourth. A new row. Another. Broken skulls. Every skeleton in the plot.

They checked our dead to see if they were gods touched, Old Fang had said while looking at Astra's and Cobel's crushed skulls.

A shiver travels up my spine.

There's an old well near the graveyard, and I check it on a whim. Bone-dry. Sheltered in a sliver of shade, I lean against its bricks and feed Baby.

✦ ✦ ✦

By noon, there's a trickle of liquid running down the center of the riverbed's wide girth, and the scrub along the banks looks less like tumbleweed and more like actual scrub. Maybe Flint wasn't lying. By Powder Town, I might see a real, proper tree.

But that won't be until tomorrow. Powder Town is fifty clicks from Dead River, and I'm not even at West Tower yet, which marks the halfway point. Like the rig near Zuly's Ark, it'll be raised above the dirt—a good place to stop for the night. Away from scavengers and raiders. Sheltered in case a storm blows through. And I'll need shelter. Far to the east, between Dead River and Alkali Lake, you can find a few settlements where the land is fertile enough for planting. Then Zuly's Ark to the south and Powder Town to the north.

But that's it. Everywhere else there's a whole lot of nothing. Dry ocean beds, sweltering desert, or worse—Burning Ground, where liquid bubbles to the surface, so hot it can kill you. Flint says the earth will warn you of it. You can see the steam rising and the wastes themselves shifting into wild colors—orange and rust and sometimes even a blue brighter than the sky. But I still have nightmares of taking missteps in that dangerous land.

Not that I've ever headed toward it before. Not until today.

You have to get to West Tower first, and then Powder Town, I tell myself. *No sense worrying about what lies beyond.*

I take it one step at a time. One foot in front of the other. One dry-mouthed sip from the waterskin to every feeding session for Baby. By the time West Tower comes into view, I'm drenched in sweat and the sun is setting.

Like Zuly's rig, West Tower has a platform that can be reached by ladders, but that's where the similarities end. Instead of a hut on stilts, this is a spike on a platform. The structure is impossibly tall, reaching up into the sky as if it means to stab it. I can't even guess at how the thing was built. Everything about the Old World puzzles me.

Still, it will do fine for the night. I can climb to the rusted platform and sleep with some shelter over my head. At my first thought of rest, Baby, of course, begins crying.

"I swear to the gods you are lucky I don't desert you," I grumble at her.

She wails louder.

"Oh, shut it. We'll eat after I climb."

That's when a voice croaks out, "Help."

I freeze, squinting through the twilight.

"Up here! Help! Please."

I scan the tower until I find a figure on the eastern edge, secured to a section of metal that extends into the sky. A skirt waves along the girl's shins. The rest of her is in shadow, too difficult to make out in the sun.

Trap! my brain shouts. But looking out across the desert, I can't find a single puff of dust or any other movement that might suggest a raiding party is closing in on their bait.

"Please," the girl says again. Her voice, low and parched, cracks on the word. Her throat is surely caked with dust. "Please. I need water."

The girl goes on begging and Baby goes on crying, and the truth remains the same: I need a place to sleep. It's on West Tower or in the open. I leave the goat and dragger, draw my bone knife, and scurry up the ladder, with Baby still wailing in the sling.

Once on the platform, I turn in a quick circle. No movement in the shadows. No hidden threats. The girl faces out toward the desert — it's how she saw me coming — and I pad toward her back, shocked at how tall she is. At least a head taller than I am, and I'm not short. It's then I notice that what I mistook for a skirt is really just bindings. Pieces of rope swaying as he struggles. Because it's a guy tied to the tower. The width of his shoulders; the size of his hands, tied behind his back; the shadow of scruff along the side of his jaw, where his scarf has slipped.

My pulse kicks faster. Baby must sense a change in my demeanor because she finally shuts up.

I edge toward the man and put my blade to his back. He arches, every muscle tensing.

"Where are your friends?"

"No f-friends," he stammers. "I was robbed two days ago. I just want water and to be cut loose. *Please.*"

I glance over my shoulder, down to the goat, out toward the horizon. Everything is as it should be, calm, undisturbed. That raid back home has rattled me good, scudded up my judgment and left me fearing everyone. This guy's no better off than I am: a victim of bad circumstance.

I cut the bindings at his arms, and he brings them to his front, massaging his wrists. I step around him and drop to his feet. These ropes are thicker and will take a bit of sawing.

"Thank you," he says as I work. "A trader passed by yesterday and didn't stop."

"I've seen enough bad in the past day to last a lifetime. You're lucky I feel like doing some good to counter things."

"That baby yours?" He sounds sad about it.

I glance up. The goggles he wears have been tinted somehow, and though I can tell he's looking at me, I can't see his eyes. He flinches. As if looking at me properly has burned him.

"You have to leave," he says, his voice at a whisper.

I stop sawing at his ankle ropes and stand. "You said you were alone."

"I lied."

I don't know why he's suddenly warning me. Maybe so I race from the tower and flee into an ambush. I yank his scarf down and put my blade to his throat.

"Please just go. I'm not lying about this. Go!"

There's a whoosh from above, and I look up to see a pair of boots descending. Their wearer is coming down fast, thanks to a pulley system farther up the tower—the only place I hadn't checked for enemies. Of course they'd come from the heavens. From the stars.

I hunch over, instinctively protecting the worthless, always hungry, never sleeping baby in the sling. Heels connect with my back, and I go sprawling forward. I hear my attacker land on the platform. Then a second set of boots. There's two of them. Two, plus the bait. I roll over, Baby still nestled against my chest. She's wailing now, and I palm the back of her small head, like my lone hand has any chance of actually protecting her. A young man towers over us with a blade pointed at me. *My* blade. I dropped it when I fell.

"Skies, it's a young one. With a baby, too!"

His companion lets out a whoop. "We'll get paid good for this. Nice catch, Asher." He claps the bait on the shoulder and I think I must have heard him wrong. I think also that surely more than one person has that name. I've never met another before, but it's possible.

But then the bait lifts his goggles and I'm staring into a set of eyes I haven't seen since childhood—staring at a ghost.

He's lost the youth in his cheeks, and his hair has faded from brilliant sunshine to dull straw. His jaw has hardened, his mouth grown thin. Everything about him has changed, sharpened, steeled, but those eyes are the same, bluer than the sky. Calmer than the still after a storm. The color of the ocean that once was.

"Asher?" I manage. I'm shocked and relieved and furious in the same breath. "What the hell?"

"Wait, don't!" he shouts, lurching for his companion. But the man's boot comes out of nowhere, knocking my head so hard I see stars.

Stars, stars everywhere. Worthless, deserting gods.

The world goes dark.

CHAPTER SEVEN

When I come to, I'm in a small wagon that they must have kept hidden around the back side of the tower. Woven scrub and driftwood arch over me, trapping me inside like a caged animal. Baby is with me, but my knives are gone. We're moving beneath the black of night, and the goat follows the wagon, towing my dragger and gear.

I curse up a storm, kick at the sideboards, make threats I have no ability to carry out. When that gets no response, I try a more tactful approach, offering my captors the jars stashed in my pack, the goat, *everything* on the dragger. The only thing I don't mention is the lodestone. The two men at the yoke haven't slowed their pace since they started hauling the wagon from West Tower, and it's clear that I'm the prize. If I offer up the lodestone, they'll just take it and sell me anyway.

I hope the bastards make a misstep into Burning Ground. Maybe I can break out in the chaos, assuming that Asher finds his conscience and helps me.

I look at him now. He's walking alongside the wagon, mouth set in a crooked grimace, and his fingers curled around an Old World rifle modified to shoot black powder. Every few paces he glances over his shoulder to make sure the goat is still following with my gear.

I can't believe he's alive. All those years we assumed him dead, and here he is, walking beside the wagon, whole and well. I should be elated, relieved—and a part of me is—but a larger part is furious. He's trafficking servants! Which I fear is what I'm about to become. Powder Town might be where people go for security, but word among the smaller, more paranoid packs is that the security comes at a price, that people there aren't quite free, and that a working class keeps the place running while the folks who founded it live comfortably.

It's part of why Ma never wanted to make the trip, why she clung to Dead River with an iron fist.

Guess I'm about to find out the truth.

"This what you've been up to all those years, Asher?" Baby doesn't even flinch when I break the silence. The wagon's rocking like a cradle and she's sleeping the best she ever has against my chest.

Asher gives me a narrow sideways glance and plods on.

"You escaped that raid at Alkali Lake to trap people like game? Silla would be disgusted."

"My mother is *dead*," he snaps, turning on me. Those blue eyes don't look calm anymore, but rimmed with fire. "And you don't know anything about me."

"I knew—"

"You knew a *kid*. That Asher's been gone since your half of the pack left."

"The kid I knew was at least kind," I point out. "He set animals free when our traps brought in more than we needed. He didn't like gutting game, so I did it for him. He picked wildflowers off the scrub for his mother, and he *never* would have resorted to something like this."

"He also grew up the moment he watched his pack die for him, and he went on growing up alone and abused and imprisoned. He didn't have anybody, so he became what he needed to survive. I'm sorry you don't like that, but I don't give a rusted damn how you judge me. You always thought you knew best, Delta, and sometimes you did, but not about this. You know nothing about what I went through."

I bite the inside of my cheek because he's right about that last bit. The traders talked about Alkali pack-members shot in the heart, floating bloated in the lake, burned alive in their huts. I assumed Asher was among them. I never imagined he got away. Or rather, that the raid got him.

His buddies chuckle up front. It's dead silent in these wastes — nothing but the creak of the wheels and their occasional grunts as they drag the wagon over a stubborn rut — and our voices have carried. Apparently they've never caught a sale that has history with one of them, and this is amusing.

"How'd you know it was me?" I ask Asher quietly.

"The scar above your eye."

He put it there when we were wrestling one summer. A hard tackle, my head striking a sharp rock. Ma said I was lucky it wasn't worse, that I could have died if I'd fallen differently. I wear that luck daily now, in the form of a pale scar that bisects my right brow.

I catch Asher watching me. His eyes seem huge, his jaw slack. For the briefest moment he looks like a version of the boy I once knew. It makes the relief I felt at West Tower come surging back. Then he frowns, and the magic is lost. He's just someone who's conned me.

"What are you playing at, Asher? You trying to make me feel like we share something? That you're not carting me off to be sold?"

"No, I just..." He sighs and looks away. "I've been looking for you—for the pack—since I got out."

I pause, turning this unexpected answer over in my mind. "How long's that been?"

"Six moons."

"Where were you before?"

His throat bobs as he swallows, but he refuses to make eye contact.

"Who are your buddies?"

Again, he stays quiet.

I glance through the cage and into the heavens. The Gods' Star shines to the north, mocking me with its brilliance. As the seasons change, the other stars rotate around it, reminding us that every fate, every path, is tied back to our gods. This was true before they deserted us. It will be true even if they never return. Like my lodestone, the Gods' Star shows the way north. The problem is we're moving away from it. The wagon isn't tracking north toward Powder Town, but almost due east.

"Asher, where are we going?"

"Don't answer that," one of the men snaps from the front.

"Where the hell are you taking me?"

"Tell her to shut up before I make her," the other says.

"Shut up, Delta." Asher's voice is callous and firm. It could be an act, a way to keep the men happy. But it could also be who Asher is now. Like he said, I don't know him anymore.

"If you know what's good for you," he goes on, "you'll keep your mouth closed and not fight us. I swear to the gods . . ." His mouth curls into a snarl, and I don't recognize him in the slightest. Not even his eyes. Whatever happened to him at Alkali Lake, whatever happened to him after . . . It's changed him. The Asher I knew is dead, and I can't trust the ghost walking in his place.

✦ ✦ ✦

Several hours later, not even the rocking of the wagon can keep Baby asleep. She wakes with a vengeance, howling to be fed.

"She needs to eat," I announce. "And I should change her wrappings, too."

The wagon doesn't slow.

"She'll just go on crying until she's fed. All night, even."

"Bain, the baby needs to eat," Asher says eventually. "Let's stop."

The bulkier of the two, Bain, grunts. "What's the point in stopping? Just keep your rifle on them both. I don't trust the girl."

My hands are bound together in my lap, but not completely useless. Asher glances at the sling for Baby, my leather jacket and wool shirt, the bulk that implies layers.

"Can you get them off without help?" he asks.

I suddenly realize what they've all assumed. "I can't feed her.

She's not mine. I need the goat's milk and the feeding pot packed with my gear."

Bain says, "We're not stopping."

"Gotta make good time," the other adds.

Baby howls louder. Her nose is pink with cold. The wastes cool off fast without the sun, and even the warmth of my body and the sling doesn't seem to be enough anymore. It's a miracle any newborn lives. Fragile, weak things.

I rock her lightly, trying to distract her from the hunger pangs. It only makes her cry harder.

"We can spare a few minutes," Asher argues to his friends. "Besides, the baby's not worth anything if it's dead, and weaklings don't draw the same bids."

That does the trick. Bain and his buddy straighten at the yoke, and the wagon halts. "Find the feeding pot and milk the goat," Bain says to Asher. "And do it fast. I don't like sitting still in the open." Then he stalks off, muttering about taking a piss. His friend follows.

As soon as the guys are gone, I lunge for the cage, grabbing the driftwood bars. "Let me go, Asher. I can run."

"To where?" He grunts from where he's stooped to milk the goat. "There's nothing for dozens of clicks, and they'd murder me for setting you loose."

"Then come with me. Or I can knock you good with that rifle, make it look convincing—like I got a jump on you."

"They'd just catch us again. And if you go alone, you'll end up lost and dead of thirst."

"You guys are the lost ones, heading east. There's nothing east of West Tower."

"That's what I thought once too. Couldn't be more wrong." He stands and passes me the feeding pot. I accept it through the bars of the cage. I know I shouldn't trust him, but curiosity gnaws at me.

"There's settlements east of West Tower? In Burning Ground?"

He raises a brow in that knowing way he always had as a kid. Same look he gave me when I nagged him for not wearing his shirt that day.

"Where are we going, Asher? We were friends once. Please."

Hurt glances his features. "We're still friends."

"Really? This is what friends do to each other?" I rattle the bars of the cage.

Asher searches for his buddies, and after confirming that they're still out of earshot, he turns back to me.

"*Beyond* Burning Ground," he says at a whisper. "We're side-stepping it, aiming for a place called the Barrel. You'll be out of there in a matter of days if you play it right, with a real chance of escape. Nothing like what I can offer you here. Let Bain and Cree get a payload from you, and get yourself moved to a new house. Servants have access to most parts of a home, especially the kitchen. Kitchens have knives. And you've always been good with a knife." His face has that youthful look again, a sliver of the Asher I once knew. I wonder if this means his words are sincere. If everything else is an act. He's a stranger, yet he's not. I don't know what to believe.

"I'm not staying in the Barrel long," Asher goes on. "It was just for this last job, to pay off a debt to Bain, and then I'm leaving. But I'll wait for you. We can head west together."

Wait for me to murder whoever buys me, or to simply threaten my way free with a blade. Still, it sounds like a plan that has a chance of success. I'd rather run now, but Asher's right. I don't have the supplies to get anywhere safe.

"Say I manage all this and get myself free. How would I even find you?"

"The Vulture's Roost. It's a pub. I'll stop in daily, at high noon."

"What's a pub?"

"A place that sells moonblitz and chow, but mostly moonblitz."

Moonblitz was always at the bottom of our list for trading needs at Dead River. It could clean wounds fine and was a nice treat to sip on during a holiday, but it was never something we went out of our way to secure. To think there's a place that sells it and that people actually trade valuables for the drink regularly sounds laughable.

Baby gurgles on the milk, drinking too quickly, and I pull the pot back to give her a chance to breathe. "Why are you helping me suddenly?"

"I was always helping you. At West Tower, the moment I knew it was you, I tried to help. And what I said earlier . . . It was only because Bain and Cree were listening."

The quiet holds between us. His eyes gleam in the weak moonlight.

"They came for me at Dead River," I blurt out.

Fear washes over him. "And you got away?"

"I was at Zuly's."

"The others?"

"Old Fang, Astra, and Cobel were murdered. They took the rest. You know where they took them, don't you?"

He shakes his head and looks away — at the stars, the horizon, anything but me.

"Asher, where did they take them?"

"You can't go there."

"Who did it?" My voice cracks. "Who took them, and where are they going?"

"It's a dead end. One way in, no way out. He controls everything. Let them go, Delta. Get sold in the Barrel, break loose, and find me at the Vulture's Roost. I'm going to Powder Town. It's the last free place in the wastes."

"Let them go?" I stare at him, my stomach churning. The Asher I knew would never give that advice. "Just *leave* them? They're my pack!"

"You don't understand what it's like there, Delta."

"I would if you'd tell me!"

"You can't do anything for them without damning yourself."

There's a muffle in the distance as Bain and Cree come into view. Asher steps away from the wagon.

"Ready to move?" Bain calls. Asher turns to me and holds out a hand, waiting for the now empty feeding pot. I feel like cracking it against the wagon, but I pass it through the bars. He might be trying to protect me, but all he's doing is sending me forward blind and uninformed.

He slides a clean rag between the bars for Baby. "What's her name?"

"Ba—" Suddenly I don't want to admit that I haven't named my own niece. "Bay," I amend.

"And if she's not yours . . ."

"Indie's. She died during the birthing."

He frowns, eyes cutting into me, and I feel like he's saying something else in the silence that stretches between us, something I can't hear.

The wagon lurches as Bain and Cree lean into the yoke, and Asher falls into step. He says nothing else, but steals a glance my way now and then. I burp Bay over my shoulder as we rock eastward, wishing I could hear all the things he refuses to speak.

✦ ✦ ✦

At some point during the night we stop at a rocky outcropping that breaks from the earth like the bow of a sinking ship. The scrub surrounding it is barren, but the rocks provide a bit of shelter from the cold. There are signs of a camp: dark soot from an old fire, a canopy made of threadbare cotton supported by driftwood poles. They've stopped here before.

Bain gets a flame going in the empty fire pit. Cree throws meat on, pulled from a trap that was set somewhere nearby. My stomach growls viciously as they dig in. My gear gets raided, too, and the jerky I intended to eat over two days is gone within minutes.

"You can have a bite for a kiss," Bain calls when he catches me watching.

"Scud off," I answer.

"Aw, come on. Just a single kiss before you're out of my world forever." He smiles, running his tongue over his teeth.

"Leave her be," Asher says.

"Old flame still flickering?" Bain elbows Asher with a wicked grin. "Yeah, I heard you guys talking. Childhood friends of some sort, maybe more. Well, we share everything in this crew."

Asher lurches to his feet, putting himself between the fire pit and the wagon. Bain and Cree are both bulkier than he is, a few years older too, but his shoulders are squared—like he thinks he stands a chance.

Bain buckles over, laughing. Cree grins around a mouthful of squab.

"Messing around with the catch will just make her look like damaged goods," Asher says.

"You ain't never cared how much our catch fetched before this one," Cree says, squinting at Asher.

"Well, this is the first girl," Asher says, as if this makes his aiding in selling people more palatable.

"Still," Cree goes on. "Why you care so much about this one? What's she to you?"

It's quiet for a moment. What *am* I to him? Lost family? An old friend? Someone he simply feels guilty about trapping?

I wait for his answer, but it never comes.

"Eh, let him get all sentimental." Bain spits into the fire. "I was only fooling. And I ain't wasting meat on that scrawny thing." His eyes dart my way. "I just wanna keep her scared."

I wish it wasn't working, but I look away, not wanting him to see the fear in my eyes.

They say little after that. I'm allowed to feed Bay but given nothing for myself, and by her second feeding of the night, my stomach is growling so fiercely, I nab a sip of goat's milk from the feeding pot.

Someone's always on watch, making sure I can't break a bar on the wagon's cage and slip free. When it's Asher's turn and the others are sleeping, he drops a squab wing at my feet. I eat like a heathen, then toss the bone into nearby scrub, causing the goat to bleat at me before she returns to munching on the greenery. I sleep eventually, exhaustion pulling me under.

We start moving again just before dawn. A headache throbs between my eyes. I haven't had any water since before West Tower, I realize. Haven't needed to pee either. I'm dehydrated.

I lie on my side in the bed of the wagon, curling myself around Bay, and try to ignore the scratchiness in my throat.

CHAPTER EIGHT

It goes on like that for another two days. Traveling across desolate land. Spending nights at camps the boys seem to be familiar with. I never see Burning Ground, so we must be staying well away from it. Asher says little to me, but he always gives me a bite to eat during his evening watch. In the worst heat of the day, Bain even allows me to have water. A corpse won't fetch him much when we get to the Barrel.

To keep from going mad, I talk to Bay. I tell her about the dying earth and the deserting gods and the stars that judge us. I even sing her a lullaby Ma used to sing to me. It calms my nerves as much as hers.

By noon on the third day, the sun is high in the sky, red-angry and gleaming, and the land has changed.

Sand and dirt have all but vanished, giving way to hard rock. Not packed, dry earth like the land near Dead River, but honest-to-gods rock. Rock everywhere, rolling and bucking and spreading north, with shallow ruts worn into their surface. Ahead of us, a wall of it sprouts for the heavens, rock stretching east and west for several clicks, as solid as can be, save for one narrow pass.

"A mesa," Asher says when he sees me staring.

"Huh?"

"That's what you call a rock formation like that. A mesa."

I wonder if he was as awestruck as I am when he saw one for the first time. I'm about to ask him where he learned the term, but Bain glares at us over his shoulder and Asher falls back.

Squinting, I can make out sun-bleached canopies stretching over the pass that cuts through the mesa and a series of wooden bridges snaking back and forth along the rim. Below, additional platforms and walkways seem to be built on top of one another, lining the sides of the pass like a skeleton stairway.

I blink, concerned that I'm seeing things. I've been feeling dizzy and feverish for most of the day, and I know I'm terribly dehydrated. But as we draw nearer, the image remains unchanged. I stare, slack-jawed, marveling at the ingenuity of it all. I'm not sure how people managed to raise these wall-clinging structures, but there's no denying that it's impressive.

Soon we're slipping beneath idle flags that mark the mouth of the canyon and entering the pass. Just behind the flags is a raised iron gate, its post ends sharpened to spikes. I shiver when I picture the gate coming down, cutting off the passageway. This is not a place I'd want to be trapped.

Huts and shanties are built along the canyon's base, serving as the foundation for the walkways that climb the surrounding walls. A blacksmith's tool clangs somewhere in the distance. When I tilt my head back and look up through the wagon's cage, I spot gunners along the rim line, scarves wrapped over their mouths and gunpowder satchels slung across their shoulders. Their modified rifles sweep the chasm as our wagon creeps forward.

I understand now why this place is called the Barrel. We are the bullet, moving through the barrel of a gun. There is only one course of travel, and it cannot be altered. I envy the falcon I spot flying high overhead, sunlight cutting through its wingtips.

The pass widens and eventually opens onto a bustling oblong clearing. Here, traders have set up a market, their wares spread over their mules and displayed in their rickshaws. There are more permanent structures too — booths and tables stocked with textiles, baking goods, leather. Pens of chickens and livestock. Pale canopies provide shelter for the sellers, who squabble with buyers over price.

I've never seen a settlement so big. This can't have cropped up recently. The complexity of the walkways and the bridges that span the pass, the scale of the market, and the sheer number of wares . . . This place has been growing for years, and it seems impossible that our pack never heard of it.

Nestled in the shadows, behind the bustling market and against the mesa wall, sits a ramshackle shanty with a faded cloth door. A blitzed-looking man staggers from within, blinking in the afternoon sun, and I wonder if this place might be the Vulture's Roost that Asher mentioned.

Bain and Cree set the yoke down across from the maybe pub, just outside a particularly unstable looking shanty. Like the Vulture's Roost, it has a threadbare cloth door and leans into the rock walls like a weary vagrant. The uneven boards that make up the siding sport ugly gaps, and the roof is a series of decaying wooden planks that look as brittle as old cornhusks.

Asher hauls me from the wagon. Bay is secure in the sling, but I instinctively cup the back of her head to keep her from jostling.

"Don't fight them," he whispers, pulling me close. "Speak only if spoken to, keep your head down, and don't make a move until you've been assigned somewhere. You know where to find me when—"

A foreign set of hands grabs me from Asher and shoves me toward the doorway, where Bain is arguing about payment with a rotund, balding man. I get one final glance at Asher—standing in the market, arms at his sides and gaze rooted on me—before I'm yanked into the shanty and the cloth door falls back in place.

Fingers pinch my cheeks, forcing my mouth open. A woman with deep-set eyes and wrinkled skin examines my teeth. She pushes my jaw up, and I find myself staring at the sagging ceiling. Next, she pokes and prods, checking ears, eyes, combing through my hair. There are two other people being inspected in the hut, a boy and a girl, both around my age.

Heat laces my cheek, and my head snaps sideways. It takes me a minute to realize I've been slapped. "Only thing that should interest you is your feet."

"Yes, ma'am," I say, and stare at the rock floor. I don't have the energy to fight her. Even now, the room seems to be spinning.

The woman moves on to my neck, shoulders, ribs. When the sling gets in her way, she unfastens it and sets Bay on the floor, where the tiny girl immediately starts crying. I've never wanted to coddle her, but I'm suddenly overwhelmed by the urge to scoop her up. The rock floor is hard and likely cold. The sling has fallen open. Bay should be in my arms, nestled against the heat of my body. Her little face wrinkles as she howls, and it takes all my effort to keep my mouth shut as the woman ignores the crying and continues prodding her way down my body. "Take this one to the wagon for Bedrock," she says to another worker after no part of me has been left untouched.

I risk a glance up, pulse kicking. Asher never mentioned any Bedrock settlement, and the Vulture's Roost is here, in the Barrel. I was supposed to be assigned somewhere here. The worker stoops near my feet, and I realize the woman was never talking about me.

"Wait!" I shout as he picks up Bay. "We have to stay together."

"She ain't yours," the woman says, "and even if she was, there's wet nurses and goats."

"But she's my niece, my blood." I move to follow Bay, but the woman yanks me back.

"Go on," she says, waving the man off.

"You can't just take her from me!"

The woman's hand comes up, and this time I see the blow coming. I grab her at the wrist, stopping her cold. She's all bark and growl, with no real meat on her, and with a bit of pressure at the right angle, her arm folds in and she crumples. "The poker!" she cries out.

The other inspector abandons the girl she's examining and grabs a poker from the fire. As she turns the red-hot end toward me, something roars to life in my gut, a flame in the pit of my empty stomach. Suddenly it doesn't matter that I'm weary and dehydrated; when the woman lunges, I drop low. The poker sails over my shoulder, and I tackle her around the waist, bringing her to the ground. She coughs out all her air, and the poker clatters aside. I snatch it up and turn, wheeling on the first woman. She's clutching her wrist. I wonder briefly if I broke it, but as soon as she starts screaming for backup, I run. Out of the shanty. Into the open market.

I see only one thing: the man carrying Bay. He's moving toward a caged wagon in the center of the market, this one drawn by mules. I race after him as the women scream for me to be stopped. Their voices are a distant hum. Bay is almost back in my grasp. Another three steps, and the man will be within reach. I wind up with the poker, ready to strike.

Something collides with my side.

I crash to the hard earth and lose all the air in my lungs. Hands pin my wrists down by my ears. Knees pin my thighs firm. The poker is ripped away as I gasp.

"You realize I don't get paid if you run, right?" Bain smiles above me. Standing behind him, Cree now holds the poker, glowing end pointed at my face. I thrash beneath Bain, but even with the rage burning in my chest, I'm no match for his strength.

"Get her up!" comes a shout.

Bain hoists me to my feet.

"Jacket off." It's the balding man Bain had been bartering with.

I crane my neck, trying to find Bay, but my jacket is already being stripped from my shoulders. Bain shoves me, and I stagger forward, barely catching myself on the wagon he used to tow me into the Barrel.

The balding man unfurls a whip, and dread coils in my chest when I realize what's about to happen.

Show it to no one.

A fist gathers my shirt at the back of my neck.

Unless you trust them with your own life, keep it hidden. Always.

With a yank, the worn fabric tears like Old World paper and hangs on my shoulders, my front shielded, but my back exposed. Sun kisses my skin. My flesh prickles with the strangeness of the sensation. I flinch at the whoosh of the whip being raised in the air.

"Wait!" someone shouts from above.

I look up. It's one of the gunners along the rim of the mesa. His clothes are cleaner than the others, and he wears a ram-skull mask while the rest do not. Like all the gunners who have stopped to watch the whipping, his rifle is aimed at my back. "Those markings can't be ruined." The falcon I spotted earlier turns in circles high above his head.

"I'll decide how to punish my property, Loyalist," the man with the whip snaps.

"I'm not making a suggestion, I'm giving orders. Put her in the wagon for Bedrock. The General will see her."

✦ ✦ ✦

Even with my jacket back on, I feel exposed, naked. The leather kisses my bare skin. It's another odd sensation, a reminder that all those years I spent following rules are now meaningless. My shirt was ripped. Everyone has seen my back. Everyone has seen the brand.

The wagon they drag me toward is part Old World tech. The bed is made from the chassis of a salvaged rover. Wooden wheels have been mounted where the Old World variety have failed, and a yoke designed for mules is attached to the front so the wagon can be towed by animals. Bars of woven scrub form the cage, and I'm thrown inside with four other prisoners. One is a boy of about fifteen. Two females are twice that. Their eyes drift to my shoulders, the side of my torso, eager to get a glimpse of the markings now hidden beneath my jacket. The last prisoner is Bay.

She is the only thing that keeps me from physically shaking with fear. I scoop her up, gather her into my chest. She's smarter than she lets on, and if I tremble or cry, she'll pick up on it.

Curse you, I feel like saying to her. *Look what you made happen.*

She's got some sort of hold on me, a dark magic. Just a few days ago I wanted Zuly to take her. All I wanted when I met her was for her be someone else's burden, and when the moment finally came, I fought it like a rusted idiot. Now we're in another cage, headed to Bedrock, to the General.

Images of my pack's smoldering huts flash when I close my eyes.

"Delta?"

I turn and find Asher behind me, his fingers curled around the scrub-woven bars that separate us. "Don't drink anything they give you. Promise me this, Delta."

Someone yells for him to get away from the wagon. The gunner from the rim. He's approaching, rifle at the ready.

"Promise me!" Pure terror sparks in Asher's eyes. He hasn't confirmed it, but I know I'm headed for wherever he was taken after Alkali Lake. Raiders in black. Old Fang's mention of a general. It's all connected. And Asher survived—he escaped—only because of the warning he's giving me now.

"I promise."

He lets go of the bars and slips toward the Vulture's Roost.

The gunner reaches the wagon. Honey-colored eyes gleam at me from behind his mask. "Did he give you something? Show me your hands."

I shake my head adamantly, hold out my palms.

"What did he say to you?"

"That I cost him. That by running, he doesn't get paid, and I'm lucky I'm in this cage or he'd kill me."

The gunner glances toward the pub, then puts his thumb and forefinger in his mouth, producing a high-pitched whistle. The falcon I saw earlier dives from the sky and lands on his gloved fist. With his free hand the gunner holds up a small leather pouch, which the bird snatches in its claws. Then, with a flap of its sandy wings, the creature is airborne again, climbing above the rock of the Barrel and flying north.

The gunner mounts his horse, gives a nod to the driver of the wagon. Reins snap, and the mules plod forward. I look toward the Vulture's Roost, but Asher is nowhere to be found.

The wagon leaves the market and continues through a final stretch of narrow canyon, the gunner following us on a saddled mare. When we break from the pass, I blink in the afternoon brilliance.

The falcon is ahead of us, now a dark smudge against the cloudless sky. Perhaps two clicks ahead is a monstrous mesa. Twice as tall as the Barrel's, and running farther in either direction. Water rushes over its edge, clearer and heavier-flowing than any I've ever seen.

As we draw nearer, I can tell that the falls spill past residences that are built directly into the mesa's rock face. The smooth stone façades practically gleam in the sunlight.

This must be Bedrock.

The place looks like heaven. A sanctuary. An answer to the dying state of the land.

Is *this* the Verdant?

Surrounding the settlement and stopping the flow of water from traveling into the wastes is a towering stone- and mud-packed dam. Like a corral, it runs around Bedrock in a half circle. Only a stream of water breaches the barrier, drying long before it can reach the Barrel. The rutted trail our wagon follows leads to a ramp that climbs to the top of the dam, where a guarded entrance allows access to the fortified settlement beyond.

One way in, no way out. He controls everything.

I realize suddenly why Asher looked so terrified. Even with his warning, he fears I won't survive this.

II

BEDROCK

CHAPTER NINE

Before we reach the ramp to the dam, a cloth sack is thrown over my head and I'm left leaning against the side of the wagon's bed, trying to make sense of things as Bay squirms in my arms.

The wagon pitches during the climb, is momentarily level, and then pitches again as we descend into the space beyond the dam. Once on flat ground, the mule's hooves clomp over hard earth. A few instructions are spoken to our driver, but despite Bedrock's scale, the place is eerily quiet. No voices or laughter. Just the distant roar of the crashing waterfall and the creak of the wagon's wheels.

Despite the sack blocking most of my light, things suddenly go darker still. The mule's hooves echo—we've rolled into an enclosed space, a large stable of some sort, if I had to guess—then lurch to a stop. I'm pulled from the wagon.

"Those three go to the fields, the girl straight to the General's meeting chambers. And the baby goes to the nursery."

Bay is lifted from my arms. "No!" I grasp blindly for her, tugging against my escort, but I can't see anything, and I feel like an empty husk of myself. My limbs are heavy, my head clouded. Any fight I had in the Barrel scudded off when Bain tackled me. If the person holding me now let go of my arm, I might topple over.

They push, guiding me roughly, and like a particle of dust in a storm, I'm swept away.

✦ ✦ ✦

I'm sitting in a chair, hands bound in my lap, when the sack finally comes off my head.

I blink, momentarily stunned by the brightness of the room. The ceiling is too high, and the weathered table stretching before me is massive. It could easily seat twelve. Guards line the perimeter of the room, yet the place doesn't feel crowded. It's unnatural. Too large. Too open.

Candles and torches burn throughout the space, casting the stone walls in flickering shadows. To my right there's a window framed with thin curtains, but from where I'm seated, all I can see beyond it is sky. At the far end of the table is the room's only doorway. A curtain of beaded ropes hangs from the top frame.

The beads part without warning, and a man steps through. Tall and broad-shouldered, he wears pale garments and a sleeveless leather robe that falls to his heels. A chain of metal pendants hangs around his neck, and a falcon is perched on his shoulder. Its plumage is sandy, like the bird belonging to the gunner from the Barrel, but this creature is larger.

The guards along the walls stand straighter as the man approaches the table.

This must be the General.

I steel my expression, raise my chin.

"Delta, was it?" he asks, as though he doesn't already know. As if his men hadn't attacked my home. "Of where?" Two additional guards enter behind him, both wearing ram-skull masks like the gunner from the Barrel, and position themselves on either side of the door.

"I didn't say."

The General smiles as if I've made a joke, and it causes thin lines to appear around his eyes. He's Ma's age, probably, perhaps a bit younger. "Please, have something to drink." He motions to a clay pitcher on the table and the small cup beside it, but I don't miss that there is a second pitcher at the General's seat. Two pitchers. Two different drinks. Asher's warning echoes in my mind.

When I don't move, the General's eyes drift to my hands. He waves for a guard. "Cut her bindings, won't you?"

"I'm not thirsty." Even as I say it, my voice, parched and dry, cracks on the words. I can practically taste the cool relief the drink will provide.

"Cut her bindings anyway. She is no prisoner here."

A guard moves forward and severs my ties with an Old World knife. I rub my wrists as the General sits opposite me.

His face is youthful, almost handsome, but I imagine it's easy not to get beaten down by the land when you rule from a sheltered paradise. Dark hair is cropped close to his head, and a beard obscures most of his mouth, which makes me wonder if he's smiling at me or sneering. The clothes he wears are impeccably clean: a spotless pale shirt tucked into neatly tailored pants. The long, sleeveless robe is the only article that has a patch — a strange faded symbol sewn over his heart. It's an odd place to need mending. Seams tend to give out first, or holes find their way into the elbows or knees, none of which the long vest-robe has. He's clearly never seen a day of work in his life—or at least not since he rose to power within Bedrock.

"It's Delta of Dead River, sir." A face pokes through the beaded curtain door—the gunner from the Barrel who brought me in. "The man trading her confirmed it."

"Thank you, Reed. That will be all." The gunner named Reed disappears, and the General's eyes slide back to me. "Welcome to Bedrock, Delta of Dead River. Now please, have some water. You must be parched."

I stare at him, unblinking. His falcon stares back with a beady, glass-eyed gaze. I pour myself a drink and raise the cup to my mouth. I fake a sip—feel the heavenly wetness on my lips—then swallow to sell the act. The General smiles.

"You must have many questions, such as who I am and—"

"You're the General," I spit out, "and I want to know why your men attacked Dead River and abducted my pack."

He puts a hand to his chest. The slender, thumb-size pendants on his chain clink beneath his palm. Some are rusted, but newer additions gleam in the candlelight. "I would never authorize such actions," he says. "You saw this happen?"

"Well, no," I admit. "Old Fang did."

"I believe my troops were near Dead River during a silent storm. Is this Old Fang elderly? Is it possible the storm influenced his grip on reality?"

"He'd been shot," I practically snarl. "Silent storms don't shoot bullets. And our midwife and her son were killed too, had their skulls smashed in."

The falcon hops onto the table, and the General strokes the bird's cream-brown feathers. "There's been a misunderstanding, clearly. Come. I'd like to show you something."

He stands and moves to the window.

This is the General. His men attacked my camp, killed some of my pack. I should want to claw his eyes out. If I had my knives, I'd be throwing them into his back, but I lost them to Bain days ago and all I can do is stare at my cup of water, thinking about how good it would taste. Because I don't trust myself to sit within an arm's reach of it any longer, I stand wearily and join the General at the window.

Up close he smells of clean linen—a smell I have only encountered during the actual act of washing laundry. As soon as our sheets and clothes are thrown onto the line, they begin to gather dust. Dirt is the scent of a person in the wastes. Dirt and sand and sweat. Dirt is in everything, and the fact that the General doesn't wear it just proves the wrongness about him.

"What do you see?" His falcon jumps from the ledge and spreads her wings, gliding in the open air beyond the window. I look past the creature, down to the land, and nearly lose my breath.

We must be at the very top of the residences I saw built into the mesa. The General's haven extends far below, a jumbled blanket of green and brown. The green is so startling, so foreign, it takes me a moment to realize that I'm looking at crop fields and not a patchwork quilt. From this height, the laboring workers are no bigger than small beads as they weed and harvest. I search for Ma and my pack, but it's pointless. Everyone is too tiny.

Bisecting the fields is a dirt path that leads from the General's towering mesa residence to the dam that corrals his kingdom. Gunners move along the rim, guarding the ramp that provides access to and from Bedrock and pacing between large wooden contraptions that must serve as some type of defense mechanism.

Running beside the dirt path is a puzzling river. It is raised off the ground, water passing through what looks like the crosscut of a wooden straw supported by stilts. Additional half straws branch off the main channel, leading to the fields, but no water flows through them.

"Aqueducts," the General says when he notices me staring. "There's a dam above us, controlling the flow of the falls. We use the aqueducts to direct the water to the fields, opening and closing channels as necessary. Any overflow carries on past the lower dam."

From my vantage point, I can see how the dam wall serves as an aqueduct of sorts itself. Its top is hollowed out and holds water supplied by the rest of the aqueduct system, with metal grates laid over the opening so that guards can patrol there with ease. Barely any water from this strange contained river makes it beyond the General's stronghold. He's using it all. If the river flowed freely, would it stretch through the Barrel and past Burning Ground? Did its water once meet up with Dead River and supply our pack's lake?

"As you can see, I have no need to abduct people. Water. Greens. Shelter. Bedrock is a haven, and people come here freely. Your pack-member Old Fang misspoke."

"You must need hundreds of hands to maintain these fields."

"Thousands, actually. Last time we counted, Bedrock was nearly three thousand strong."

"And you haven't forced any of them into work?"

"If a traveler told you of this place, would you not willingly relocate? Would you not be happy to tend to crops so that your pack would have plentiful food and water?"

I would. Of course I would. This is the type of place I've longed to find for ages. But that's exactly why it's so disturbing. Flint has never mentioned Bedrock, and he trades all over the wastes. Not even Clay, who spouts lies and bumbles about cities across the ocean beds, has spoken of it. The only explanation is that if they knew about Bedrock at all, they've seen it as a place to avoid. And if workers were here freely, they wouldn't need to be driven into Bedrock in caged wagons.

"I have sent my Loyalists far and wide into the wastes," the General goes on. "Each time they find a new settlement, they are instructed to inform the inhabitants about Bedrock and extend an invitation to join us in this paradise. It sounds like your pack eagerly agreed—and that a few of them, including Old Fang, did not. Perhaps they got violent. If my soldiers were attacked, they'd respond with force. It's never ideal, and I will speak to them about this incident, but it does happen."

Lie, lie, lie! my brain shouts. But Old Fang was our leader, and a stubborn one at that. For the first time, I consider what might have happened if he opposed something the majority of the pack wanted. If they all pleaded to relocate and he refused, would they have fought him on it? And, out of shame, would he have lied to me about what happened?

"What does it mean to be gods touched?" I ask. "Old Fang said you were searching for people like that."

"We welcome everyone to Bedrock, but the gods touched are our most valued." He gives me a thin smile. "There was a time when all our ancestors were marked by the gods."

My back prickles. "Marked how?"

"Here." The General taps his temple, and I relax slightly. "Our ancestors were in tune with the earth and the stars, could read the Old World symbols and communicate directly with the gods. I believe that if the gods touched walk among us again in great numbers, our gods are more likely to return." He strokes the metal pendants on his chain absent-mindedly and smiles down on his workers.

"My pack would have waited for me," I insist. "If they wanted to come to Bedrock, they would have asked your men for directions and made the trip once I'd returned from . . ."

I pause, and the General's eyes snap to me. He doesn't ask for it, but I know he's waiting for a location. Just as I didn't know what waited beyond Dead River, he must not know what waits in the desolate stretches of the wastes. I'm not giving up Zuly and her Ark.

Sensing my hesitation, the General's shoulders deflate. "You can speak to your family tomorrow. Confirm my side of the story with them yourself, see that they are here by choice. I'll arrange for the visit."

"So they're here?" My heart swells. I'm relieved . . . and also uneasy.

"Yes, and quite happy about it."

I glance at him sideways. He's watching his falcon ride the wind, face glowing in the setting sun. "Most people would lock down a place like this," I say, "not seek out others to share it with."

"Ah . . . *that* is why the gods abandoned us. Greed. Selfishness. A disrespect for nature. The more people who join us and the more we tend to the land, the more clearly we prove that we are worthy of the gods' blessings. And when we've proved that, when the gods touched walk among us once more, the gods will return from the stars. They will descend on this land and make it green. Water will be so plentiful, I'll be able to open the dams, let it flow across all the wastes. But until then, we must be loyal to the earth and the stars. And if I must dam the water to do that, the least I can offer those beyond Bedrock is a chance to join our cause."

The General whistles, and his falcon returns, landing on the ledge and tucking her wings in place. A beady eye stays rooted on me.

"You don't believe me," he says as he strokes the bird.

"I was bound, brought here in a caged wagon, and shoved into these meeting chambers with a bag over my head."

"Yes. I'm sorry about that, but it was a necessity. Reed believes you are quite valuable to our cause, and I happen to agree. We couldn't risk your refusing to join us."

The map on my skin prickles. He hasn't asked to see it yet, but we're getting there. "Why's that?"

A small smile. "Reed tells me you have a scar on your back. I'd very much like to see it."

I step away from the window. "I'd rather not."

"I wasn't asking."

He signals to the guards lining the room, and before I can shout in protest, fingers pinch my shoulder.

I clasp the front of the jacket, squeezing the buttons. Another guard is immediately at my side, grabbing my arms and yanking them behind my back. In a single exhale, the jacket is ripped away and I'm thrown face-down on the wooden table. The pitcher topples, spilling water and soaking my torn shirt. I don't have a scrap of energy left. I'm held there, pinned down, my brand bared to the men.

The General's clean smell floats over me, and then a finger touches my bare skin. I hiss out a breath as he traces the raised parts of the brand, memorizing my secret, seeing everything I've been told to keep hidden.

"I've seen this map before," he croons, "and I was not careful enough with it. I will not make the same mistake twice."

A sheet of scrap metal is slapped down on the table, the edge nearly taking off my nose. I'm held in place as a guard copies the map, each squeal of his knife on the material like a wedge digging into my skull.

When he's finished, I'm yanked upright and spun around to face the General.

"Read it to me," he demands.

I take in the map properly for the first time in my life. I've never seen it in such clarity. Our hut in Dead River had a sliver of mirrored glass salvaged from an Old World rover and I've peeked once or twice during washes over the years, but it looks different on the sheet metal. I can see the whole of it, every curve and line and dash, and none of it reversed as in a mirror. It's even clearer than what I saw on Asher's back that day at Alkali Lake—still and unmoving and staring back at me.

"I can't," I say.

The General bends forward, his nose a knuckle's width from my cheek. "Tell me what it says."

I shake my head, helpless. I wouldn't know where to begin even if I wanted to. Nothing on the map makes sense. It's just a swirl of random lines. There's no pattern, no purpose. I recognize nothing.

"This here." He points to an Old World symbol. A vertical line with three smaller lines branching off it. "What does it say?" I shake my head. He moves his hand farther to the right, where the same symbol is repeated.

"I don't know."

Another curve. A dash. A series of waves.

"I'm sorry."

The General slams a hand on the table, his face red with rage. "The gods will only return if we are loyal, Delta. Be loyal to the cause. Tell me what it says!"

"I *can't.*"

He whistles twice, and the falcon lands on my shoulder, then brings her beak dangerously close to my eye. "One more whistle, and I can leave you blind. Read me the map!"

"I don't know how! Even if I wanted, I can't," I gasp. "I don't know how to read it. No one in my pack does."

I wait for the final whistle, brace for him to prove a point, but he snaps his fingers and the falcon returns to his shoulder.

"You were supposed to be gods touched," he snarls. "You were supposed to know how to read."

"And you said the gods will only return if you're loyal to the earth. Why do you care about this map if the only way to salvation is through servitude to the stars?"

"I answer to no one but the gods, Delta. You do not get to question me." He turns to the guard holding the scrap metal. "Put it in the library and keep it patrolled. I won't have a repeat of last time."

"Sir, metal can't burn."

"Keep it guarded!" he screams.

"Yes, sir." The man hurries out with the map.

"Everyone is here by choice, Delta," the General says coolly. "Even you. So here is your choice: stop lying and tell me how to read the map, or in three days' time, your mother will be executed."

CHAPTER TEN

I am visibly shaking as the gunner from the Barrel—Reed, the General had called him—leads me to my quarters. His falcon is perched on his shoulder, its head tilted so it can keep an eye on me.

I walk with my jacket clutched to my chest, my shirt still hanging open at my back. Even having shown the brand to the General, even knowing that a copy of it now sits somewhere in his fortress, it pains me to walk with my skin exposed. But Reed's pace is nearly beyond my means, and I worry that if I stop to pull on the jacket, I'll fall behind and anger him. And I heard the General's orders when he stormed from the meeting room. If I try to run, if I attempt to undermine the Loyalist agenda, if I upset anyone in *any* way, I am to be punished in whatever way my current guard deems fit, so long as it doesn't damage the map. I take it that means anything but a whipping. I don't want to find out.

Bedrock is a maze of stone corridors and stairways. Windows line most of the halls on one side, but the setting sun basks everything in a brilliant glow, and I'm hopelessly lost within minutes. We've descended several flights of stairs when Reed passes through a cloth doorway and into a bedroom. A window framed by sheer curtains overlooks Bedrock, and a small nightstand sits beside an honest-to-gods mattress. I've slept only on bed mats my whole life.

"Is this some type of joke?"

Reed frowns. His ram-skull mask is pushed back on his forehead, revealing that he is young—not much older than I am. I wonder how a person ends up working for the General. If he was born into this or if he believes all that Loyalist garbage the General spews. My pack was loyal to the gods, too, and we didn't hold people against their will.

"The General wants you to be comfortable," Reed says, and his expression is so sincere, I feel like punching him.

"Sure he does. Right up until he murders my mother for something I can't give him. I'm not lying. I don't know how to read the map."

Reed swallows and nods, almost sadly. "If that's the story you decide to go by, it's your choice."

"It's not a choice, you rusted idiot. Not when he holds all the power and I literally can't win."

If Reed is bothered that I've insulted him, he doesn't show it. Expression calm, he walks to the nightstand, where a pitcher and cup wait, and peers inside. "There's water here. I'll make sure someone brings you dinner."

"Is this how every prisoner is treated, or am I special?"

"Your pack lives with the other fieldworkers in the shanties along the lower dam. Backbone housing is only for the General and his top Loyalists."

"Backbone?"

"The mesa that these rooms have been built into."

"Right. Best conditions for the army, and shanties for the workers. But everyone's here by choice, so my pack must have picked that."

Reed sighs heavily. "You're making this harder than it has to be. Just give the General what he wants and you'll all be able to live in these conditions permanently. You and every member of your pack, if you request it."

"See how that requires me to give him something first—how I don't have a choice? Or is this too complex for you?"

"I think you should drink some water. You're not feeling well."

I actually laugh a little. He's right. I'm not feeling well. In fact, the room is slightly blurry, and when I blink, the edges of my window seem to ripple. Curse Asher and his rotten advice. How am I supposed to stay alive if I can't drink anything?

My gaze trails to the waterskin on Reed's hip. It hangs from a braided strap slung across his torso, and by the way the pouch puckers, I'd guess it's half full. The dryness in my mouth becomes unbearable.

Don't drink anything given to me, sure. But water the General and his soldiers willingly drink . . .

"I'll be stationed outside your room all night, so don't try to run," Reed says. "And don't bother with the window. No one has ever escaped that way without falling to their death."

Adjusting his grip on his rifle, he gives me a curt nod and strides for the exit. Before I can think too much about the consequences, I grab the waterskin and yank it with the little strength I have left. My efforts combined with his quick pace is enough. The braided cord snaps, and the skin is mine. I raise it to my lips as Reed's falcon lifts from his shoulder in surprise. I choke and sputter on the drink, half of it splashing down my front. My throat is so raw I've nearly forgotten how to swallow.

"Hey!" Reed grabs my wrist and pulls me nearer, pinning my arm and the waterskin between our fronts. With the ram-skull still on his forehead, he seems impossibly tall. My ripped shirt has slipped off one shoulder, and his gaze dips to my front, lingers a second, comes back to my face.

I drop the waterskin, suddenly wanting nothing to do with it, Asher's warning be damned.

Reed is bone still as water leaks from the skin and onto the floor. "I'm going to pretend this didn't happen," he says slowly, "but I won't pretend again." He drops my arm, and I collapse to my knees. Then he retrieves his waterskin, beckons for his bird, and is gone.

It's only when the cloth door falls shut that I begin shaking. I sop water from the floor with my palm, rubbing where his fingers had squeezed over my wrist, scrubbing as though I can wipe away the feeling. The tears come next, or at least the act of crying does. I sob, but I'm so dehydrated, nothing falls from my burning eyes. At this realization, I drink what I can of the spilled water, lapping it from the stone floor like an animal. When I get more grit than water on my tongue, I sit back, clutching my jacket in my hands. The brand burns on my back. The lodestone weighs heavy on my heart.

I crawl to the window and use the ledge to pull myself up. The shanties along the dam are now cloaked in shadow, the fields quiet. Ma's down there somewhere, and the General will kill her if I don't tell him what he wants to hear.

There is no choice for me, no good outcome. Part of me wonders if he knows this.

Skies damn Asher and Bain and Cree. This is their fault. They conned me, caught me, let me be led into this trap. I know Asher never intended for my imprisonment to extend beyond the Barrel, but he knew what waited here in Bedrock, and he did nothing to prepare me for it. He could have told me what to expect, how he escaped, what he did to survive. Instead he only told me not to drink anything I'm given.

I grab the pitcher. The water inside smells faintly sweet, but looks clear. I dip my pointer in, lick the liquid from the pad of my finger. Seems normal—glorious and tasteless and *wet*. But that scent is still there, lingering like a lazy fog. My mouth wants the water even when my brain screams that clean water shouldn't have a smell.

I collapse on the bed before my thirst makes me do something I'll regret.

✦ ✦ ✦

When I wake, it's dark, but a plate of cured meat, bread, and fresh peas still in their pods sits on the nightstand. The bread is tinted green, a telltale sign that the soda that helped make it was harvested from the rich beds at Alkali Lake. Of course the General would have the best of everything. He has water and crops and even the wastes' best baking soda. He can't leave just one thing to the outside settlements.

I eat ravenously, but I don't touch the pitcher. I can't bring myself to ignore the one piece of advice Asher bothered to give. Not yet, at least. My mouth is chalky and dry, and the food tastes like dust in my mouth, but I clear the plate. My goggles rest beside it, moonlight reflecting off the eyepiece.

The eyepiece.

I sit straighter, an idea hitting me. I glance over the items on the table again. My goggles. The tall, narrow pitcher made of clay. The metal Old World cup. I pick up the cup and hold it above the pitcher. It will fit inside, just barely.

In a flash, I'm at the window. The sun will rise behind the Backbone, meaning there won't be much heat on this window ledge until near noon, but I can't not try.

I dump the pitcher's contents, watching as the liquid rains past windows and splats on a stone awning several levels below. The water I stole from Reed has refilled my bladder some, and I relieve myself into the pitcher, then carefully set the Old World cup inside.

Next I rest my goggles atop the pitcher so that the curved, clear eyepiece faces down. The goggles are wide enough — and the pitcher narrow enough — that it creates a decent seal.

I set the whole thing on the window ledge and step back. When the sun finally shines on Bedrock, it will heat up the urine in the pitcher. Water will rise, gather on my goggles, drip down the sloped shape of the eyepiece, then fall into the Old World cup, which waits below. Separate from the urine. Clean, drinkable water.

Gods, am I grateful that I once heckled Flint about his travels in the wastes. I wanted to know how he spent so many days between settlements, how his water lasted so long. He admitted that some days it didn't, that in the worst of the heat he'd move during the night and stay still during the day to collect water. Flint carried a piece of Old World tech he called *plas*. He showed it to me once. Clear like glass, but foggier and flexible, it could be crumbled into a ball or smoothed flat like a blanket. During the day, he'd stretch the plas across a hole in the ground and set a small stone at the center so the plas bowed slightly. Beneath, in the hole, was his own piss and an empty Old World jar, waiting patiently below the stone.

"And you can drink what you collect?" I'd asked, disgusted.

"Yeah. Fresh water droplets gather on the underside of the plas, then slide to the lowest point—where I placed my stone—and drip right into the jar."

"Scud off."

"I'm serious, Delta. Every trader knows the inverted well trick and has relied on it while trekking between the most remote settlements. It yields drinkable water that won't make you sick. You'd do it too, if you were ever in a situation that required it."

I glance at my goggles now. They're not like Flint's plas, but they're clear and curved enough to guide the water true. Eons ago they might have blocked out the worst of the sun's rays—at least that's the rumor I've heard about Old World eyewear—but I squint plenty when I wear them. They only shield me from dust and rubble now.

Meaning this just might work.

It has to, or I'm dead.

I draw the thin curtains, hiding the inverted well from view, and collapse onto the mattress.

CHAPTER ELEVEN

I sleep like the dead but wake early.

First light filters through the sheer curtain, the pitcher a suspicious dark silhouette behind the material. I leap from the mattress and check the cup. Nothing's collected yet, but the worst of the day's heat is still a ways off.

In the hall, I find a new Loyalist guard on duty. When I ask him to see my family, he says he knows nothing about that. When I ask where Reed went, he says he's unsure. When I ask him if there's anything he actually *does* know, he ignores me.

I pace my room for the better part of the morning, rewarded with a sip from the cup around noon. The gathered water is no deeper than the height of my pinkie nail, but it is clean and odorless, and I gulp it down with confidence. I've only just dropped the curtain in place when Reed strides into the room carrying a plate of food, his ram-skull mask still pushed back on his forehead. I'm beginning to wonder if he ever actually wears it outside gunner patrol. I take a step away from him, my hip grazing the window ledge, not sure which I'm more afraid of: his presence or the possibility of him finding the inverted well.

"I've been told to take you to see your family," he says dryly.

I'm surprised I didn't have to fight to see them, and it must read on my face, because he adds, "The General keeps his promises. All of them." He says this last bit with a pointed look, and I know he's talking about the threat against my mother. "Food first, before we go." Reed holds out the plate of melon and a single fried egg. It smells divine, and I hate that my traitorous stomach growls at the sight of it. I doubt my pack is eating so well.

"I'll eat while we walk," I say, wanting to put distance between us and the pitcher on my window ledge.

He shrugs, and I follow him through the halls, shoveling food into my mouth as we go. I can't remember the last time I had melon. Maybe as a kid of four or five? The traders haven't brought it in ages, and we sure couldn't grow it at Dead River. I lick my lips after eating, practically moaning. To think something this ripe and sweet grew from wasteland soil just several days' journey from my home.

When we step from the Backbone's sprawling network of tunnels, Reed pulls his ram-skull mask down to shield his eyes. I squint.

A shrill *kree-kree* sounds overhead, and a shadow flicks over the ground before Reed's falcon settles on his shoulder. He turns toward the animal, and I catch a smile on his face as the bird nips playfully at the nose of his mask. "Go on, get outta here." He jerks his arm, and the bird lifts back into the sky.

"You get a pet if you do all the General's bidding?" I ask.

He ignores me.

Making our way up the large dirt path that divides the crop fields, I take him in properly for the first time. He's about a head taller than I am, but the horns on his skull make it feel like more. Unlike the General's clothes, Reed's are stained with dust and dirt. There's a patch on his left elbow. His boots have been mended several times, and the leather ties that wrap up his calves are varying shades. A modified rifle hangs across his back. I've never shot one, but it's tempting to imagine taking it from him. Of course, there are gunners positioned along the rim of the dam, surrounding all of Bedrock, their eyes and barrels scanning the masses. In my weakened state, I probably couldn't even get the weapon from Reed. Along his shoulders and elbows, there are spikes secured into his leather jacket. One well-placed jab, and I'd go down.

One way in, no way out. He controls everything.

I glance over my shoulder. The Backbone is dizzying from this angle, a towering city that climbs toward the heavens. In the uppermost window, just beside the waterfall, I can make out a figure. Something glints in the sunlight, along the person's front. The General. His chain necklace.

I look away, scanning the other windows quickly as I bring my gaze back to level ground. There must be hundreds of these windows, and many of the ledges hold what appear to be potted plants. It's a small bright spot. My pitcher setup will be almost impossible for a guard along the dam to find suspicious.

"This way," Reed says, stepping from the dirt road onto a network of paths that snake through the fields. I follow him through a patch of melons, then tomatoes, peppers, and squash. Stalks of corn. Potato and turnip plants that look twice as healthy as ours back home, and another patch of vines with deep green leaves and orange flowers the size of my hand. The petals are long and slender, almost paper-thin. I've never seen such a plant, and I wonder what sort of fruit the flower will yield.

It's a miracle, all this food. Not only that it is growing, but the sheer variety of it. More than I've ever seen in a single settlement. More than seems possible to maintain.

Overseers patrol the fields, flicking switches at workers who dawdle. Reed steps around them, nodding to the guards but never bothering to look at the people huddled near his feet.

Women workers easily outnumber the men, and they range from young to old, whereas most of the men appear elderly. Probably because the Loyalist army absorbs the younger, agile men. All the workers wear threadbare clothes stained with sweat. The backs of their necks have darkened to deep russet and brown. A few wear broad-brimmed woven hats to fend off the rays, but what they really need is the protection the guards get; brush-made canopies shield the overseers, allowing them to bark orders from the shade.

The General claimed that everyone is here willingly, but no one with choices elects to get whacked with a switch.

"Almost there," Reed says, stepping over the heels of a young worker who has knelt to gather pea pods. She glances up at me, and when the brim of her hat lifts, I'm struck by the lifelessness in her eyes. They don't communicate fear or helplessness. They're not even tired. Her eyes just look . . . empty. As if she's already left this life and is halfway to another.

"Do you want to see them or not?" Reed snaps.

I look up, realizing that I have stopped in my tracks. Reed is several paces ahead, beneath the shade of the next canopy. The overseer is even deeper in the fields, jabbing his switch into the side of one of the workers.

The woman straightens, brushing sweat from her brow with her forearm. Her clothes are caked with dust, and the yellowed remnants of a bad bruise encircles one of her eyes.

It's Ma.

I run, leaping over the legs of workers and straight into her arms. With my cheek against her chest, I listen to the thrum of her heart, the very realness of her. She's okay. Her arms come around me, and she holds me for a moment before pushing me back so she can cup my face with her hands. "Indie?" she asks.

I shake my head, and tears gather in her eyes. I feel a brief jolt of relief; at least she's hydrated enough to cry.

"The baby?"

"A girl. I've been calling her Bay. The General has her somewhere. A guard mentioned a nursery when I was brought in."

"How'd you find us?"

"I was traveling to Powder Town to ask after you. Got caught along the way." I can't bring myself to say Asher was involved. Mentioning that he's alive will only prompt her to ask questions, and I have too many of my own that need to be answered first. "They tried to sell me in the Barrel, but a gunner saw the brand, brought me to the General."

I expect her eyes to widen at this, expect fear to lace her features, but she barely even blinks. Her gaze has skirted back to the peas she's been gathering, her basket nearly full. She kneels and begins harvesting again. I drop beside her.

"What happened, Ma? Old Fang mentioned an attack. Why did they attack?"

She pinches off another pod, tosses it into the basket. Scoots to the side, gathers more.

"The General said he gave you a choice. But you didn't choose this, right? There's no way you chose this."

"We did." She glances up at me, a calmness about her expression. She was sad when I told her about Indie, but not about this. "It was die with Old Fang or relocate. It's not terrible, though, Delta, truly. Look at this place." She nods toward the waterfall, the crop fields. "If we work the land, we get a share of the resources. We have shelter, small homes not unlike Dead River, but at least the land's not dying here. The traders have kept this place secret from us. They've never wanted us to know, because if we did, we'd move, and then where would their business go?"

"Maybe they didn't know Bedrock was here. No one ventures beyond Burning Ground. And even if they *did* know, maybe there's a reason they didn't tell us. Maybe this place isn't the haven the General pretends it is. Maybe there's a reason traders like Flint and Clay choose the wastes over Bedrock."

She goes on plucking pods from the bush.

"Can you at least look at me when we talk? Ma!" I shake her, forcing her to turn. Her eyes seem distant, lost. "You can't really want to stay here, working every hour of the day."

"I worked every hour of the day at Dead River. Only difference now is I do it for a decent payoff."

"No. You do it because someone has forced you to, *ordered* you to."

"I do it because this is the way to redemption, Delta." Her voice is firm, almost annoyed. "This land is fertile because people here are loyal to the General. He's gods touched. Did you see his chain? The stars that line it? He is close to them, and he believes they will return soon. If we continue to do as he says, they'll come back. This paradise will extend beyond Bedrock. All the wastes will be reborn."

"What the hell are you talking about? If he was gods touched, he'd be able to read. And I know he can't, because yesterday he couldn't read the map."

She doesn't even seem concerned that the map I've been told to protect my whole life has been exposed. She just looks bored.

"The gods' blessing manifests in many forms. Now, where is your basket? If you don't pull your share, you won't get as much water."

"Ma, we have to get out of here. You, me, the rest of the pack. You're in danger, and I can't protect you here. We need to leave."

A girl a row ahead of us turns and whispers, "You're gonna get the switch if you don't— Oh, hi, Delta." It's Pewter. Her cheeks are red with sunburn, and, like Ma, her eyes seem dazed. "Where's your basket? Why aren't you working?"

"I don't want a damn basket!" I practically screech. "Pewter, you trust me, right? I taught you how to dam the lake, how to mend a saddle and patch a tear. I wouldn't lie to you."

She considers this a moment, but turns away as the clanking toll of a wooden bell floats over the fields. Every worker jolts at the noise, heads snapping up. A mule-driven wagon is approaching. Several guards sit in the back, along with a series of barrels. "High noon water call," one of the Loyalists shouts. "Three ladles for a met quota, one for everyone else."

The workers grab their baskets and race for the wagon. I stand there dumbfounded, watching as they battle for positions in line, pushing and shoving. Some grab harvest from the basket of a neighbor, attempting to boost their own haul. Several fights break out, and guards patrol the line, pulling quarrelers apart.

When Ma gets to the wagon, she dumps her peas into a large barrel. From a different barrel, a guard ladles out three scoops of water. She drinks directly from the spoon, then touches her forehead in thanks and carries her empty basket back to the field. Without so much as glancing at me, she kneels and returns to harvesting.

"Ma, don't you want to know where Bay is? Or why the General is after the brand on my back? Don't you care that he killed Old Fang, Astra, and Cobel just to recruit you here?" She goes on picking pods. "Ma! Look at me, dammit."

I grab her shoulder and force her to turn. Her face is slack, almost expressionless. There's a sweet aroma about her now that drowns out the stench of sweat, and her eyes are more detached than ever. She looks toward me, but not at me. "Find your basket and tend to the land, Delta," she says blandly. "Be loyal to the cause, or I'll report you."

Be loyal to the cause. The same words the General snarled while his men held me down and copied the brand on my back. I back away from Ma. She watches me indifferently for a moment, then returns her attention to the crop.

I flee down the row. I'm not even out of the pea field when

Reed tackles me around the waist. I crash to the ground. The fertile land smells like wet earth — completely natural, no sweetness like the water in the barrel Ma drank from.

The truth strikes like a knife to the heart.

The General is tending to the land but drugging his workers. I will never get through to Ma. And if I don't start pretending to be drugged also, the General is going to force the tainted water on me too.

CHAPTER TWELVE

Back in my room, the inverted well has yielded nearly a full cup of water. I drink it slowly, savoring each drop as I watch shadows creep across the fields.

Does Ma know the water she drinks has been tampered with?

We're used to stagnant water in the wastes. Murky, cloudy, sometimes even a touch brackish, but our purified fare was always odorless after boiling. Clean. It's hard to imagine that she didn't notice the sweet undertone to the General's water. Or maybe she just didn't care. Like every worker in those fields, it was drink the strange water or die, and she doesn't have a warning from Asher echoing in her mind.

I'm not sure what the drug is. Moonblitz can fog a person up good, but Ma's dazed state was different. A blitzed drinker will stagger, stutter, sometimes even pass out, but the workers today were competent, seemingly healthy in all ways except their logic. And even wasteland remedies like nightshade and humweed, which can force sleep or dull pain, don't match Ma's symptoms. I don't know of anything addictive that can keep a person func-tional *and* subdued. Which means I have no idea how quickly the drug can take hold of a person, or how long it takes to get out of one's system.

I dump out the pitcher and reset the well for tomorrow. Surviving on such a small amount of water is absurd. Even now my throat scratches, angry at the tease the cup provided.

I'll never be able to help the pack if I give in to thirst and end up fogged like the rest of them. And even if I don't, I can't help Ma. I don't know how to read the map. I sink into bed, my stomach reeling. No matter what I do, I lose.

✦ ✦ ✦

When morning arrives, I have a plan, or at least the very crudest makings of one.

"I need to see the map," I tell Reed as he arrives with my breakfast.

He scowls. "I'll have a mirror brought."

"No mirror. That's how I've seen it my whole life. I need to look at it properly. Maybe I'll be able to make sense of it if I can actually study it."

Reed's brow pitches up, but he turns and leads me from the room. Let him believe that I think I can do this. Let all the Loyalists believe it. If the General thinks I'm *trying* to read the map, perhaps I can buy more time for Ma.

Instead of working our way down through the Backbone as we had yesterday, Reed leads the way up several flights, then through a curtained doorway guarded by two Loyalists. Inside, I find a windowless room crowded with Old World artifacts. Shelves teem with salvaged tech, tarnished and worn. I can make out the door of a rusted rover and a sloped piece of scrap metal bearing a faded birdlike emblem leaning against the far wall. Dowels near the ceiling hold scraps of brittle paper. Countless crates are stacked haphazardly beneath them, their contents hidden from view.

It's a treasure room, a scavenger's paradise. I've never seen so much Old World tech in one place. And yet despite the wide array of items, none of them seem terribly useful. There are no goggles, like my trusted pair. No Old World rifles or the exceedingly rare Old World bullets. Not even plas, like I've seen Flint carry. Instead, everything looks like scrap. Garbage. Pieces of history rather than valuable assets. But all the junk has something in common: the Old World language, long lost to us, graces each item.

A lone woman sits at a table in the center of the room, head bent as she observes something before her.

"Oracle," Reed says in greeting.

The woman looks up. She is young—perhaps just a few years older than I am—and she wears a long, sweeping dress the color of straw. Her braided hair is knotted atop her head with dark strips of cloth.

"Reed," she says with a small smile. "I'm surprised to see you. I thought you'd been granted a station in the Barrel for a moon's time."

"Plans change." He grunts. "This is Delta of Dead River, and she would like to study the map. Perhaps you can tell her what you've learned, and it will loosen her tongue. She's withholding from the General."

Withholding. I could spit on him.

"She is welcome to study with me," the Oracle says, and she raises a pale, willowy hand to beckon us nearer. Reed nudges my back, forcing me into the room.

I approach the table slowly. The Oracle is studying the sheet of metal that the General had the brand copied onto. Beside her is a shallow tray of damp dirt, and she has scraped symbols into it with a twig. Some seem to match the markings of the map. Others are new shapes, illegible swirls and curves. She brings a palm to the dirt, wiping the surface clean before I can get a closer look.

"Guards remain stationed at the library door, so staging an escape would be futile," Reed says to the woman. "I'll be back in a few hours." Despite his blunt tone, he nods to the Oracle and touches his forehead in respect, then leaves without another word.

The Oracle motions to the chair beside her. As I sit, I notice her necklace. Its chain is shorter than the General's, and it holds just one pendant, but the style and size of the metal is the same. Slender and smooth, the length of my thumb. A star, my mother had called it yesterday.

"Did you help someone escape once?" I ask, still thinking of Reed's warning to the woman.

"My father did. He was the Oracle before me."

"What happened?"

"There was a fire. My father burned some of the General's most prized relics. But that's not what you came here for, is it?" She angles the map toward me. "What do you see?"

The markings shine up at me from the carved scrap metal, foreign and strange. Crisscrossed lines. Swirling curves. Dots and specks. "A thicket. A dust storm. An unreadable constellation."

"You cannot read it?"

"Can you?"

The Oracle frowns. "This is an *E*." She points to a symbol

115

in the top left of the map, the line I'd noticed the other day with three smaller lines branching from it. "It repeats here." She moves her finger to the right, where the symbol appears again. "Nothing else makes sense."

"What's an *E?*"

"A letter of the Old World language. When combined with others, the letters form words that can tell stories, reveal correspondences, give directions." She scowls at the map and returns to writing in the damp dirt beside her. "My father never cracked the map in his time, and all his research was lost in the fire, along with the original map."

Sir, the guard had said to the General yesterday. *Metal can't burn.*

He had the map before, only to lose it. The Oracle's father had helped the bearer escape.

Asher.

"Where's your father now?" I ask.

"Dead. The General had him proved a fraud and executed." The Oracle is stoic, seemingly unbothered by this tale of lost family. Her eyes search mine. "Are you sure you can't read it?"

"It means nothing to me." I take in the strange markings, lingering on the letters she says are *E*s.

"Maybe there's a cipher or a key," she says. "Some way to unlock it." My confusion must show on my face because she adds, "Those would be ways to make a message appear, to change something from scrambled to legible. Think, Delta. Please. Is there anything you were told when receiving the map, anything that might unlock its truth?"

"Just to keep it hidden. Always."

"*Always*," the Oracle muses, and scribbles something into her damp dirt. I watch her work for a moment, writing additional lines and symbols, her brow furrowed.

"How was he a fraud?"

"Hmm?"

"Your father."

"He wasn't gods touched."

"But I thought anyone who could read was gods touched. Isn't that alone proof that—"

"After his execution, they opened his skull. There was no star, no sign of the gods' blessing."

Opened his skull . . . stars on a chain . . . gods touched.

I think of Astra and Cobel, their crushed skulls. The grave-yard to the north, where all the skeletons bore the same fate. The blood on Old Fang's crown, as though he'd been struck before the General's men abruptly dispersed.

I swallow slowly, feeling ill.

The General has been searching for physical proof that marks one as blessed by the gods.

"His chain," I say softly. "That means that . . . each of those pendants . . ."

The Oracle nods. "He's collected them over the years. From graves and salvages, from traders who don't know what they've found. They are a thing of the past, I fear, though many believe that a man with so many stars must be gods touched himself, or at least close to the gods. The star chain marks the General as mighty—as someone worth following."

My eyes drift to the Oracle's necklace. "And your chain?"

"It's been passed down through my family for generations. The star is from a distant relative. Perhaps the last of the gods touched in our bloodline, but since the General can't confirm that I'm gods touched without killing me, and because I'm the last person in Bedrock with knowledge of the Old World language, he holds out hope that my bloodline may have been touched by the gods again. That a star could burn within me. Just as he had hoped with my father." She swallows heavily. "What about here? See these repeating waves?" She points to the center of the map, where three vertical lines have been etched. Unlike the vertical line of the *E*, these wiggle, like the path a snake makes when slithering across sand.

"I don't know. I'm sorry. They're not another letter?"

She shakes her head. "No. Aside from the two *E*s, nothing on this entire map is a letter—at least not one that I know. There was a time when our ancestors spoke multiple languages. Maybe the map is written in one of those."

"There must be someone else who can help, someone who knows these other languages."

"No one here can read as I do, let alone read a second language. I am not allowed to teach letters, and neither was my father. He taught me when I was a child, long before we came to Bedrock and the General began overseeing our lives. Even the children in our nursery, who represent a better future, are not permitted to learn from me. If they one day wake up able to read, or to prophesize the weather, or to handle Old World tech without instruction, *that* will be proof that the gods have blessed a mortal again."

118

"This nursery," I say, my voice almost cracking. "Where is it?"

"You care for one of them?"

I blink rapidly, silently cursing the water that builds in my eyes. "I was brought here with her. She's just a baby."

"The pups receive some of the best care in Bedrock," she says reassuringly. "They could be our future gods touched, after all. I visit them with each full moon, speak with the older ones and administer tests. If they aren't showing signs of being gods touched, I sort them into the working staff or Loyalist army, but not until they turn seven. Yours will be fine for many years, so long as you don't let him see your fondness for the girl. He will use it against you."

I let out a gasp that is part relief, part agony. Seven years in this place. Seven years of a childhood that isn't a childhood before Bay is sorted like a piece of Old World tech at market. "She's not mine," I manage.

"Oh," the Oracle says, her eyes heavy with sadness. "I think she is."

I glance away. If I look at her a moment longer, I will lose all my composure. I still don't know how it came to this. Life at Dead River was hard, but fine. I didn't realize how ideal it was, even with the storms and the drying lake and the backbreaking work. I didn't know I'd miss it until it was wrenched away.

I stare at the map. Each dash and curve, every line and symbol. If the Oracle can't read it, how in the scorched skies am I supposed to?

"I don't know how to fix this," I mutter. "If I don't tell him how to read it by tomorrow, he's going to kill my ma."

"I will try to find something—anything—to buy you time before then, but I'm not hopeful."

She's honest, at least. That's more than many can say.

I nod my thanks. "Do you think you could take a message to the nursery for me? Tell Bay I will make everything all right. I don't know how, but I'll find a way. I promise."

"I'll tell her . . ."

"But?" I ask, sensing the Oracle's hesitation.

"A promise you can't uphold is a dangerous thing. The General, for all his faults, upholds his. If your mother is the first target in his quest to get answers from you, he will eventually turn his sights to Bay. Seven years may sound long now, but it is merely an exhale in the cosmos."

She stands quickly, her gaze fixed on something over my shoulder. I turn to find Reed in the doorway. It hasn't been several hours, let alone one.

"Time's up," he says.

I've taken just one step toward him when the Oracle's hand closes over my wrist. "Tread carefully, Delta of Dead River. If there is something you're keeping from me—if you think of *anything* that might help me decode this map—I urge you to speak before it is too late."

CHAPTER THIRTEEN

That night, beneath a blanket of gods-forsaken stars, I sip a fresh cup of water and stare at the dam that surrounds Bedrock. I study the Loyalists, learning the pattern of changing guards by watching torches shift. They patrol between the massive wooden contraptions I noticed while in the General's meeting chambers—objects that I assume can help defend the settlement, though I've never seen anything like them before. I consider the dizzying descent down the Backbone and wonder if I could make it with nothing but my bare hands. There are plenty of windows, but very few with stone awnings, and even fewer balconies. I would likely fall to my death, just as Reed warned on my first night.

And even if I made it to the fields, what do I truly expect? That I can waltz into the workers' quarters, round up my pack, and slip into the wastes unseen? Ma will probably fight me, tell me to be loyal to the cause. The guards will see me enter the shanties, and if they don't, they'll certainly catch us trying to cross the dam. And if by some gods-granted luck we make it out, bullets will find our backs within minutes. Sentry posts overlook the land beyond Bedrock, which is unsheltered and sprawling, with nowhere to go but south through the Barrel. Through a bottleneck. Through hell.

We'd be caught.

We'd never make it.

But still I run through scenarios. I plot and plan, because I know that tomorrow my time is up. I even comb through every childhood memory I can recall, wondering if the Oracle may be correct. Perhaps I know something that unlocks the map—a cipher or a key, as she called it. I start with the day I was branded, a suffocatingly hot summer day, and move through the days that followed. Nothing stands out. Our pack was so concerned with keeping the map hidden, so eager to please the gods with blind faith and trust, that we rarely spoke of the brands Asher and I wore. There's nothing. Nothing outside the rule we lived by.

Show it to no one. Unless you trust them with your own life, keep it hidden. Always.

When the sun rises, I am still at the window, still staring at the dam, still at a loss for how I will possibly spare Ma from her fate.

✦ ✦ ✦

At first light I request a visit with the Oracle. Reed escorts me, the ram-skull mask resting on his forehead. His falcon is not with him today.

"Are you a Barrel gunner or a Bedrock guard?" I ask him. "I can't figure it out."

"I'm a Loyalist," he says dryly. "And the General's fourth."

"Fourth?"

"It means I'm *just* unimportant enough to get stationed in the Barrel for a moon, but important enough to get dragged back to my regular duties when you showed up. Some reward for locating a map to the Verdant."

"Maybe you should have kept your mouth shut. Might have been better for both of us."

"Yeah, maybe," he grumbles. He actually sounds like he means it.

As we walk, I consider what his number might mean. That Reed is one of General's most trusted advisers? That he is fourth in a line of succession? By blood or by chance? Reed is sweeping aside the curtain to the library before I can settle on a theory.

I step through to find the Oracle where I left her yesterday. Her pale hair is still knotted atop her head, but her clothes are different. Today she wears a faded top tucked into a skirt of many layers, some so sheer that lower sections of fabric bleed through like a sunset.

"Delta of Dead River. You've thought of something?"

"*Show it to no one,*" I recite. "*Unless you trust them with your own life, keep it hidden. Always.* That was the only rule of the map, the full rule. I thought maybe the exact wording might help."

"Sit." She nods at the chair. "Let's break this down together."

Reed leaves us to the task. I lose track of time as the Oracle scribbles in her dirt tray and wipes it clear and scribbles again. She mumbles and studies and asks me to repeat the rule multiple times, but throughout it all, her brow remains creased. Eventually she adds a few drops of water to her tray to keep the dirt from drying out. I watch the soil suck up the liquid, my mouth watering. I almost ask the Oracle for a drink—it seems unlikely that water she uses in this manner would be drugged—but I am afraid the question will look suspicious. I don't want her to mention anything to Reed, so I bite my lip and try to ignore the scratching in my throat.

"Why do you help him—the General?" I ask, finally breaking the silence.

She glances at me sternly. She can't be far into her twenties, but I feel like a child under her scrutinizing gaze. "Know this, Delta: we are all prisoners here in Bedrock. It is not lost on me that my imprisonment brings more privilege and comfort than those who work the fields. But everyone who was brought to Bedrock has been robbed of their choices. I was brought here as a child. My father stayed because he saw shelter and water and food."

"And you?"

She glances at the curtained door and drops her voice to a whisper. "I stay because I see that the General's resources are fading. I am provided with less water than I was years ago. The rations have grown smaller. Most may not have noticed, but I see the truth, especially in the water that flows over the Backbone. It was wider in my childhood, the falls broad and beautiful. Now its volume has lessened, and not merely because of the upper dam. His paradise is truly on borrowed time. If I cannot read this map, if the gods are not timely in their return and we do not find the Verdant soon, we will all perish. Everyone within Bedrock. And only a few men here deserve that fate. I refuse to doom everyone for the sins of a handful."

It makes sense, finally—the General's obsession with the map. I don't doubt that he believes in the gods, but he is worried they won't return in time, and the Verdant is his backup plan. I hate that I have something in common with him, that I can understand how he is torn between faith and practicality. I have always felt that same tug, self-preservation telling me to move the pack to Powder Town, gods be damned.

"Does anyone else know? Or at least suspect?"

She shakes her head. "Not outside the General and his Four. They are his closest advisers. They wear masks to mark themselves as such, and they communicate by falcon. Not with the Old Language, but with a short code they've developed."

That solves one mystery about Reed. I picture the leather pouch he'd passed to his falcon that day in the Barrel, how the bird had flown ahead to Bedrock, surely carrying some type of message to the General. It makes me consider what the Oracle said the other day about forgotten languages. These short codes used by the General and his Four are a language, in a way. Could something similar mark my back? A code that my pack doesn't know how to read, but someone, somewhere on the wastes, does?

"How can you sit on this secret about the water?" I ask the Oracle.

"Do not shame me. And keep your voice low. If I were to speak of this openly, the General would execute me for blasphemy."

I wonder briefly why she's being so honest with me—a complete stranger. Maybe it's a calculated risk; she shares secrets with me in hopes that I'll share a secret about my brand.

"If he executes you, he'd have no one to read the map," I point out.

"I can't seem to read it as it is." She sighs heavily. "And the truth is, he'd rather maintain the illusion that he is all-knowing, all-powerful—and that the gods are returning because of what he's done for this land—than admit that Bedrock is failing and the gods are as absent as ever." She wipes her dirt clean and stares again at the map. "He needs me, but only because I'm convenient. If I betray him, if I make him look weak, he will dispose of me swiftly, just as he did my father. Besides, his Loyalist army is substantial. He'd send them into the wastes in search of another Oracle. The skill to read is rare, but they'd find someone. Just as he found you."

Or Asher. Taken at nine, his world shattered.

"Your father helped a map-bearer like me once. Didn't he?"

Something pained graces the Oracle's features. Regret, perhaps. "I didn't understand at the time. He helped that boy escape when he never once tried to save me from this prison. My father couldn't read the map, and he believed all his work to be in vain. He set that fire as a diversion while the boy fled." She glances at me briefly, hurt in her eyes. "But I can't help you, Delta, not the way he did for that boy. The map is too important now. I must protect it in order to protect Bedrock's people. At least I must try."

The curtain parts, and Reed enters. His mouth is thin, his expression unreadable. "The General would like to see you."

Dread coils in my stomach. He wants an answer I still don't have.

"Be strong, Delta of Dead River," the Oracle says. "Even knowing what comes next will not lessen the pain."

✦ ✦ ✦

Reed brings me to the nursery, where light shines through the room's three windows.

Babies sleep in cradles, toddlers play with wooden blocks on the floor, and young children scurry between them, chasing and laughing and being *children*. The space feels separate from the rest of Bedrock, a room filled with hope and innocence and purity. Several caregivers drift around, handing out snacks of cornbread and honey. Another stoops over a cradle to comfort a crying babe.

Bay must be here. My heart beats faster just knowing it. I can speak to her in person, not rely on the Oracle to deliver a message.

Even still, I don't look for her among the children. I can't seem to look anywhere but at the General once I spot him. He stands before the room's central window, his posture rigid and his eyes unfeeling. Two men flank him. Like Reed, they both wear ram-skull masks. Advisers. Two more of his Four.

"Delta of Dead River," the General says, motioning for me to join him. Reed has to nudge between my shoulder blades to get my feet moving. Once I'm at the window, the General's two guards step back, giving us space. "It's beautiful, yes? The only room with a better view is my own, a floor above us."

The General's falcon screeches outside the window. Shadows move on the sill when she flaps her wings, but I can't bring myself to look anywhere but at him, afraid of what I might find outside.

"Go on. Look." He pinches my chin and angles my head. I can see all of Bedrock, but my eyes find her immediately, as if they don't know where else to settle. She's been forced to her knees atop the dam, arms bound behind her back. Several Loyalists surround her, but only one holds a blade to my mother's throat. It glints in the afternoon sun.

I hadn't understood what the Oracle meant about knowing not lessening the pain. I do now.

"You said I had three days," I gasp. "It hasn't been three days."

"You were brought to Bedrock in the morning. By noon the brand had been copied, and three evenings have passed since then. I was very clear with my words. Three days. Not three and a half. Now tell me what I want to hear."

"But a day doesn't end until sunset. This is still the third day."

"And will another few hours make a difference?"

"Maybe. I told the Oracle everything I know. She could discover something."

He bats a hand. "She is as useless as her father. If she could read it, she would have done so on the day you arrived. Now, tell me the brand's secret or your mother's blood will paint the side of the dam."

The guards must have told her where to look, because her face is turned toward the window, as though she expected to find me standing in its frame. Her hair hangs limp around her face. I imagine her expression as pleading, though she's too far away to be certain.

"I don't know how to read it. If you give me more time, I can figure it out."

"You are out of time." The General pulls a square of red cloth from his vest pocket and raises it above his head. I'm trying to think of a lie — something, anything that might spare her — when he brings the cloth down and the Loyalist on the dam draws his blade across my mother's neck.

She goes slack, crumples to the ground. I make a noise I don't recognize, something guttural and wild. The guard grabs her at the shoulders while a second Loyalist gathers her feet. With a single heave and swing, they throw her from the dam, and she disappears as a ripple of cloth and hair.

I stare, heart in my throat. He said it would come to this. Promised it. And still I'd thought there'd be another way, a reasonable compromise. Surely if I didn't waver, the General would trust that I was being honest, that I had no clue how to read the map. But she's gone.

I turn on him. His guards have me by the wrists before I can strike. I could tear that glinting star chain from his neck. I could gouge the star pendants into his eyes. "I needed more time!" I scream. "I could have solved it with more time."

"It's quite possible," the General says calmly.

"Then why did you kill her?"

"So you understand how serious I am." A glance at his guards. "Bring her to the baby."

Not Bay. Not Bay, you monster. I'm dragged from the window, shoved toward one of the cradles.

She's swaddled in a pale cloth, sleeping soundly. It doesn't seem possible that she could have changed in just three days, but her cheeks seem fuller, her eyelids a bit less translucent.

"This child represents the future of your pack," he says.

It is not a question, but I nod, fear gripping me. I don't know how to unlock the map. I can't give him what he wants, and he's going to kill Bay for it. I'll have to lie. There has to be something I can say, something I can do . . .

"You want more time?"

"Yes, please," I gasp. I'm on my knees beside the cradle now, begging with a devil. "Please, I just need more time."

"Then you will have more—three days for each of your pack-members. At noon every third day we will convene in this nursery. You will look across the dam at the oldest surviving member of your pack, and if I do not hear what I want, they will fly like your mother. I'll work my way down to this child"—he nods at the cradle—"and if, by the time her blood is spilled, you still haven't come clean, perhaps I will believe that you've been honest. That you do not know how to read it."

"I *don't* know how."

The General pulls a knife from a sheath at his hip and rolls the handle idly in his palm. "So I should just kill her now?" The blade dips toward Bay. "Not even bother with the new time I've afforded you?"

"No—wait! It's a code!" I blurt out. "Your Oracle can't read it because it's not written in the Old World language."

The General lifts a brow. "Go on."

"I can't decode it from here, I need ..." *Asher.* The Vulture's Roost. He'll know what to do. "I need to leave," I tell the General, "and I will get you answers if you promise that my pack will be safe until I return."

"Whatever you need, we can acquire it. Name the objects or person who can decode the map, and we'll bring them to Bedrock."

I open my mouth, pause.

"You're lying." The General smiles slyly. "You know the code. You know how to read it and you're keeping it to yourself." His smile morphs into a scowl. "Remember this, Delta: whoever finds the Verdant controls who can access it. *You* won't be leaving Bed-rock unless I allow it, and you and your pack won't be granted access to the Verdant unless I allow it either. Give me what I want, and your pack can have a future. Do you understand?"

I consider lying again — calling out a random location where the Verdant might be and sending him searching the wastes. But he'd only return furious, happy to spill more of my pack's blood.

So I nod, numbly.

"Wonderful. Reed?" The General looks behind me. "Give her a few minutes with the baby. Let the full weight of the situation register."

"Yes, sir," Reed replies.

"And Delta?" he adds.

I force myself to look at the General. His voice is even, but there is a smile in his eyes. He's enjoying this.

"Tonight is your last evening in your quarters. I'm short a fieldworker now, and you will take your mother's place at first light."

He whistles for his falcon, and it sweeps into the nursery to land on his shoulder. As the General strides out with his two guards, the bird watches me with a gleaming golden eye.

I'm not certain how I remain standing, not when the earth has given out beneath me. Ma, dead. My remaining pack-members all facing the same potential fate, even Bay. And my new work assign-ments. How will I keep my head when I'm moved to the fields? I doubt the shanties have water pitchers. There will be no way to set up an inverted well.

Everyone in the nursery is staring at me. I spot Wren, Brooke's girl of just four, fiddling nervously with the end of her braid, her eyes wider than the moon.

This was a calculated move on the General's part. He could have let me watch my mother's murder from his own room or the meeting chambers, or anywhere in Bedrock, but it took place here in the nursery so that these children see what happens when you cross him. If they are not gods touched, they will end up in the General's fields or army. He is teaching them with fear and threats, cruelty and submission. He is bending them to his will now so that they are easier to control later.

"Here," Reed says gruffly, nudging me toward the cradle.

I glance down, and there she is, eyelids fluttering open. "Hey," I whisper, crouching beside her. "Hi, Bay." Her gaze flits around idly. "I am going to get you out of here. I don't know how, but I will make it right. I promise. The Oracle told me not to make promises that I can't keep, but I *have* to keep this one. I won't be able to live with myself otherwise." Bay wriggles, arms popping free of the swaddle. I touch her small hand, let her fingers curl around my pinkie.

I think of the stories Ma told me when I was little, passed down from her ma and the ma before that. Stories about water —rivers and streams, coves and canals, oceans and inlets. So many formations lost to us, so many we wish the gods would resurrect.

"We're stuck together now, the only bit of blood we each have left," I whisper. "I'm the delta and you're the bay. I lead to you. You depend on me. We're a team, and I'm not gonna let anything change that. Understand?"

She gurgles softly.

When Reed hauls me to my feet, it's a blessing to have someone guide me. I'm not sure my feet would work if I weren't being told where to step.

✦ ✦ ✦

Back in my quarters, as soon as the curtain falls into place and Reed's footsteps fade off, I race to the window. There's a full cup of water in the well. I pull it out, sip gingerly. Instinct tells me to gulp it down, but I also know it's likely to be my last clean drink. I should save some for the morning.

I'm taking a final sip when the curtain parts and Reed steps into the room. "I just wanted to say—" He freezes. "What the hell is that?"

I set the cup on the ledge and drop the curtain, as though hiding the inverted well behind it will make it disappear.

He stalks to the window and peers into the pitcher, nose wrinkling. Then he picks up the cup, sniffs the water. No curled lip, no fowl expression. Slowly, he dips a finger in and tastes the liquid, his eyes locked with mine. He swallows. A muscle ticks in the side of his jaw. He's going to dump it. My final drink of clean water and he's going to pour it out. As though I haven't lost enough already. As if my world isn't coming apart at the seams.

"Don't," I beg softly. "Please. I won't have any starting tomorrow."

Time sticks, and for what feels like an eternity he stands there glaring at me. Then he places the cup on the ledge and heads for the door without another word.

"What will you tell him?" I ask as he reaches the curtain.

He pauses. "Nothing. Like you said, you won't have any more starting tomorrow." He brushes the curtain aside and slips from the room. I hear him say something to the guards on duty; then his boots fade off.

I grab the cup and gulp down the drink before Reed can change his mind and return to toss it. The water is warm and glorious. As it wets my mouth and slides down my throat, I remind myself that what Reed did was not born of compassion. When my traps yield catch, I killed them immediately. It is kinder that way. Less suffering. Reed granted me a drink, then left me in the cage to perish slowly.

I crawl onto the mattress and try to sleep, but all I can see is the blade coming across Ma's neck, her limp body falling from the dam. My brain jumps ahead in time, showing me the others, leaving out no details, not even for poor Bay.

Although I can't afford to waste water, the tears break loose. I come apart, sobbing into the mattress, the knowledge that I am going to fail my pack unbearably heavy. Just as I failed Indie, just as I failed Ma. I don't have the power to save them.

CHAPTER FOURTEEN

The fields are blistering hot.

I joined the workers at sunrise, unceremoniously. I was allowed to bring what I could wear, so I put it all on, ensuring that nothing could be confiscated. Now, as the sun nears its peak in the sky, I harvest beans with my goggles on to avoid the dust that is kicked up by the shuffling workers. The back of my neck aches. Even with my jacket collar flipped up, I can't escape being cooked.

To my right, Pewter keeps her attention on the crop. To my left, Brooke does the same. I can't avoid talking about it any longer. "I'm so sorry," I blurt out. "I'm so sorry about Marin." They just stare at me with glassy eyes, blinking.

"Who's Marin?" Pewter asks. It is the only thing she's said to me all day. Like all the other workers, she is focused on filling her basket, her fingers picking and plucking, the plant leaves rustling as she moves through the row.

"What do you mean, who's Marin? My ma. Marin. The General executed her."

Pewter blinks at me.

"Didn't any of you notice she's missing?" I turn around, waiting for someone to confirm it. Maybe their grief is too immense to discuss things right now. Maybe throwing themselves into the work is all that's holding them together.

I drop a handful of beans into my basket and angle my head toward Brooke. "Who's the oldest in our pack now?" I whisper. "Is it Alder or Vee?"

"Get back to work."

Worry gnaws at me. "You know who they are, don't you? Alder and Vee?"

She remains quiet.

"Your daughter. Where is she?"

Brooke glances about briefly, then frowns.

"Do you even remember her name?"

A crease appears in her brow. "Be loyal to the cause . . ." She studies me, searching for my name, but she can't place that either. Eventually she just shrugs and goes back to harvesting.

Whatever's in the water isn't merely numbing the General's workforce, it's chipping away at their minds, their memories, their very souls.

I hope Ma had forgotten me by the time they dragged her onto the dam. I hope she looked at my face and saw a stranger framed in the nursery window. I can't bear to think that she died knowing her daughter was the one to forsake her.

✦ ✦ ✦

By noon, I have sweated through my undershirt and am feeling faint. Heat rash speckles my palms, but when the wagon comes with the water, I've harvested only enough to earn one ladle. I accept the drink, nod my thanks, and hold the water in my mouth until I'm back in the fields and out of the guards' sight. There, I drop to my knees and spit it all out. I watch the soil soak it up, my throat dry and scratchy.

After the water wagon leaves, we're instructed to shift from harvesting to weeding, tossing anything we pull into our baskets so they can be dried out and used for textiles or fuel. The surface dirt is bone-dry, but when I pull my first weed, damp earth clings to the roots. The General must have the fields watered in the evening, when the workers are back at the shanties, spent from the day and dreaming whatever fogged dreams the drugged water induces. If I can sneak out to the fields then . . . If I capture runoff from those watering sessions . . .

Shouts from the dam pull me from my thoughts, and I look up to see a convoy rolling into Bedrock. I push to my feet for a better view. At first I think it's some division of the General's army, men back from pillaging another poor settlement, new workers for the fields in tow. But the procession of wagons is mismatched—some built entirely of worn wood, others part Old World rover—and no one with the unit wears a ram-skull mask or the Loyalist black. In fact, the people with this convoy look as disheveled as those from any settlement in the wastes. Slapdash goggles are pulled over their eyes, threadbare scarves wrapped around their necks and noses. I can make out woven wool shirts and the occasional leather jacket. Harnessed mules tow the wagons, whose payload is hidden beneath sheets that are pulled over the bed. Ropes and braided rags cinch the fabric down tightly, but by the bulking shape, it's obvious that there's a lot of whatever they're moving.

The dark-skinned driver at the front of the procession cracks a whip, guiding the way down Bedrock's dirt street. Gunners are positioned around the bed of each wagon, long barrels resting against their shoulders now that they've entered Bedrock and left the dangerous wastes behind. A handful even hold bows, the quivers slung across their backs.

Only the lead wagon is marked in any way—a pale flag with the symbol of some type of instrument stitched onto its face. A hammer perhaps, or a pick. The flag flaps too much for me to be sure.

Loyalists meet the convoy just before the Backbone, and the wagons roll beneath the lowest canopies, disappearing from view.

A shadow falls over me. "Weed," the guard barks.

I'm too parched to argue, and after standing upright for so long, dropping to all fours is a relief. I return to my work, considering how a soul can end up broken, with or without drugged water.

✦ ✦ ✦

I'm in a bad place by late afternoon. My vision swims, and even moving my basket of weeds leaves me winded. I should have had some of the water, maybe just a sip. I can't help my pack if I'm dead, and that's where I'm driving myself.

I glance up, praying to find the water wagon nearby. Instead I see a familiar face on the dirt road.

I squint, certain the heat is playing tricks on me, but the figure remains unchanged. Dark hair and broad shoulders and a slight limp in his step from a broken ankle that never healed right. *Flint.* I blink several times. It's him. The problem is he's wearing the Loyalist garb—black from head to toe. He's even carrying a rifle.

In all the years I've known him, he's rolled into Dead River to trade with nothing but a pair of Old World knives and a slingshot.

I bolt to my feet and am running before the shock of such movement registers with my body. I nearly wipe out a couple of rows from where I was weeding, but I manage to keep my feet beneath me. A guard shouts for me to stop, but I'm already bursting onto the dirt path.

Flint starts at my sudden appearance. His weapon comes up, and he freezes when he recognizes me.

"What the hell is this?" I say, grabbing his dark shirt and balling it in my fist. "My pack . . . Flint, my pack is here and you're . . . how are you . . ."

"That won't be necessary," he says, his gaze drifting over my shoulder, and I can only imagine that the guard who'd been chasing me has a weapon aimed at my back. If I turn to check, I fear I might pass out. Skies, if I let go of Flint's shirt, I might pass out.

"Delta," he says, eyeing me up and down. "You look awful. Have you had anything to drink?"

I squeeze the cloth harder. "You're a Loyalist?"

He shrugs in the indifferent way he's always had about him. Flint was never much of a talker.

I drop his shirt in disgust. "What happened to trading?"

"It got too hard. Barely scraping by. Always a day away from starving. Running tonics and meds for settlements instead of seeing to myself. I went where things were better."

"But you never mentioned this place. Not once. How long have you known about it?"

He swallows and looks up. This has always been his tell: a gaze skyward instead of at me meant he was lying, or at least withholding. He's known for ages. He's kept it from me, from the pack.

"You rusted-up, scudding—"

"I couldn't tell you," he blurts out. "I was trying to protect you, but things got hard. I found myself in a bad place, and it was this or work even worse than trading." He glances at the fields.

"They killed Old Fang, Astra, and Cobel. Did they tell you that when you joined? They abducted our entire pack!"

"I know."

"Abducted, Flint! Forced to work these fields and—"

"I KNOW!"

I freeze. He's looking away again, refusing to make eye contact. "I made the deal I had to make," he mutters.

In the span of a blink, I'm reliving the night we rolled beneath the stars on the outskirts of camp. I'd been straddling him, and his hands had roamed, slipping beneath the hem of my shirt. "What's that?" he'd asked when his fingers grazed the scars.

"Nothing," I'd said.

His hands climbed. "They're everywhere."

"Shut up, or we don't do this." I grabbed his hands and moved them to my front. I kept the shirt on, but we fell asleep after, and when I stirred, he was already awake, making a fire.

I stagger away from him now, unable to believe it. He saw my back, must have looked when I was asleep. He knows what happened to our Dead River pack because he's the one who pointed out the way for the General. I don't know what led him to be cornered by the Loyalists, but when faced with working the fields—a life even more demanding than trading—he spilled my secret, spoke of scars that could be a map.

I made the deal I had to make.

They came looking for me at Dead River because he betrayed our entire pack.

"You bastard." I swing a fist, but I'm so sluggish and heat-sick that he easily dodges the blow. I crumple to my knees, bracing my palms against the dirt. Something hard connects with my torso, and I roll onto my side, wheezing.

"Dammit. I said I had things under control," Flint snaps.

"She attacked you," the other guard says.

"And I dodged it. You didn't have to kick her."

"Can't let field varmint openly attack a Loyalist without punishment. It sets a bad example."

"The others are so ilked-up they don't notice anything but the coming and going of the drink wagon. She'll be the same by tomorrow. Let it go."

There's a creak, and a shadow rolls over me. "You lot are in the way," a new voice says.

I get an elbow beneath me. Lift my head. The convoy is back, and the lead wagon has stopped just paces from where I lie on the ground. The dark-skinned driver at the reins nods in my direction. "Well, are you gonna move her?"

"Drive over her if she doesn't move herself," the guard says. "Come on, Flint."

And Flint goes. Doesn't even argue. The traitorous ass turns his back and leaves me in the dirt, dizzy and weak. What Indie once said about lying with a person—how it makes you blind

141

to their faults—rattles in my ears. Was I really that naive? Flint never talked much, and I had to get him blitzed before he ever shared anything useful, but he wasn't always this awful person. He was just private, quiet. He wasn't trying to hurt anyone.

He was selfish and always has been, my brain hisses. *You had to get him blitzed because he was keeping secrets. He didn't want you to know the way to Zuly's Ark, because then you could go for meds on your own. He wasn't eager to tell you about the inverted well, because then you wouldn't be tied to Dead River. Anything that might have made you independent and erased the need for a trader, he kept secret until you pushed and begged for him to share it. He was always protecting himself, right until the moment he told the Loyalists about your brand.*

I shake my head, and the world streaks white. I think I'm going to be sick.

"Get out of the way, girl," the driver calls.

I try to stand but everything goes sideways. Dirt scratches my cheek. Running to confront Flint has left me empty. I'm not sure I could sit even if I want to.

A pair of leather boots enters my vision. Next thing I know, someone is slapping my cheek. "Hey, girl. Come back. That's it. Open your eyes."

The driver comes into focus slowly. Deep brown skin and hair cut close to her scalp. A woman. I hadn't noticed that at first, but the height of her cheekbones and the smooth slope of her neck give it away. One of her eyes is hidden behind a patch. The other sweeps over me, honey-brown and wide.

"You got the right idea, though," she says, drawing my arm

behind her neck. "Only way out of here is with the dead." She hoists me to my feet and all but drags me from the path.

"Help me," I croak out. "Please."

"I just did." She climbs back into the driver's seat, and with a crack at the reins, the wagon lurches forward. I watch the convoy go, the wagon beds looking as full as when they'd arrived. They've traded something, though I can't guess what. The General doesn't *need* anything.

I force myself to move, crawling slowly back to my basket. The sun beats down, merciless.

By the time the evening water wagon shows up at the end of the day, losing my mind to the General's water doesn't sound so terrible. I just want to forget. All of it. Ma's death, and how the rest of the pack is doomed, and how Flint betrayed me.

My basket of weeds is sufficient enough for one ladle of water. I drink it eagerly, waiting for my wretched memories to be lost.

CHAPTER FIFTEEN

The memories don't fade, but instead become sharp, like a blade in my side.

Ma's limp body as she was shoved from the dam. Brooke's fogged eyes as she failed to recall her daughter's name. Flint's utter indifference at what his cowardly decisions have caused. It's all still there, only now I'm thirstier than ever.

Lying on a bed mat with a weed-stuffed pillow beneath my head, I stare at the shanty's crooked ceiling. My body already craves more of the drugged drink. It's all I can think of, even when my muscles ache and my head throbs.

I've stripped down to my lowest layers in an effort to cool off. Everything else hangs above me on lines that run the length of the shanty. The clothes of my pack hang from these lines too, drying out the sweat while they sleep.

No one spoke after leaving the fields, just shuffled like mules to the shanties, receiving dinner from the guards on the way. A knob of corn. A scoop of beans. A chunk of dry bread.

I ate ravenously as I followed the others to our quarters, hoping my pack would come alive after the meal. Maybe once the guards were at a more formal distance for the night, life would return to their eyes and they'd speak in whispers, plotting escape.

I should have known better.

After eating, everyone promptly hung up their clothes and collapsed on their mats. Now, in the quiet, I lie on mine, thinking about how one of these mats will be empty each third day, and still, all I want is to taste that sweet-smelling water again.

I fall asleep deciding that I will work hard tomorrow and earn myself three full ladles by midday. The sooner I forget, the less it will hurt to lose the only family I know.

✦ ✦ ✦

"Delta." A firm hand on my shoulder drags me from a deathlike sleep. "Delta, wake up."

I force my eyes open, finding a monster before me—curled horns and dark eyes. I bolt upright, pulse pounding.

"Hey, it's me. It's just me."

The ram skull lifts. Reed. Here in the shanty. I frown. It's dark still—the middle of the night—and my pack sleeps soundlessly. Before I can ask him what he wants, he holds up his waterskin. I snatch it and down several gulps.

"Slowly," he warns, "or you'll make yourself sick."

"It's clean," I say, ashamed at the disappointment in my voice. While my brain craves the drugged drink, my body wants water of any kind, so I down a few more gulps, then pause. Behind Reed, his falcon has perched on the clothesline. She pecks at a button on my jacket.

"Rune. No." The bird—Rune, I guess—ruffles its feathers

and snaps its beak at Reed, but leaves my jacket alone. "Another sip," he urges me. "Slowly this time."

"Why are you helping me?"

"I actually want to find the Verdant, and I don't see how getting you drugged out of your mind helps things." He glances past me, as though he's looking through the thin shanty walls toward the waterfall that the Oracle claims is waning.

"You want me to help the General find the Verdant? Tell him to lift the threat against my pack."

"I can't do that."

"You haven't even tried."

"He won't listen."

"Let me escape, then. Sneak me through the dam. Maybe I can find answers in the wastes."

He snorts. "The Loyalists have been looking for answers for years. The answer is on your back. If you just tell us how to read it, use that code you mentioned."

"I made that up," I snap, then laugh, because it all seems ridiculous now — how I thought I could fool him.

Brooke grunts in her sleep.

"Keep your voice down," Reed whispers.

"If you want to help me, help me. None of this half-rusted crap."

"I'm giving you clean water."

"Yeah, keeping me sharp and focused so I can watch my entire pack die, one by one. How is that helpful?"

"He won't kill Bay. She has seven years, at least."

"Oh, I feel so much better." I consider throwing the waterskin across the shanty, but my cursed body betrays me, and I drink from it again. "Why are you even here, Reed? You don't actually want me to find the Verdant at any cost. You want me to find it *here*, under his thumb, so you and your precious Loyalists get salvation while everyone else continues to suffer in conditions no better than the wastes."

"You know nothing about me, Delta."

"Well, tell me, then. Why are you here?"

We're both standing. I don't know when it happened, but I'm off the mat, my chin jutting up so I can look him in the eye. His gaze dips to my neck, where the cord of the lodestone is visible.

"I'm here," he sneers, "because two guards got into a fight over a game of dice and now one of them's dead and I have to load him onto the burial wagon. That's all. Coming here was a mistake." He snatches the waterskin back. "Enjoy the ilked-up water tomorrow."

He strides for the door.

"What were you going to say the other night?" I call out. He pauses, but doesn't twist to face me. "When you came back to my room and found the inverted well, you were going to say something."

His head turns just slightly, so I can see his profile. "That I was sorry about your mother."

"Oh." It's not at all what I was expecting.

He shoves out of view, Rune flaps after him, and I stand there, dumbstruck, rage and confusion battling in my mind. It's only when I'm settling back onto my mat that it slams into me.

You got the right idea, though. Only way out of here is with the dead.

I lurch to action, the fresh water rolling in my belly as I gather up my goggles and throw on my outer layers. I pad to the door and look back only once. My pack sleeps like the dead. Some of them will be dead if I do this. But *all* of them will be dead if I stay.

Before I can change my mind, I slip from the shanty.

Sticking to the shadows, I steal between the ramshackle residences, moving toward the only sounds I can make out — muffled chatter coming from a few buildings over.

"Firing shots over a game of dice," a Loyalist grumbles. "General's gonna have a fit."

"Just get the corpse on the wagon." This from Reed. "It leaves at first light."

I creep nearer, pausing at the edge of the next shanty. Beyond the dirt path that bisects the working fields is a stable. It doesn't hold animals, but a wagon filled with corpses. I can make out the prone form of the deceased even from a distance. Reed holds a torch while two Loyalists heave the dead man into the wagon. Rune circles overhead, the glow of the torch illuminating her white belly. I push flat against the shanty.

"Still wish we could burn them here," one of the men goes on. "Big waste hauling bodies out every week."

"The General doesn't like the smell of burning bodies," the other says.

"And this is better?"

Even from where I'm standing, the smell is awful. Based on what they've said, the deceased have been piling up for a week. The General wants all his people to be loyal to the gods, but for the convenience of not having to smell their burning flesh, he risks damning their souls when they die. If the workers' minds weren't cloudy from the drugged water, maybe they'd see the hypocrisy in it.

"Are you done yet?" Reed grunts.

The men yank a sheet over the wagon, hiding the bodies from view, then follow Reed as he heads for the Backbone. I watch their torches drift off, Rune flying with them. Soon the only light left is that of the moon and a few flickering torches high along the dam wall where security details patrol. It's a blessing that these men don't have falcons. They really should, though maybe the birds are a pain to train, a resource reserved only for the General and his Four. More likely, he doesn't want to teach his code to more people. If they can communicate on their own, they can keep secrets from him.

I stand still, waiting for a change in the guards. When their backs are turned, their attention slightly lowered, I dart for the cart. Lifting the sheet, I dive beneath and yank it back into place.

The stench is horrific. I gag, nearly losing the little food in my stomach as I wedge my way between the stiff bodies. The guard who died during the scuffle over dice is still warm, his body the easiest to move. Something sticky trails across my arm. I bite my bottom lip to hold in a cry. Turn away from the wetness. Find myself staring into a set of lifeless eyes. It's an old man with wrinkled, sun-browned skin. He probably died from exhaustion in the fields, but blood marks his crown. There's a gaping hole in his skull.

They've checked to see if he was gods touched. I glance around. Everyone in the wagon has been checked.

I wrap my scarf over my nose, hoping to block the smell. It still presses in on me, heavy and rotten and warm. I squeeze my eyes shut, trying to ignore what I've seen.

I don't have to weather it for long. Just until first light. Then the wagon will be moving.

The only way out is with the dead.

CHAPTER SIXTEEN

Sleeping with the dead seems like tempting the gods to render me a corpse as well, so I don't risk it.

When the wagon creaks to life, dawn's early glow is just beginning to fill the sky. I can make it out through the paper-thin rag of a blanket that hides me. What I can't hide from are the flies. They found the bodies as soon as the heat began to climb.

It doesn't smell as bad anymore. Or maybe I've gotten used to it.

I exhale sharply, chasing a fly from my nose. I don't dare move a hand to swat it, not with the Loyalists so near. I can hear their chatter in the front of the wagon. Two men, it sounds like, joking above the clacking of their steeds' shoes.

We climb the ramp to the dam, and I hold my breath as they speak to a guard on watch. Then the wagon is descending again. Leaving Bedrock behind. Traveling into the wastes.

I expect relief, and in some way I find it; I'm breathing easily again. But guilt coils in my stomach and dread stretches through my limbs. I am deserting everyone I love, and if I can't find someone who can read whatever language makes up my brand, they will all be dead when I return.

If you return. You have to get out of this wagon first—and through the Barrel—unseen.

I clamp my eyes shut, thinking. Climbing into the wagon was the extent of my plan. I hadn't considered how to get out of it. And now there are two guards. Two men, likely armed, while I have nothing but the clothes on my back.

We roll to a stop all too soon.

The men dismount, dirt crunching beneath their heels. I tense, waiting for the blanket to be ripped from overhead, but they move away.

It's ungodly hot in the wagon. Sweat beads on my forehead and is dripping between my breasts when the unmistakable scent of smoke reaches me.

They're lighting the whole wagon on fire.

They're burning the entire lot.

Panic seizes me. I'm about to throw off the blanket and run when the crackle of burning wood makes me pause. It's distant. A dozen paces off, maybe more.

Footsteps approach.

"You can't take off, Twill. How am I supposed to tow the wagon back with just one horse?"

"The wagon will be empty when you're done with the bodies, dunce. One horse'll be enough."

"But it'll take me twice as long to move the corpses working solo."

"Good. That buys me more time to visit my girl. You know they keep turning down my request to get reassigned to the Barrel. This is my only chance."

"They're gonna ask where you went," the first Loyalist says. "When I return alone, they're gonna ask questions. We could both face the firing squad for this."

"Then wait right here." A shuffle of fabric. "Take my water rations, use the blanket to make a shade canopy, and I'll meet you in a few hours. We can head back together. Tell them the tinder was wet and the pyre took ages to get started. Please?"

I bite my lip in the delay, praying the Loyalist agrees. One man, I stand a chance against. Two are out of the question.

"Fine," he says finally. "Be quick about it. And you owe me half your dinner rations for the next week."

"You're the best." The horse whinnies as Twill presumably spurs him to action. Hooves pound on the hard rock. "I'll see you in a bit . . ." A fading shout.

The remaining Loyalist grumbles to himself as his shadow descends on the wagon. I sling my arm across my eyes a heartbeat before the blanket is ripped away.

There's a creak near my feet—a board on the wagon being lowered so that unloading the bed will be easier. The deceased man to my right shifts. There's a meaty slap as the corpse falls from the wagon and hits the ground. I listen to the struggle and the grunts as the Loyalist tugs the body toward the fire. The scent of smoke isn't as thick now, but the crackling wood is hungry.

I risk a quick glance over the edge of the wagon. The pyre is several paces away, flames licking toward the sky. Bedrock's mesa, dam, and waterfall have all seemingly disappeared. We didn't travel far, though, so we must be in a valley of some sort, the settlement hidden from view. I can't see the Barrel either. I'll have to use the wagon tracks to puzzle out which way to travel once I'm running. But first . . .

I return my focus to the Loyalist, who's rolling the corpse into the fire. The man is taller than I am, but scrawny, and I'll have the element of surprise. There's a long rifle strapped to his back, but I doubt I can get my hands on it quickly enough. On his hips, though, I spot the familiar shape of a knife hilt.

You've always been good with a knife.

That I have.

The Loyalist straightens at the fire, and I lie back down, return my arm over my eyes.

I hear him move nearer, feel his shadow fall over me. "Huh," he says, and I know he's looking at me now, wondering why my skull hasn't been opened like the others. He grabs me at the ankles, and I remain limp as he tugs. When I'm halfway from the bed, my legs hanging from the wagon but my torso still being dragged over the corpses, I lurch upright.

"What the—" The Loyalist is so startled, he staggers back. But I've anticipated this, and I scoot off the wagon bed, racing at him. He reaches over his shoulder for his weapon, but I'm already diving low, my sights on his hip. I grab the blade there and tug it free, ducking into a forward roll that carries me past him. Then my feet are beneath me. I spin around, my arm arched to throw.

He raises his weapon.

But I've already let go of the knife.

The blade buries into his chest. He looks down at it, shocked.

He still has enough life in him to shoot me, but he's so surprised at what's unfolded that he just stands there staring as blood begins to soak his shirt. By the time he looks up, ready to fire, I'm already directly before him. I grab the hilt, yank the knife free.

"Rest easy."

I slice the blade across his neck.

Hot blood splays my cheek as he crumples to the ground.

I strip off his black shirt, knowing it will do me little good as a disguise if it's completely soaked in blood. It's only after I've pulled it over my jacket that the horror of it catches up with me.

I look at his pale torso gleaming in the sun.

I've never killed a person. Quail and fish and jackrabbits and the occasional desert mule, but never this. His eyes still hold the fear that filled his face as my blade drew across his neck.

I retch, not managing to look away quickly enough.

I need to move. Need to leave.

His horse is still harnessed to the wagon.

It's then that my eyes catch another horror. There in the wagon, the very corpse I'd been lying on, is Ma. The line on her neck, the state of her skull . . . it's too much. This time I really am sick.

A shadow flicks over my arm, dancing over the dirt. I look up, fearing one of the Four's falcons, but it's only vultures, already circling overhead, ready to eat.

Using the Loyalist's waterskin, I wash the bile from my mouth. Then I drag Ma to the pyre and roll her into the flames. She is the fourth of my own pack that I've burned, but unlike Old

Fang, Astra, and Cobel at Dead River, hers is the only death I can claim responsibility for. This happened because of me—because of what I can't do.

The brand on my back practically burns, taunting me with its unreadable markings.

"Rest easy," I manage, tears stinging my eyes.

I turn away from the flames, from the smell.

I can't stay here.

I need to be in the Barrel before Twill leaves. If I cross him on the wastes, everything will fall apart.

My pants are dark enough to be Loyalist black, but I pull up the hood of the Loyalist's shirt, hoping it will hide my hair and help me pass as one of the General's men when I get to the Barrel. Then I sling the Loyalist's long rifle across my back and lower the wagon from his horse. I take his knife and waterskin, too, then ride.

✦ ✦ ✦

Riding a horse is foreign to me, and I nearly fall from the creature the moment it breaks into a trot. I sink into a rhythm with time, but my body is beaten weary. I squeeze the horse's torso with my legs, thighs aching. My palms burn as the reins rub them raw. My tailbone and back throb.

The pyre was indeed in a rocky valley. Following the hoof-prints of Twill's steed, it doesn't take me long to climb back to level land. From here, Bedrock is easy to spot but far enough off that, with any luck, I look like nothing but a wasteland vagrant to any bino-sporting Loyalists on watch from the dam.

"I'll be back for you, Bay," I whisper. "I promise." Then I slap the reins, urging the horse to go faster.

The temperatures are blistering, and I'm sweating like mad beneath all my layers, but I make remarkable time. No wonder the Loyalists prefer horses for their mounts. A mule can't move like this—so swift and smooth—and I imagine that with a saddle, the riding would be even easier.

Like the southern entrance of the Barrel, the northern pass is marked by faded flags along the rim of the canyon. Gunners wearing Loyalist black patrol the walkways, staring down on me as I approach. I touch a hand to my forehead as I saw Reed do once in the fields. I'm in black, riding a steed, just another Loyalist. The man overhead returns the gesture, and I nudge the horse with my knees, entering the chasm.

Shadows engulf me. It's immediately cooler between the rocks, but instead of feeling relieved, I only feel trapped. I keep my head down, knowing that showing my face will lead to questions I can't answer. I don't look up until I'm in the open-air market, the chatter of bartering townsfolk echoing off the rocks.

My eyes lock with a familiar establishment: the Vulture's Roost.

I check the sun. It's nearly high noon.

I slip from the horse, secure the reins on a rickety fence, and lift the doorway curtain.

CHAPTER SEVENTEEN

Dried grass and wood chips cover the floor, but the scent of murky moonblitz, urine, and days' old vomit lingers. Tables are spaced sporadically through the pub, a single candle flickering atop each. Seems risky, given the chips at my feet. Maybe they're so damp they'd never catch.

Several faces snap up to greet me, but when the curtain falls at my back, I realize folks are more bothered by the light that momentarily sliced into the Roost than by my actual presence. They hunch back over their drinks, pull their glass jars of blitz nearer. A man standing behind a waist-high counter with a dirty rag slung over his shoulder is the only person to keep me in his sights.

"You gonna order a drink or you gonna stand there like deadwood?" Jars of moonblitz line the shelves behind him. Some batches clear, other tinted amber or gold.

I scan the room. Asher's not here—not yet at least—and it's only a matter of time before the General realizes I've escaped and sends his army after me.

Still, I find myself saying, "I'm waiting for a friend."

"This ain't a meetinghouse, it's a pub. Order something or get out."

"Moonblitz." I walk to the counter that divides us, wood chips flexing beneath my boots, then slide onto a crudely carved wooden stool. The man just peers at me. "Please?" I add.

He slaps the rag onto the counter, fisting the material, and drones, "What's your *trade?*"

"Oh. My friend is bringing it."

"This ain't a charity, Loyalist."

"It'll be worth your time, promise."

A brow cocks with interest. "You get the weak stuff till he arrives." He wipes out a glass jar with his rag, grabs one of the batches of moonblitz off the shelf, and pours me a drink.

I raise it to him in thanks and take the smallest sip. The blitz scorches my throat, liquid fire that I barely manage to swallow without hacking up a lung. If this is the weak stuff, I don't want to taste his strong batches.

Smiling smugly, the man returns his attention to wiping out dirty glassware.

I spin my blitz-filled jar on the counter, worry building. If Asher doesn't show, I have no way of paying for the drink. And even if he *does* show, it's possible he'll have nothing to trade for the drink either. There's no way the owner will let me go without paying. Even now he's watching like a hawk, one eye on me while he goes about his cleaning.

The back of my neck prickles. Asher should be here by now. What if he's stopped coming? What if he gave up on me the moment the wagon carted me off to Bedrock?

Light slices through the Roost as the curtain lifts. I glance over my shoulder. It's a pair of Loyalist gunners. Dread coils down my limbs. I release what's become a death grip on my blitz and thumb the rim in a manner that I hope looks lazy.

The men walk into the room, their eyes flitting over the patrons. I hunch over my drink like everyone else, praying I fit in. *I'm just a Loyalist, another bored blitz drinker. Nothing to see here.*

"We're looking for a girl," the men call to the owner. "Maybe sixteen, seventeen years."

Behind the counter the man frowns. "Can't say I've seen her."

"You, brother?" A hand slaps down on my shoulder.

"Oh," I manage, side-eyeing the men. The one with his hand on me is stocky and broad, at least twice my weight. His friend is larger still. "No. Haven't seen any girl."

Stocky Loyalist's eyes narrow as he squints beneath the hood of my stolen garb. I probably stink of the corpse wagon, but maybe that helps my lie. My hair is hidden. Dust is probably stuck to my cheeks from my ride on the horse. I have the rifle slung across my back still, and the Loyalist uniform isn't so much of a uniform but a mismatched set of black clothing. It could be convincing enough. The pub owner didn't say anything, after all.

"You should get back to your post," the Loyalist finally says. I nearly gasp when he lets go of my shoulder. "There's an order coming from Bedrock."

"Sure. Nearly done here."

Stocky Loyalist grunts to his partner, and they head out. My head sags forward, relieved.

There's another slice of light as the men leave the pub. But then, footsteps, right on top of me. They've come back. They know.

Fingers clamp around my wrist, and I spring from my seat, clenching my free hand into a fist and swinging it at the Loyalist with all the strength I can muster. I crack him square between the eyes, and he doubles over, swearing. I twist, looking for the second man, but there isn't one.

"Dammit, Delta," a familiar voice says.

Asher.

I glance at the doorway. The curtain is still swaying. He must have entered just as the Loyalists left.

"What the hell?" Asher straightens, and I'm rewarded with a view of the damage. His nose is bleeding. The front of his dark shirt is wet with blood.

"Sorry," I mutter. "I thought you were someone else."

He wipes at the blood with the back of his thumb, wincing. "They're locking down the Barrel. We have to go."

My stomach drops away.

He grabs my arm, and this time I let him tow me from the seat. Then we're sprinting for the door as the pub owner yells after us about payment. When we don't slow, he gets louder, screaming to anyone who will listen about our theft. I just pray everyone is too preoccupied with the lockdown to really listen.

The midday sunlight assaults us when we spill from the Roost. It's high overhead, an angry orb beating down on the Barrel.

"The mare!" I protest as Asher blows past my horse.

"Too big. Won't help us where we're going."

"*I'm* going into the wastes. Are you with me?"

He stares, as if I've made a ridiculous suggestion.

"The General is going to kill them, Asher. My entire pack.

Even Bay. They're dead if I don't figure out how to read the map. The mare will help us make good time. If I just get out of here . . . Find another gods touched, someone who can read whatever language most of the brand is in . . ."

"The mare will get you caught."

"You owe me this, Asher. You helped *sell* me, dammit."

Regret glints in his eyes. "I did," he admits. "And I'm so sorry. No amount of apologizing will make up for it. But I've shown up at the Vulture's Roost every day since they took you to Bedrock. I showed up even though I never expected to see you again. And now that I have, I'm not throwing away a second chance." He swallows, looks at me pleadingly. "I know how to get us out of here, Delta. Into the wastes, just like you want. It's just not through the southern pass."

I frown. That's what makes the Barrel the Barrel. A single passageway through the mesa. It wouldn't be a barrel if other routes branch off it.

"Do you trust me?" Asher asks.

I answer honestly. "I don't have much of a choice."

✦ ✦ ✦

Asher leads.

The Loyalists are in a frenzy of activity — questioning people in the market, storming shacks and shanties in the Barrel. On the gunner walkways overhead, their weapons scan for a girl with a branded back.

Thanks to our dark ensembles, Asher and I blend in on the canyon floor. He even has a skull mask. Stolen, most likely. He must have been holding it when he found me in the Roost, and a good thing, too. If he'd been wearing it, I'd have cracked it in two when punching him, and it wouldn't be diverting eyes from us as it is now. Among the chaos, we're just two more Loyalists sweeping the Barrel.

A boom echoes from the southern end, far out of sight.

"What was that?"

"The gate," Asher says. I remember the raised gate I saw when I first entered the Barrel, the spikes that are now surely buried in dirt. "No one will leave until they've found you—or until they're convinced you were never here to begin with."

He darts behind a shanty and pulls me to a crouch alongside a pile of storage crates. Just ahead is a single Loyalist guard, standing watch before a woven blanket that hangs against the canyon wall.

Asher puts a finger to his lips, then reaches behind his back, procuring a hand sling from the waistband of his pants. He can't be serious.

I motion to the black powder rifle on my shoulders. The weapon is a pain to load, but it will be more reliable than the sling, especially at this range.

Too loud, Asher mouths. He jerks his head back toward the way we've come. He's worried about the activity in the main pass, that the shot will draw other Loyalists to us.

I reach for the rifle anyway, only to realize that in my hurry to take it off the Loyalist at the pyre, I never took his powder horn. I've been carrying an unusable weapon.

Asher stoops, his fingers grazing over rubble along the chasm floor until he turns over a relatively smooth rock that fits nicely into the sling's pouch. Biting his bottom lip in concentration, he stands and begins to swing the sling overhead, building momentum. By the time the guard catches the movement and turns toward us, Asher has let the stone fly.

Its aim is true.

The rock clips the Loyalist on the side of the head, and he drops like a sack of potatoes. He's unconscious, maybe even dead.

I stand there, stunned. I hate slings. They take years of practice to master, plus an ungodly amount of patience, and even after carrying one for most of my childhood, I brought down only a few quail with the weapon. Swinging a sling alerts your target of your presence, and aiming accurately is virtually impossible. If you don't hit your mark on the first try, you've lost your advantage, usually your prey, too. When we were kids, Asher was even worse with a sling than I was, and now he's struck down this Loyalist as easily as blinking.

I'm still staring as he rushes forward and checks the man. "Knocked out," he whispers, then hooks an arm beneath the blanket hanging against the rock face and draws it aside. A gaping dark hole waits behind the material. I shuffle nearer, and a breeze touches my cheeks.

"There are iron mines to the northwest," Asher explains. "The tunnels were dug for easy transport."

I glance down at the Loyalist. His brow is bleeding, his chest rises and falls shallowly. I peer back into the tunnel. "Shouldn't it be guarded by more men?"

"Everyone's been pulled off to sweep the Barrel."

I hesitate. The tunnel is wide, but I wonder what will happen when we get deeper. Will we be hunched to half height? How will we see? How long will we be stuck in the darkness, and what will we eat once we are? It's not like I had the opportunity to pack supplies before I ran.

"I know someone who can help you," Asher insists. "Someone who can help *them*." His eyes flit in the direction of Bedrock.

I picture Bay in that tiny cradle. Brooke, Wren, Pewter. Alder. Vee. All of them. I picture the dam and the knife that was drawn across my mother's neck.

"Who?" I ask.

"She's called Kara the Prime. She runs Powder Town."

"The last free place in the wastes?"

He nods. "I know the way there. I can get you to her safely."

Just paces away, Loyalists are shouting. It's only a matter of time before their search brings them toward these tunnels.

I nod at the entrance. "Lead."

CHAPTER EIGHTEEN

We gag the guard, tie his hands behind his back, then lug him into the tunnel—far enough from the entrance that a Loyalist peering behind the blanket won't see him, but not so far that we break a sweat.

It's cool inside the mesa, and dark.

Asher swipes a flint and candle from the unconscious guard and gets a flame going. I follow his flickering form deeper into the tunnel.

"If we move fast, we'll be out the other side by nightfall. We *have* to be out by nightfall."

The tunnel will be searched eventually, and if Loyalists flood it while we're still in here, there will be no escaping. Suddenly, *this* feels like the true barrel, not the town we're leaving behind.

"You've been through this way before?"

He nods. "When I escaped Bedrock. The Oracle told me about it."

"He's dead now."

Asher's head ticks to the side. "I worried that might be the case. Don't know why he helped me."

"His daughter mentioned that he was executed for it."

"Isla," he says at a whisper.

He knew her before she was the Oracle, when she was her own person, with a name and dreams and wishes. Now she's just another of the General's tools.

It's not such a mystery anymore why her father helped Asher. Freedom exists only if we can make our own choices.

"How'd you escape?" I ask. "During the fire."

He doesn't ask how I know about the fire, doesn't even slow his step. "Those aqueducts that bring water to the crops? There's similar piping that brings waste out of Bedrock. The Oracle told me how to access them." He shudders slightly, as though the ghost of sewage still lingers on his skin. And it did linger, I'm sure. Water isn't easy to come by once out of Bedrock. "The Oracle set the fire on midwinter night, so getting into the Barrel wasn't too difficult. All of Bedrock was celebrating, and there was a festival in the Barrel's market. I was probably through this tunnel before they realized I was missing. On the other side, I headed west. Made my way to Powder Town."

He glances over his shoulder at me. I nod, as if this explains everything, even though I want to ask about Bain and Cree and how he ever managed to fall in with those rusted asses. How he went from the boy I once knew to one who would help con people into wagon cages.

Asher pauses. "I should have told you about the sewers, but there was so little time, and if you drank the water, you'd have forgotten my advice within a day." He bites his lip. Shadows dance over the creases in his forehead. "You're smart, Delta. Always have been. I knew that if you just kept your wits, you'd figure a way out."

A day.

A single day.

I shudder, thinking how close I was to losing my memories, to having my life fog up before my eyes.

I don't tell him that I nearly broke. Instead I say, "It smelled sweet, like a syrup. I've never seen anything like it."

"Ilkcorolla seed, also known as sleeping ilk. The plant grows right there in Bedrock. The orange flowers drop white seeds that can be ground into a powder. And the powder is . . . potent. Makes folks numb and forgetful."

I think of the vine plant I didn't recognize that day I followed Reed through the fields. I'd thought it was beautiful, those massive flowers, their long, delicate petals.

"Do the memories come back if someone's not"—I search for the term I'd heard in Bedrock—"ilked-up?"

Asher shrugs. "They did for me. The Oracle told me to stop drinking the water, started bringing me his own." He pauses. "It was hard at first. My body craved the drug, but eventually I was clean. But then I could remember what the Loyalists did to me . . . The torture, the abuse. In some ways it was easier to be lost in my own mind."

I don't know what to say. I've spent so long focused on the con he pulled on me that I've failed to truly consider what he's endured these past years.

He lowers the candle a little, peering at my face. "Did they hurt you, Delta? Gods, I could kill myself for watching you go there. It was supposed to end in the Barrel. If they hadn't found the map . . . If you'd just been placed in a home . . ." His thumb grazes my cheek, and I flinch away from him.

"We're wasting time. We should be walking."

His face does that thing where it flickers between the boy I once knew and the stranger who let Bain and Cree put me in a cage.

"Asher, we don't have time for this," I insist. I snatch the candle and shove past him, taking the lead.

"I'm so sorry, Delta. Truly."

His tone, honest and vulnerable, brings me back to when we were kids. When I glance back at him, his eyes are pleading. I feel bad for him. Worse, I feel guilty, as if his pain is somehow *my* fault. Asher always had this power over me. Like that day when the Loyalists spotted his scar from across Alkali Lake. He was the idiot who took his rusted shirt off, yet for months after—years, even—I felt like it was my fault. If only I'd made him put it back on sooner, if only I'd never let him take it off, the pack wouldn't have split. Those men never would have come. Everyone would have lived.

"Asher was careless with the map, not you," Ma told me the night we learned of the massacre. "Is it awful? Yes. Do we wish it didn't happen? Of course. But do not carry the mistakes of others as though they are your own. Life is hard enough already."

He's still staring at me now, as though I can somehow relieve whatever pain he bears. As if I can change the past.

"I know," I say finally. "And if you get us to Powder Town, maybe I'll forgive you completely. But right now, every minute I waste is a minute closer to one of my pack dying. So no more talk till we're at the iron mines."

He nods, and we carry on in silence.

✦ ✦ ✦

The tunnel gets smaller, but not by much. Shallow ruts on the ground show where modest cargo wagons have been pushed through this space over and over, carrying iron from the mines to the Barrel. For about a click I have to walk with my head ducked down, but otherwise I can move upright.

When my legs are aching and the lack of sleep from the night in the corpse wagon is catching up with me, Asher's hand closes over my wrist. He puts a finger to his lips, nods ahead.

Squinting, I can see it—a faint glow.

He blows out the candle, and the tunnel is swallowed in darkness. After a few breaths, our eyes have adjusted and we creep forward ever so slowly. By the time we reach the tunnel exit, I'm squinting fiercely even though the sky has bruised into a deep shade of purple. It's dusk, and I'm glad for it. Were it midday, my eyes would be burning from the brightness.

The tunnel opens onto a ledge where two Loyalist guards sit with their backs to us, eating dinner. My stomach rumbles so loudly I'm shocked they don't hear it. Beyond them, the ledge tumbles and rolls away like an awkward sloping staircase. At the bottom, tents and shanties speckle a valley, and wisps of camp-fire smoke dance toward the darkening sky. A few tools clank, metal hitting rock, but the bulk of the day's work appears to be over.

Asher pulls out his sling, and in a flash, the two Loyalist guards are unconscious.

"When the hell did you get so good with that thing?" I mutter.

He flashes a grin, then runs forward and pockets the guards' dinner.

"This way," he whispers, and scurries to the left, watching his footing on the rugged terrain. I grab a set of binos from the knocked-out Loyalists and follow.

If word of my escape hasn't made it to the mine yet, it will as soon as these guards wake up. Outrunning them will be near impossible once we make it back to the wastes. The General's men will be well rested, well fed. They'll have horses. I try not to dwell on it, instead focusing on following Asher in the fading daylight.

We make our way west until it's so dark that continuing on in only the moonlight would be dangerous. Too afraid to make a fire, we sit with our backs against a boulder and share the Loyalists' jerky. There's a bit of hard cheese also, which Asher asks me to cut.

"Cut how?"

His hand disappears inside his jacket and reemerges with my knives — the Old World one from Astra's hut and my trusty bone blade, too. "Bartered them off Bain. Told him he could have the goat, but I was owed these — that I wanted something to remember you by. 'Course, I always intended to give them back to you."

The hilt of my bone knife fits my hand like a memory. It makes me miss Bay — how her body in the sling was just starting to feel familiar when she was taken from me.

"Thank you . . ." I manage.

He nods, then lays out the waterskins—his, along with the one I stole before riding for the Barrel, plus a third we lifted off the Loyalist guards. It's a downright feast.

I drink eagerly, savoring each drop.

"Easy," Asher says, pushing my waterskin aside. "Long way to go still." He's right. I wipe water from my chin, grumbling. "Just being honest," he chides. "And smart." He gives me the smuggest grin I've ever seen grace his features.

I grab the jar of jerky he's eating from and screw on the lid. "Better save this too."

Asher's grin tilts sidewise. "You trifling with me?"

"Don't flatter yourself. We need to ration food just as carefully as we ration the water." I turn around, wanting to stash the jar, only to realize I have nowhere to put it. Asher holds his jacket open, showing me a spacious pocket stitched into the inside of the garment—probably where my knives had been stowed. I hand the jar over begrudgingly.

He's still smiling. I turn my head to the stars because I don't want to give him the satisfaction of knowing he's almost made me smile, too.

"You can see Ation this time of year," he says, nodding up at the sky.

The constellation seems brighter than usual, or maybe it's just that I rarely see her without a fire or a torch glowing nearby. The goddess's head tips down to watch us, her dress sweeping behind her like a flowing river.

"She's beautiful, don't you think?"

"Are you serious?" I glance at Asher. His cheeks are awash with starlight, his eyes wonderstruck. "She deserted us. They all did."

"The blue and green stars appeared last summer, though," he says. "Signs of fertility. They both passed by Feder—straight through his armor. And this spring I heard someone say there was a yellow comet over the North Star. And a star shower over Ation."

"So?"

"Comets are sparks of life, and a star shower means rain."

"And Ation is the goddess of earth and a shower fell above her. I know what it means."

"But you're not hopeful," he says. It's a statement, not a question.

I shrug.

"Delta, the signs couldn't be clearer. This means a rebirth is coming."

I stare at him incredulously. "You really believe that?"

"Of course. Don't you?"

"Teleios is the goddess of water, and a comet or star shower hasn't touched her in Old Fang's lifetime," I point out. It's the same argument I made when Ma grew excited about the signs Asher mentioned, but she also said that a sign of rain over the goddess of water meant nothing. It was like saying that the sun is hot or water is wet. It was a sign of rain over *earth* that we needed, and when it appeared, stars streaked above Ation's bowed head for nearly two days. A week earlier we had seen a comet flying by the North Star, and a week before that, the blue and green stars —unnamed gods that always appear without warning, often with decades of absence in between—had lit up the sky.

Their message was clear: hope, a rebirth, the return of the gods.

I wonder, sometimes, if I could have convinced Ma to move to Powder Town that winter, had those colored stars not passed through Feder's shield. We were getting desperate, but once she saw those signs burning in the night sky, any doubt she had when it came to her faith had vanished.

I sneak a glance at Asher. He's had it worse than anyone I know. After all he's been through, after the Loyalists raided Alkali Lake and killed his family, after the General had him tortured, after a lifetime of failing crops and dust storms, of sand squalls and baked-out earth, I'd have thought his faith would be shattered. Weakened, at the very least. But no, he's sitting here beside me, still speaking of salvation coming, as though it's a guarantee.

It's depressing.

And the thought of him experiencing yet another disappointment makes my chest quake.

"It's a scudding lie, Asher. You know that, right? The gods deserted us, and they're never coming back. No combination of stars in the sky is going to bring green back to these wastes. All those signs of fertility—comets and star showers appearing at certain times? They're meaningless. It's just us trying to make sense of this rusted life, grasping for something—anything—to make us feel less alone. The gods might as well be yelling at us to scud off, and we're still putting faith in them. It's pathetic. And then for parents to feed all those lies to their kids? It's cruel. I wish my ma never told me about the gods. I wish she—"

I stop abruptly, tears burning my eyes. Ma believed in them until the moment she died. I want to call her foolish for having such faith, but she's gone, and I can't bear to speak ill of the dead.

What would I tell Bay if she asked about the stars one day? Is it better to tell a lie if it helps people feel safe or hopeful? Or is it better to be honest, even if the truth hurts?

Asher's still frowning. "You shouldn't talk like that."

"You sound like Indie." The lump in my throat grows larger, because she's gone, too. I flop down and roll away from Asher, tucking my hands beneath my cheek.

It's deathly still for a moment. Somewhere far off, an owl screeches.

"Maybe rebirth isn't coming," Asher says quietly. "Maybe the gods have deserted us for good, and the stars are just lights in the sky, and green only exists in a Verdant we can't find. I still think having hope can't hurt. It got me through the darkest moments of my life. Maybe it will get you through yours."

I grunt, unconvinced. Hope won't save me. Action will. I need to get to Powder Town. Find someone who can read the map. Trade the knowledge with the General in exchange for my pack's freedom and guaranteed entry into the Verdant—if it even exists. Only that will bring order back to my life.

I can feel Asher looking at me, waiting for a response. The brand practically tingles.

"Delta?"

I stay still, pretending to be asleep.

"I'll take first watch," he says finally. There's a rustle of clothing, then the crunch of gravel as he walks to the outskirts of our small camp.

The night falls silent and I shiver, suddenly lonely.

Is it possible to miss someone even when they're right beside you? I'd ask the gods, if only there were any up there, listening.

CHAPTER NINETEEN

We rise early—before the sun is truly up and the world is a hazy hue of russet red—and hike in silence. By late morning we're out of the worst of the mountains and looking down at the foothills that stretch out into the wastes.

I flip up the collar of my jacket, protecting the tender skin on the back of my neck from the climbing sun. "What now?" I ask. The land ahead is flat and sprawling. If the General's men show up in saddles, they'll catch us in no time.

"Let me see those binos," Asher says. I lift the strap over my head and drop the pair I stole from the Loyalists into his outstretched hand. He scans the open terrain. "If we head due west, we'll hit the Serpent River. That's the same river you call Dead River—Powder Town just has a different name for it. Once we hit the Serpent, we can follow it south into town."

"But?" I say, sensing a catch.

"But that's what the General will expect. And we'll be an easy target on open ground."

"I told you we should have taken the horse," I grumble.

"It wouldn't have fit through the tunnel and probably would have lamed itself climbing out of the mountains at the pace we were moving." Asher hands back the binos. "We'll take the most direct route. Go southwest."

I peer through the binos. The land to the southwest is just as flat, just as open, and the air is rippling. It's not a mirage, I realize. It's steam. I catch movement in the corner of the eyepiece. Scalding water shoots toward the heavens, billowing and spouting.

"Through Burning Ground? Are you crazy?"

"They won't expect it."

"Because it's a deathtrap."

"Taking a horse through will be impossible. They won't be able to follow in the saddle. That means we can keep our lead."

The geyser stops erupting, and I lower the binos. "We're going to die," I grouse.

"I know you've got no faith in the gods, but what about me, Delta? An experienced guide." He flashes me that boyish smile again, crooked and sly.

"You've been through this way before?"

"How else do you think I got to Powder Town without getting caught?"

I don't mention that surviving Burning Ground once is already a miracle and entering a second time is probably pushing his luck. We're out of options. I shrug and wave a hand at the dangers awaiting us.

Again, Asher leads.

✦ ✦ ✦

Despite being a traitorous leech, Flint told the truth about Burning Ground; there *are* obvious signs that warn a traveler of dangers.

The pools of water look magical—crystalline, so blue they

are almost green, clear enough that you can gaze straight into their rocky depths. It's the most beautiful thing I've ever seen. I try to imagine an entire ocean this color, Zuly's tanker floating on it. How serene this world must have been before the gods turned their backs on it—on us.

But as beautiful as the pools are, they are also deadly, so hot they can boil you alive, and the warning is obvious along their edges, where rings of rust red and sunset orange and honey yellow encircle the water. Steam billows off the surface, disrupting the otherwise perfect reflection of the sky. A smell lingers in the air, rotten, like bad eggs.

We give each pool a wide berth, but they are often fed by tributaries from other pools, creating a cobwebbed maze of hot water. We hop over what we can, but sometimes we are forced to zigzag along a runoff until we find a safe place for crossing.

So much for our lead.

I keep glancing over my shoulder, but the wastes behind us are empty, and even when I use the bios to scan the mountains, there's no sign of activity. Maybe the Loyalists gave up their search. It doesn't seem likely, but I let myself believe it. We have enough to worry about.

The heat in Burning Ground is even worse than the heat of the wastes, which isn't a thing I thought possible. My under layers are drenched, and even the air seems sweaty. I feel like I'm standing in the cookhouse at Dead River, right alongside a pot of boiling stew, steam coating my limbs.

"There's one thing I can't figure," I say as we walk.

Asher hops a forearm-wide tributary. "What's that?"

"You escaped Bedrock," I say, leaping after him, "made it through the tunnel and out of the mountains, crossed Burning Ground, *and* arrived safely in Powder Town?"

He nods.

"So when the hell—or maybe I should ask *why* the hell—did you fall in with Bain and Cree?"

He flinches, but keeps leading without comment.

"I asked you a question, Asher."

He exhales loudly. Asher knows me. I'm not going to let this die.

"I wasn't at Powder Town long," he admits. "Roughly two moons. Soon as it felt safe enough, I left to search out your pack. I'd heard talk that there were a few groups living west of Powder Town"—this is news to me—"and another to the south, half-way between West Tower and the Old Coast. I went west first. Maybe if I hadn't, I'd have made it to you guys. To you." His head twists to the side briefly, but he doesn't make eye contact. "I got jumped by Bain and Cree three days after leaving Powder Town. They took all my gear, were talking about bringing me to the Barrel to trade. I couldn't go there. If anyone saw the brand, I'd end up back in Bedrock, and I knew I wouldn't escape a second time. The General would make sure of it. So I made Bain an offer. Told him I would help him bring in ten times what I might have been worth in the Barrel, so long as we could part ways after."

"And he agreed?"

"Not at first. He wanted to know what I was running from. Probably trying to decide if he could get even more from me by turning me in. I just said I'd already worked in the Barrel once and couldn't do it again. Turns out, he had, too."

"You'd think that would make him want to help the vulnerable, not work against them."

Asher grunts. "You don't know Bain. He likes assets, comfort. I thought for sure he wouldn't take my offer, but Cree started arguing that it wouldn't be bad to have an extra set of hands setting up camp and making meals, and that it would make cons easier to pull off."

He jumps a particularly wide tributary and turns back to wait for me. I don't know if I can make this one, but as far as I can see, Asher's found the narrowest place to cross. I bite my lip, get a bit of a running start. As soon as I leap, I know I'm not going to make it.

My heel hits the edge of the tributary. I don't feel the heat through my boots, but the rock beneath the water is slick. My foot skids out from under me. Asher rushes forward. His arms hook beneath my shoulders, and I collide with his chest.

"I got you." He staggers, pulling me upright. We're so close, my nose nearly brushes his chin when I look up. There's a small scar by his bottom lip that I don't remember from when we were kids. I wonder how he got it.

He straightens his arms, putting distance between us. "Anyway, I worked with them for about four moons. You were the last job before I could cut loose, the last trade I owed them." His throat bobs. "Gods, I wish it hadn't been you."

My face feels flush from being so close to him. I don't like it, so I tell myself it's from the heat of the day and not his nearness. "If it wasn't me, we wouldn't have reunited," I say with a shrug.

"Yes, we would."

"You don't know that. I could have been taken when the Loyalists raided Dead River. Or we could have both wandered the wastes for the rest of our lives, never crossing paths."

"I would have found you again," he says surely, and I believe him. Asher has faith even when he shouldn't. He believes wholeheartedly.

He turns and begins leading again. I watch where he steps, but I watch his back, too. Beneath that shirt, we are still alike, even if everything else has changed.

✦ ✦ ✦

My mood sours quickly in the afternoon, and it's not only because we won't be out of Burning Ground by nightfall. Asher keeps trying to make conversation. By the way he steals glances over his shoulder, I can tell he's trying to cheer me up, but nothing will help.

I remind myself that this was necessary. That staying wouldn't have solved anything. That the only way to help them was to leave.

It doesn't lessen the guilt.

Asher comes to a halt at dusk. There's a pool to our rear and another one ahead, but enough dry land between that we're not in danger of rolling into boiling water while sleeping. He sits on a small boulder and complains about his aching feet. I've had blisters on mine since morning, but the pain has been a welcome punishment. I deserve it, and more.

Asher hands me some jerky. I eat silently, barely looking at him.

"Did you swallow your tongue?" he teases.

"One of them is dead," I snap. He couldn't have known, and he was only trying to lighten the mood, but I can't steady my voice. "At noon. Every third day at noon the General will execute another of my pack."

Asher's face pales. "I'm sorry. I didn't know."

I stare straight ahead, chewing on my jerky.

"Who?" he asks.

"Alder or Vee. Whoever was oldest."

"Vee," Asher says, and of course he would remember more than I do about my own pack, despite being away from them for so long. Of *course* he has to make me feel even more like a failure than I already do.

"Vee, then. Vee's dead. Because I couldn't read the map." I knead my hands together—my useless, worthless hands. Hands that did nothing. Suddenly I'm furious. "Dammit, Asher. If you hadn't conned me, none of this would have happened."

"This is on the General, Delta, and you know it." Asher's mouth is a thin line. There's a crease in his brow to match it. "And Bain and Cree conned me first."

"I know, but you should have fought back. You should have killed them."

"You say that like killing is easy."

I don't tell him that it is, shockingly so. Instead, I look away. The Gods' Star glints to the north.

"Oh gods, Delta," Asher says. "When? *Why?*"

"I had to. I wouldn't have gotten away if I didn't." I risk a glance at him, afraid he'll be looking at me like I'm a stranger, like he's terrified of me. But it's the opposite. He's looking at me like he wants to take away the hurt, like what I've said has cracked him open.

"There was a cart of corpses," I explain. "Two Loyalists were taking it out of Bedrock to a pyre. I hid under the blanket. *The only way out is with the dead.*"

"Or with the sewage."

Despite everything, I feel the corner of my lip twitch into a smile. "One of the Loyalists left early. I killed the other once he was alone, and I took his horse."

"Are you okay?"

"Yeah, sure."

"You're a rotten liar."

"No, really. He was a Loyalist. He worked for the General. I didn't like the blood, how easy it was, or the rush I felt in the moment. But it's not like he didn't deserve it."

"He was just trying to get by," Asher says, taking a swig from his waterskin. "We all are."

"So we're just supposed to forgive them? Pretend they don't have blood on their hands? No, they *chose* to fall in line with the General, Asher. That Loyalist *chose* his path."

"Maybe only because it was the better of two terrible options. Maybe, if there was a way he could pay for his crimes, he could be forgiven, earn his place beneath the stars again. Not right now. Nothing is in place for such practices. But maybe someday."

I stare at him long and hard. He means it. He believes that no one is too damned to be redeemed. He has hope that some future version of this world exists, where the right people will rule, where the guilty can pay for their crimes and maybe even start over.

"You're a better person than me."

"Nah. I really don't think that's true." Asher side-eyes me from where he's sitting, forearms resting on his knees, hair falling into his lashes. I'm reminded of a moment when we were kids. I'd told him to scud off during a hunt because he was spooking all the game. When I found him afterward, he was sitting on a rock, just as he is now. His body has changed, but his expression hasn't.

"Let's drink to Vee," I say, raising my waterskin.

Asher nods, lifts his as well.

"Rest easy, Vee," I say to the stars. "I'm sorry I failed you."

We drink, then sit in silence for what feels like forever.

"You didn't fail her," Asher says a while later. "The gods did."

"I thought you had full faith in the gods."

"I do. That doesn't mean I always understand how they work. And this isn't solely your fault, Delta. It's the General's, and the Loyalists', and mine by extension, as you pointed out, and Bain's and Cree's, because who are we all but children of the gods? They could change everything, save any soul they want to spare. I don't understand why life is the way it is, but I believe it will all make sense in time."

"That was beautiful, Asher."

His brow wrinkles. "You making fun of me?"

"No. I'm serious. If my ma or Indie, or really anyone, ever admitted to me that they didn't understand the gods, maybe I would have struggled less with my faith." I take another sip from my waterskin. "Life is strange, isn't it?"

He nods. "Life is strange."

A chill settles over the wastes as night lengthens. Again, we don't have a fire, for fear of giving away our position. I curl into my jacket and tuck my hands beneath my cheek. The earth is hard. The ground has taken in the night's cold.

I hope Bay is warm, wherever she is. I pray she's in a cradle in the nursery, blissfully unaware of all that is happening around her. Of course she's unaware, I tell myself. She's a baby. Something pangs in my ribs, and I realize I miss her. I wish she was sleeping in the sling right now, snuggled against my chest, our bodies warming each other.

I will get back to her. Even if it takes me forever—even if I fail everyone else in my pack and she is the only one left—I will not let the General destroy my entire family.

I fall asleep repeating this vendetta and wake only once, shivering. Something tightens near my stomach. I look for Bay, the sling, but of course she's not there. It's Asher's arm. He's moved beside me in the night, curled his body around mine. I almost elbow him off, but he's warm, a comfort.

I nuzzle nearer, soaking up his heat, and in the morning I shift away before he wakes and can see that I needed him.

CHAPTER TWENTY

A shadow falls over us by midmorning. I put a hand to my forehead, shielding my eyes, and tip my head back.

"Vulture?" I suggest. The bird is a dark silhouette against the sky. It doesn't look big enough to be a vulture, but I don't know why any other animal would waste energy following us.

"Looks more like a falcon," Asher answers. "Maybe one of the General's."

"Well, that would be unfortunate."

We're trying to make light of things, but we both search the horizon as we pause to drink from our waterskins. There's no sign of anyone following us. Perhaps it's a wild falcon, scavenging like every living thing in the wastes. We finished the last of the jerky this morning and my lips are now blistered and raw. If we don't make it to Powder Town today, the bird might be rewarded with two corpses to pick at.

I stuff my hands into my jacket pockets, protecting them from the sun. "How much longer?"

"Hard to say. Soon, I think." Asher pauses at a tributary. It's wide, deep even. I peer through the rust-colored water and feel like I'm looking into a crevice. The strange coloring plays tricks on the eye.

As we start looking for a place to cross, a gust of hot air hits my sunburned cheeks. The bird screeches overhead and peels away. I'm wondering what's spooked the creature, when the ground erupts. Water shoots from the crevice and into the sky, roaring like a beast.

"Geyser!" I scream. I grab Asher at the wrist and haul him back. The water erupts like a wall, pushing up through the crevice. A droplet scalds the back of my hand, but I don't dare take another step away. A hot pool waits right behind us.

Still gripping Asher's arm, I watch the cascading wall of water peter out as it moves through the crevice. When it's not trying to kill you, it's almost pretty.

"That bird nearly got his meal early," Asher says once things are quiet.

I twist, searching the skies, but the bird has vanished. Scared off by the geyser, I think, but then I spot the truth to the east: dust. Not a true storm, from the width of it, but a decent squall. It's bearing down on us fast.

"Asher!" I shout. He's already jumped the crevice. "Goggles. Put on your goggles!"

He glances over his shoulder, and his eyes track beyond me, going wide when they find the squall. He reaches for the skull mask he's had hanging between his shoulder blades on a piece of rope.

"You don't have goggles?" I yank mine on, pull up my scarf. It's second nature, these movements.

Asher shakes his head. With the ram skull on, he looks like Reed, and it's a terrifying reminder that the Loyalists are still searching for us. But Asher's blue eyes shine through the open eyeholes in the skull. Eyes that will go blind from the dust.

We need a blanket, something to shield him. We need—

I shrug out of my jacket, leap across the crevice, and fling the leather over his head before tugging him to a crouch. As I'm holding his head to my chest, the squall hits. Dust and rubble claw at us. The wind howls. We're knocked off our feet, tumble sidewise.

I wait for the excruciating sting of burning water, but we get lucky and fall on dry land. I keep the jacket pinched beneath Asher's chin. Not so tight that he won't be able to breathe, but firm enough to keep the dust out.

The wind roars with one final blast of intensity, then vanishes. I let go of the jacket. My clothes are covered with dust. Grains of sand have made it through my scarf and into my hair. I take a swig of water and spit, cleaning out my mouth, but the grit remains in my nose. I exhale hard through my nostrils. No such luck. The only way to be rid of it will be a good bath. I'm not wasting drinking water.

Asher stands. When he pushes back the ram-skull mask, his face and hair are much cleaner than mine. Leather will always stand up to a squall better than a scarf.

He balls up the jacket and hands it over. "Thank you."

"You saved my knives. I saved your eyesight," I say with a shrug. "We're even now."

"Oh, is that the only reason you did it?" He extends a hand and helps tug me to my feet, smiling the whole time like he knows it's not true.

"If you already know the answer, why bother asking? Gods, you're insufferable."

"And you're—"

"Lost," I say, cutting him off. Our tracks have been swept over by the squall, and there are cobwebbed tributaries running everywhere. I can no longer tell which one erupted with the geyser.

Asher looks up. The sun is high overhead, making it impossible to determine directions. "If we wait a bit, we'll know which way to head."

"I don't have hours to spare," I grumble. And then I do something I've never done before. I pull out the lodestone in front of someone. It shivers in the air, then locks on to north. "This way," I say, pointing us west.

"How do you know?" His tone is doubtful.

"The lodestone always finds north. Even in the gods-sent silent storms. A trader gave it to me."

Asher frowns. I know he doesn't believe me, and he still looks doubtful a few hours later, when the sun starts to dip for the horizon ahead of us.

"How can you still not believe me?" I grumble.

"Oh, I believed you from the beginning. Why would you lie about that? It was very specific." His eyes twitch to my neck, where the lodestone's cord is hidden beneath my layers. "I'm confused about why you told me. Tech like that is something people would kill for. Betray friends for."

"That what you're going to do to me?"

"No," he rushes to say. "I guess I figured that if you were being so honest, you must trust me again. At least a little."

Between the gods deserting us and everything I've experienced since Indie died, I'm not sure I trust anyone fully. I've been going it alone since I came home to find Dead River raided. I'm about to tell Asher as much when he puts a hand on my shoulder. "There," he says, pointing. "See it?"

Squinting, I can make out something along the horizon. A pale, stout structure, definitely man-made, like a plank of wood resting atop Burning Ground. It stretches away from us, switchbacking toward the sinking sun.

"Boardwalks," Asher explains. "They'll lead us to Powder Town."

✦ ✦ ✦

As the sun nears the horizon, we step out of Burning Ground and onto the raised walkway. The wooden planks glow golden, but they feel worn beneath my boots, smoothed from years of wind and sandstorms.

The walkway cuts almost due west, spanning narrow tributaries and turning only when a large hot pool demands it. Occasionally the path branches off and dead-ends right before one of these pools of water, though I can't understand why and am too tired to ask. We're making remarkable time. I'd forgotten how freeing it is to not have to worry where you step, to just . . . *walk*.

It doesn't take long for Powder Town to appear in the distance.

The first things I notice are the trees. A rocky rise looms at the settlement's rear, and real, living trees pepper the landmass. They twist like scrub, hunched and beaten by storms, but they have undeniable trunks, nearly straw thin from this distance.

Pines, Asher calls them when he notices me staring. They are so vibrant, so bright, they seem impossible.

Powder Town itself is hidden behind a wooden defense wall that looms around the settlement. Sharpened spears are angled outward at the top, encouraging incomers to avoid climbing. Watch points are positioned along the wall also. It reminds me of a smaller Bedrock, and I wonder if I've simply traded one prison settlement for another.

The shrill cry of a bird pierces the afternoon.

Two birds now circle overhead, flying lower than the one that tailed us earlier. They are definitely falcons, and I've seen one of them before. It's Rune, I realize with sickening dread. Reed's bird. The creature turns a beady eye toward me and opens its bill. Another cry cuts through Burning Ground.

There's a far-off response, eerie and foreign.

"Asher, do you hear that?" I tilt my head, listening. It's like the beating of a million hearts, the flapping of a thousand wings.

To the north, a cloud of dust mushrooms, but it's not a storm. It's an army. I can't make out the individual horses yet, or the riders—too much dirt has been kicked up—but I know it's them. They tracked us with the birds, stayed north of Burning Ground and then turned south with the hope of cutting us off here, less than a click from salvation.

"Run!" Asher yells.

After two days in Burning Ground, my legs are all but useless, but I surge forward. My boots pound on the boardwalk planks. The frenzied hoofbeats of the Loyalist army rattle in my ears. I don't dare check how close they are. Not even when the board-walk ends and we're running the final half click of wasteland to Powder Town.

When we reach the defense wall, we skid to a stop. It's made from the same wood as the boardwalk, and here, two beams extend higher than the rest. A brace connects them, and a series of pulleys are mounted in the corners. I follow the ropes to the watch point. There's a figure there, but they're looking north, toward the army.

Asher pounds on the wooden wall. "Let us in!" he shouts. This section can be raised, I realize, much like the gates of the Barrel.

I risk a glance north. The Loyalists are only a few clicks off.

"You've brought trouble," the figure in the watchtower shouts down. Her short hair is as dark as my lodestone. "We don't want trouble."

"Saph, please!" Asher says.

I'm as surprised as she is that he knows her name. Her gaze snaps back to us, then widens with recognition. "Asher," she grits out. "You are not welcome here. You know that."

If it weren't for the pounding of hooves closing in on us, I'd be picking apart the story Asher told me earlier, trying to figure out which pieces were lies. The Loyalists are barely a click away now. They'll be on us in no time.

"I'm sorry. I can explain everything. Just let us in, Saph. *Please.*"

"I should consult with the Prime first—"

"We don't have time!" I erupt.

"Then he should have thought of that before—"

"I seek refuge from Kara the Prime," Asher shouts. "I invoke the right to work for the Trinity!" He looks to me, eyes urgent. "Say it. Repeat those exact words."

"I seek refuge from Kara the Prime," I recite desperately. "I invoke the right to work for the Trinity."

Saph turns away, and for a second I think we're doomed. Then the doorway creaks. As soon as it is raised enough to squeeze beneath, Asher and I drop to the dirt and roll into the settlement. I get one final look at the wastes—the legs of an army of horses galloping into view—before Saph lets the door fall back in place.

III

POWDER
TOWN

CHAPTER TWENTY-ONE

The hooves pound nearer, then slow as commands are shouted. Horses whinny and snort. The Loyalist army is gathered just beyond Powder Town's wall, and we're on the inside, sitting in the dirt just a stone's throw from being captured.

Up in the watchtower, Saph is wiping dust off her goggles. "You have no business here," she calls down to the army. I don't know where she finds the strength to keep her voice steady. She's lucky she hasn't been shot dead.

"You have something that belongs to us," a Loyalist responds, and I freeze. *Reed.* I can picture him sitting in the saddle, that ram-skull mask pulled over his eyes, Rune settled proudly on his shoulder. He never wanted to help me. All he cares about is finding the Verdant, and the things he said in the shanty that night —the clean water he provided—were just a means to break me. He thinks I truly know how to read the map, that I'm withholding. I must be shaking, because Asher puts an arm around me, pulling me nearer.

"People cannot be owned," Saph snarls. "This is where our people and yours have always disagreed."

"She has something that belongs to us," Reed amends. "The General wants it back."

"Then the General should request an audience with the Prime, not bring an army to our door." A pause. "Does he request an audience?"

"He's not with us," Reed answers.

"Of course he's not. He never leaves his stone fortress."

On the other side of the wall, there's a muffled discussion. Reed arguing with another of the General's Four, perhaps, whoever owns the second falcon we saw. Then, silence. The world goes deathly still as Saph cautiously raises her hands. They must have their weapons on her now.

Someone races past Asher and me and ascends the ladder to the watchtower opposite Saph with catlike speed. As fast as she's moving, she's seemingly silent, and when she reaches the landing, the rifle that was slung across her shoulders moves soundlessly into her hands. She aims at the army. "If you fire that weapon, your arrangement with Powder Town will be null and void, I can guarantee it. I can't imagine that's a risk the General would want you to take."

"Says you, or the Prime?"

"Says I, though I know the Prime will agree. We bring you shipments once a moon, and you don't meddle in our affairs. That includes not demanding that we hand over townsfolk."

"And you are . . ."

"Luce the Reaper. One of the Trinity."

"Oh." Another pause. "I will see if the General would like to request an audience."

"Good choice."

And then, miraculously, Reed gives an order to move out.

The hooves retreat. Overhead, the falcons lift back into the sky, screeching as they soar east.

The woman who called herself Luce the Reaper swings a rust-colored braid over her shoulder and gives a nod to Saph, who quickly descends the watchtower ladder. "Your declarations have earned you entry," she says to me and Asher, "but to stay, you'll have to plead your case to the Prime."

I nod, dumbfounded. Who the hell are these people, and how do they have the power to turn away the General's army with only a few words?

✦ ✦ ✦

When Asher helps haul me to my feet, I find that a crowd has gathered in the clearing behind us. The group is made up of mostly women but there are men, also, and children. They peer from behind the legs of their parents, wide-eyed and curious.

Like Saph, their clothes are threadbare and mismatched, but something in these people's eyes feels lighter, younger. Hope, I realize. These people haven't lost hope. After Dead River, the wastes, the ilked-up state of the General's workers, it's a beautiful sight.

Behind the crowd, huts and shanties huddle together, separated only by crooked dirt paths that cut between them. It's so quiet, I can hear the distant bleating of a goat and a gurgle that can only be the Serpent River Asher mentioned.

"High alert over," the Reaper announces from her perch. "Everyone can return to their normal duties."

The crowd disperses at that, chattering among themselves.

One girl lingers, blocking Saph's way. She looks about five

years old, and she wears a basket attached to her back with shoulder straps.

"Are you a god?" she asks me. "Is that why the devil's men were chasing you?"

"No," I say. "Of course not."

"Him?" She glances at Asher.

"No."

"You must be gods touched, then."

"I'm nobody. I'm just trying to get by."

The girl frowns. "Armies don't chase nobodies."

Saph clears her throat.

"Sorry. I'll go now." The girl runs after a woman who wears a similar basket on her back.

"This way," Saph says, and leads us through a patchwork of shanty homes. She seems taller now that she's on the ground with us—Asher's height, maybe even a knuckle or two more. With her goggles pushed onto her forehead, her short hair sticks out at odd angles beneath the pull of the strap.

Though the crowd has broken up, I spot faces peering at us from behind the curtained doorways of several shanties.

"Is this normal?" I whisper to Asher.

"Pleading a case to the Prime, yes. Having the entire town watch your arrival, no."

"What about pleading a case twice?"

He keeps his eyes locked on Saph.

"Asher, why didn't she want to let you in?"

He shakes his head, as if this alone is an acceptable answer. There's little color in his cheeks. Something in the story he told me isn't true, but rather than being angry with him, I find myself terrified at the prospect that he might get turned away. That we *both* might. That can't happen. Powder Town is where I'm going to find answers, and I don't have the supplies to make it anywhere else if we're thrown back into the wastes.

We reach a bridge that extends across the murky brown water of the Serpent. To the south, I can make out a dam. The stones look relatively new, clean of moss or growth, which explains why our water supply at Dead River started fading so enthusiastically.

On the opposite side of the bridge is the largest building I've seen since entering Powder Town. Unlike most of the shanties, this one has numerous open windows, a mud-tiled roof, and four stone slabs that serve as steps to the entrance.

"Prime Hall," Asher whispers to me.

There's a flag hanging idly from the corner of the building. Without a breeze, the emblem stitched in the cloth is clear: two picks, their shafts overlapping.

I freeze. I've seen this flag before, flying from the wagon patrol that came to Bedrock while I worked in the fields. I glance over my shoulder. The same flag flies along the perimeter wall. I'd been too concerned with the Loyalist army to notice it earlier.

The sound of Saph knocking pulls me back to the present. I turn around in time to see Prime Hall's door swinging open.

A dark-skinned woman emerges from the shadows. Her head is shaved. A patch obscures her right eye.

It's the woman from Bedrock, the caravan leader.

She's Kara the Prime.

CHAPTER TWENTY-TWO

"**Y**ou?" I mutter.

Asher stomps on my foot and gives me a glare so fierce it could kill. But the Prime only smiles.

"Me." Her eye flicks up and down my frame. "I've never heard a plea from a ghost before. But there are firsts for everything. Tell me your name."

"Delta. Of Dead River."

"I'm glad my advice served you well, Delta of Dead River. And *you*." Her voice cools as she turns to Asher. "I granted you refuge once, and you ran. I do not open my doors to just anyone, Asher of Alkali Lake. To come here—to agree to be a part of Powder Town—means working to make it stronger. Not weakening it by leaving."

I seek refuge from Kara the Prime. I invoke the right to work for the Trinity.

What have I promised—what has Asher made me promise—without me even knowing it? I can't stay here and work for the Trinity, whatever that is. I need to decode the map and return to Bedrock, or my pack is dead.

"Still"—the Prime sighs—"I will hear both your cases. Come in."

I expect the building to be regal, full of luxuries the rest of Powder Town lacks, but Prime Hall is virtually empty. Several tables fill one corner of the room. Thick wooden shutters flank each window, and candles—currently unlit—sit on clay dishes that hang from the ceiling. The Prime is tall—even taller than Asher—and has to duck on occasion to avoid knocking into a candle.

"You expected something fancier," she says as she leads the way toward the sitting area. "But how can I expect my people to give their sweat and blood to me if I do not sweat and bleed alongside them?"

"That's a very elaborate way of saying the Prime has her own home in town, just like everyone else," Saph explains. "Prime Hall is a communal room, used for meetings, like this one, or for shelter during storms."

The space doesn't seem big enough to hold all the people I saw earlier, but maybe there are multiple buildings like this throughout the town.

The Prime motions at a table, and I all but collapse into a chair. A smooth seat, my shoulders on a backrest . . . after several days in the wastes, it feels magnificent.

"You seek refuge," the Prime says, slipping into her own seat. "I am willing to provide it, so long as you are willing to work in a division of the Trinity—production, prosperity, or security. These are the pillars that keep Powder Town strong."

"And do you feed your workers ilked-up water like the General and call it a choice?"

"Delta," Asher hisses.

"What? I have a right to know. She was at Bedrock when I was there. She *traded* with that monster."

"Of course we trade with him," the Prime says. "How do you think Luce the Reaper turned away his army with just a few words? We have something he desperately needs. We trade it in exchange for certain goods, mainly iron and water, and the understanding that he will not touch a soul behind Powder Town's perimeter or our agreement is forfeited."

"He could take whatever he wanted," I insist. "He has the numbers."

"But he doesn't have *this*." The Prime touches the side of her head. "We produce something here, something that only a few of us know how to make. If we die, or end up on sleeping ilk, the method of producing this valuable substance vanishes, and then the General's army is powerless."

"I don't understand."

"They carry modified rifles, don't they?"

"Yes."

"And what do those weapons require in order to fire?"

"Black powder."

"And what is the name of this town?"

My mouth falls open. "You make black powder here?"

"It has to come from somewhere." The Prime smiles. "Powder Town was founded when the first Prime discovered how to make black powder years ago. They made it in secret, for a while, and by the time the General rose to power, the town had leverage: a product that the General couldn't rule without. Our arrangement is a cautious one, but he will not meddle in my affairs if I continue to haul a shipment of powder to Bedrock each moon." She leans back in her chair, hangs her wrists from the armrests. "So tell me, Delta of Dead River: Why should you be granted refuge in this haven?"

I consider this a moment. I could beg for my life, plead for mercy, but after begging the General and his Loyalists for these very things, I'm beyond requesting that people treat me decently.

"The General is after me," I admit.

"So I've been told. I may not have a black-dressed army to do my bidding, but Luce the Reaper is a third of my Trinity. She oversees security, and her scouts saw the Loyalists coming long before you did. We know they are after you. What I want to know is *why?*"

I glance at Asher. He raises his brows as if to say, *Your call.*

"He thinks I'm gods touched. He thinks I can read something, when I can't." It's a piece of the truth. "He's holding my entire pack at Bedrock. If I can't figure out how to read what he wants me to, he's going to kill them all. I came here hoping to find help."

"We do not get involved in Bedrock affairs," she responds. "I can offer you help by way of refuge. That is all."

"But if I don't—"

"Refuge in exchange for work. Take it or leave it."

I can't step back into the wastes—not without learning how to read the map. If I do, my pack's fate is as good as sealed. But here in Powder Town, I can work hard and honestly for a few days. Maybe in the process I'll even meet someone who can read the map's language. And then . . .

"Fine," I say.

"Security reports to Luce the Reaper, and you already got a glimpse of that job. The prosperity division is made of doctors and farmers, stewards to the body and earth. Amari the Tender oversees it. And then there's —"

"Production," I say. "I'll work in production." If there's a recipe for black powder written down anywhere, people who can read will work in this division — people who know the Old Language and maybe even others.

The Prime nods. "Bronx the Chemist manages all aspects of powder production. Saph will let her know you've chosen to serve her pillar. It's good to have you with us, Delta of Dead River."

"What about Asher?"

"What about Asher?" she echoes. The Prime's eyes slide to my friend. "You agreed to work for the Chemist once too, but then you ran."

"To try to find my old pack," he says. "I only wanted temporary asylum until I was strong enough to travel again. I told you I had no intention of staying, and you gave me no choice but to lie. It was go back into the wastes to be captured or to die, or say I would work for the Trinity and leave when it was safe."

The Prime frowns. "We are one here, Asher of Alkali Lake. We are unified. Your heart is not with us — it wasn't then, and it isn't now — and so you may not stay."

Saph grabs the meaty part of Asher's arm, tugs him from his seat.

"He'll stay," I blurt out. "This time, he'll stay."

The Prime raises her brows. "Why's that?"

"Because of me. That's why he left last time—to find me, my people. But I'm here now, with him, so he won't run."

Asher stares at me as if I've told the Prime a terrible secret.

She looks between us, coolly. Her lone eye has an intensity that unsettles me, as though she can see every truth I've refused to share. But then the corner of her mouth lifts slightly, and she says, "This is your final chance, Asher of Alkali Lake. Report to the Chemist alongside Delta. If you run again, you will not be welcomed back."

"Thank you," he murmurs, bowing his head to her. "Thank you."

"Show them off, please," she says to Saph. "And tell Amari I'll see her about the water report now."

✦ ✦ ✦

We take the bridge across the river and thread our way north through town. It's quieter now, all the spectators who gathered in the clearing when we arrived having cleared out. The scent of fresh bread and cooked vegetables wafts through the streets. Saph stops before a home with a single, eastern-facing window and jerks her head at a heavy woven blanket hanging in the doorframe. "You can stay with my sister while we raise a new structure."

"Cleo hates me," Asher says.

"Well, she has reason to, doesn't she?" Saph gives Asher a particularly pointed glare. She looks only a few years older than we are, but when she steels her eyes, Asher folds like a baby.

"I'm sorry, Saph. Really. But I had to go. You all *knew* that. I had to try to find them."

Now Saph's gaze drifts to me. "Seems you were successful."

"Not really," Asher spits out. "One, when I should have found more than a dozen? That's not a success. He has the Loyalists combing the wastes now. Did the Reaper tell you that? Does she tell you that while everyone is safe here, everyone outside the walls suffers?"

"Don't make this about me. You're the one who left."

"You could barely stand me any more than Cleo."

"I was trying!" Saph snaps. "Which is more than you can say—"

"I'm sorry," I cut in. "But how, exactly, do you two know each other?"

Saph levels her gaze to mine. "We were sharing a bed." She spins on her heel and stalks off, and I stare after her, dumbstruck. When she's disappeared between shanties, I turn to Asher. His face is blanched and his mouth stuck in a small circle. Well, good. He *should* be mortified! He'd finally managed to find some safety after Bedrock, and what's the first thing he does? Ditch his clothes and expose the map to a complete stranger, all for a few minutes of pleasure.

"You move fast" is all I can think to say.

"It wasn't like that, Delta. I slept *beside* her. That's it. I was gone before it could go anywhere."

"I don't care. You can roll with whoever you want."

"Amari the Tender pushed us together, had us sharing a home," Asher goes on. "I don't know why."

"Because there aren't many young men in Powder Town," a voice says as the doorway's blanket is pulled back. The woman standing in the frame has hair that falls to her hips, but otherwise she is so strikingly like Saph that I wonder if they're twins. "The Loyalist army has swallowed most of the wastes' men, even the once-decent ones, and a town can only continue to thrive if it continues to reproduce." She jerks her head at Asher. "This one was decent and free of the General's influence. My sister is of prime childbearing age. The Tender saw a good match and encouraged it."

Asher beams. "Cleo, you just called me decent."

"I still hate you. Come inside."

We slip into the one-room home. It is dark, even with a few candles burning. Half the space is filled with bed mats and pillows. The other holds a small eating area overflowing with the scents of fresh bread and a flavorful stew. My stomach immediately growls.

"She cried when you left, you know," Cleo says as she surveys Asher. "I've never seen my sister cry."

Asher looks genuinely confused. "She hated me. She was furious when the Tender suggested that we lie together. I think her exact words were, 'You can't tell me what to do, Tender. I am my own person to give to who I want. I'd rather gouge my eyes out than share a bed with that piece of driftsand.'"

Cleo sighs. "You're a decent man, Asher, and decent is hard to come by. After almost two moons, you were growing on her. I think maybe she was starting to picture a future she never imagined possible."

I glance at Asher. I used to know him so well, but this person before me is full of secrets, and he looks conflicted now. It makes me wonder if maybe he didn't mind Saph so much either—that if he hadn't felt an obligation to look for my pack, he could have grown fond of her too. The thought makes my stomach uneasy.

"Thank you for taking us in," I say to Cleo. "We won't be any trouble."

"I believe that of you. Not so sure about this one." She jabs a finger in Asher's direction, but she's smiling now. "I just came back from the market. Are you hungry?"

Asher practically drools. "I thought you'd never ask."

CHAPTER TWENTY-THREE

After we've cleaned quickly at the dry sink, Cleo stuffs us with food. Warm bread and a potato stew so flavorful I moan through half the meal. When we've had our fill, Cleo tells us to get some shuteye. "Lots to do tomorrow. I'll show you around, teach you the ropes." She pulls a tie near the low ceiling, and a blanket that had been rolled and secured there unfurls, separating the sleeping mats from the rest of the space. From the sound of it, she's clearing the dishes before she joins us.

The mats look terribly close. Asher's already collapsed on the middle one, so no matter which I pick, I'll be beside him, our bodies just a palm's width apart. We already slept curled together that night in Burning Ground, but this feels different. There will be walls around us, for one.

"Did you stay here last time?" I ask as I sprawl out on the mat.

Asher shakes his head. "At Saph's."

"Right. How could I forget?" I picture a cramped sleeping space like this, Asher and Saph lying so close that their sides are pressed together, and my cheeks get warm.

"Nothing happened between us," he says again.

"The more you insist that, the less I believe you. Besides, why should I care? You're a grown man. You're free to do what you want."

His brow creases. "I just thought you'd want to know I didn't do *that*."

"It's none of my business. I just hope you kept your shirt on. Taking it off that time when we were kids didn't lead to anything good, and I'd've thought you learned your lesson."

Asher looks at me for a long beat, then says, "I remember you being blunt and honest. I don't remember you being mean."

He rolls away from me, and I'm left in the darkness, stomach churning in a way that makes me wonder if something was wrong with the stew.

✦ ✦ ✦

Cleo wakes me at the crack of dawn. At least it feels that way. But Asher's bed mat is empty, and when I duck beneath the curtain that divides the sleeping area from the rest of the hut and get a view out the lone window, I can tell it's already past noon.

"You let me sleep in."

"You'll thank me for it later. Now eat so I can show you the ropes." She shoves a biscuit slathered with honey in my direction. My stomach has settled since last night—actually, it's growling all over again, as if I haven't eaten in ages.

"Where's Asher?" I ask through a mouthful of flaky biscuit.

"Already at work. He doesn't need a tour."

"Is that your job—giving newcomers tours?"

"Nah, I'm in production, same as you. Bronx the Chemist stopped by early this morning and asked me to get you up to speed. It's hard work, though, so I figured you could use a bit more shuteye." She squints at me. "You don't know how to work a loom, do you? Or knit? I hear the textile gals can chat all day. It's not too late to switch to the prosperity pillar."

I shake my head. Knitting and handiwork may be one of my strong suits, but I need to stay where my odds of meeting someone who can read are highest.

"No matter. Just figured I'd ask. Let's go." Cleo leads me out the door and through the narrow dirt streets. I can hear a blacksmith's tools clanging. Cleo says something about markets and livestock fields, hands waving in various directions. Presumably she's pointing out their locations, but all I can see are the worn sides of the crowded shanties. "At the southern end of town is the lumberyard and the charcoal pits," she goes on. "That's where we make the charcoal. Can't produce black powder without it. And on the northern end we've got three saltpeter beds, all at various stages of development. Plus the kitchen, where we make the black powder, and the pantry, where it's stored. And once we go out the front gate—"

"What's saltpeter?" I interrupt.

"Another ingredient we need to make black powder. And be glad you're harvesting sulfur and not working the saltpeter beds. It's nothing but turning over manure and straw for weeks on end, until the saltpeter comes to the surface, and a decent amount of urine is involved to keep things moist. It's disgusting."

"Sounds it."

"Not that harvesting sulfur is a picnic. We work two shifts: one in the early morning and one in the afternoon, taking a lie-down at midday, when the heat is the worst."

"And you let me sleep until second shift? But not Asher." This embarrasses me for some reason.

Cleo shrugs. "He got up early, and who am I to stop him? But don't go thinking he's just some selfless hard worker."

I frown, because he is. At least the Asher from my childhood was.

"He's got lots to make up for," Cleo clarifies. When we reach the front gate, she shouts up to the guard on watch, and the door rises with a creak.

Beyond Powder Town's wall, evidence of the Loyalists' visit still lingers. Hoofprints mar the dry earth, but the horizon to the north — the way they'd ridden in — is blessedly quiet, and the sky is an open pool of blue, no falcons in sight. The sun has already crested its climb and is starting to dip toward the mountains at the town's rear.

Cleo leads the way onto the boardwalks, and soon I can make out the workers. They're all clustered near the dead ends, only their torsos and heads visible. They're not standing on the walkways, I realize as we draw nearer. They've only used the planks to gain easy access to the hot pools.

When we come to one of the boardwalk's dead ends, Cleo flicks a pair of leather gloves against my chest. "Put these on," she says.

Several workers are already here, breaking growth from the edge of the steaming pool and lowering their harvest into glass jars. The stench of rotten eggs is more pungent than ever. I loosen my scarf and pull it over my nose with a gag.

"You'll get used to the smell," Cleo says, and it must be true because no one else has bothered to shield their nose with their garments.

Cleo lowers herself off the boardwalk and creeps toward the pool. At the edge, she points to the pale yellow growth. "Sulfur. The third and final ingredient in black powder."

"I expected you to be more secretive about all this," I admit.

"Ingredients are the easy part, and everyone here knows the three materials necessary for production. The real secret is in how they are combined—the precise ratios and measurements, the order in which they are mixed. *That* is something only the Chemist and the Prime know."

"Where is this Chemist? I want to meet her." *So I can ask if the black powder recipe is written down somewhere—if it's written in the Old World language or something else entirely, and if she knows how to read it,* I add mentally.

"She checks in on us occasionally, but most days she's in the kitchen. She does all the mixing, actually *makes* the powder. They don't call her the Chemist for nothing."

So if anyone can read, it's this woman. Maybe I can get Asher to show me where the kitchen is later.

"Now quit delaying and get over here," Cleo says, beckoning with a finger.

I eye the pool hesitantly. "What about geysers?"

"This one never blows. Pool three erupts daily during our lie-down. Pool seven every third morning. We've got charts to keep track of everything. Now, let's go. It's safe."

No one else along the pool's edge looks remotely nervous, and from what the Prime said last night, her people have been harvesting like this for ages. I quit stalling and scramble down to join Cleo. She demonstrates how to break the sulfur growth free and how to stack the pieces inside a glass jar so it can be easily transported back to Powder Town.

I go to task alongside her, the sun beating down on our shoulders. It isn't hard work, exactly. The sulfur is lightweight and brittle, and it doesn't take much effort to break it free. It's the hunching over at an awkward angle that wears on me. I have a stiff neck and an aching lower back in no time. The work reminds me of harvesting at Alkali Lake as a kid and also of that day in the General's field, weeding alongside my ilked-up pack. Their fogged eyes, the threat the General holds against them . . .

I wonder briefly if I've made a mistake. Harvesting sulfur isn't going to save them.

Members of the Reaper's security team stand watch along the boardwalk. Cleo assures me that there's nothing to fear; sulfur is typically harvested without any sort of protection. The Prime simply insisted on a few days of added security after the Loyalist army made a surprise appearance.

If I look east, across my pool and to the next, I can see Asher tucking sulfur into his jar. If he glanced up, he'd see me staring, but he's too busy chatting with Saph as he harvests. She's standing on the boardwalk to his right, a rifle griped across her chest. He keeps smiling at whatever she's saying. It's a familiar smile, crooked and all-knowing, as if he's in on a joke just the two of them know. I thought that smile was something Asher gave only to me, but of course not. The truth is, I barely know him anymore, especially not the person he is now.

"You two have a lot of history?" Cleo asks, and I realize she's caught me staring. Saph must have told her what I said to the Prime yesterday — how Asher wouldn't run now that he'd found me.

"We grew up together, that's all. I barely know him anymore." I tuck a piece of sulfur into my jar and use my forearm to wipe sweat from my brow. Cleo looks unconvinced.

Asher is standing now, arms stretched overhead. He tilts his head to the side, transferring weight from one leg to the other, stretching his hips. I've only seen him close-up since he reappeared in my life, and as he loosens stiff muscles, I can't help but take in how much he's changed. The narrow of his waist, the span of his shoulders . . .

He catches me watching and flashes that crooked smile. Something pinches in my stomach, and I drop my head, embarrassed. That my eyes wandered? That he caught me staring? That I've missed him all these years, even when the person he is now is a stranger?

When he walked back into my life, I wanted him to be this perfect version of himself, an image I'd made up in my head. It was an impossible image, of course, because I created it from childhood memories, from the people we were when we were innocent and small. But we're not children anymore. We're not innocent, we've both done things we regret, and because of it all, Asher is a complete mystery to me. He's a mystery, and I hate it.

Even still, I want to trust him again. Even after everything. Because I can't deny that his time with Bain and Cree seems like the exception. Everything he's shown me since then falls in line with the Asher I knew — a boy who was kind and considerate. A boy who put others before himself, who never lost faith, who took risks but never with bad intentions.

I want to be willing to confide in him as I did when we were kids, to know exactly what he's thinking before he says a word. I want all that, and after our time together in the mountains and crossing Burning Ground, a part of me thinks it may actually be possible.

My stomach churns, and this time I have enough sense to know it's got nothing to do with the food I ate earlier. I felt this same giddy unease the very first time Flint touched my arm in Dead River and asked if I wanted to go for a walk after he unloaded his rickshaw. This feeling leads to nothing good. I turn back to the sulfur and don't look at Asher for the rest of the day.

When my shadow has stretched long and the sun nearly skims the horizon, the workers at our hot pool call it quits.

"You almost done? I'll walk in with you." I look up to find Asher waiting at the edge of my boardwalk. "Your nose got sunburned," he adds, pointing.

I'm amazed there's anything left on me that wasn't burned already. "You go ahead," I hear myself saying.

"With Saph?" He almost sounds disappointed. She's lingering a bit farther back on the boardwalk, smoothing the short hairs at the back of her neck.

"Yeah. I'm going to finish filling this jar and then I'll head in with Cleo."

"Okay." He frowns, but turns around and jogs off.

When I glance toward Cleo, she's rolling her eyes. "I've got no pity for idiots who say one thing when they mean another."

"I can't be with anyone," I insist. "And I'm not sure I fully trust him."

"No one fully trusts anyone in the wastes. But you're in Powder Town now, and you won't be leaving, so if you've got something to say to that young man, I suggest you say it before he moves on to someone showing him interest."

I break off a final piece of sulfur and snap it again so it can fit into the jar.

"I'm not kidding, Delta," Cleo continues. "Men don't do subtle well. You gotta lay things out for them, and I promise you, Saph's gonna lay it out. I've never seen her fold and forgive someone so quickly."

"I don't get it." I screw the lid on my jar and stand. "Saph's your sister. Don't you want her to be happy?"

"Not if the person she's happy with would be happiest with someone else. Not if what she's chasing is doomed for failure."

"It's complicated," I say.

Cleo shrugs. "It always is."

CHAPTER TWENTY-FOUR

That evening, I convince Asher to introduce me to Bronx the Chemist.

"She likes to work late—and alone. She's not going to want to see us," he says.

But Saph is at some mandatory meeting at the defense barracks and Cleo went to see a friend, and even with my aching muscles after a day of harvesting sulfur, *anything* sounds better than lying on those cramped bed mats alone with Asher. So I insist. Tomorrow marks six days since my mother's execution, and Alder will die at noon. I'm too late to save her, but if I act now —if I find answers—I might be able to make it back to Bedrock in time to stop the following execution.

As we leave Cleo's, Powder Town is peaceful beneath a blanket of stars. The sounds of families chatting and laughing flood the streets. Candlelight flickers through slats of shuttered windows. There's a sense of ease here, of safety. People are truly relaxed. I've never come across anything like it, not outside Zuly's tanker. It gives me hope that even without our gods, people might be able to live together. If we just pool resources—if we work together instead of tearing each other apart—there might be hope of a future worth seeing.

"Those three buildings house the saltpeter beds," Asher says, pointing. The smallest building is on our side of the glistening Serpent River, and a narrow bridge leads to two larger buildings on the other bank.

"I think I can smell the manure from here," I say, wrinkling my nose.

"You can. It's a scudding bad job, the saltpeter beds." He shudders, like he's shaking off a bad memory, then pauses. "And here's the kitchen."

A building nearly as large as Prime Hall looms before us, but unlike the Prime's meeting quarters, this building has no windows. I expect it to be guarded, but there's not even a door, just a massive opening where several familiar wagons are stationed — the very same ones that made up the convoy I saw when working the fields in Bedrock.

"I thought it would be more . . . secure," I say.

Asher shrugs. "Only way out with a wagon is through the front gate. Which is always guarded."

I glance over my shoulder toward the rocky foothills that butt up against the rear of the town. There's no wall, but the Serpent River and various rock forms create a natural barrier — one that can only be crossed on foot, and even then, not easily. Plus, there are patrols in the foothills, members serving the Reaper's pillar who stand watch. I can see a few of their torches bobbing in the dark.

Asher leads the way inside, telling me about the pantry — the cool, dark cellar that holds jars upon jars of powder — and the kitchen on the ground level, where we'll find Bronx the Chemist.

Asher has pulled a candle out so we can see where we're going, and I try not to think about all the stores of black powder waiting below our open flame. Spare wagon wheels and axles hang on the room's walls, along with carpentry tools for repairs. There's a strange clay tube pushed to one corner, like the barrel of a rifle, only five times larger. It would take several people to move it. Before I can ask Asher what it is, we're entering a new room.

Here, floor-to-ceiling shelves are stocked with jars—some glass, some clay. From what I can make out, they hold one of three things: charcoal, sulfur, or a white, crystalline substance that looks an awful lot like salt. It must be saltpeter. These are the ingredients for black powder.

When we pass what must be the tenth shelf, we come upon a work area. Here, a woman with ghostly white skin is bent over a wide wooden desk. Glass jars hold candles that cast faint light on the ingredients she carefully measures and mixes. Her head is shaved like the Prime's, but the short, stubby growth of hair on her scalp is a brilliant white. The eyepieces of the goggles she wears are tinted despite the already dim lighting, and another piece of eye equipment perches on her nose—two glass disks encased in frames that she looks through, all held in place by a wire that extends from the frames and hooks behind her ears.

"I like to work alone," the Chemist says as we step nearer, her focus still locked firmly on her work.

"I told her that," Asher says, "but she insisted on meeting you."

"Asher of Alkali Lake," she murmurs, finally looking up. "I received a report from the saltpeter beds this afternoon. You didn't put in your time."

"I decided to harvest sulfur from now on. If that's okay?"

"It's not. You were assigned to the beds during your first visit, and that's where you'll stay. You don't get to upgrade — especially not after running." The Chemist takes the wire-framed eye thing off, sets it on the table, and turns her attention to me. "You must be Delta of Dead River."

I nod.

"I can spare you a few minutes. Come sit." She nods to a chair in the corner of the room, almost behind her desk. "Asher, that is all."

He lingers a moment, but in the end doesn't argue. After I'm seated in the small chair, the Chemist turns away from the candles and lifts the tinted goggles to her forehead. Her eyelashes are as brilliant a white as her shorn hair, and her eyes are the lightest shade of blue, almost violet along the edges. The whites of her eyes are slightly pink, as though she's rubbed them fiercely and is in desperate need of sleep.

"They're tinted," I say, pointing to her goggles.

"Yes. My eyes are very sensitive. And the glasses" — she glances at the wire-framed instrument on the desk — "make everything a bit bigger, which helps with the measuring. A trader came to town with them ages ago; he found them in an old rover. I was lucky to be out that day. I'm usually here, in the kitchen." Her eyes flick upward with the memory, and for a moment, she's lost in it. "I'm rambling. Was there something you needed?"

I look over her desk, hoping to spot paper or scrap metal filled with symbols — Old World or otherwise. But there is nothing other than unmarked measuring cups and mixing bowls, jars of ingredients, and the completed black powder, dark inside sealed jars.

"Is there a recipe that you have to follow?" I ask. "Instructions for mixing?"

"Yes. It's been passed from Chemist to Chemist."

"So it's not written down anywhere?"

The Chemist laughs, her violet eyes twinkling. "What good would that do? No one here can read, and then that rusted General would try to steal the recipe so his Oracle can tell him how to make powder."

I lick my lips and nod, trying to mask my disappointment. "Wouldn't it be easier to just . . . get rid of him?"

She cocks a pale eyebrow at me. "We are safe only because we have something he needs. We could never truly overthrow him."

"You have all the black powder in the wastes! You could stockpile it. Bring in an explosive during a delivery!"

Her features suddenly harden. "You speak of certain death, Delta of Dead River. Annihilation. The gods turned their backs on the people of the wastes, but the Prime and the Trinity will not turn their backs on the people of Powder Town."

"But I have to do something. He has my pack. There are only nine of them left, and they will die if I don't—"

She holds up a hand, cutting me off. "Whatever he wants, give it to him. And if you can't, make peace with the fact that you will lose your pack. It is cruel and unfair, but that is the way of the wastes. You cannot best him, and Powder Town will not sacrifice thousands to save nine."

I stand up so quickly the chair skids back. "This was supposed to be the last free place in the wastes, a haven for the needy."

"And it is. You were granted refuge, weren't you? You no longer have reason to fear." The Chemist lowers her tinted goggles back into place. "If you'll excuse me, I have some mixing to do."

She puts her glasses back on and returns to measuring and pouring. I watch her, wanting to flip the rusted table and spoil her work. But there are candles aflame, and black powder, and I do not have a death wish. Not this evening, at least.

I leave, defeated, the walls that surround Powder Town feeling shockingly similar to the dam at Bedrock. I'm trapped, my service pledged to people who cannot help me read the map— people who intend to sit still while a monster rules the wastes.

We could never truly overthrow him, the Chemist had said. But what if they could? I need to convince the Prime that she *can* take on the General. If she doesn't, my pack is as good as dead.

CHAPTER TWENTY-FIVE

The following morning, Cleo wakes us before the sun. This time, Asher is beside me, as grumpy and bleary-eyed as I feel. We stagger out of bed and pull on our outer layers.

After a trip to the outhouse and a quick breakfast with Cleo, we split ways. Asher heads for the saltpeter beds, a slouch to his shoulders, and I follow Cleo to the main gates. Back in Burning Ground, we harvest sulfur as the sun starts its climb. I miss Asher's presence, though I'd never tell him. By the looks of Saph's flat mouth, she's missing him too. She's on watch again, along with a few other guards who patrol the boardwalk, though their numbers are half of yesterday's.

My thoughts drift to what Cleo said about Asher, and I come to the same conclusion: I will say nothing. I won't be forthcoming *or* subtle. I'll be silent. If Asher and Saph decide to give things another shot, it's for the best. My heart belongs to my pack, and when it comes down to it, if I can't convince the Prime to attack Bedrock, I'll just be turning my back on Asher—and Powder Town. Regardless of what I've pledged, I won't stay here while my pack is slowly executed.

When we started our morning harvest, Cleo had said that the

Prime was likely to make an appearance—she checks in with her workers every few weeks—but as we retire for the midday lie-down, the woman has yet to appear.

Rather than resting, I spend all of our break searching for her, but she's not at Prime Hall, and no one I speak to has seen her all day. The summer solstice is approaching, and the town is a flurry of activity and excitement. Three nights from now, as the sun sets on the longest day of the year, there will be a celebration—a feast in the town's center, and dances and prayers performed for the gods. The Prime is likely busy with preparations.

It feels silly to celebrate anything right now. I've already been gone longer than I ever planned, and every day I'm away is a day closer to losing another pack-member.

Soon the sun is high in the sky, and I find myself on the central bridge, tears in my eyes as I watch the Serpent River snake south.

"What's the matter?" a small voice asks.

I look down to find the girl who asked me if I was a god that day I arrived in town. She's gripping the leather straps of her woven backpack and peering up at me with wide eyes.

I swipe at a tear with the back of my hand. "Someone I know just died."

"They did? But I didn't hear the funeral bell. Does the Prime know? We always have a pyre."

I force a thin-lipped smile. "It was a woman named Alder. She's not in Powder Town."

The girl looks confused. "Are you sure you're not a god?"

"Positive."

"Then how can you know someone is dead when they're not even here?"

"She was executed. It was scheduled, and I couldn't stop it."

She wrinkles up her nose. "What's *executed*?"

I can't help it; I smile. What a blessing, not to know what an execution is. To have lived in such safety that she is blissfully ignorant of the way the wastes operate. To not know about raids or death or murder. My thoughts switch instantly to Bay. How long does she have until she learns the cruel way of the world?

"I think you're gods touched," the girl concludes. "You just don't know it yet."

"That would be nice, actually. I wish I was."

"You are. Or will be. I can feel it."

"What was your name?" I ask.

"Rain. My mamma named me after what we need most. She said it's the most fitting name ever because now that I'm here, she doesn't even need rain, just me." She grins proudly. "Okay, bye now!"

The girl runs off, and I stand there thinking about how many people I know named after some form of water—this small girl, myself, Brooke, Bay. Our gods deserted us and so we started looking for hope in one another, choosing names that remind us of what we've lost, hopeful that a loved one with that name might make us feel closer to what we so desperately need.

"There you are!" Cleo is standing at the edge of the bridge, hands on her hips. "Did you eat? Or even rest? We're due back."

The sun has long since crested the sky. It's midafternoon. Time to harvest again.

I follow Cleo to the boardwalks, my heart heavy. The days will keep passing, no matter how much I wish to slow them, and harvesting sulfur is not going to save the people I love.

✦ ✦ ✦

On the way back into Powder Town, I hear a familiar voice. "And the newest prototype?" I crane my neck, searching, and there, just inside the main gate and standing at the base of a watchtower ladder, is the Prime.

"Still untested," Luce the Reaper answers.

"That's unacceptable."

"I have watchtowers to man, general training to oversee, boardwalks you now have me patrolling. We can't do everything at once."

The Prime's shoulders pull back. "Drop the boardwalks and postpone training for a week. This needs to be a priority."

The Reaper nods, and the rust-colored braid hanging down her back twitches in response. "It will be done."

"Thank you." The Prime places a hand on the back of Luce's neck and draws the other woman closer, until their foreheads are touching. There's something intimate about the moment, the way they're looking at each other.

When they part ways, I break away from Cleo. "Prime!" I call out, jogging after her. She looks up, startled. Behind me, Cleo is hissing something about protocol. I take it you need to request an audience with the Prime, that you can't just run at her like a heathen, but I couldn't care less about norms anymore. "I need to speak with you."

"I have some time tomorrow. Come to Prime Hall during your lie-down."

"No. It has to be right now. Right here."

I'm not sure what does it. Maybe my tone, or the desperation that's certainly showing on my face. Maybe it's simply that the Prime is the type of ruler the General will never be—firm but kind, someone who truly cares about her people. Whatever it is, I watch her opinion shift, her face softening.

"Reaper," she says, calling over her shoulder, "may we borrow a watchtower?"

"Whatever you need," the woman replies.

Orders are shouted, and in a blink the Prime and I are ascending a ladder to relieve one of the guards. The watchtower is small, and with the Prime less than an arm's length away, her annoyance with me is as obvious as an incoming dust storm. "What is it?" she asks bluntly.

"I need your help taking on Bedrock. My pack is dying. *Everyone* there is dying. The sleeping ilk keeps them slow and weak. The General works them until they fail."

"And you think this is news to me? That I do not see it every moon when I bring him a shipment of powder?"

"Then why don't you *do* something?"

"We *are* doing something," the Prime says. "I take people in. I keep them safe. I bargain with the devil until I can do more than bargain." Her eyes flit away from me, toward the Reaper below us.

"What's the prototype? Is it something that can stop him?"

"Maybe. But not yet."

"What do you need? I'll do anything to help."

"We need time, Delta. You can help by harvesting sulfur and letting me do my job."

"But there *isn't* any time. Don't you get it?"

"It is *you* who does not get it," the Prime snarls. "I have one shot at this. One. If I act before we are ready, if I take him on with even a sliver in my armor, he will find it and he will destroy us. That's how perfect our execution has to be. I will attack only when that attack will be a success, because if I fail again, it will be more than an eye that I'll lose."

I shudder, recalling the moment the General's falcon held his beak near my face, how a mere whistle would have cost me an eye. How my compliance saved it.

"What happened?" I ask the Prime.

"I tried to undermine him several years ago. He was growing too strong, eating up the exposed packs, swallowing the wastes' good men and turning them into Loyalists. The Reaper suggested we bring an explosive in with one of our deliveries. Detonate it while in his storeroom, call it an accident. Then, with his supplies destroyed, we could bring fighters in during our next powder delivery. Hide them beneath the wagon covers and take the General out." She pauses for a moment. "One of his Four caught us lighting the explosive. Reed, I think he was called. He smothered the fuse, turned us over to the General."

The Prime glances east, in the direction of Bedrock.

"He killed my accomplice immediately. Then two more of the

231

Reaper's soldiers for good measure. It's a good thing Luce stays behind to defend Powder Town during deliveries or she'd be dead too." Genuine fear flits across her features, and I know I am right about what I saw earlier. Luce the Reaper is more than a soldier to the Prime.

"And me?" she goes on. "It all happened so fast. The whistle, the pain." She touches the eye patch lightly. "'If you try anything like this again, our agreement is void,' he told me. 'I will march on Powder Town and overrun you. Wipe out your people. Bring mine in to take over powder production. Torture your Chemist until she reveals how it is made. And I will keep you alive to witness it all. Only you. So that you know, every day, how much you failed them.'"

She turns back to me, and there is a terrible heaviness to her good eye. Whatever responsibility I am feeling for my pack, she feels the same thing for the people of Powder Town. I was foolish to ever think otherwise.

"I am sorry about your pack, Delta of Dead River, I am. But I cannot help you save them at this time. I *will* take on the General someday, but only when we are absolutely prepared to confront him. When I know with certainty that we will not fail. And I fear that day will be long after he's executed your family."

I nod, feeling numb. I don't like it, and I hate that she can't help, but I don't hate *her*. She's only doing what I would in her place—protecting her pack, defending her home.

"What's the prototype?" I ask again, curious.

"I'm afraid that is for only me to know. Me, the Reaper, and the select few she chooses to help test it. The fewer people who know about it, the less likely that information about it will slip into the wrong hands." She raises a brow as she studies me. "What is it that the General wants you to read?"

"I'm afraid that is for only me to know," I repeat.

A small smile breaks across the Prime's face. "Well, I can't fault you there." A pause. "Then again, he has his Oracle. She's bound to figure it out eventually, and then he'll drop the threat against your pack. Unless, of course, you *stole* what he wants you to read." The Prime looks at me deeply, the way she did that day in the fields at Bedrock. She's too close to the truth. I don't think she'd use me to get to the General, but I know how far I'd go for my pack. Perhaps she is the same.

"I didn't steal anything," I say, and it's not a lie. The map is mine, the brand a part of my skin. My body is my own, and no one else's. If anyone is a thief, it's the General. Stealing people. Stealing hope. And besides, he has a copy. This is about power and control. About thinking I know the language of the brand and wanting to force me to reveal its secrets.

The Prime nods slowly. I think she believes me, but I think she also knows that I'm sharing only a portion of the truth.

"I knew a woman who could read, once. She was a trader, came to Powder Town when I was just toddling. Zuly, I think her name was. Real good with tonics and tinctures. Been a long time since she visited here." The Prime touches her lips in remembrance. "Another gods touched lost to the wastes. I wonder who the General will turn to when they all pass."

My eyes flick south, toward the Old Coast. Zuly, the healer. Gods touched and living on an oil tanker. *I thought he'd be the key to*

233

our salvation, she'd said of Asher. The truth hits me like a blow to the chest. She *had* seen his back that day she treated him as a child. And she could read it. Zuly knows whatever language makes up the brand.

I'm stunned. Shocked. The answer to my problems has been twenty clicks south of Dead River all this time.

The Prime puts a hand to my shoulder. "I'm sorry I cannot help right now, Delta. But I promise you this: when we are ready to take on the General, you will be among the first to know."

It is a kind gesture, and I am grateful for it. But it does me no good.

I nod my thanks, knowing full well that I'm going to break my pledge to Kara the Prime. As soon as I figure out how to run without being caught, I'm heading south.

CHAPTER TWENTY-SIX

Part of me is tempted to pack a bag and run while everyone is harvesting sulfur. Who's going to follow me into the wastes without supplies? But the boardwalks can be easily seen from Powder Town's watchtowers, and someone is sure to come after me on horseback if I leave in broad daylight. As I head out with Cleo just before dawn, I make a promise to myself: at lie-down, I will confront Asher—make him explain how he split last time without anyone catching him.

It's another morning of backbreaking work, though my shoulders are starting to get used to spending half the day hunched over. When we head inside, I see a familiar face towing a rickshaw toward the market.

"Clay?" I run after him.

He turns toward my voice and shoots me a toothy grin. "Delta!" He scoops me up and squeezes me around the middle like we're family. "Gods, are you a sight. I passed through Dead River recently, and it's burned. All the huts leveled. Is Indie with you?" He searches behind me, barely seeming to notice that I'm shaking my head. "Did she end up in Bedrock with the others? I ran into Vee a few days ago and she told me you brought Indie to Zuly."

"Vee's alive?"

"She was"—he ticks out his fingers, counting—"three days ago, when I saw her in the Barrel. I went there after finding Dead River raided. Heard that's where raiders sometimes bring folks they take alive."

Three days ago is a whole day *after* the General promised to execute the eldest in my pack—which would have been Vee. What Clay's claiming can't possibly be true. "It must have been someone else you saw," I tell him. "Vee was in Bedrock."

"Nah, she's waiting for you in the Barrel . . . Is supposed to bring you in when she finds you, whatever that means."

Bring me in . . . to the General. He's pulled her off sleeping ilk and planted her in the Barrel. He's using her as bait in case I pass back through, hoping I'll make contact with someone I expect to be dead. I bet a dozen Loyalists are shadowing Vee's every move.

"I don't know what you did to anger the General, Delta, but you have to make it right. Vee said he paused the executions for now, but he'll start them again if he needs to. I don't know what she was talking about." He scratches his chin. "Maybe I should have asked."

Bless Clay. He never was the brightest, but this is the best news I've heard in ages. The General needs leverage over me if he catches me—or for when I return. If he's killed everyone I love, that leverage dies too. He probably paused the executions the instant he learned I'd escaped into the wastes.

"You're *sure* it was Vee?" I pry, even though too much of Clay's story lines up with what happened.

"Course. I never forget a face. Now, where's Indie?" Again he searches behind me. "Vee said you took her to Zuly's before the raid, but she didn't know what happened after that."

Meaning Ma never updated the rest of the pack after speaking to me in the fields. Maybe she wanted to spare them the pain, or maybe she was too ilked-up by the time she had a chance to talk with them. Whatever the reason, it doesn't change the fact that Clay doesn't know.

I'm not sure how to break it to him, so I just come out and say it. "Indie's dead."

"Good one!" He laughs.

"I'm serious, Clay. She didn't make it."

"Nah, that can't be." He stares, dumbfounded. "You took her to Zuly's. She's fine. 'Cus you got her help. She's—"

"I'm sorry, Clay."

"No."

He says it a few more times, eyes pleading, hoping I'll change my story, and when I don't, I watch him come undone. The gasps, ragged. His eyes, wet. He sinks to his knees, and I feel like a scudding fool for ever teasing Indie about lying with him. It's obvious that he cared about her. He'd passed through Dead River, hoping to be with her when the baby came. He made her happy, was so blessedly *decent,* and that should have been enough for me to be happy for both of them.

"The baby?" he manages.

"In Bedrock with the others. I named her Bay."

He nods, still in a bit of a trance. "Whatever the General

wants, you have to give it to him, Delta," he says, glancing up at me. "You have to get her back."

Fathers don't always stick around in the wastes—I never knew mine—but if Clay was hoping to be with Indie during the birth, maybe he also intended to be a part of Bay's life. A bittersweet sensation floods through me—relief that Bay won't have to grow up parentless, apprehension at what this will mean as she grows older. Will she choose to live with him, traveling the wastes? Will she stay with me . . . wherever I end up settling? It's hard to think that far ahead, but she's also made it impossible for me not to. That child has her hooks in me.

"I'll get her back," I tell Clay firmly. "Just . . . give me a few weeks. A moon. Don't tell the General we spoke, or Bay and the others will be at risk. Can you promise me that?"

Clay bites his lip, nods. "I'll check in with you each time I pass through. Maybe soon you'll have good news."

He staggers for the market with his rickshaw, not bothering with a proper goodbye. I've given him terrible news while he's given me the opposite. Sure, my pack remains ilked-up and working the General's fields. Vee is a prisoner as bait. Bay is still held hostage in that nursery. But the executions have been paused. I don't have to worry about one of them dying every third day, which means I can push to Zuly's at a safe pace. If she can read the map, I'll have time to think up a solid plan, figure out a way to use the info to barter my pack free.

I sprint for Cleo's and find her at the table with Saph, both of them snickering through mouthfuls of their lunch.

"Where's Asher?" I ask.

Saph stifles a laugh. "I stopped by to see him over my break. Let's just say he's got his hands full."

I frown, mostly because I don't know what she's talking about but maybe also because the thought of them chatting between shifts makes my stomach twist in ways I don't like. "Full how?"

"With shit," Saph says.

"Literally," Cleo amends.

"There are these raised slats that extend across the saltpeter beds," Saph explains. "You stand on them when you turn over the manure and straw. They're narrow, kinda wobbly."

Asher has never been the most sure-footed. "He fell in, didn't he?"

The sisters glance at each other and burst into laughter.

"Happens to someone every few weeks," Saph says between gasps. "Never gets old, though."

✦ ✦ ✦

The horrific stench of the saltpeter beds puts sulfur harvesting to shame. I had nothing to complain about on the boardwalks.

Nose scrunched, I walk through the first facility, asking after Asher. Someone tells me he was working at the third bed, but when I arrive there, he's nowhere to be found. A pair of workers who are turning over the manure with long rakes mention a changing room in the rear of the building. I thank them and dart off, passing a wash area that reeks of shit before the hall dead-ends at a curtained doorway. I grab the fabric and burst through, finding a clean but shirtless Asher drying his hair with a thread-bare towel.

He twists, turning his back away from the doorway and holding the towel in front of his chest. The moment he sees it's me, the fear in his eyes shifts to annoyance. "Gods, Delta. You don't just barge in on someone like that."

I eye the clean pants he's wearing, the pink-scrubbed skin of his arms. "And you'd think someone with a secret branded on his back would put his shirt on first, not his pants," I hiss quietly.

"Guess I'm lucky it's just you then," he says, and goes back to drying his hair. "Nothing you haven't seen."

Yet that couldn't be further from the truth, because as he lifts the towel to dry his hair, I can see his time at Bedrock as plain as day. Long, pale scars mar his stomach and chest, overlapping, crisscrossing. Too uniform to be from a whip. A hot poker, maybe. A blade.

"They couldn't very well mess up my back," he says, catching me staring.

I want to ask him how it happened. Was it all at once or was it one burn a day for the course of many? Did they do it before they got him on sleeping ilk or after? I want to ask why he didn't tell me. But all I can do is follow the scars as they stretch across his chest, my heart aching for him. Is this what would have happened to me if I hadn't escaped the General so quickly? Would our fronts have matched just like our backs?

He's broader now than when we were kids. Stronger, too. My eyes find lines of strength among his scars. On his arms, his chest, his stomach. There's a V of muscle cut off by his pants.

My cheeks flush, and I don't know where to look. His face, the floor, my hands—none of it seems good. Asher rubs his mouth, trying to hide a smile behind his fingers. Then he turns for the wall, lifts his shirt from a hook.

I freeze at the sight of his brand. "Stop!" I practically yell. "Don't put that on."

With his arms threaded through the sleeves and the shirt still held to his chest, he glances over his shoulder. I walk toward him in a trance. I never got a good look at his brand that day when we were kids. Never got a good look at it ever. But now, standing so close . . .

"Delta?" he whispers.

I'm a hand's width from him, studying two Old World symbols on his left shoulder blade. I have two in this same spot. *E*s, the Oracle had called them. But the symbols on Asher are not *E*s. One is partially curved, the other made of three sharp lines.

I raise a finger and touch the pale, puckered skin on his back.

He sucks in a breath.

"Sorry," I murmur, but I let my finger trace the Old World marking, mesmerized. Asher shudders, his skin prickling beneath my finger, and twists abruptly to face me.

I step back.

His throat bobs.

Something hangs between us, heavy and dangerous.

"Asher, can I trust you?" I ask quietly.

"Yes," he says immediately. "Always."

"With my life?"

"Yes, of course. Why would you even ask that?"

"'Show it to no one,'" I recite. *"'Unless you trust them with your own life, keep it hidden. Always.'"*

He frowns. "There's nothing to hide from me. We're the same where that's concerned."

"We're not."

He stares.

"I saw what they copied off me in Bedrock. And I just saw your back. Part of your brand is different. *Here,*" I say, walking behind him and touching the strange symbols on his left shoulder blade. He sucks in a breath again, and it makes my heart beat faster.

"Is that it?"

I swallow, try to ignore the moths in my belly. "And here." I trace my finger down the planes of his back to the shallow curve above his waistband. "Maybe here?" I pull my hand away. "I don't know. It's similar, really similar, but I think it's different."

I toe the dirt floor of the changing room. It's loose enough to track footprints.

"Stay there," I say, and I start copying his brand into the floor the way the Oracle had copied sections of my brand into her tray of damp earth.

"Have you lost your mind?" he whispers when he realizes what I'm doing.

"We'll clear it before we leave." I peer out through the curtain. The muffled chatter of the people raking the beds can be heard, but there's no one in the hall. I cinch the fabric tight and finish my work.

"Done," I tell Asher.

He turns and surveys the markings on the floor. "It's just a bunch of lines."

"Maybe. But maybe not." I slide off my jacket and toss it aside, then pull off my scarf, lift my overshirt over my head.

Asher stiffens as I grab the hem of my final layer. "What are you doing?"

His question makes me pause.

There will be no going back from this, but if I had to show it to someone in the wastes, I'd pick Asher. Even after everything, I'd pick him.

"Trusting you." I turn around and tug the sleeveless shirt off, baring my brand to him. Clenching the shirt to my chest, I hear him move nearer. The air on my skin is shocking, but not as much as his touch. It starts on my left shoulder blade, the faintest pressure, featherlight and warm. He traces the Old World symbols there, so different from his, and I bite my lip, shudder against my will.

"Sorry," he says, but he doesn't stop tracing the brand, and I don't ask him to. A lifetime of being told to keep it hidden, and his mere touch makes me want to keep my shirt off forever.

His finger trails down to the small of my back, and I suddenly feel lightheaded. Sucking in a breath, I step out of his reach. "Draw it on the floor," I say. "Find what's the same, so you can line things up, and then fill in what's different."

I hear him working behind me. "Done," he says a while later.

I pull my sleeveless shirt on and turn around to face him. Despite the enormity of what waits on the floor by our feet, neither of us looks down. Our eyes are locked. His gaze dips to my mouth. Something would happen between us if I let it. The energy in the room feels tight and magnetic, the space between us quivering like my lodestone when I hold it out to spin freely. I could let myself be drawn to him if I wanted.

"The map," I say, nodding to the floor. The air is normal again, the magic broken.

He steps beside me, and we stare at the dirt together. It is finally, most definitely a map.

The markings at our feet are no longer mere waves or harsh angles. They make sense at last, creating something coherent, and I can see now what our pack has forgotten. All those years ago, when our ancestors chose to brand two people, they didn't create two copies of the map. They created two halves of a whole.

Our brands are just pieces. But together, overlapped . . .

"That's Burning Ground," Asher says, pointing to the waves in the center, flames of heat and rising air.

"That's the Old Coast," I say, motioning toward the obvious shore near our feet. "The Barrel." I point to another set of lines.

We call out more landmarks. The rig near Zuly's. East Tower. West Tower. The Backbone of the General's domain.

"Then what's that?" Asher asks.

He's pointing toward a circle with an *X* through it — what would have been on both our left shoulder blades. It's far north of Powder Town and northwest of Bedrock, beyond a barren stretch of desert waste that no living soul has ever dared to cross. Above the marked circle are four Old World symbols, two of which are *E*s, two others from Asher's brand.

EDEN

I stare at the marked location, heart hammering against my ribs.

"That's the Verdant," I say. "Asher, we just figured out how to read the map."

CHAPTER TWENTY-SEVEN

I was wrong about Zuly, I realize.

She couldn't have read Asher's brand, because it was never a complete map to be read. She simply sensed that it was important—that *he* was. Maybe Silla even told Zuly that the brand was to be kept secret, begged her to not speak of it for fear that harm would befall Asher if word got out.

We never needed Zuly to read the map, or an Oracle, or any gods touched. We just needed each other.

"We have to go there," I say, staring at the E D E N mark. "Immediately."

Asher cringes. "We invoked the right to work for the Trinity. We made a pledge in exchange for refuge. The Prime won't let us leave."

"We don't need her blessing. We can go alone, sneak out together."

"These distances aren't exactly accurate, Delta." Asher points to Dead River, which is positioned evenly between Powder Town and the Old Coast, despite the fact that Powder Town is nearly fifty clicks from Dead River and the Old Coast only about half that.

"So things are a bit off." I shrug. "The brand's been copied so

246

many times, and everyone who wore the brand grew while carrying it. Things are bound to have spread and shifted a little."

"But who knows by how much."

I watch Asher's eyes drift to the desert waste that separates Powder Town from the Verdant. How large is it truly? Doesn't matter. I have to keep moving forward.

"Maybe if we tell the Prime, she'll lend us some mules," Asher offers. "She could even send the Reaper and a defense unit with us, in case we run into trouble along the way."

I shake my head. "*Show it to no one. Unless you trust them with your own life, keep it hidden.* And besides, if all the rumors about the Verdant are true, we should be the first to access it. *We* get there first, *we* wield control over who can enter paradise. I don't trust that to anyone else, not even the Prime, and certainly not the General. Plus, the Prime is busy at the moment."

I relay my conversation with her earlier—how she refuses to take on Bedrock until the prototype is ready and she's certain she can best him.

"I don't need the Prime," I tell Asher firmly. "I don't need help from her or the Trinity or anyone in Powder Town. I just need you. The map. Us together."

He squints at me, mouth in a conflicted grimace.

"We know the way now, Asher. We can go there ourselves, see it with our own eyes. If I shove a fistful of green earth into a jar —if I bring the General proof that the Verdant is real—he'll let my pack go."

"Not if you don't also promise him access to it," Asher points out.

"Then I will."

"You'd allow him entry? The last green place in the world, and you'd invite in a monster?"

"No. I'd bluff. I'd promise him and his Four access to the Verdant in exchange for my pack's freedom."

Asher stares at the dirt. "I don't know, Delta. I think he'll expect that, and we're safe here. I think we should stay put."

"What about my pack? You left Powder Town to try to find us, but now you suddenly don't care?"

"Of course I care. But who knows how long it will take to even reach the Verdant. They could all be executed by then."

"They won't be." I tell him about what I learned from Clay, how the executions have paused and this is a perfect opportunity for us to venture north.

"That's even more reason to stay put. Let the Prime test her prototype. Wait until she's ready to attack."

"And let my pack live in those conditions for potential *years*? While we just sit here?"

"It's hard to swallow. I get it. But they're relatively safe. And if we wait until the Prime is ready to attack, we have an actual shot at freeing them. The Prime might even send a scouting group to the Verdant in the meantime. But this plan of yours . . ." He shakes his head. "It's not going to go the way you think. Finding the Verdant, using it to barter with the General . . . It's not going to save your pack."

"Yes it will. This is the way."

"You think he's going to want to share the Verdant, Delta? He won't even share Bedrock! You use it to try to barter your pack free and he'll hold them hostage until you grant him access to the Verdant—or worse, the power to control its border. Either way, he'll end up with the prize and you'll have nothing. Everyone in the wastes will have *nothing*."

"Then help me figure this out! We can come up with a solution while we travel."

He sucks his bottom lip.

"Asher."

But he doesn't respond, just goes on shaking his head, refusing to look at me, his eyes rooted on the map between our feet.

Suddenly it's all clear.

"All that talk about the Prime being able to help me," I say, "about how we should agree to her terms now and do what we need to do later ... You never meant it. You never planned on leaving this place again."

"I was lucky to be allowed back this time. If I leave Powder Town again ..."

"What about the Verdant? We know where it is!"

"Yeah, beyond a stretch of desert that no one's ever crossed. Because it's probably too scudding big to survive!" He drags a hand through his hair. "Delta, this might be as close to a Verdant as we're ever going to get. This. Here." He flings his arm at the walls around us. "They've got food, shelter, protection from the General. There's a future here."

I take a step away. "You're being selfish."

His face blanches. "That's not fair."

"You're selfish, just like everyone else in the wastes."

"I left to find your pack," he insists, features steeling.

"And now you're giving up on them."

"I risked everything for you, Delta! The Barrel wasn't safe for me, and I stayed. Even after everything I suffered at the General's hands, I stayed in a hornet's nest for *you*. I came to the Vulture's Roost every day. You should be thanking me. I helped you escape and I brought you here, to safety."

"No. You as good as conned me again!" I shout back. "You put me in a cage, with no way out, and you expect me to be grateful for it. Well, I'm not. You don't want to help me *or* my pack. You want to help yourself." I jab him in the chest with a finger. "You only care about yourself."

I turn away and drag my heel through the map, back and forth, obscuring the markings. It's burned into my mind now. Having finally seen the map, I'll never forget it. I move faster, wildly, until there's nothing left but loose earth.

"Delta," he says softly. "Delta, come on." His hand closes over my forearm, and I yank it free.

"Don't touch me, Asher."

"You're being ridiculous."

"You're being a coward."

His face goes blank, his arm falls to his side, and he stands there staring at me in disbelief. He looks young suddenly, like a child. "So what are you gonna do, run? Alone?"

"Yes." I push through the curtain and into the hall.

"You don't even know how to sneak out of Powder Town," he says, hurrying after me.

"No thanks to you."

"The Prime might not let you back. If you go, it's over. Delta, please don't do this."

I pick up my pace.

"Delta, stop."

But I don't.

I keep moving, and he lets me go.

✦ ✦ ✦

I wait until they're sleeping.

Cleo crashes almost immediately, but Asher takes longer. He didn't say a word to me through dinner, and though he hasn't looked my way once since we lay down on the bedrolls, I know he's waiting. Waiting for me to get up. Waiting so he can stop me.

Finally, when my eyelids are heavy and near impossible to hold open, he drifts off. I can tell it by his breathing, how it lengthens, slows.

I ease soundlessly off the mat and pull on my jacket, gather my things. I swipe a bag from Cleo and fill it with food and water, plus a pitcher and cup that will allow me to set up an inverted well with my goggles as I did in Bedrock. I feel a touch guilty at taking her supplies, but I don't dwell on it. This is Powder Town. She'll be able to secure more. A theft here won't break a person the way it might on the wastes.

I pause briefly in the doorway, glancing at Asher's prone form.

It was a mistake to trust him. It's always a mistake. Better to go it alone, count only on your own two hands.

I don't understand how he could leave Powder Town once, turning his back on safety to find our pack, only to abandon that very pack when he learned that saving them was too hard. Indie would say something like, *People are complicated, Delta. Stitched together all sorts of which ways, and when they come apart at the seams, you can't just patch them up like a pair of gloves.*

Maybe Asher needs mending, or maybe he's too far gone to be saved. I just know that if a pair of gloves keeps failing, you don't stitch them up endlessly. Eventually you throw them out and make a new pair. I can't rely on him anymore. He helped all he could, and this is where we part ways.

On the streets, Powder Town is quiet, a bit of moon lighting my way. Almost too quiet. For the briefest moment I consider returning to Cleo's and waiting for the solstice to make my move. The town will be rowdier then, the guards more distracted. But everyone will also be awake late into the night come midsummer, and the thought of slipping away without Asher or Cleo or *someone* noticing my absence feels impossible.

I shuffle for the saltpeter beds, sticking to the shadows until I have to cut across the Serpent River. Once on the opposite bank, I crouch low, observing the foothills.

Torches flicker on the rise, the Reaper's sentries patrolling Powder Town's vulnerable perimeter. They are fairly spread out, the closest one a quarter click to my left. The next a bit farther to my right. If I just stay low and move slowly, blending in with the boulders, I should be able to make my way up the foothills without being seen. After all, Asher mentioned that he went west when he ran from Powder Town. Perhaps sneaking past these very guards. At the crest of the bluff I should be well out of sight. From there, I can scale back down as I head north. I've got my lodestone to see me true. Once I've put distance between me and Powder Town, it'll get easier.

Grasping the straps of the stolen rucksack, I sprint for the nearest boulder and duck alongside it.

No shouts, no whistles.

I watch the torches a moment, making sure that they are staying at their posts.

Then I grab my rucksack straps and do it again. Soon my legs are burning from the steady ascent. But the torches wink far below me, almost out of sight, and I can practically feel the wastes calling to me.

I stand, face the hillside, and barrel into something as I begin to run. I go down hard on my rump. Pain shoots up my spine.

A shadowy figure bends down to inspect me. A broad-shouldered woman with a braid that encircles her head like a crown.

"You didn't think we only patrolled along the river, did you?"

I gape.

"Oh, you did. That's cute." She puts her forefinger and thumb into her mouth and produces a shrill whistle. "Deserter on the northern foothills!" she shouts.

The torches below jostle to action along the river. More flicker to life to the east and west, sentries who patrol from the shadows becoming visible. The whistle is repeated, rolling away into Powder Town, causing lights to wink to life throughout the shanties.

It's fine, I tell myself. *The Prime turning you out won't change anything. So long as they let you keep your supplies, everything can carry on like you planned.*

I repeat it as the sentry guides me down the hill I just worked so hard to ascend, back through the streets, and to the clearing just inside Powder Town's wall. I truly think it will be fine, even as the crowd gathers, bleary-eyed with sleep but curious to see who could possibly want to escape this haven. I still think it's fine as the Prime steps through the crowd, dark skin aglow in the moonlight, expression sharp enough to cut. I think it's fine right until the Reaper steps into view behind her, towing Asher by the meaty part of his arm.

She shoves, and he staggers forward, joining me in the clearing.

"What did you do?" he hisses.

"For breaching their pledges to me and the Trinity," the Prime announces, "for making our pillars weaker rather than stronger, Delta of Dead River and Asher of Alkali Lake are banished from Powder Town immediately."

"But only I ran," I argue, my stomach twisting. "Asher had nothing to do with it."

"You told me he would stay because of you. If you're leaving, he goes with you."

"He didn't want to leave. I asked him to, and he wanted to stay. He . . ." I glance at Asher. His mouth is a thin line, his eyes like fire.

"You are both banished," the Prime repeats.

Before I can get out another word, the Reaper's sentries are dragging us from the clearing and into the wastes. With a shove, I go sprawling, my chin glancing the ground.

I'm spitting dirt from my mouth when the gate slams closed behind us.

CHAPTER TWENTY-EIGHT

"**H**as your brain rusted?" Asher screams.

I stand wordlessly, dusting the dirt from my pants.

"Have you lost your scudding mind?" he goes on. "I don't even have my gear. I hope you're happy, Delta. I hope you're prepared to die on the wastes and be picked apart by vultures, 'cus that's what's going to happen to us."

I feel for the straps of my rucksack, confirming that it's still there, that the Prime didn't confiscate it.

"I have some supplies," I say. "We can share."

"Scud off." He starts walking south. I can see his slingshot poking from the back of his waistband, so he did manage to grab *some* gear, or maybe that always stays stowed within arm's reach. He's got no jacket, though, to stave off the cold nights. No scarf or goggles for unexpected squalls. And nothing to eat.

"Where are you going?" I call after him.

"Wherever you're not."

"Asher, I didn't mean for this to happen. I went alone."

He keeps walking.

"You think I want to be out here with you?" I yell. "Some lying bit of dirt who conned me and lied to me and doesn't care about my pack? We could save them, Asher. We could save them and make things better for everyone in the wastes, and you don't care."

He spins around hastily, and there's a glint in his eyes, something detached and menacing. It reminds me of the version of him I saw that first night in Bain's and Cree's wagon. The kind parts of him buried beneath a callous heart.

"I'm only alive because I put myself first," he snarls. "That's how I survived Bedrock. It's how I survived the wastes. The moment I got soft—the moment I decided to try to find you and the pack—everything fell apart. So when I found you at the Vulture's Roost, I told myself *no more.* Just get to safety. Lie low. Breathe a little. *Live.* I got us to safety. We could have stayed in Powder Town, Delta. We could have stayed!" His eyes flit up and down my frame. "Do you think you're special in your guilt? That you're the first person to feel responsible for your pack? I watched mine get slaughtered. Burned. Beheaded. Shot through the chest. You lose people on the wastes. You can't save everyone. I learned that lesson at nine. It's about time you learned it, too."

"So what? You just give up on people?" I scream back. "You run?"

"If you have to, yes. And you pray to the gods for forgiveness. And you try not to drown in your guilt. And when you find a bit of safety, you don't spit in its eye. Especially not when you've been given a second chance." He glances at the Powder Town wall, then back to me. "Gods damn you."

He turns and strides off.

"Where are you going?" I call again.

"South. To Zuly's. Maybe she'll take me in."

"You'll never make it without supplies."

"I've got you to thank for that."

"Asher, don't be stupid."

"Scud off," he says again, and he keeps going, slipping into the shadows.

"Fine! Go!" I scream into the darkness. "It's not like I want you around anyway, you coward. I'll find it on my own. I'll save them on my own. And since I have supplies, I'll be just fine, and you'll be the one picked apart by vultures."

My words echo back to me, and I stand there a moment, feeling like a toddler throwing a tantrum. Still, I expect him to emerge from the shadows, drawn back by logic. He won't even make it to West Tower without water. But he doesn't return, and I'm left alone with the darkness, the guilt.

I face north.

It's like Ma said all those years ago. Asher's his own person, free to make his own choices. I didn't mean to get him cast from Powder Town, but it happened, and I can't change it, and I certainly can't beat myself up over his choosing to walk to certain death instead of staying with the rucksack filled with provisions.

That's his call.

He's choosing himself. I'm choosing my pack.

That's all there is to it.

✦ ✦ ✦

Despite the late hour, I'm wide-awake, high-strung and focused. Might as well take advantage of my energy and the coolness of night.

I follow Powder Town's wall as it ropes around the settlement. Where it butts up to the foothills, I continue north. For a while I can see the Serpent to my left, winking in the moonlight, but it flows down the hills from the west and is soon behind me. I wonder if it's the last free-flowing water I'll see between here and the Verdant.

I walk well into the night, until the foothills start to fade out. There, I curl against one of the last boulders and sleep briefly. Just enough to feel rested. When I wake, dawn's first light is spilling over the wastes.

I fish the binos from my rucksack — the same pair Asher and I lifted off the Loyalists after escaping from the Barrel. As I scan the horizon, my heart beats rapidly at the prospect of the Verdant in the distance, a swatch of brilliant, fertile green. Instead, all I can see is sand-colored earth stretching on forever. Of course. The map wasn't to scale, and at minimum, I probably have fifty clicks to go.

I glance over my shoulder.

Asher's trailing me, his hair brilliant in the morning sun.

I don't slow down, but I don't try to lose him either.

✦ ✦ ✦

By the worst heat of the day, I rest. Sit down on the cobweb-cracked earth right in the middle of the wastes and drape my scarf over my face. It's as hot as all can be. Sweat drips over every crevice in my body. I should sleep now, and I must, because suddenly a boot's nudging my side and I'm dragging my eyes open.

I sit up, hand going for my blade, but it's only Asher, caught up to me finally.

"What happened to Zuly's?" I ask. His lips are parched and cracked, like the ground I sit on.

"Decided I didn't want to be vulture food."

I nod and pass him my waterskin. He drinks greedily.

"Slower," I warn.

He wipes his mouth on his sleeve and sits beside me. A moment later he takes another small sip, then lies back. "Wake me when you want to move again?"

I nod.

The wild, wary side of me wants to sit watch. But Powder Town is easily twenty clicks behind us. The General's mines are far to the east, maybe eighty clicks or so, given how much Asher and I traveled after leaving them. There's nothing around these parts. No one to even keep watch against.

I lie down beside Asher and doze. When there's still plenty of light left but the worst of the heat has passed, I nudge his shoulder. We walk the rest of the day in silence, passing the water between us and eating as we move.

✦ ✦ ✦

It goes on like that through the evening and into the next morning —the summer solstice. We walk when we have the energy and rest when we don't. Still, I think we might be pushing too hard. I keep seeing Indie and Ma in the heat. Sometimes they're ahead, urging me to hurry. Other times they're behind me, on a horse of all things, waving their arms and begging me not to leave.

By midday, these figures are a constant smudge on the horizon to the south, and I start to wonder if maybe they're not a figment of my imagination. If there is truly someone following us.

"You see that?" I ask Asher.

He stares back the way we came. "Probably one of the Reaper's soldiers. Confirming that we're not going to circle around and sneak back in."

"We've been walking long enough that they know we're not coming back," I say. "Think it's a Loyalist?"

"Nah." He jerks his head toward the sky, which is quiet and sprawling, no birds in sight. I don't point out that it's only the General's Four who use the falcons and that this shadow of ours could still be working for him. "Maybe just another vagrant wandering the wastes," Asher goes on, "hoping we drop dead so they can strip us of our gear. We keep on, we'll outpace them. Honestly, they'll turn back as soon as they realize they don't have the supplies to keep dogging us."

I pinch the waterskin, checking its fullness. Half left. "See that outcropping ahead?" I point to a disruption on the horizon, a small bluff surrounded by rocks and boulders that break up the otherwise flat plane. "We should set up an inverted well and rest there. Get more water before we head back out. Maybe even let our friends catch up so we can take them out if they're trouble."

"Yeah," Asher agrees. "Sounds good."

And with that, we plod on.

I don't like the quiet between us. It's awkward, uneasy. Neither of us has apologized since our fight, and I worry that if I try, it will only lead to more yelling.

As we close in on the rocky outcropping, two strange, foreign shapes appear just beyond it. They're unnaturally straight, like wooden posts, but far too tall. Thin, shadowy wisps hang from them like spider's threads.

"North Tower?" Asher asks.

I shake my head. "North Tower was closer to the Backbone on the map, and east of the Verdant. Sure looks man-made, though."

A shiver travels the length of my spine. A man-made structure means people, and out here, in an uncharted section of the wastes, that means people we can't trust. People who could be Loyalist spies or opportunist trappers like Bain and Cree.

Asher and I glance at each other. I draw my two blades, passing the Old World model to him, and we creep forward, cautious.

The structure gets larger with each step, until we're rounding the rock outcropping and staring at the strangest construction I've ever seen.

The posts are as thick as tree trunks. Ropes and pulleys hang from them, attaching to a thinner, horizontal post that bisects each vertical one. Pale, bunched fabric is cinched here, against the wood. The vertical posts are secured to a wooden wagon that could easily hold a dozen people. The sideboards aren't tall — maybe knee-high — and the bed has been modified so that it is narrower at the front than at the back. The entire thing sits atop two metal axles salvaged from a rover. One wheel is still the Old World variety, made of some strange foreign material. The other three are wooden.

We scan the area quickly, then move closer.

I walk around the vehicle — I assume it's a vehicle of some sort, since it has wheels — and stare up at the towering posts. Why

261

would anyone want massive treelike posts aboard their vessel? It makes the wagon needlessly top-heavy.

"Someone must have abandoned it," Asher says.

I use one of the wheels as a foothold and pull myself up and over the siding. Aside from additional roping and a lever near the front, the wagon is virtually empty. Where is the yoke for hooking up mules? Where are the reins and harnesses? The thing certainly can't be pulled like a rickshaw.

Asher climbs in and steps beside me, shielding his eyes as he gazes up the posts. Even cinched, the pale cloth flutters slightly, toyed by a breeze we can't feel in the wagon's bed.

"What is it?" he asks.

I shake my head. "It makes no sense. It's like a wagon, but shaped all wrong. And these posts will only make it top-heavy. Whoever built it is an idiot."

"That idiot is about to shoot you," a voice announces.

We twist toward it. Nestled against the foot of the outcropping, standing in the crooked doorframe of a ramshackle hut we hadn't noticed in our first sweep, is a wrinkled old woman. She has a rifle aimed at our heads.

"Now, if you don't mind," she says, motioning with the weapon, "get your tired asses off my wind wagon."

CHAPTER TWENTY-NINE

"**W**e don't mean trouble," Asher says, raising his hands. "Just passing through."

"That's a lie," the woman croaks, squinting at us. "There's nothing around these parts, so there's nowhere to be passing through to."

"Wind wagon, you called it?" I say, thinking about the posts behind us, the giant swaths of fabric that could catch the breeze if uncinched. Like my flags back at Dead River, hung out to warn of incoming storms. "That's genius."

"Modeled it after a sailboat," the woman says.

Zuly's tanker surfaces in my mind. I can see the resemblance between her hull and this wagon's bed. The tall posts are another matter.

"Not much use for boats anymore," Asher says.

"There's lots about the Old World people have chosen to forget. Doesn't mean they can't still serve a purpose," the woman replies. "Now, what're you doing here?"

"Like we said, just passing through," Asher repeats.

"And like I said, there ain't nowhere past here to pass along to."

"You can't believe that," I say. "You built a wind wagon.

263

Clearly you intend to cross the wastes. Which means you think there's something out there."

The woman's eyes narrow. She looks about Old Fang's age —ancient for the wastes—but I don't doubt for a second that she could end my life. There's a fire to her stare. "It doesn't work," she says finally. "Not yet at least."

"Where are the others?" I ask.

Asher startles beside me, but he hasn't noticed what I have seen beyond the woman: the remnants of a small pack. Several huts are built along the rocks, sheltered in alcoves. They're dilapidated now, caved in. Sand and dust have gathered at their frames. Only the woman's home is anywhere near habitable, and even that is a stretch. The entire structure leans to the side, as though it may collapse any day.

"Gone. Left about a year ago, to head to Powder Town. Not sure if they made it or not. Hope so, though. They thought I was crazy wanting to go north and were tired of waiting for me to prove I wasn't. Still, I don't wish them any ill will."

"You just said there was nothing around here," Asher points out.

"There ain't," the woman says. "When I founded Harlie's Hope, it was home to a thriving pack of ten, and we explored every which direction from this here center." She stomps a foot on the parched ground. "Powder Town's to the south, and according to the folks living there, there's nowhere worth living beyond it. To the east, we found iron mines belonging to men I don't trust. And desert to the north and west. Days of it. Farthest we ever got on horseback was four days. Then we had to turn back."

My heart sinks. We won't last four days on foot in barren desert. We'll run out of water, supplies. And who knows how far the Verdant is, truly. The possibility that he was right about everything gnaws at me.

"We couldn't risk exploring any farther," the woman goes on, "not with binos showing nothing as far as we could see and our animals growing weak, so we came back, let the horses recover. We tried a few more times, with different headings. Still nothing. And now the horses are gone too, south to Powder Town with the others."

"But you stayed," I say.

"I think there's green out there," she says with a shrug, and her weapon lowers with the motion, no longer aimed at our heads but at the dirt that separates us. "This whole world can't be rock. I don't blame the others for giving up on me and the wind wagon, though. I crashed more often than I sailed, and even if I get it working someday, there's no guarantee I won't sail myself into an endless desert and starve. But I've dug my heels in so far on this one, I can't quit. Once the rusted thing works, I'm not looking back."

This is our ride, I realize, this crazy wind wagon I'm standing on. If we get it working, we can cross the desert. We can find the Verdant. I just need to convince this woman to take us.

"I'm Delta," I say. "This is Asher. We're headed north."

She eyes me skeptically. "You won't get far on foot."

"I know. That's why I'm going to help you get your wind wagon working."

"Is that so?"

"Unless you don't want help."

She peers up at me, a glimmer in her eye.

"Delta's real good with gadgets and contraptions," Asher adds. "I bet the two of you can figure it out."

"So, Harlie," I say to the woman. "What do you think?"

"How'd you know my name?"

"Just a guess, since you said you founded this place. Now what do you think?"

"I think your minds might be mucked-up, and you got as much sense as a chicken running headless. But I ain't turning away help. Climb down, and we'll get started."

✦ ✦ ✦

There's not much left to Harlie's Hope. A well that pulls less water each day, a designated outhouse away from the well, and Harlie's ramshackle hut. She hasn't bothered to repair it in nearly five years, and it shows.

"Can't afford to," she explains with a shrug. "Any bit of wood I get my hands on goes toward the wind wagon."

She's been working on it for the last three years. Her pack originally lived closer to Powder Town, but when Kara the Prime took power and began building a defense wall around the settlement, Harlie's people were in the way. The Prime offered them safety behind their wall, but Harlie prided herself on being independent. She also believed the answer to defeating the bad men taking over the wastes wasn't to hide behind walls, but to beat them to the Verdant. She moved her people north, to the edge of what proved to be an uncrossable desert. They brought wagons full of lumber and supplies with them, and for the first ten years, traders visited Harlie's Hope regularly. They come less frequently now, once a season if she's lucky.

She survives on the water from the well—meager, but enough now that she's the only person calling the place home—as well as tubes and weeds that grow in a shaded section on the south side of the rock outcropping. She also shoots whatever birds she can. If she falls sick, if bad weather hits at the wrong time, if a trader doesn't make it to her, she'll be dead. It's so bad, it makes Dead River look like a paradise.

"If I don't get the wind wagon working by winter, I'll be heading for Powder Town with my tail between my legs," Harlie says. "I'm not sure my pride can handle that, but I also know this place is dying. I won't last."

While Asher rests in a sliver of shade beside Harlie's hut, she shows me inside. The walls are awash with markings, her plans for the wind wagon carved right into her home.

"Most everything I needed—pulleys, rope, lumber—I had to trade for, which is part of why it's taken me so long. The wagon was mine, made the move up here with me. It used to have two Old World tires, but I had to replace one."

"We'll want spares when we head north," I say.

"What do you take me for—some bright-eyed babe? I've got two spares already stowed beneath the deck."

"Deck?"

"The wagon bed—the wood you stood on. That would be called the deck on a boat."

"I've been on a boat. It was nothing like your wind wagon. Metal-made, massive. And it didn't have those weird post things." I make a motion up and down, illustrating their height.

"The masts? Girl, those are what will let us sail." She tugs me toward a different drawing, where the fabric I saw cinched against the posts—masts—is unfurled. "They'll catch the wind."

She walks me through her plans. Soon I know all about rigging and sails, how a boat has a starboard and port side, how the bow is narrower to cut through the water—or, in our case, simply to create less drag as we move over the earth. The lever I saw near the front of the boat—a tiller, she calls it—will steer the wagon by forcing the axle to turn left or right.

"Real trouble is, I can't stop safely. Winds can get the wagon moving pretty fast, which is a risk for rolling. And turning can only be done at slower speeds. I rolled last time I took the thing out, busted the portside and part of the mainmast. That was a year ago, when my pack left. Been repairing ever since. Gotta say, I'm a bit terrified to take it out again. If something goes wrong, I might have to walk away from it."

"And you're too proud for that," I conclude.

Harlie smiles. Her lips are paper-thin and her face full of wrinkles, but her expression exudes youth.

"Where'd you learn all this?" I ask.

Her eyes twinkle. "My ma passed it to me through stories, and her ma did the same for her. Someone must have sailed in our family, eons ago, back in the Old World when the ocean wasn't dry."

"How'd they stop *their* vessels?"

"Combination of things. Turning into the wind and lowering sails, mainly. But my wagon's not on water and can't turn quickly. They also had anchors—big, heavy hooks you could throw overboard to drag along the ground and stop the boat, but that won't work for us either. I had one on my first model. Flipped the whole wagon when I dropped it. Nearly killed myself. We gotta brake another way."

She explains everything she's tried. Mostly it involves the sails.

I stare at her plans, mind racing. Mule-drawn wagons stop because the power ceases. The beast stops moving, so the cart does as well, with the yoke and line bracing against the animal. But closing the sails hasn't slowed Harlie's wagon quickly enough. We need to slow the wheels, too, not just take away the wind. An anchor feels like the obvious solution, but Harlie says it's unsafe. If we can't use an anchor and we can't use the sails, what *can* we use?

I sort through every wheeled contraption I've ever encountered. Wheelbarrows, rickshaws, rovers. I don't know how the Old World rovers worked, but presumably they had an easy way to cut off the power, force the wheels to stop turning. Otherwise they'd slide down hills or slopes.

This makes me think of the time I extended the dock at Dead River, how my dragger holding supplies kept slipping down the bank. I propped rocks against it to hold it in place. I've seen traders do the same thing with their rickshaws after lowering them, positioning a rock behind the wheels so the cart can't slide.

We can't put a rock beneath the wind wagon wheels while moving—that would be disastrous—but we *can* press something

269

against the wheels. And if we press hard enough, the wheels will turn slower and slower and eventually . . . stop.

I plop myself down right in the middle of Harlie's hut and start drawing in the dirt.

✦ ✦ ✦

At some point my eyes start to hurt and I realize it's because the sun is setting. Asher lights a candle on the room's lone table.

"Onto something?" he asks.

I nod.

"You should eat."

I nod to that too.

"We have a fire going. Harlie's sharing some fowl and a bit of moonblitz, too, to celebrate the solstice."

"Maybe in a minute," I say, but I know it will be far longer.

Later, when I can no longer hear the warm timbre of Asher's voice or Harlie laughing at his stories, there is a creak behind me. "You should sleep," the woman says. "Your friend is."

"I think this might work," I say, standing. After sketching and wiping the dirt clean and sketching again, I finally have something promising.

"Girl, you cannot show up here and solve a problem I've been battling for years in one day. It's not pos—" She stops, staring at the dirt.

"We make a lever like your tiller, but over the back axle. And if we build it like this"—I point to the drawing, which shows how beams can run beneath the wagon bed and make contact with the wheels when the lever is pushed—"the drag should slow the wheels."

270

Harlie shakes her head, brow furrowed.

"It should work," I insist.

"I know it should. I'm just mad I didn't think of it first."

"You did all the hard work, figured out all the ways it *couldn't* be done. That made it easier for me to find the way it can." I stand, smack my dirty fingers against my thighs. "Do you have any lumber left? Enough to make this?"

"A little. We can start tomorrow."

But she's looking at me . . . like maybe she doesn't want to start, like finishing the wagon is a thing she's only ever dreamed of accomplishing.

"Why do you want to cross that desert so badly?" she asks.

"Same as you. Just hoping to find a place worth living."

"Delta, I've only got a few years left on this scorched, gods-forsaken earth. If there's nothing out there, if I die with only the sun and the vultures there to witness it, I won't be losing much. But you . . . you're young. Go back to Powder Town, settle down with that boy, have a family the way they did in the Old World. *Live.*"

"I've seen the way of things in these wastes. It's not a world to bring a kid into. And besides, I don't need kids to live. I don't need to settle down with Asher—or anybody—to have my life mean something."

Harlie touches her lip, grimaces. "You're right. I wasn't being fair."

"Besides, whatever you think there is between Asher and me, you're wrong. He doesn't want to be here with me; he just got stuck with me. Big difference."

"Sometimes you're too close to a thing to see it clearly. Like me with the wind wagon. You get what I'm saying?"

I know exactly what she's implying, and I don't like it.

She sighs and adds, "When you have a shot at making a home for yourself in a place like Powder Town with someone who cares about you, you don't throw it away."

I don't know how to tell her that I'm not throwing anything away. That I'm doing all this for the life I already have, the people I already love. My pack, Bay . . . This is all for them. And when the Verdant becomes our home—when I've saved them and we live there together—all this will have been worthwhile. But if I share this with Harlie, she'll have questions about why the General is holding them as leverage over me. She may consider traveling with me too much of a risk and turn me away. Above all, I think I'm scared she'll try to convince me that Asher could be my family and home as much as my pack and the Verdant.

And maybe that's true. Maybe if Asher and I stopped arguing long enough to apologize and forgive, we could be happy. We could start again, just the two of us. But I can't dwell on that. As long as a single member of my pack lives and breathes in Bedrock, I am going to try to reach the Verdant. And I need to find it before the General does.

"I have to do this, Harlie," I say firmly. "And I know it will work."

"The braking system or the trip across the desert?"

"Both."

A crooked smile stretches across her lips. "Spoken with the confidence of the gods."

CHAPTER THIRTY

We wake early the next morning and—after a meager meal of rubbery tubes and leftover pickings from the fowl—go straight to work on the wind wagon. Harlie drags out her tools and lumber and spreads them out beneath the baking sun. I'm sizing it all up, figuring where to make our first cuts, when a shadow flicks over the wood. I throw my head back, and my stomach sinks.

A falcon. Sandy in coloring, with dark wingtips and white on its throat.

The shadow tailing us yesterday. It wasn't a vagrant, and they didn't turn back.

I twist in a frantic circle, scanning the rocks that border Harlie's Hope. There's a whistle nearby, and there he is. Not a stone's throw from Harlie's ramshackle hut, crouched low in the rocks, binos in hand, watching us. *Reed*. The horns of his ram-skull mask scrape at the sky. His rifle, slung across his back, is visible over his shoulder, but his horse must be hidden on the other side of the rocks.

My stomach coils as I realize what happened. He never went back to Bedrock. He sent the others back, but he waited at a distance, watched. And when I was cast out of Powder Town, he followed.

I know what will happen now, remember the leather pouch Reed gave his bird when I sat caged in the Barrel. He sent a message with his falcon that day, using the short codes the Oracle told me about. If Reed sends Rune to Bedrock with a message now, an army will descend on Harlie's Hope.

"Asher!" I shout, pointing. The falcon is soaring for Reed, who has his arm outstretched, waiting for the bird to land.

Asher drops the file he's been using to sharpen a handsaw. Standing quickly, he draws his slingshot from the back of his pants, winds up, and lets a rock fly. It slices through the air like a bullet, clipping the bird. The falcon plummets, one wing flapping, desperate, the other hanging useless as it falls. It hits the dry earth with a thud.

Reed bolts upright, shouting the bird's name as I sprint for it.

One wing is broken, bent at a wrong angle, and Rune flails the other, turning in circles in the dirt. Working quickly, I use my knife to cut a length of braided hair from my head and tie the falcon's legs together. It nips and snaps at me, but is too disoriented to do any real damage. Once I've tied a second knot for good measure, I stand, holding the braid out by the end, with the falcon hanging an arm's length before me. She twists on the line, her injured wing grazing the ground.

"Easy there, boy," Harlie says to Reed. She's got her rifle aimed at him and he's got his aimed back. "You might shoot me, but my friend's got a knife, and he'll lodge it in your chest before you can reload." Asher has my Old World blade held out, the slingshot dropped at his feet, useless until he finds another stone for it.

Reed looks between them, anxious; then his eyes flick to me. Rune chirps pitifully as she dangles. I lower the falcon to the ground, press my boot lightly to her body, pinning her in place, and draw my bone blade. I hold it at her neck. Her golden eyes lock on me and she doesn't try to bite me again, as though she can guess what's to come.

"Don't," Reed shouts from the rocks.

"Toss your gun," I call back.

He throws it, and it clatters to a standstill before Harlie's shack. Asher inches forward and grabs the weapon.

"Get on your knees," I tell Reed. "Hands up, toward the gods."

He does as he's told, and Asher and Harlie approach slowly. After a bit of careful maneuvering, Reed's hands are bound. They tear off his mask and drag him from the outcropping, dumping him before me. His bound hands are pressed together before his heart, almost as if he were praying.

"I can explain," he says. "Just don't hurt Rune."

"Explain what? That you were tracking me? That you plan to drag me back to the General?"

"No!" he insists. Then, hurriedly, he adds, "He paused the executions."

"I already knew that."

He swallows, fear in his eyes. He thought this would buy him time or sympathies.

"We should just kill him now," Asher says. "You can't trust a Loyalist, especially not one of the Four."

"Not yet." I give Reed a pointed glare. "Are you alone?"

"Yes."

"Does the General know you've been following me?"

"Yes. I sent word that I'd stay behind. But it's not what you think. It's — *Don't!*" Pure terror flickers in his eyes as I press down on the blade. The bird thrashes beneath me. I can feel her body swell and deflate beneath my boot, breathing uneasily, desperate to flee.

"Check his pockets, his belt," I say to Harlie and Asher. "He'll have a leather pouch."

"He's got three," Harlie says, holding them up. "Only one's full."

"Empty it. What's inside?"

Harlie turns the pouch over, and a bunch of wooden tiles fall out. They're small, about the size of my thumbnail, and marks are burned into their faces. Dashes and arrows, mostly. And a few other symbols I don't understand.

"What do these mean?" I ask Reed.

"It's how we communicate. If I planned on returning to Bedrock in three days, I'd send the tile with the symbol for homecoming and the tile with three dashes. If I needed aid, I could send the tile with the symbol for aid and then my location."

"Location how?" I ask.

"Show us," Asher nudges him with his foot.

Wrists still bound, Reed extends his hands and selects a few tiles. On one, I can make out the symbol that graces Powder Town's flags. The next tile has an arrow, and four others are identical, each with five dashes on their face.

"Twenty clicks north of Powder Town," Reed says, nodding to his selected tiles.

"But that arrow could point any direction," I say.

"There's a dot on all the tiles that have arrows. When you read them, the dot always goes on the bottom. That's how you know the right heading."

I can see it now, a small dot burned into the tile's face. The arrow points up from the dot. On the other unused tiles I can easily discern additional directions. West. Southeast. Northwest. It's genius, this method of communicating. Simple but effective.

And terrifying.

My heartbeat ratchets up in my chest as I realize how close Reed had been to sending a message to the General. If Asher's aim had been off, if he hadn't struck the bird . . .

"He was about to send a message for help," I say, glancing between Reed and his falcon.

"No, I wasn't. If you just let me explain."

"I don't trust him," Asher says. "Kill them both."

"Don't hurt Rune, please," Reed begs, eyes glossy as he watches his injured falcon squirm. I think he might actually cry for the creature, and compassion is something he almost showed me once, too. It nearly makes me pause. But then I think of the Prime's story, how Reed was the one who caught her people trying to destroy Bedrock's black powder. How *he's* the reason the Prime lost an eye.

"Will she recover?" I ask Reed.

"Was she bleeding from the head at all? Can she move her neck?" He cranes his, trying to get a better look.

"It's just her wing," I say. "Broken, I think."

Reed gasps in relief, brings his bound hands to his mouth. "She should be all right then. She'll heal."

"That's what I feared," I say, and I end the bird with one quick slash of my blade.

"No!" Reed shouts as the blood spills. A tear breaks loose, trailing down his cheek. "She wasn't a threat. She couldn't even fly. Why would you do that?"

"I didn't make it this far to go soft," I say through gritted teeth. "I can't risk her recovering and you sending word to the General. Forgive me for not being sympathetic to a Loyalist who serves a monster. You killed my mother. I killed your bird." I take my boot off the creature, now limp, and approach Reed. I put my blade beneath his chin. "Now, you wanted to explain something? Go ahead. Explain before I slit your throat, too."

Reed's still staring beyond me, toward Rune, his eyes impossibly wide.

I twist the blade minimally against his neck and a bead of his blood wells up.

"I came to help," he grits out. "When the Reaper turned us away at Powder Town, I sent the Loyalists home and said I'd wait behind. Told them to tell the General that I didn't expect you to sit still long, not with your pack's lives on the line, and that I would bring you in as soon as you ran. But clearly, I didn't. I followed you. I was going to reveal myself this morning, but Rune got antsy and took off flying, and then you spotted her before I could explain myself, and it all rusted up."

I bark out a laugh. "You expect me to believe that?"

His brow furrows. "It's the truth."

"You're here to *help?* You didn't help when the General murdered my mother. You didn't help my pack stay off sleeping ilk. You didn't even quit chasing me to Powder Town until the Reaper threatened to cancel Bedrock's trade agreement!"

"I was always being watched then. I had to play a part."

I shake my head.

"I kept your secret about the inverted well, and I brought you clean water the first night you worked the fields," he goes on. "I want to help you find the Verdant. That's why you're here, right? You know something."

"If I did, I wouldn't tell you. And I think you're full of shit. I think you were sent to spy on me. You were supposed to follow me to the Verdant and report back to the General, but you got yourself caught and are trying to trick me with the shallowest lie the wastes has ever seen."

"So you know where it is?" he asks, eyes brightening. "The Verdant?"

"Goodbye, Reed. Rest easy."

His bound arms come up expertly fast, swiping in a circle and knocking my blade aside. Harlie and Asher sharpen their aim with the rifles. I recover the knife. But before I can strike, Reed draws something from beneath his shirt that freezes me solid.

"Don't shoot!" I yell to the others.

I stand there, staring. Barely able to believe it.

Hooked on Reed's thumbs is a leather cord, and hanging from it, quivering between us as it finds north, is a lodestone.

✦ ✦ ✦

I drag him to Harlie's shanty and shove him inside. Asher grabs my wrist. "You shouldn't be alone with him," he says thinly. "I don't trust him."

"Then stand watch. I'll shout if I need help." I shake Asher off and push through the fabric that serves as the door. Reed is standing against the far wall.

"Explain," I say, eyes on his chest. The lodestone still rests there, identical to mine. As black as night. A luster of shine, even in this dim lighting. An indentation to mark north.

"I got it from a trader when I was eight," he says, tucking it beneath his shirt. "I was living with a pack near East Tower at the time. The trader said there was a man named the General gaining power to the north, that I should leave my pack and head there, pledge my loyalty to him. I didn't understand, but the trader insisted that I would need to be in Bedrock. That someday, a girl might arrive. She'd have a lodestone to match mine, and he said I needed to help her."

"Why?" I ask.

"Because we're blood, Delta. Half-siblings. The trader claimed he was our father."

The room seems to swim. Reed's eyes flit to the center of my chest, where my lodestone rests beneath my shirt. He'd seen it that day in Bedrock, I realize. When I stole his waterskin and he grabbed me, pulling me close, he'd glanced it down the front of my shirt.

That was the day he discovered who I was.

"What did he look like?" I demand.

"Dark hair, patchy beard. Was riding a horse bareback, and

most of his gear was beat, but he had a real nice pair of goggles."
Reed's gaze flicks to the pair propped on my forehead.

This is an impeccable description—exactly how I remember that trader looking as well, and I never spoke of him to anyone. There's no way Reed could be making this up.

"Our father suspected that the General would become dangerous," he says, "and that you would be the key to finding the Verdant. He said I should help you, but only so long as I never lost the General's trust. That part was key, and it's why I didn't help as much as I could have when I first realized who you were. Bedrock's water is drying. I thought finding the Verdant would save humanity. I tried to help you while also helping the General understand the map. I'm sorry. But I'm here now, and it's just like our father wanted. The General still thinks I'm loyal to him. He thinks I'm a faithful spy, watching you, waiting. But I'm here to help."

This is too much. That washed-up trader who gave me my lodestone was my *father*. Reed's father, too. We're half-siblings. I stare at him. I feel like I can see the resemblance now. We have similar noses—our father's nose.

Suddenly I'm furious at this man I never knew. For abandoning us. For leaving. If he suspected that the General would become so dangerous, why did he seek us out only to give us lodestones and disappear? If he knew we'd need help, why didn't he stay to provide it?

"Do you know how to find the Verdant?" Reed asks.

I nod.

"You can read the map?"

281

I nod again.

"Where is it? How far from here?" His eyes gleam with hope.

"This is a lot to take in, Reed. I'll keep those answers to myself for now."

"What about your friend? Does he know?"

"Asher?"

"Ash . . ." Reed glances toward the door, understanding flickering on his face. "Rust and rot. We thought he died when he ran. Are there more of you? Branded with the map?"

"Just us two," I say.

"How did you figure out how to read it?"

"I'm not telling you that either." *Show it to no one. Unless you trust them with your own life, keep it hidden.*

"I have no way of communicating with Bedrock, Delta. You slaughtered my falcon."

"You'd have done the same in my position."

"Probably. But I'm unarmed now. Rune is dead. I have a lodestone. I'm your *brother.*"

"Half brother."

"I'm on your side," he insists. "If I know anything about this gods-forsaken world, it's that you don't turn away help. That's how you end up a vagrant, wandering the wastes, hopeless. Please, Delta. You can trust me."

"I don't trust anyone. Not even Asher."

"But he knows how to read the map. You trust him enough to travel to the Verdant with him."

I can see the hypocrisy of it, and if I stand here letting Reed fill me with more doubts, I'll come undone. I've got to trust my intuition. It's the only thing left that seems to guide me true. That and my lodestone.

I glare at Reed. "You can come with us, and I'll share what I want to share, when I want to share it. Or we leave you here, anchored to a boulder for the vultures to pick apart. Your choice."

He stares for a long beat, then says thinly, "It's not a choice when you hold all the power and I can't win."

I said these same words to him at Bedrock, only about the General. I almost smile.

"If you're thirsty, there's a well that still pulls a little water. Asher will show you to it. Then you'll help us with the wind wagon."

He doesn't ask what a wind wagon is, just nods.

"I'm sorry about your falcon," I add, and slip from the shanty.

CHAPTER THIRTY-ONE

I didn't ask about my father much when I was a child. Most of our pack was female, and it was odder to have a father in your pack than not. Men ran goods and traded. They came into camps often, but they rarely stayed.

Ma said she knew my pa would never stay—the day she met him, she sensed he was too wild to be rooted anywhere. "He had a far-off look in his eyes," she once told me. "Like he was always thinking ahead, like he was already halfway to whatever place he'd rather be."

Everything I know about him, I learned in pieces, in fragments of memories Ma shared and I stitched together. They met at midsummer the year after Indie was born. Our pack had invited one of the neighboring groups to celebrate with us at Alkali Lake, and he'd arrived with them. The way Ma tells it, laughter floated across the lake and a star shower rained in the night sky. They shared a drink of moonblitz, and she was in love with him by the morning. When the visiting pack rolled out, he didn't saddle his horse. Not until a few moons after I arrived.

"He wanted to see you born," Ma once said, half lost in a memory. "I was right that he wouldn't stay, but he lingered far longer than I expected."

"Did you ever see him again?" I'd asked.

"A few times. He'd appear without warning, riding into camp with goods to trade, then disappear just as quietly. Those visits were magical, but he was always searching for something. He spoke of a group that was mining to the northwest. He wanted to look into the earth, too, and was more focused on the rocks beneath our feet than on our gods among the stars." She exhaled sadly. "The last time he visited, we'd just learned that you'd be branded in the coming days. I never saw him after that. I'm sorry I never let him see you—and that I didn't tell you who he was. His visits were so short, so fleeting. I thought it would be crueler to meet your father and lose him, than to never know him at all."

He could never read the future in the stars, I realize. What he said that day when he gifted me with the lodestone was merely poetic, a way to capture my attention.

He didn't know what would happen, only what he *hoped* would. So he put the wheels in motion. He found the children he fathered and gave them lodestones, pushed them in certain directions. Reed to Bedrock, in case the worst came to pass.

I reach for my lodestone now, turn the cool stone between my fingers.

Where did he find it? Was this powerful compass why he showed interest in mining and was always looking at the dirt beneath his boots? And if he truly cared about what happened to me—if he feared the General's growing power—why did he disappear? He should have stayed to help.

"I don't trust Reed," Asher says, dragging me from my thoughts. "We should leave him behind."

I shake my head. "Who knows when he last communicated with Bedrock. If they have his position as being near Powder Town—or, gods help us, *north* of Powder Town—Loyalists might come looking for him. Better to take him with us."

"To the Verdant?" Asher says skeptically. "You want to take a Loyalist to the Verdant?"

"Shh," I hiss, but Harlie's already heard.

"If you wanted your destination to be a secret, you should have lowered your voice to a whisper when chatting with that half brother of yours." She scans my frame from where she stands, leaning against her wind wagon. "You got a map, huh?"

"Up here," I say, touching my temple.

Harlie frowns. If she heard me discussing things with Reed, she certainly heard him mention a brand, but Harlie just squints north, a smile spreading over her lips. "Always knew there was more out that way, and by gods, we're gonna find it."

"Still don't think he should come with us," Asher grumbles.

"Oh, rust, Asher. I think every god in the sky knows how you feel at this point. You've said you don't trust Reed about a hundred times since he showed up. You think I trust him any more?"

"You wanna bring him with us, so yeah."

"I'm bringing him so I can keep my eyes on him. Better to have him on the wagon than running back to the General." I glance at Rune's cooling body, wondering if I should have spared the bird. We could have healed her up, sent her east with a fake message. But it's too late for second-guessing. What's done is done.

"You told him he could stay behind," Asher points out.

"He'll choose to come," I say surely. "I didn't really give him a choice, just the illusion of one. Now, how about we get started on this wind wagon?"

"Thank the gods," Harlie says. "A person could die of boredom listening to you two argue."

✦ ✦ ✦

We spend the next several days working on the wagon. I measure and mark. Harlie cuts. Asher lugs supplies and is a fantastic sport about doing our bidding, even when it includes lying under the wind wagon and holding things in place for hours while Harlie and I see to fastening and securing.

All the while, Reed lumbers around camp, wrists still tied together. He hasn't tried to run, which is the first thing that makes me consider that he might be telling the truth. The fact that no Loyalists come looking for him is another. I almost feel guilty about the first night he spent with us, the look he shot me as he sat in the dirt while Asher, Harlie, and I ate dinner.

"We couldn't waste fresh meat," I'd said to him. "You know how it is."

"I'm still not eating her." He glanced at the spit extending over the fire, and the pain he was feeling touched his eyes.

We could have burned Rune, but putting fresh meat on a pyre is like sowing fresh seeds and never watering them; you might as well pray to the gods to end you. And it wasn't as if Harlie's Hope had plentiful food to spare.

Still, I couldn't shake the guilt. It was my own weakness, or perhaps proof that Reed's story was true. Blood is the strangest bond; it makes you do wild things. Like trek through the ocean bed to bring your sister to a healer, or make an impossible promise to a baby you barely know.

When Harlie and I don't need Asher's help on the wagon, he works on curing meat for the upcoming trip. Reed's steed won't make the journey across the wastes, and much like with his falcon, it makes no sense to send the horse trotting for Powder Town. Reed theorizes that the horse will break west as soon as it's free, travel back to Bedrock. If it shows up without a rider, Loyalists will be sent looking for him. Plus, our wagon needs to be loaded with rations.

"I'll put it down," I'd offered, remembering how Asher couldn't stand killing game as a kid.

"Nah, you focus with Harlie," Asher said. A bit later, he came back from the side of the outcropping where he'd butchered the steed, blood covering his front, giant flanks of meat loaded on a dragger to be smoked. His mouth was thin. His voice didn't waver when he said it was done.

Maybe it will be different in the Verdant, but out here, the wastes harden everyone in time. Even boys who pick scrub flowers for their mas.

✦ ✦ ✦

On our third morning in Harlie's Hope, Harlie says it's time to test the newly installed brakes.

We all scramble into the wagon, which faces north. Reed sits near the stern, arms still bound, and Harlie barks out instructions for me and Asher to raise sails and tighten rigging. There's a tailwind, as there's been every day since we arrived — it seems to blow in from the southwest without fail—and the sails quickly snap tight, cupped with air. The wheels lurch beneath us, creaking as they get going. Harlie leans on the tiller, aligning us with the wind, toward barren desert.

The wheels keep turning, slowly, then faster, and soon we're bumping across the plain at the clip of a galloping horse. I squint, marveling at the speed, then laugh and throw my arms out. My scarf flutters at the nape of my neck. This must be what it feels like to fly.

"Here goes nothing!" Harlie calls from the tiller. Her white hair whips behind her like a current. She looks back to where I stand near the brake, her eyes flashing behind her goggles. "Grab on to something and pull, girl. Let's see if she stops as well as she sails."

I yank on the lever. Beneath the deck, the wheels cry in protest, squeaking and grinding against the weight of the brake. Immediately, we start to slow, and my palms burn hot. I'll need to wear gloves next time.

"See to the sails!" Harlie shouts to Asher. "Drop them fast." She leans into the tiller, angling us back the way we came as he works the rigging.

The wagon turns in a wide arc. The back wheels skid across the dirt, trying to keep up with the front. When the wind can no longer fill the sails, our speed is cut drastically and my work at the brake becomes easier. I squeeze tighter, listen to the wheels lock firm. By the time we're angled into the headwind, Asher has completely dropped the mainsail.

The wind wagon slows to a crawl.

Asher pants, the ropes still wrapped around his palms. Harlie steps away from the tiller, laughing as we roll to a stop. "It works," she gasps. "It scudding works!"

We look at each other in amazement, then raise the sails. It takes nearly twice as long to return to Harlie's Hope, because we're now sailing against a headwind and have to zigzag to keep wind in our sails at all, but we return — and brake — without issue.

"Tomorrow?" I say, glancing north.

"Yes," Harlie agrees, "but she needs a name first. All good boats have one."

"*Gods Touched*," Reed proposes. It's the first thing he's said all morning — one of the few things he's said since the day he told me we shared blood. Now, as he stands with a hand against the side rail looking out across the wastes, there's a spark to his eyes. Hope. Faith.

He thinks this might work. He *wants* it to.

And this name choice . . .

Does it mean he is still loyal to a man who wears a pendant of stars and believes only the gods touched will save us? Or does it prove that Reed has faith in something larger than the General, that he wants this boat to deliver all of us from our suffering?

"I like it," Asher says, and he looks mad about it — annoyed that he agrees with Reed on something.

"The *Gods Touched*," Harlie says, gazing up the mast. "She'll find the way when no one else has, because she's touched by the gods."

A few weeks earlier I'd have hated the name. But now I like the idea of our wind wagon being blessed by the gods. They've abandoned us, but I'm starting to wonder if they may return after all. Because if the map is real and readable, all the rumors about the Verdant must be too. The gods will reappear and grant us the power to control the Verdant's borders. Power to keep the General out of it forever. And our gods touched vessel will make this moment possible.

+ + +

Come dawn, we're ready.

The previous night was spent loading the wagon, and everything of use that Harlie owned is now aboard the *Gods Touched*. Enough food for nearly a moon, thanks to Reed's butchered horse. The animal provided even more, but Harlie had only so many jars to spare for storing the smoked meat. The others are filled with water; enough for eight days, maybe ten max if we really ration it. We also have a few empties and some plas that we can use to set up inverted wells, gathering water while we work our way through the stocked jars. The rest of her lumber, rope, and tools go belowdecks, along with some blankets for the evenings and a few jars of moonblitz that Harlie had been saving.

"I figure it'll get used one way or another," she says. "In celebration, or desperation. Guess it all depends on what we find."

I shrug into my jacket and smack dust from my hair. Since arriving, we've been sleeping under the stars, and even with my scarf wrapped around my head, the desert has managed to work its way into every nook and cranny. Once my bag is packed and my goggles are pulled into place, I scramble onto the wagon.

Asher is already aboard, showing Reed how to coil up extra rope and adjust the rigging so that he can help us on the wastes.

Once we get moving, we've agreed that he can finally be freed of his bindings; it's not as if there will be anywhere for him to run.

Harlie is at the tiller, looking over her home one last time. "Goodbye, Harlie's Hope," she says. "You are where my granddaughter lost faith in me, and even if she was the last to do so, she hurt the most. I won't miss you."

It's bittersweet, almost depressing, but I understand more than she knows. I also miss my pack, but not Dead River itself. Dead River was just a place we lived for a while.

"Nice tailwind again," Harlie says. "I say we ride it and head northeast."

"No, we have to go northwest," I say, the *Es* on my back practically tingling. The Verdant lies in that direction. I can see the complete map in my mind.

"Will be a bit slower than heading northeast," she warns, letting the breeze pass through her fingers, "but I bet we can manage if you're sure about this."

I glance at Asher. He nods. "Oh, I'm sure."

"Is it you that's gods touched, or my wind wagon?" Harlie says with a wink.

I roll my eyes.

"Asher, hoist the mainsail!" Harlie announces, her eyes sparkling. "Reed, you see to the headsail. Delta, I want you at the brake, just in case it's needed."

We lurch to action.

And just like that, unceremoniously, we head into foreign territory, the sun beating down on our necks.

IV

EDEN

CHAPTER THIRTY-TWO

We fall into a rhythm by the second day, taking turns at the tiller and on watch at night. Reed is the only one who gets to sleep straight through the evenings. Though he's held us on course during the day, none of us trust him enough to let him man the tiller with only the moon for company.

By the evening of our third day, Harlie estimates that we've traveled as far as her pack ever explored. It feels like we are in truly uncharted territory, but the map Asher and I share means someone has been through this stretch of wastes before.

The ground is hard-packed and mostly level now, the wind having smoothed the rock over with dirt and dust. When I'm not taking a turn at the tiller, I spend most of my time at the bow, binos to my face, scanning the horizon.

There is nothing. Just endless earth that stretches before us like a blanket.

I keep waiting to see green in the distance, for trees or scrub to pop up, and the anticipation is ruining me. I'm jittery and jumpy and can barely sleep at night.

During the fifth day of continuous travel, Harlie asks, "Are you still sure, Gods Touched?"

She's started to call me this, joking that my confidence in our destination must mean that *I'm* gods touched, not the wind wagon. Asher smiles every time I bristle at the nickname, and it makes me want to kick something.

"Yes," I say without hesitation. "We're on course."

"How much longer, then?"

The trouble is, I don't know. I've checked our heading with my lodestone almost daily. Reed has checked with his, too. We are heading in the right direction.

"Soon," I tell the woman.

"Good, because I'm tired of peeing in a jar," she grouses. "The men have it so easy."

I don't mention that my moon bleeding started the day we set sail, and I'm sick of cramps and having to sacrifice spare clothes for rags. She's seen me tearing strips and can probably guess. And besides, she just wants to vent. Complaining is sometimes the best remedy for crossness.

"Even once we stop, you'll still be peeing in a jar," Reed points out. He glances at the inverted wells we've set up on the deck using some of Harlie's spare jars and plas. "But if you want to turn around, you should do it this very second. Your water rations will barely get you back to Harlie's Hope as it is, and those wells aren't producing at the rate you're drinking."

This is another thing Reed has been doing that makes me want to trust him: refusing ownership over the wagon and our journey. He never refers to the water as his. He never assumes anything. He's letting us lead and is happy to do so, as if he has no concern for his own well-being.

"We're not turning around," I insist.

Harlie nods. Reed shrugs. Asher just looks at me, frowning.

I can't tell if they trust me or think I'm crazy. Maybe it's both at the same time. The answer doesn't matter. There's no turning back. I touch my lodestone, feel a shiver pass over my brand. This is how I save my pack. It's going to work.

✦ ✦ ✦

That evening I sit at the tiller while the others sleep. Everything is shadowed and purple-black, so dark that if it weren't for the stars, it would be nearly impossible to tell where the sky ended and the earth began.

Ation dances above me, her long dress fanning behind her like a river. Feder waits halfway across the sky, his shield lowered, as if the sight of the goddess has stolen his breath. They both steal mine again now, and it seems ridiculous that I can hate them but still find them so beautiful. That I want to believe in them again, even after everything.

"Do you trust him?" Asher says beside me, and I let go of the tiller in surprise. Just a moment ago he was lying with the others.

"Rusting rot, you scared me." I scramble to recover the tiller before we drift too far off course.

"Reed," he goes on. "He's been acting strange. Talking like he doesn't care what happens. He's up to something."

"If he was still loyal to the General, an army would have shown up at Harlie's Hope long before we left it."

"Maybe they'll be waiting for us when we return. *If* we return."

I sigh. "The way he's been talking . . . I think he's just trying to show that he's loyal to us now. It's a sacrifice, of sorts. A surrender."

"It's reckless," Asher responds. "Brash. The kind of behavior that gets you killed."

I cock up a brow. "Like running from Powder Town to follow a map through uncrossable desert?"

"Exactly like that. Preservation would have meant staying in Powder Town, but I'm just a coward. A coward who keeps chasing his best chance at staying alive."

It's the closest we've come to discussing that night since it happened. He followed me to Harlie's Hope because I had water and food. But that's not why he's here now. Once Reed showed up and his horse was butchered, there were enough rations to easily last a moon. Asher could have stayed in Harlie's Hope, pulling enough from the well each day to get by. But he followed me.

"I'm sorry about what happened at Powder Town," I say. "You know that, right?"

He looks at me for a long beat. "I'm not sure what I know anymore, Delta. You were my pack. We used to be easy."

"Nothing's easy in the wastes. It never has been."

"I know. That's not what I meant."

"What did you mean, then?" I can hear my voice rising, getting defensive, though I'm not sure why. He holds a finger to his lips, nodding at Harlie and Reed, still asleep near the bow. I adjust my grip on the tiller.

"Do you regret that we reconnected?" he asks a moment later.

"No," I answer truthfully. "I wish it had happened another way. I wish I still had Bay, and that the General didn't know about my brand, and that we started working together to get my pack out of Bedrock the very same day we met. But how could I ever regret running into you, Asher?" I steal a glance at him.

"Well, I got you into quite a bind."

"Then you helped get me out of it. And I—" I stare at the horizon for a moment. It's murky and muddled, like my thoughts. I wish words were easier.

"I missed you every single day since Alkali Lake," I admit finally. "I thought you were dead. I thought you died alone, and I felt like it was my fault, because we left. But you're here now. I don't like what you did back at West Tower, but I understand how you thought you had no other options. Just like I thought I had no other option than to run from Powder Town once we could read the map. And I see now that the wastes turn us brutish and short-sighted. All any of us try to do is survive, and that means doing what feels right from moment to moment. I did what I had to. You did the same. And I forgive you."

He raises a brow. "You do?"

"Yes. Is that so hard to believe?"

"You have a will like granite, Delta. You are the most stubborn person I know."

"Well, maybe Bay started to soften me. And maybe that's not such a bad thing."

"I never said it was."

"Oh, so you're happy I'm softening up. You thought I was too strong-willed?"

"I didn't say that either. I think you're . . . I wouldn't change . . ." He puts his fist to his mouth, blows a muffled breath into his hand.

"I thought about you every day when I was at Bedrock," he says finally. "At least when I could. There were years in the middle when I was on the sleeping ilk and everything was hazy. But in the beginning, every time they beat me or burned me or cracked a rib to try to get me to read the map, I thought of you. Every day they let me heal, every time I realized I was never going to get out of there—that I couldn't give the General the answer he wanted because I didn't have the answer to begin with—I thought about you. I could picture you in my head, standing on that rock at Alkali Lake, your dark braid shining in the sun, your eyes cutting into me, yelling at me to put my shirt back on. You were right. I thought every day about how you were right. If I'd only listened . . ."

"That's a horrible memory to be stuck reliving. I'm surprised you don't hate me."

"No. You got me through it," he insists. "You were so scared that day when we were kids, and nothing scared you. I saw it on your face, and I tried to shrug it off, but you were terrified for me. And when things were at their worst at Bedrock, I pictured how much you cared. And it made me realize how much I cared about you. How if I ever got out, I'd find you again and tell you that you were what got me through it. Then the sleeping ilk happened, and I forgot everything, until the Oracle helped me get clean. And that's when the *if* became a *when*—*when* I got out. You gave me a reason to keep going."

He glances at me, eyes glistening.

"And you did get out," I say.

"I did. But when I saw you there on West Tower . . . Delta, I

300

think my heart broke. I was finally with you again, and the first thing I saw in your eyes after all those years was disgust. You recognized me, realized the con I had pulled. You hated me."

"I don't hate you, Asher."

"You did in that moment."

"And you hated me in the moment we were thrown from Powder Town. We fought as kids sometimes, too, but we always came back together."

"You trusted me enough to show me your map," he says, "and then I didn't help you. You were right to call me a coward. I'm sorry, Delta. I spent so long trying to find you—to find the pack—that once I had you again, I was afraid to let go. Afraid to lose anything. There's so little good in the wastes, it's hard not to keep a death grip on the few bright bits. You know?"

"I know."

"I was trapping you, just like you said. But I don't want you to feel trapped. I want you to feel . . ."—his eyes search mine—"whatever it is you want to feel."

He seems closer, suddenly. Or maybe it's the wind wagon's side rails that have constricted, or the sky lowered, the air thickened. Everything is closing in, shrinking. He touches my hand. I feel that same pull I did in the saltpeter changing rooms, an energy tugging between us, quivering, like my lodestone finding north. I wonder, briefly, if it's always been trying to lead me back to him.

"I want to trust you," I whisper. "It's just hard."

"I get it," he says. "I trust you so much, and that's why everything is difficult."

But trust should make things easy. Trust should be as simple as breathing.

He lets go of my hand, nods at the tiller. "You go lie down. I'll take over."

I fall asleep feeling uncentered, wondering what I have failed to understand.

✦ ✦ ✦

The next morning, our sixth day on the wind wagon, we wake to find a storm chasing us. Big wall of dust drummed up by the wind current we're riding. Billowing and churning and sparking with lightning.

"We should be able to outrun it," Harlie says. "For now." But she keeps looking over her shoulder, squinting. Eventually she asks Asher to climb up the mast to try to get a better gauge of its distance.

This is bad. We're in the middle of nowhere, supplies dwindling, and if a storm hits us—if we tip or wreck—we're dead. I twist in a circle, scanning the horizon, but there's nothing but the same bone-bleached, rock-hard earth we've seen since leaving Harlie's Hope.

The first tendril of real fear unfurls in my gut.

What if I've doomed us all? What if the map is wrong? What if we never reach the Verdant—or worse, what if the Verdant is gone too, dried up, turned to dust, vanished with the gods?

I join Reed at the starboard rail, needing a distraction. "Where did he go?" I muse aloud.

"Who?"

"The trader with the lodestone. Our father."

Reed blows out a breath. "Probably somewhere he could avoid the General. People say there's a town across the ocean."

"They do?" The only person I've heard say something remotely similar is Clay, and I never put much weight in his stories.

"Sure. Traders, here and there. Loyalists who feel trapped by their pledge to the General." Reed rubs the inside of his wrist with a thumb. He hasn't been bound in days, but a rope burn lingers. "It's just talk, people looking for hope outside of the Verdant. There's no way to travel that course without dying — least that was true before wind wagons — but maybe our father tried anyway."

Something Zuly said surfaces in my mind. *I see in you someone I once knew. They were stubborn also, defiant. Wanted the world to make sense and for life to be easy.*

Maybe it was all too much for my father, this world. He might have passed through Zuly's before trying to cross the ocean and escape the wastes. Perhaps she saw *him* when she looked into my eyes. I think also about what Ma said to me — how my father couldn't sit still, how he was always searching for something, digging, unearthing.

You are meant to have this lodestone, and I am meant to find another.

He was after the stone itself, searching for the rare material that acted as a compass in all weather, even the silent storms. I'm certain of it now.

He never really knew anything about the future, he just hoped. He hoped so hard that he tried to will it into existence. And for the most part, the future he wished for has come to pass. Reed went to Bedrock. I reconnected with him. We're working together, against the General, on our way to find the Verdant. And my father, presumably, went looking for more lodestones beyond the dried ocean beds. It strikes me as selfish, irresponsible. Like the gods who abandoned us instead of offering guidance.

"What kind of parent leaves his kids to deal with a mess he saw coming?"

Reed doesn't have an answer for that. It's quiet for a moment. "You trust me yet?" he asks finally.

"I'm getting there. A cautious, uneasy sort of trust."

"That's not trust."

I half smile. "What are you gonna do after this, Reed?"

"Whatever I can to help." He says it like it's obvious. Like it's easy.

"You won't be able to go back to Bedrock. Not if he knows you defected."

"He doesn't. And he won't. We'll figure it out."

I wonder, briefly, if I even need the Verdant to barter my pack free. Reed is one of the General's Four. Surely the General would want him back, would long to punish a defector. Could I trade Reed for the safety of my pack?

Reed's face stills, his brow furrowing sharply.

He's heard my thoughts somehow, sensed this betrayal. But then he extends a finger, pointing beyond the wagon's bow.

On the horizon, a small dark shape separates the blue sky from the bone-bleached earth.

I push off the rail. "Straight ahead!" I shout. "There's something straight ahead." I scramble for our gear, grab the binos. But even with them, we're too far off to make any sense of the object. It's darker than I expected the Verdant to be, more black than green, but maybe that's just the distance contorting things. There's a smoothness to the shape that bothers me, like a pebble rounded by a stream.

Harlie and Asher, busy watching the storm on our tail, twist toward the bow. Harlie shouts orders. Asher climbs down the mainmast at a dangerous clip and I move to the brake, my heart pounding in my throat.

With the *Gods Touched* sailing at full speed, we close in on the strange object. It's no bigger than Zuly's tanker, but is rectangular in shape, with a rounded roof. It's dull gray, like scrap metal, but somehow not a single flake of rust graces its sides.

There's no green surrounding it, not in any direction.

This is wrong, all wrong.

"It must be a marker," I reason aloud, "a sign that we're headed the right way."

Harlie gives me a skeptical look.

"Let's get as close as we can and stop a minute," I say.

"The storm," she warns.

"If this place holds directions that weren't on my map and we pass it by, we're doomed. We pause here."

She turns us against the wind. As Asher and Reed lower the sails, I work the brake. We slow steadily, then sag to a stop a quarter click from the structure. I vault over the wagon's sideboard and sprint ahead, pausing in the sand that has gathered at the base of the dark formation.

Its sheer size gives it away as Old World–made, a relic of the past. I walk around it, dumbfounded. It's pocked and cratered up close, made of something more akin to rock than metal. Certain areas are darkened black, as though they've burned.

On the eastern side, there's a recessed doorway, tall and wide enough to allow passage to the wind wagon, but it's caved in. Rock and rubble are piled in the entranceway, sand and dirt blown between every crevice.

I don't know what this place is, but it's definitely not the Verdant.

But then I look up toward the roofline, and I freeze.

Above the collapsed doorway, four Old World letters are etched into the stone.

EDEN

CHAPTER THIRTY-THREE

Asher steps up behind me.

"Look." I point to the letters.

"Like on our map," he murmurs.

"I don't get it. This isn't the Verdant. The map was supposed to show the way to the Verdant." A sickening sensation twists in my stomach. I feel like I'm still back on the wind wagon, bucking and swaying over the hard-packed earth.

"Maybe the rest of the directions are inside," Asher suggests. "Like you said earlier."

I nod silently. That must be it. It has to be.

"Think we can fit through there?" He points to a small gap of darkness in the corner of the doorframe, just above the giant pile of rubble.

"Maybe. And if not, we can widen it."

I glance back toward the wind wagon. Harlie is still wrestling with the excess rope, tying everything down in case the storm doesn't peter out before it reaches us. Reed helps.

"Let's get started," I tell Asher. "They'll catch up when they're done."

We climb the rubble, which is more difficult than expected because everything is half covered in dirt. It skids out beneath our heels, sending our boots sliding. More than once I nearly twist an ankle. Finally we reach the opening. I peer into the darkness, but can't make much out. Even after Asher gets a candle going with a flint, I still can't see more than an arm's length ahead.

"I think I can fit if we move this one," I say, toeing a rock the size of my head. With a good deal of grunting and huffing, we dislodge it and roll it aside. It keeps on rolling, crashing down the rubble hillside.

"Watch it!" comes Reed's voice from below.

"No more clearing anything till we join you," Harlie hollers. "I didn't come all this way to be crushed by a boulder."

But we don't have to move anything else because the opening is now wide enough for me.

I go in headfirst, if only so I can see what I'm getting myself into. There's a pile of rubble on this side, too. The air is stale and heavy, old. Despite the stuffiness, I hug myself, rubbing warmth into my arms.

Asher passes the candle through. "What do you see?"

The light flickers over the rocks. "I'm standing on another huge pile of rubble, same as outside." I hold out the candle, and the flame dances over the smooth walls that surround me. There's one overhead, too. "It's like a chamber. And at the base of these rocks there's . . ." A shiver sends my hair on end. "It looks like a door."

Its face is as smooth as the walls, its frame perfectly straight. No plane can shave this evenly, no saw cut so clean. The Old World tech I've seen before — jars and deserted rovers and rifles

—have smooth edges, organic shapes, but this ... It's divine, otherworldly. The work of gods.

I have a wild, terrifying thought.

Maybe the gods didn't desert us. Maybe they've been testing us, just like Ma always claimed, but we've been going about it all wrong. We've been praying to the stars and working the land, trying to prove that we are worthy of a green earth when we should have been working to find this. *EDEN*.

Maybe this is a doorway to the gods.

"Stay right there," Asher says. "We're coming, too. Soon as we move another few rocks."

✦ ✦ ✦

Some time later, after a bit of a scare when rocks went tumbling on their side and I feared one of them would be swept away in the fall, Asher's face appears through the widened gap. Reed comes after him and then Harlie.

"You don't want to stay with the wagon?" I ask.

"Storm's almost on us," she says. "Better to be inside. Hopefully she doesn't get too banged up in the winds."

We descend the pile of rocks carefully, making our way toward the door. There's a wheel protruding from it, perfectly round, like the opening of an Old World jar. Asher touches it, pauses. "I think you should do it," he says to me.

I shake my head. "Together."

The wheel is cool beneath my palm, firm. It reminds me of scrap metal or the side of Zuly's tanker, but it's smooth, barely rusted. When we try to turn it, it won't budge. "Help with this,"

I say, motioning for Reed. It takes the three of us to get the thing turning. Metal groans on the other side of the door. There's a click and an echo. It sounds like a secret being whispered.

"Now," I say. "Pull now."

We open the door about three boot lengths before it hits the base of the rubble pile. There will be no opening it farther. But it's wide enough for passage.

I cross the threshold cautiously, hold out the candle.

There's a set of stairs leading down into darkness.

It's the opposite of everything I expect. Instead of brilliant rivers and teeming green and calm skies beneath a radiant sun, there's just this stairwell. Leading into the ground. Behind a locked door.

Nothing could grow in here.

But the secrecy of it makes my heart beat wildly. We are close. The Verdant waits at the bottom of this staircase. The gods would never take so many precautions unless they were protecting something truly vital.

I worry, briefly, if they will let me reach it. If my lack of faith is a thing they can sense, will they keep the truth from me? I glance at Asher, glad he's here. His faith is so enormous, it should be enough for both of us.

I lead the way down the stairwell. There's another door at the bottom. Again, we work a wheel. It groans. The door opens, and we step into more darkness.

In the candlelight I can make out a dark material beneath our feet, even and smooth.

After we take a few steps forward, there's a rapid flashing, like lightning, followed by a clicking sound. The space fills with harsh blue light, almost as though our very presence caused it to appear. I throw my hands up, cower.

There is no viselike grip on my neck.

No booming voices of the gods.

Just a faint, steady hum.

I look up. Sheets of scrap metal glow overhead with blue-white light, illuminating what is easily the largest room I have ever stood in. The walls are curved. The floor is slick and shiny. An emblem marks the center, some type of winged creature that is vaguely familiar. I've seen it in the General's library, I realize. It marked some of the Old World tech he'd hoarded.

Areas to rest—seats and benches, tables and chairs—are spread throughout the room. "What is this place?" Reed asks behind me. I shake my head, uncertain, and we move forward, crossing the emblem on the floor and entering a hallway.

The first doorway we come to has Old World symbols— *CENTRAL COMMAND*—above the frame. Inside, there are rows of tables and chairs. Hundreds of small squares line the tables, each one marked with an Old World symbol. There are levers too, knobs. A strange silver thing shaped like a curved squash with a cord coming off one end. And standing at eye-level on the table, across from each chair, is a dark window. When I brush away the dust that has gathered on one of the surfaces, I can see my reflection in the frame.

There are more rooms off the main hall. A storage hold, stocked with boxes and labels I can't read. A kitchen, though I can only reason this from the few plates and bowls left on the table.

An outhouse that was certainly referred to as something else by the people who lived here, seeing as it's very much inside. Bathing rooms, with a tub five times the size of the bucket I wash in at Dead River. Then bedrooms.

The first few we pass have just one bed per room, but the last one holds hundreds. Maybe thousands. They are stacked on top of one another, three high, with ladders to reach the upper mattresses. The air in the room is stagnant. It reminds me of being under the deck on Zuly's tanker, only worse.

"Oh," Harlie says.

I turn toward her and gasp, clamping a hand over my mouth.

There's a body on the bed, swimming in clothes that are now too big for the bones that remain. Asher turns away from the sight, only to inhale sharply. There's another pair of skeletons in the bed behind us. They are curled together, as if they died in an embrace.

"What is this place?" Reed asks again.

I glance at Asher. He looks as shocked as I feel. "Where's the Verdant?" he asks.

"Here," I murmur, turning in circles. "It was supposed to be here."

CHAPTER THIRTY-FOUR

We split up to search more thoroughly. Maybe this isn't the Verdant, just a place on the way to it. Maybe there's a map somewhere.

After Harlie and I search the massive sleeping room to no avail, she mentions needing a rest. I head to the first room alone —the one with the dark, dusty windows and strange tabletops. I can hear Asher and Reed across the hall, rummaging through gear in the storeroom, but I'm starting to fear that we might not find anything.

Don't think it, not even for a second, I snap at myself. *There has to be a map somewhere.*

There has to, because if it's not, we're all dead.

We have maybe three days of water left, if we really try to stretch it. Our limited supplies weren't going to be an issue because this was supposed to be the Verdant.

I collapse at one of the tables, exhausted. The seat is the softest thing I have ever sat in, plush, contoured to hold me. I nearly moan. If I'm going to die stranded here, at least I have this chair.

I hang my head forward, eyelids heavy. I'm thinking of Bay in the General's nursery, and the rest of my pack, and how I've failed them all, when I suddenly doze off. My head lurches forward, hits the table. I shoot upright, rubbing my brow, and freeze.

The black window above the table now has white Old World symbols on it. I brush dust from the frame with my palm and stare at the strange shapes.

Code Red Protocol Enacted 127,385 days ago.

Touch any key to play back recorded logs.

I don't have a clue what any of it means. I'm not even sure why it appeared. Maybe when my head hit the strange toggle on the table. I reach out and touch the one closest to me — a long, narrow one without markings.

The window flashes, and the symbols are gone, replaced with a view of exactly where I'm sitting, yet it's not me in the chair, but a man with dark skin and haunted eyes. I yelp and jump to my feet. Twist around. It's just me in the room.

I turn back toward the window, and he's still there, rubbing the thick beard that covers his jaw. "I'm not really sure where to start," he says, "so I'm just gonna come out with it: I'm stranded here."

I must be dehydrated, on the verge of sun sickness. I grab my waterskin from my side, guzzle some down, splash a bit more on my face.

The man remains. "Hello?" I wave a hand at him, but his eyes never connect with mine. He's looking toward me, but not *at* me. I take in the brilliance of the deep blue clothes he wears, tailored tighter than what makes sense for the wastes. There are decorative gold lines across his arms and a leather patch on his chest that holds more Old World symbols: *GENERAL*. It's oddly familiar. It . . .

I lower myself into the chair, feeling sick.

The General at Bedrock had a patch like this, aged and worn, stitched into his floor-length robe. It looked just like this man's.

"Asher!" I shout at the top of my lungs. "Reed! Get in here!"

"Things were fine at first," the man says as their boots come pounding up the hall. "Eden was built with no issue. Mining and harvesting got under way. For fifteen months, things went smoothly. This rock was rich with harvestable fuel, just as our research said, and without a native species, we were taking all we could."

Asher sinks into a chair beside me and shoots me a stricken look. Reed waves at the man like I did, dumbfounded at his lack of response.

"Then the geomagnetic storm hit. Scouting reports had claimed that the sun's next active phase wouldn't be for several hundred years. Our math was wrong, or the active cycle kicked off early. Whatever the case, we weren't prepared. All our tech malfunctioned: GPS failed, radios went down, satellites began to drop out of orbit. Not a single compass worked, and the mag-rifles were completely worthless what with magnets powering the barrel rail."

I glance at the boys. They look as confused as I am. I have no clue what this man is talking about.

"But the worst of it," the man goes on, "were the workers. Their cerebral chips malfunctioned, and they snapped free. I don't know if they could suddenly see all the ways they'd been mistreated and used, or if they simply saw a rock that they could colonize and make their own. Perhaps it was a little of both. But when they revolted ..." The man blows out a breath. "Workers outnumber Federation guards a hundred to one on these ops—it's not like brainwashed and chip-controlled workers typically need much oversight—and it was a massacre. They overran us at drill sites and water harvest points. Killed every Federal foreperson they could get their hands on, and used anything they could get their hands on to do it: wrenches, hammers, drill gear. It was brutal. They used the mag-rifles as clubs, and once they got to our rovers and the semi-autos stored in the trunks, well ... Then it was easy. Like shooting fish in a barrel.

"Most of the senior personnel were lucky—in a meeting up on the orbiting ship. All but me. I'd decided to oversee some stuff on the ground that morning. Only reason I'm not dead now is because I made a deal with the workers who attacked me—promised I'd code them into Eden if they let me live. Whoever ends up reviewing this will probably think I'm a coward, teaming up with the side that was killing mine, but my people ..." He exhales heavily. "Those Federation bastards are lucky they were already in orbit when the uprising happened. The ship's shields protected them from the worst of the storm, and once they realized they'd been slaughtered on the ground—that the op was a dud and the planet too dangerous to return to—they cut their losses and tried to bury it all. It's a miracle I got to Eden in time. The sound of the bombs was awful."

The man pauses here, glancing toward the hall that leads to the bedrooms.

"There's over two thousand of us here now. The workers have been celebrating their victory since we sealed the doors a few hours ago — drinking and hollering and singing "The Federation of the Free." They mostly ignore me, but I'm waiting for that to change. I'm still a Fed, and they're still incarcerated criminals, and even though the Federation uses only criminals with minor infractions for these types of harvesting gigs, I don't think I'll sleep much tonight. There's no way they fully trust me. I got them in here safely, but once I stop serving a purpose, they'll turn on me.

"I hailed the Federation just before recording this log. The bunker's defenses protected the tech here, so I'm praying my message got out. I can't imagine that Eden's solar array survived the bombing, though, which means we're running only on whatever energy is stored up. I'll report back when I know more."

The image cuts out. When the man reappears, he looks even more tired than before.

"It's been forty hours since the bombing, and I've yet to hear from the Federation. I'm choosing to believe my message never reached them, not that they've decided to abandon me.

"The incarcerated aren't nearly as animated anymore. There's been a lot less singing, and they're starting to shuffle around the way they did before the storm, when the chips worked. I'd think they rebooted and were functioning properly if it weren't for the fact that I've caught them asking each other where they are. Some have even asked me who I am. It's like they're losing their memories, like the chips, so deeply embedded in their brains, are atrophying." The man rubs his chin in thought. "It's not a far stretch. Pacemakers can fail with magnetic interference, the heart failing with it. The cerebral chip is similar—an electrical device implanted in the body. Maybe the magnetic interference from the storm was too much, and now that the chip is dead, it's taking certain memories with it."

Another flash in the image.

This time, the man's beard has been shaved. He still looks tired, but also younger without the facial hair.

"One hundred sixty hours post uprising, and no word from the Federation. I doubt they're coming back. We've got plenty of supplies here, but Eden's generator and battery stores will last us only another few days. Staying put is a death wish. Out there, however . . ." His eyes flick toward the ceiling. "This rock has always been desolate, and we stripped it pretty well before things went south, but there's life. It will be a hard one, but I think we can make it. We have to try.

"The bombing did some damage to the outer door and caused a cave-in. All the rovers parked there are buried. Could be some out and about, of course. Our unit was stretched between Eden and the coast. We could find them, see if they're operable or if the geostorm fried them altogether. There's plenty of gear we can take with us from Eden, too—tools and apparel. Med kits. The storeroom has thousands of jars of canned food. The mag-rifles aren't reliable on this rock, but the semi-autos the Federation brought will serve us fine. At least until ammo runs out. Still, I'd rather die out there, trying to live, then die in here, praying to be rescued."

The man leans forward, resting his forearms on his knees. He nods a few times, almost to himself. "The workers' minds are seemingly wiped. They know their names and their friendships with others, but they don't know why they're here. They've forgotten the uprising, their time in Federation prisons. They barely know themselves, but they're making their own decisions now, even with a chip still in their heads, and that would scare the Federation shitless." He barks out a laugh. "Look at me, talking like I wasn't employed by them. I was just as guilty. Funny, how these people are suddenly my only hope. They've been looking to me for answers, asking me what happened. I told them there'd been a war outside, that we're the only survivors and we're waiting for it to be safe to leave. It's been safe since the Federation left, of course — it's not like they nuked us — but I needed some time to figure out what to say."

A pause.

"I've caught them praying a lot. They have no memories, yet they sit on their bunks with their hands clasped together, whispering to unseen powers, and it's given me an idea . . ." He rubs his mouth, sighs through his fingers. "I think I'll tell them that our gods left us; that they flew into the sky and might one day come back. Those Federation bastards don't deserve getting turned into immortal legends, but I need these people hopeful. If they know there's no chance that we'll be saved, if they don't have hope, we're doomed. I'm in this with them now. We're all we have." He nods, the idea solidifying. "I'll tell them what I have to, and that story will become our history. Right now, for us to survive, having hope is more important than knowing the truth."

He clasps his hands. "I'll put some supporting references at the end of these logs in case anyone ever finds them." Then he looks up, eyes boring into me as he says, "This is General David Amory of the Federation's Department of Energy, signing off from Planet CIX-b."

The man—Amory—reaches forward, and the window goes blank.

I've barely blinked before a new visual appears: a hand holding something silver and curved, the size of a thumb. With sickening realization, I recognize it as one of the General's stars on his chain. A sign of the gods touched.

"This is the cerebral chip that failed during geostorms and then caused amnesia in the chipped workers in the following days," Amory's voice says. "It's a model FLU5.1, as you can see here." His hand pries the star open to expose a green board and copper wires, where tiny Old World symbols are etched into the green.

"The op manifest is on the hard drive. I marked who died in the uprising as best I could, as well as who was aboard our ship when they bailed. Lastly, here's a shot of those bastards leaving. It was the last bit of footage Eden's topside cam captured."

The black window changes to a view of the wastes. In the distance, a winged tubelike shape hovers in the air, floating in the most unnatural manner I have ever seen. Unlike a bird, its wings are rigid, and it moves faster than any bird can travel, drawn up by an invisible thread. Something falls from it, moving closer and closer to us, the viewers. It fills the whole window, and everything shutters and splinters, hundreds of colors streaking across the frame. Then it goes dark.

"I think that says just about everything."

General Amory falls silent.

The window stays dark.

There is nothing else.

I push my chair away from the table, feeling sick. The truth slides into place, Amory's story reshaping my world.

There is no such thing as the gods touched. The stars the General collects are just tech that was put into the heads of prisoners ages ago to control them. There are no gods either. Amory made them up. He invented them to encourage the people to leave Eden, to eke out a living, to keep surviving.

They must have left Eden and never looked back. They took what they needed, including the jars Amory mentioned, a resource we still use to this day. They left the malfunctioning mag-rifles and took the Old World rifles we've since modified to shoot black powder, and they traveled south and east. To the Barrel, Powder Town, Alakali Lake, the coast. They made do and kept waiting for the gods to come back, and somewhere along the way they began to whisper about a paradise — a haven where life was easy and evil could be locked out.

When my pack's ancestors found a map in a deserted rover, they thought it led to this forgotten paradise. But it just led back here, to Eden. To this bunker. To the truth that died with Amory:

There is no Verdant.

It's a giant scudding lie.

It never existed.

My heart ratchets wildly. I can't breathe. I need air.

I turn away from Asher, vaguely aware that he's calling my name. I sprint past Reed. Bolt into the hall. Climb the stairs. Scramble up the rubble. Tumble out into the setting sun. Heat envelopes me, and the wind whips dirt at my face. Dirt and grit and grime, endless and everywhere, as far as the eye can see.

I was born of this dust, and I am never going to escape it. I'm going to die right here, starved in this barren wasteland, on the threshold of the Verdant that never was.

I scream at the horizon, the sound of a dying, desperate animal. I scream and scream, and the sun beats on, indifferent.

CHAPTER THIRTY-FIVE

I grab a rock near my feet and hurl it toward the sun.

"Delta."

Another rock.

"Delta, stop."

A third, but this time I throw it at the rusted wind wagon that sailed us to our deaths.

"Delta!"

Asher grabs my arm, spins me to face him. I collapse against his chest and sob. He holds me there, one hand in my hair, the other around my back. "It's going to be okay," he whispers, which is the biggest scudding lie I have ever heard.

"Asher, we are going to die here," I say into his shirt. "We don't have the supplies to get back."

"Sure we do."

"It took us six days to get here *with* a tailwind. Going back will take twice that. Maybe more. We only have a few days of water left, and the inverted wells work too slowly to save us."

"The storeroom has water. Not a lot, but enough. Bottled and sealed up in some way I've never seen. It might be safe, and we can boil it to be sure."

I step away from him. "Do you hear yourself, Asher?" His

brows pull down, wounded. "What's the point? Even if we make it back to Harlie's Hope, what then? Go back to Powder Town when we have no way of regaining entry? Return to Dead River and live to die? That's all anyone can do in these wastes—bide their time until it's over. And what in the scorched skies am I supposed to do for my pack now? This place was supposed to save them." I fling a hand at Eden. "This was supposed to be the solution, but there's no Verdant. There never was. It's a scudding lie."

"We'll figure something out," he says quietly. He's looking at me like a snared animal, eyes wide and expectant, as if he's hoping I'll cut him free. But there's no escaping this storm we're caught in.

"There's no point."

"You're not the person I remember," he says coldly.

"Oh, and what person is that?" I snap.

"A person who wouldn't quit when something went wrong."

"Asher, *something* didn't go wrong. *Everything* did. Everything is a lie."

"And you're not the only one struggling to accept that!"

"Exactly. We're all screwed. So for once, quit it with the sunny optimism and bottomless hope. Just say we're knee-deep in rot. Say the dust storm is endless and we're about to be buried alive. Be *angry,* like me. And if you can't do that, leave me the hell alone."

He stares at me, slack-jawed, as if I've slapped him. For a long moment the only sound is the wind clawing over the rocks.

"Sometimes," he says, looking straight at me, "I have no idea why I trust you."

He's gone, disappeared back into Eden before the hurt of his words can even register.

"Nice going, Gods Touched," Harlie says from below me. She's sitting on a sloped bit of rock, in a scrap of shade. She must have needed fresh air, come out here at some point when I was listening to Amory spill the wastes' secrets. "You scared off the only person in the wastes who not only tolerates you, but loves you."

"He doesn't love me."

"Girl, you wouldn't know love if it rode up in a rickshaw and slapped you across the cheek."

"Oh, and you would?" I snap. "You turned your back on family so you could dedicate your life to a wind wagon that didn't sail!"

"Because I was trying to find green. So that I could save them all someday. That is the very definition of love."

"And what do you think I've been doing?" I yell at her. "Why do you think I'm here?"

"I don't know. Why are you here, Delta of Dead River? Is it to save the people you love or is it because you were trying to prove something?"

"Both."

She scoffs. "Be angry and move past it then. Stop acting like you're the only one twenty clicks from camp without a waterskin. Get over yourself, or you will lose everything you have left to live for."

I open my mouth, close it.

I don't know why I'm here anymore. I thought it was to save my family, and in many ways, that is still true, but the emptiness I feel at knowing the brand on my back is useless is harrowing. I feel hollowed out. Betrayed. The map has been a curse my whole life, a thing I've had to hide, a reason to remain small and invisible, and now the pain of carrying it hasn't even paid off.

I have nothing.

I *am* nothing.

I can't free my family, and even if I could, there is no Verdant to take them to. Just a bunker and no green. Shelter, but no water source.

Nothing viable.

Nothing but a place that's already been deserted.

I can see how the myths started now, why we all believed that the first person to find the Verdant would also have the power to control its borders. Eden has impressive defenses, doors that can lock out the world.

There are fragments of the truth in the stories we've shared. But our faith in the people who abandoned us—these gods who disappeared—kept us from seeing the biggest truth: that this is it—these wastes, this dust. This is all we have.

The thought of retreating into the bunker and facing Asher is unbearable, but I don't want to be here with Harlie, either. I just want to be alone.

I climb down the rock pile, ignoring her as she grumbles, "That's it, girl. Keep on running." I head straight for the wind wagon, which fared well in the storm and still stands proud. I pull up the slat of wood to access the storage space belowdecks. Sand slides and billows from the plank. And there it is, untouched by the bad weather: Harlie's moonblitz. I grab a jar and gulp from it like I'm dying of thirst, blitz dribbling down my chin. The liquid burns my tongue and scorches the back of my throat. My belly hums with heat.

I collapse on the bleached wood and take another slug from the jar, a third. I drink until I can no longer feel the burn, then lie down on the rubble-strewn deck and let the sun bake my face.

If there were vultures this deep in the desert, they'd be circling overhead, waiting for me to die.

✦ ✦ ✦

I wake shivering, my head throbbing. I think I might be sick.

I sit carefully, using the starlit deck of the wind wagon to push myself upright. To the east, I can see the horizon if I squint, the earth a deep purple blanket where it meets the pure black spread of the sky. I'm overwhelmed by the size of it, how it dwarfs me. I wonder if this was what it felt like to be at sea on a ship all those years ago, before the people that deserted us stripped the land of its resources.

The Federation, Amory called it.

I glance up at Feder in the sky, a god he invented, then Ation, another lie. Feder and Ation. Federation.

Ay-tee-on, we've been saying, not *Ay-shun.* I wonder if Amory changed the pronunciation when he dreamed up our gods, or if it changed over time. Like so much of the Old World, the answer is lost.

I wonder if they're out there still among the stars—the people who deserted us. I wonder where their rigid-winged bird took them, *how* it took them. I wonder, I wonder, I wonder. I've uncovered so much and still know so little.

I stand up shakily, stomach twisting. I am most definitely going to be sick. I run for the rail and heave, but nothing comes up.

Rusted moonblitz. It's the devil's drink. Serves no purpose whatsoever beyond churning a person's stomach into knots and rotting their brain. Even still, I find myself searching the deck for the jar. Folks say that more of the drink is the best way to banish a fogged head. Makes no sense, really, but I'm ready to try it. Anything to make my skull stop pounding.

"Looking for this?" Asher is sitting at the wind wagon's stern, waving the jar in my direction. It's nearly empty.

Buttoning my jacket at my throat, I stagger toward him. "Where are the others?"

"Inside."

Where we should be. It's cold on the wastes at night. I glance toward Eden's dark shape, but trying to climb the rubble while my head spins sounds self-destructive.

Asher passes me the moonblitz, and I sit beside him, then take another swig. It will only wreck me further, but at the moment, that type of pain is more welcome than the truth about Eden.

"What are you doing out here?" I ask.

Asher sucks his bottom lip, shakes his head. He takes the jar from me and downs what remains of the blitz, then turns his gaze to the stars. His eyes gleam with tears on the verge of falling.

"They didn't abandon us," he says finally. "They never existed. We're completely alone." He turns the jar over in his hands a few times. "There are no gods, Delta. How can there be no gods?" His voice cracks, and something in my chest cracks with it. I watch a tear streak down his cheek before he buries his face in his hands.

I want to take back everything I said earlier. I want his optimism now, because this is worse. Asher, broken, is so much worse.

"Delta, I don't know what to do from here. How can there be nothing? How can it be just us?"

I don't know what to say. I've never been good at comforting people. That was Indie's strength, holding me close when I had a bad dream or whispering a joke into my ear when I was upset. But a joke feels wrong now. There is nothing funny about this.

I hate Eden because of what it means for the future: that there is no Verdant, that I can't save my pack. But for Asher, he's lost everything. A future and all of his past, too. His faith. Everything he's believed in.

I take his hand, and he stills as I thread my fingers through his. His eyes find mine, and I still don't know what to say. There's nothing I can possibly say to make this better. The future I longed for is gone. His world is shattered.

"Delta," he whispers.

A ribbon unfurls in my stomach.

"I don't know where we go from here," I admit. "Maybe I can trade Reed to the General — a traitor for my pack."

Asher's brows dip. "You'd do that? Trade blood to save blood?"

"I thought you didn't trust him. Wanted him dead."

"I did, at first. But if he's been telling the truth — and it kind of seems like he has — this is a dangerous slope to stand on. All we have is our blood."

"I'm not your blood, and you tried to find me again. My whole pack."

"You and I are two halves of a whole, Delta, a branded pair.

And packs are their own unique bond. Bonds and blood. They keep us human."

I nod, knowing he's right. And though I hate that Reed didn't help me sooner, he's helping now. He's risking everything to put the safety of many before himself. And if I really do have a sibling left in this world, I shouldn't turn my back on him. A stab of guilt shoots up my side, as though the mere thought of inviting Reed into my life means turning my back on Indie.

"I can't think now," I mutter. "My head's too fogged up. Maybe tomorrow, when the blitz has worn off, things might be clearer. Maybe . . ."

I stand as a movement to the north catches my eye. Along the horizon, green ribbons of light dance and twist. Signs of a coming silent storm. I don't remember a solar flare, but maybe it happened when we were inside Eden, discovering the truth of the world.

"There's been so many lately," Asher says. "Squalls, dust storms, silent storms . . ."

The light dances, unhurried and fluid. If you didn't know what followed, you'd think it beautiful. A storm means we won't be able to leave for Powder Town for at least another day, which means our water will run even lower. We'll have to use whatever supplies Eden has to offer and hope they're safe, as Asher theorized.

The supplies!

"That's it!" I blurt out.

"What?" Asher says.

I bolt to my feet, still staring at the horizon, Amory's story repeating in my mind. I see it now: the way forward. I know how to best the General.

CHAPTER THIRTY-SIX

"**W**e have to fire a mag-rifle," I say.

Asher's brow wrinkles. "Right now?"

"That's how we defeat him."

"But Amory said they don't work during storms."

"That's exactly what I want to test."

Fighting against the dizziness of our fogged minds, we get the deck boards back in place and double- and triple-check all the sails, making sure things are cinched tight. Then I scramble up the rubble pile and into Eden, Asher on my heels. Inside, the bunker is quiet. Reed and Harlie must be sleeping.

The storeroom is larger than any hut I've ever set foot in. Shelves reach from floor to ceiling, labeled with Old World symbols that I can't comprehend. Not that it matters. I know exactly what I'm looking for.

On the far wall, rifles are stacked in narrow compartments. They look nothing like the rifles I've seen on the wastes. The semi-somethings, Amory had called them. A type of weapon that didn't fail during the geostorms, and the only type Amory let people take when they left the bunker.

But the mag-rifles . . .

Amory mentioned them when talking about compasses. Our

Old World compasses go haywire during silent storms: needles spinning, never finding north. But once the storm is over, they come back to their senses. I'm hoping the mag-rifles, for whatever reason, are the same: operable most days, useless during the storms.

I take one from a compartment and pass it to Asher.

"They're lighter than the modified rifles," he says. "Easier to load, too. Watch." He takes a dull gray box from a shelf above and feeds it into a slot where the rifle's barrel meets the grip. I take it that he figured all this out when he was doing inventory with Reed. "No more shoving bullets in with a rod, no more lighting powder. Just clip in"—he touches the gray box—"and squeeze the trigger. Why the hell did Amory leave all these behind?"

"The silent storms must have been really frequent. He mentioned something about the sun and an active period, whatever that means. If storms hit every few days back then, these would be completely useless."

"But they're not now?"

"They shouldn't be. Not till the storm gets here."

"So why do you want to give these to the General?" Asher asks, struggling to keep up.

"Come on."

I grab the mag-rifle from him and run back the way we came. Once we're out of the bunker again, perched atop the rubble, I aim the weapon at the horizon. The green-blue warning ribbons are twisting still, and I point the barrel at them, as though shooting them can banish the storm that's yet to hit.

I've never fired a rifle—not the modified and popular Old World rifle and certainly not this fancy tech in my hands—but Asher made it sound easy.

I squeeze the trigger, and the blast of the gun is nearly as bad as the way it punches into my shoulder. My ears ring. I rub near my collarbone, knowing I'll have a bruise by morning.

I take aim again, holding the weapon more firmly this time, bracing for the punch.

"It works, genius," Asher says after another deafening blast.

I look at the dancing aurora. "But in a few more hours, they won't work. At least that's what I'm hoping to prove."

"And then what?"

"Then I can bring these weapons to Bedrock. I can tell the General that I figured out how to read my map. I'll tell him the truth: there is no Verdant, just a bunker filled with Old World tech. He'll test the rifles, see that they work. I won't go to him until the weather is clear. I'll tell him he can have all the weapons if he lets my pack go."

Asher bites his lip. "I want to save them too, Delta. I do. But I'm not sure giving the General the most easily fired rifle the wastes has ever seen is the smartest way to go about it."

"He'll give them to his Loyalists, arm them all."

"Right. It makes him too powerful."

"But Powder Town will know our plans. And when the Prime sees an aurora on the horizon, she can head for Bedrock and attack the very next day, during the height of the silent storm—when the General's new weapons won't work."

"It takes more than a day to get from Powder Town to Bedrock," Asher points out.

I jerk my head toward the *Gods Touched* below us. "Not on a wind wagon."

Asher's brow peaks. Now he sees what I do.

The wind wagon fleet Powder Town can build.

The Loyalist army whose weapons will fail when they need them most.

A chance to truly overthrow the General.

"And then Bedrock is just there for the taking," he murmurs.

I nod. "We're going to steal it from him. It can be our Verdant, Asher, at least for a little while. The Oracle said the water supply is fading, but I'm sure it can be stretched further. We'd stop wasting it on ilkcorolla crops, for starters. And we could explore above the Backbone, too. See if there's more fertile land that way. Partner with Powder Town through it all." I turn toward him, my pulse pounding. "The wastes won't be so bad once the General's gone. There's enough to go around if the right people are put in charge."

Asher looks away from me toward the green tendrils of light on the horizon. "We should sleep. At least until the next test."

✦ ✦ ✦

I'm not sure how much time has passed before I wake. The sharp lines of Eden's rooms make me uneasy, and I lurch upright in the bed. Asher's arm dangles in my view, hanging over the edge of the mattress above me.

I'm reminded of my time spent on Zuly's tanker—the beds stacked on top of each other in those windowless gray rooms.

I slide from the bed. The excitement of my plan has faded, and I'm left with the aching throb of a moonblitz fog. Asher's sleeping on his stomach, head turned toward me. He looks younger in sleep, his features relaxed and his lips slightly parted. It's a face I remember from Alkali Lake, a shadow of the boy I once knew. I consider waking him, but if he had anywhere near what I did to drink, he could do with sleeping off the blitz. I guide his hand back onto the mattress and tuck it beside his body.

Then I snatch the rifle from where we'd left it beside the bed and slip from the room.

Back outside, the aurora is gone, and morning light creeps over the wastes. I aim the weapon, but when I squeeze the trigger, nothing happens. I squeeze it a second time, a third.

I detach the small box Asher had slid into the rifle. One of the narrow sides is see-through. The edges of eight bullets wink in the strengthening sunlight.

I clip the box back in. Try again.

Nothing.

It won't fire.

The aurora is gone, meaning we're in the thick of a silent storm, and the Old World tech is useless. Just like Amory claimed.

I pull my lodestone from beneath my shirt and let it shiver to a standstill. The indentation points due north.

I wonder briefly if *this* is why my father disappeared to the south — if he thought the lodestone material could be used in other ways, perhaps to power weapons. Perhaps he was trying to beat the General all along, and his plan required leaving before he could return for a final fight.

I choose to believe this possibility. Like Amory and his Federation crew, I want to believe that my father didn't abandon me without a reason.

Resting the mag-rifle on my shoulder, I go to wake the others.

✦ ✦ ✦

I explain everything. Harlie grouses and moans as she stretches, but Reed jumps from bed like a drop of water on a hot skillet. "I need to show you something," he says, dragging me back to the room where we watched Amory's confession. He points at the table made of square toggles. "I was playing around with this last night. It has arrows, like the tiles Rune could carry. Tapping the arrows brought me to different information."

He taps through until the screen fills with black Old World symbols set against crisp white. The Federation emblem—the winged bird I've seen in the General's library and on Amory's clothes—covers most of the background as well, faint enough to not demand attention, but obvious if you're looking at it. Like a stain.

"I don't know what any of this means," I say.

"Wait." Reed presses the arrows again, and a strange symbol appears. It looks a bit like a face in profile, with a rainbow turned vertical beside it.

Text to audio enabled, a voice announces.

Reed taps again, and the disembodied voice continues to read what I presume are the words on the window.

Solar Cycles of CIX: Understanding the Star's Activity and How It Affects Planet CIX-b

Compiled by Dr. Iris Rae Tollis, Federation Department of Energy

The voice reads on, and a lot of it is like babble in my ears, but the gist of it seems to be this: the sun above this wasteland has what the Federation calls an active period that strikes roughly every 116 years. Frequent flares erupt from the sun, causing geomagnetic storms of disastrous size, some lasting for days on end and occurring so frequently that they feel almost like one continuous storm. After about nine or ten moons of this, the sun will go quiet again, with the occasional dust storm or silent storm striking just a few times a year. And another 116 years later, the active period starts again.

Occasionally the solar cycle might be shorter or longer, perhaps by two or three years. There will be little warning if this happens, just an increase in flares and solar storms, kicking off the stretch of bad weather. The final warning sign will be an aurora that appears like a wide-stretching curtain, visible from the ground.

"I'm guessing that the storm Amory mentioned hit far more than two or three years early," Reed says. "Otherwise those Federation people would never have brought weapons that could malfunction in the storms."

"There must be another active period coming," I say. "There's been two silent storms just in the past two moons."

He nods. "Meaning your plan will be the easiest to carry out soon. If Powder Town can build a fleet quickly, you'll have a long stretch of silent storms to choose from when it comes to an attack on Bedrock."

"It also means more chances for the General to realize that the weapons I trade him don't work during the bad weather. If we can attack *before* the active period—maybe in the next storm or two, as the sun amps up—we might be able to pull it off. If we wait too long, we miss our chance."

+ + +

We load the wagon with all we can carry—one hundred and twenty mag-rifles, eighteen boxes stocked full of the bullet cases (each holding ten bullets), and two dozen plas bottles of water from the storeroom.

It takes all day to move the supplies onto the wind wagon. We cram what we can belowdecks, then stack the rest along the sideboards and near the stern. It weighs down the *Gods Touched* significantly. Between the load and the headwind, it's going to take us a while to cross the barren stretch of desert, and by the time we're ready to leave, the sun is setting.

"Should we wait until morning to shove off?" Asher asks.

"What's the point?" I say. "We'll take shifts—we know where we're headed. Any extra time spent here just eats into our supplies."

Harlie helps us get sailing and explains how we'll travel in switchbacks on the way home, sailing west, then east, then west, then east, slowly cutting our way south against the headwind. When Asher, Reed, and I have a handle on the process, Harlie goes for a lie-down. She's breathless and weak, meaning the silent storm is still raging.

By the third day, when Harlie's feeling more like herself, I test a mag-rifle off the *Gods Touched*'s prow. It fires effortlessly, the blast echoing across the wastes. I smile to myself, giddiness coursing through me.

This is going to work.

We're going to arm the General with weapons that will fail him at precisely the right time, and we'll overrun him for good.

I just need the sun to cooperate, but if the report back at Eden taught me anything, it's that suns are merely stars. Gods in their own right. They answer to no one but themselves.

CHAPTER THIRTY-SEVEN

By the time I spot Harlie's Hope through my binos it's a hazy morning at dawn, and nearly half a moon has passed since we left Eden. We're sunburned on the cheeks, wind-chapped from the headwind, and positively sick of smoked stallion. If I never have it again, it will be too soon.

Asher teases that I'll be eating more tonight. And again tomorrow. We'll be eating it until we reach Powder Town, but knowing we're approaching Harlie's Hope means the end is at least in sight.

I'm wiping dust from the front of my goggles when a strange shadow flits across the deck. I tilt my head up, search the sky, and spot it. A falcon. I race to the bow, bring my binos to my eyes. Sure enough, three dark figures on horseback are riding in from the south.

"Loyalists!" I call to the others.

The bird screeches above us, signaling to its team, as if our unnaturally tall mast couldn't be spotted several clicks away.

"Call them off!" Asher shouts to Reed.

"I can't! I have no way to signal them from here, and they'll only shoot me the instant they realize I've defected."

"Get one of the mag-rifles out," I shout to Asher. "Two,

actually. Harlie, you man the tiller. Reed? Stay low and see to the brakes. Asher and I will shoot as necessary."

We should have had the weapons out all along, but I never expected to see anyone out this way. It's a no man's land, a dead end.

I don't know how they found us. Maybe they've been searching for Reed ever since his communications with Bedrock went silent.

It doesn't matter how it happened, just that it did.

They've found us, and there's nowhere to hide.

Asher tosses me one of the rifles, and I catch it with two hands, then take aim. The Loyalists are still too far off. We'll never hit them, not with the wind wagon bumping over every last rut.

The Loyalists' falcon suddenly dives, plummeting for the rock outcropping that borders Harlie's home. For a second I think maybe Asher has shot it down. Then I see the telltale sign of a dust storm—a yellow haze, thick and ugly and crackling with energy just beyond the rocks that border Harlie's Hope. The outcropping is sheltering us from the worst of the wind and dust, but it will breach the obstacle soon.

"Will we make it?" I yell to Harlie.

"We're about to find out."

The Loyalists spot the storm too and kick their horses into a faster gallop. If they get to the shanties before us, we'll rot.

"Tacking back to the west!" Harlie yells from the tiller. "Forget those guns, Delta. Help Reed at the brake. I'm angling us into the storm, and those winds should slow us plenty, but I don't want to crash into the rocks."

I glance up at the masts, praying that they somehow withstand the storm. If we're close enough to the rocks, we might get lucky. We *have* to, because we can't get the Old World tech to Powder Town without a working wind wagon.

An earsplitting blast erupts, and I duck instinctively. The Loyalists are firing at us.

"Here they come!" Harlie shouts.

I glance over my shoulder. I can see their black garb now. The man in the lead sits upright in the saddle, his rifle pointed our way. Good aim will be nearly impossible while he's bouncing around on a horse like that, but I crouch low anyway.

The storm hits the rocks and roars over the ridge, the wind tangling in our sails. The *Gods Touched* immediately slows, and that's when Reed squeezes the brake. The wagon skids wildly in the rear and begins to turn to starboard, toward the rocks.

No!

If we turn too far, the dust storm's wind will fill our sails again and send us cruising the way we just came—back onto the plains, *toward* the oncoming Loyalists. I race to assist Reed, bearing down on the brake with him. Harlie counters our steering from the front.

The wagon groans in protest, and there's a splintering crack from above as one of the crossbeams breaks free of the mast.

"Harlie!" I scream, but I can't leave the brake. Not if we don't want to crash.

The woman leaps aside, but the wooden beam clips the back of her head, and she collapses onto the deck. Asher runs to her. I keep squeezing the brake, the wagon slowing to a crawl as one of the sails, now free of the rigging that attached it to the crossbeam, snaps and flails overhead.

"Get water and whatever meat you can carry," I tell Reed as the wagon sags to a stop. "We're gonna have to run for it."

Above us, dust crests the rock outcropping. Rubble stings my cheeks.

We've stopped a mere stone's throw from the rocks, which might spare the wagon from damage. I grab supplies, then vault over the side rail and sprint. Reed follows. Ahead, Asher is half carrying, half dragging an unconscious Harlie to safety. They slip into the shanty. Just as I reach the door, I risk a glance left, out across the open plains. The Loyalists' steeds are galloping like mad. They're so close I can see their eyes—all but the man in the lead, who wears a ram-skull mask. One of the General's Four.

Unlike the others, he's not looking at the storm breaking over the rocks, about to bury them alive. He's looking over my shoulder. At Reed.

Reed, who is not bound or beaten.

Reed, who is carrying supplies, obviously helping me.

Reed, who has betrayed his pledge, turned his back on the General.

"Death to the disloyal!" the man shouts, training his weapon on Reed.

We rush into Harlie's place, and Asher shoves a piece of scrap metal over the doorway. I never hear a gunshot. The storm hits with the roar of a monster, and the world becomes nothing but darkness and wind.

✦ ✦ ✦

The storm rages through the night, and by morning, a decent amount of dust has infiltrated the shanty, piling in small swells around the base of the secured curtained doorway.

Harlie is conscious again, but also violently ill. She throws up whatever food we give her and complains about pressure that feels like a fist behind her skull. She keeps asking if she'll be okay, and I can't bear to lie. Head injuries are dangerous. Back at Alkali Lake, one of our pack died from a mule kick to the head. "Time will tell" is all I'm comfortable saying.

When the storm clears, the first sound to grace our ears is the screech of a falcon. I run outside to see the Loyalist's bird streaking east. It must have found shelter among the rocks.

I yell for Asher—his slingshot—but it's Reed who emerges from the shanty first. He whistles, calling the bird to him. It lands on his outstretched fist. "Ember," he says, stroking the creature's slick wings. Then to me: "Do we still have meat? She'll work with me quickly if I spoil her."

"We're keeping her?"

"I still have my tiles. We can send a false message, buy ourselves some time. If she flies back now, empty-handed, they'll know something went wrong."

I glance across the wastes, finding the bodies of the Loyalists and their horses half buried in rubble and grit, looking like little more than lumpy rocks from this distance. They suffocated, probably. I feel bad for the horses.

While Reed takes care of the falcon called Ember, I climb aboard the *Gods Touched* and survey the damage. Her sails are shredded, but the second set Harlie had stored belowdecks will serve us fine once we string them up. And the broken crossbeam that clipped Harlie isn't beyond repair either. The real stroke of luck is that the wagon didn't tip. We can get her sailing again.

I call for Asher, and we go straight to work.

By the afternoon, we're on the move again, Harlie reclining on deck with a scarf wrapped over her eyes to help with the headache. Reed says we can probably go another day or two before the General will expect an update from Ember, so I tell him to keep the bird happy. I watch as he sits on the deck, tossing her small kernels of dried meat and laughing when she gets bored with the game and decides to fly in circles above us. His smile is genuine, but it still doesn't reach his eyes. He's thinking of his own bird, and part of me wishes I had spared it. Rune could have served the same purpose that Ember will, and it would have made Reed happier, too.

We need to stay on flat terrain, so we sail southeast for a bit. I glance in the direction of the General's iron mines, feeling antsy. They're numerous clicks off, no way for us to be spotted. "They won't catch us even if they *did* somehow see us," I mutter to myself.

"They'll catch us if we're not granted entry at Powder Town," Asher says.

I shove the possibility from my head and check the horizon. A geyser explodes to the south. Burning Ground. We're nearly there.

✦ ✦ ✦

We creep up on Powder Town at dusk.

They see us coming—we're impossible to miss—and every

watchtower along the defense wall goes alight with torches. When they realize it's me and Asher, the shouting begins.

"You've got some nerve," Saph bellows down at us.

"We will not admit you again," the Reaper says, but she's staring at the wind wagon, curiosity getting the better of her.

"You will," I announce.

"We owe nothing to deserters," she says, more firmly this time. "We opened our doors to you, and you ran. Asher, twice."

"We did, but for the right reason." I stand taller, raise my voice so that everyone along the wall can hear me. "Tell Kara the Prime I have been to the Verdant and I have seen the future. Tell her I sailed across the wastes and back because I know how to beat the General."

The Reaper and Saph look at each other, then disappear from their posts. The lights along the other watch points vanish also.

The night edges in, painfully silent.

"They won't really leave us out here," I say to Asher, "will they?"

His expression is uncertain, and just as I begin to fear that I've misjudged everything, there's a creak of hinges, the yawn of worn wood.

Powder Town's door opens to greet us.

CHAPTER THIRTY-EIGHT

The Prime calls a meeting with her Trinity.

Harlie is hauled off to get medical attention from someone in the prosperity pillar while Asher and I are left under Saph's watchful eye. She brings us to Cleo's, ties us to chairs, and paces the room, muttering to herself about our stupid, traitorous asses and how we shouldn't be given second chances. *Third* chances, on Asher's behalf. The real irony is that Reed — the person she would think to be the true threat if she knew his Loyalist history — simply leans against a wall, shrugging off her interrogation.

"Who are you?" she demands. "When did you meet up with these two? Who is the old woman you came in with?"

"I'll answer questions when Delta and Asher get to do the same," Reed says. "Or when the Prime sees us. Whichever comes first."

I'm not sure how long we sit, but my shoulders are aching in their sockets and the moon is bright in the sky when the Reaper comes to retrieve us.

"Is this where we attend our welcome party?" Asher asks. "You've been so hospitable so far."

"Shut up," the Reaper says, and nudges him in the back with her rifle.

We slip from the hut and into the night. It may be late, but the Powder Town streets are crowded with onlookers.

"There she is," someone says. "The gods touched."

"She found the Verdant."

"She'll save us all!"

"Bringer of Life!" another shouts. "Green Goddess!"

"How lush was it?"

"When can we go there?"

I keep my head down. This plan seemed foolproof when it was just the four of us at Eden — me and Asher and Harlie and Reed. But now, with all these hopeful eyes on me, the stakes weigh heavy on my conscience. They are praising me now, but if I fail them, they will hate me. Despise me. Wish me dead.

I won't be their Bringer of Life, I'll be their bearer of lies.

I won't be a goddess, just a fraud. A deceiver.

At Prime Hall, we're ushered past half a dozen soldiers at the entrance and then guided to the table where I had my first audience with the Prime. The Reaper cuts our bindings.

The Prime is seated at the head of the table. In a seat at her left, Bronx the Chemist wears a pair of darkened goggles, her eyes hidden and her pale skin glimmering in the room's candlelight. On the Prime's other side is a woman I haven't seen before, bronze-skinned, with dark hair piled high on her head. She rests her chin on her clasped hands, and her wide-sleeved sweater pools at the crook of her elbows against the table.

The Prime looks us over, her eyes narrowing when she

reaches Reed. "You," she snarls. Instantly she's drawn a knife and holds it in Reed's direction. The Reaper's rifle comes up next, followed by Saph's and those of the other guards stationed along the perimeter of the hall.

"This is the Loyalist scum who cost me my eye," the Prime announces. She stands and moves toward Reed with deliberate, slow steps. "Perhaps I should return the favor." The tip of her blade touches his neck.

"He's defected," I explain. "He's on our side."

The Prime frowns. "He's one of the General's Four. He can't be trusted."

"He," Reed says, "is standing right here and can speak for himself."

"Bind his hands," the Prime says to her guards, "and then bind those to the chair. He goes nowhere until I ask some questions." She turns to me. "You bring a Loyalist into my inner circle and expect me to trust you?"

I scowl. "I returned knowing how to beat the General. I'm willing to trust you with that knowledge, and you treat us like prisoners." The Prime returns to her seat at the head of the table, her dark eye studying me. "I feel like I'm back at Bedrock," I add.

"And yet you still want to make a deal with me. Amari the Tender has examined your wind wagon," the Prime says, nodding at the woman I hadn't recognized. "She tells me it's quite ingenious. The cargo it's carrying, however, is puzzling."

"If you let me explain, it will all make sense."

The Prime glances over her shoulder, searching out her

Reaper, who stands at attention behind the leader's chair. The woman nods encouragingly.

"Go on then," the Prime says. "Talk."

I tell them everything.

How we traveled to Harlie's Hope, learned that Reed is my half brother, and sailed to the Verdant only to discover that it doesn't exist, that our gods are an invention. There are numerous gasps from the Trinity, looks of doubt and confusion.

"How can our gods not exist?" the Tender protests.

The Reaper frowns deeply. "Why would someone make them up?"

The Prime raises a hand, silencing them. "I'm sure Delta has answers for that, too." Her gaze slides back to me, calm and patient. She's not shocked by this revelation. She barely even looks rattled. *The only way out is with the dead.* How long has it been, I wonder, since she stopped believing in the gods, since she realized that no one was coming to save us and we had to be our own salvation?

I clear my throat and continue, explaining about Amory's situation, the uprising and abandonment, his motives of instilling hope in our ancestors. How the weapons he left behind at Eden will fail during silent storms, giving the Prime the perfect opportunity to attack the General. How Bedrock can be a home for all who want it — a new Verdant that works in partnership with Powder Town — and how the wastes themselves may sprout new life when the water the General hoards is used — and shared — responsibly.

"We transported as many of the mag-rifles as the wind wagon

could carry. I'll bring the weapons to the General and trade them for the freedom of my pack. Meanwhile, you have lumber here. You can build more wind wagons—a whole fleet of them—and wait for the next silent storm. They're on the rise, a new solar cycle about to kick off. Most days, there's a strong wind on the wastes that blows southwest to northeast, which means that reaching Bedrock will be easy and fast when the time comes. You can bypass the Barrel, swing around from the east through desert too deadly for anyone on foot or horseback. He'll never expect you."

"And you think he'll turn you and your pack free when you give him the weapons?" the Prime asks.

"Yes. There's no Verdant, and if he can't have that, he'll settle for the mag-rifles."

"I think he'll hold you until he can confirm your story. He'll want directions to this Eden place, and then he'll send a scouting party to confirm what you've told him. He'll find the messages you did, learn that the mag-rifles are useless during the silent storms."

"Then I won't tell him the way to Eden," I insist.

"And then he won't trust you," she counters. I hadn't considered this, but she's right.

"He can't get to Eden without a wind wagon," I point out.

"And he'll know you couldn't have traveled that far without some foreign contraption either. Again, he will know you are hiding something, or he will assume you are lying about everything. Neither will earn his trust." She spins the blade she'd used to threaten Reed, its hilt in her palm, tip kissing the table's wood grain. "You also mention that the sun is entering some . . . active phase. That means more silent storms in the coming moons. So many that it may be impossible to time your plan. What if you bring the rifles to the General and there's a storm before our wind wagon fleet can get there? What if he learns that the mag-rifles are flawed before we can attack?"

Reed and I had discussed this. I'd assumed that if we acted quickly, it wouldn't be an issue, but with the Prime's good eye boring into me, I see how risky that is. If the General discovers the flaw in the mag-rifles before we can make our move, we've lost our only edge.

The Prime runs a hand over her jaw. "What if we keep the mag-rifles," she proposes.

"But they're how I barter my pack free."

"Your pack and all of Bedrock will be free if we do this correctly. Why give him a weapon this efficient? Why arm him when we can arm ourselves?" A pause. "If we keep the mag-rifles, build a fleet, and attack when the skies are clear, his modified rifles won't stand a chance against this new technology."

"So I just let my pack suffer until we build a fleet? That could take moons!"

"It will."

I stand, slapping the table. "I'm not waiting any longer. I traveled across the wastes, dammit. I found the Verdant. Your people are calling me gods touched. Don't I get a say in things?"

"But you're *not* gods touched, Delta." She steels me with her good eye. "No one is, according to what you found at Eden. Not even our long-lost ancestors whose skulls held what the General calls stars. Those "stars" are just tech. Old World tech. Our gods are nothing, and we are certainly not touched by them."

"How can you be so calm?" I'm still standing, practically shaking.

"Controlling perception is a necessary skill as a leader, Delta. Do not confuse my careful planning with lack of enthusiasm. I am tempered and careful because I know we have only one chance. Now, please sit, so I can continue to explain."

I glance at Asher, Reed. My half brother nods encouragingly. Asher's brows flick skyward, as if to say, *What other choice do you have?*

I flop into the seat.

"This is promising, Delta of Dead River," the Prime says evenly. "The stars are aligning, the pieces sliding into place. This is the closest I've ever felt to being ready to attack him. But even with the mag-rifles and a wind wagon fleet, there is still the issue of his dam wall—breeching it, accessing Bedrock itself . . ."

"The blast barrels will breech the wall," the Reaper offers. "We can mount them on the wind wagons, fire as we approach."

"Yes," the Chemist says, tapping her fingers against the table. "We have enough black powder to do it. It should work."

"Is this the prototype?" I ask. "It's finished?"

"You've been gone a full moon, Delta," the Prime says. "We've made progress."

"What is it? What can it do?"

"A blast barrel," she says, "is like the barrel of a rifle, but much larger, and able to fire projectiles much larger, too. We've been filing rocks into balls since the Trinity began work on the first prototype."

"We haven't tested them on something like the General's defenses," the Reaper says, "but I believe they will breach the wall."

The Prime nods in agreement. "Still, the Loyalists will have the high ground until the dam falls, plus their catapults."

"Catapults?" I echo.

"Weapons that can launch a projectile over great distances without gunpowder," the Reaper interjects. "They're positioned along his outer dam. A swinging arm launches the payload."

I saw these during my time in Bedrock, and was right to assume they provided defense.

"Even with the mag-rifles, we will not have the advantage until we've infiltrated Bedrock," the Prime continues. "And by then the General will have armed everyone, even his ilked-up workers, who will do anything he commands for another drink of water. We need to render his weapons useless."

"Which is why I thought we should give him the mag-rifles and attack during a storm," I mutter.

"His weapons can still fail him," the Prime says. "It's just a matter of doing what we already tried once, several years ago." Her gaze slides to Reed, and his eyes widen.

"The powder?" he whispers.

"Yes. If we blow his stored powder, the Loyalists will only be able to fire on us so long as their powder horns are full. Once they've used what's on their persons, they'll be powerless."

"No disrespect, my Prime, but you couldn't blow his stores years ago, when you stood right beside them," the Reaper says.

"I didn't have an inside man then." The Prime keeps her gaze rooted on Reed. "Are you truly on our side?"

"Yes," he says without hesitation. "Absolutely."

"Could you go back there and blow the powder on a decided date? Is there a story you could weave so that you're welcomed home without suspicion?"

"I'm sure we can think of something."

"Oh, please," Asher grouses. "You're going to have your entire plan hinge on this ram skull?" He flings a hand at the mask propped on Reed's forehead. "The Loyalist who cost you your eye?"

"I like to believe that we are more than the actions of our past." The Prime looks to me. "Delta, what do you think?"

I can see Asher's point. I don't know Reed, not truly. But he hasn't put even a toe out of line since he joined our party in Harlie's Hope. The moment he saw the Loyalists closing in on us yesterday, he could have held me at knifepoint, and when we captured Ember, he easily could have sent word to the General with his tiles. But he's done nothing but stand by his word.

I have to believe him.

I have to start trusting people, or the future of the wastes is going to be more of the same: fractured packs, wandering vagrants, the powerful leeching off the needy.

Distrusting is how we survive this world. But to move beyond surviving—to truly live—we need to trust each other. Not everyone, but definitely the few who show us that they care more about the greater good than about themselves.

"He's always been on our side," I say. "All this time, he's just been playing a part."

"Excellent. Now prove it." The Prime tosses a leather bag toward Reed. When it hits the table, several tiles spill onto the surface, symbols winking up at him. "Call for aid. Request what remains of the General's Four. We're taking out his most trusted Loyalists before we even put this plan in motion."

CHAPTER THIRTY-NINE

The tiles don't allow for communication as specific as the Prime has requested, but Reed thinks that at least one of the remaining Four will be sent by default. He puts a message into the leather pouch and sends it up with Ember. We watch her soar east from the steps of Prime Hall. In no time, the night sky has swallowed her from view.

Come morning, Reed will travel north to Harlie's Hope, where he asked for aid to be sent. The Reaper and a few other security details will accompany him. Asher is still grumbling his doubts when Amari the Tender asks me to show her the wind wagon. It's late, the moon high above us, but I can't come up with an excuse to delay.

I follow the Tender through the streets, grateful for their emptiness this time. The wind wagon waits in the clearing just inside Powder Town's defense wall. I show the Tender how it works, explaining the steering and the brake, the rigging and the sails. Her most trusted woodworkers shadow us, nodding in the glow of their lanterns. Building a fleet will take time, and the Tender plans to start first thing in the morning. If and when Harlie has recovered, she can help oversee things.

After I've explained all I can, and after the Tender has ordered everyone to get a good night's sleep, I stagger to Cleo's. I'm exhausted, barely able to keep my eyes open. When I duck into the small home, Asher is sitting at the table, waiting.

"Do you really trust him?" he asks. He doesn't look at me when he speaks, just at his hands, folded in his lap.

"I trust that he wants to do the right thing," I answer.

His eyes find mine. "I wish everyone would do the right thing, Delta. But if they did, the wastes wouldn't be the way they are."

"You were coming around to him when we were traveling."

"His story seems plausible," Asher says with a shrug. "That doesn't mean I think the Prime's entire plan should hinge on him. If he doesn't blow the powder, everything becomes more dangerous. And if he betrays us and spills our plans, the General will aim to strike Powder Town before the Prime can build her fleet. Trust me when I say he can overrun this place in an instant. He outnumbers us."

I lick my lips. Asher regards me quietly. Dark moons sag beneath his eyes.

"Let's see what this test brings, with Ember," I say. "We can go from there."

He rubs his mouth, sighs. "I know you're right to want to do this. I know the Prime is too. But I just ... there's a part of me that wants to stay here forever. In Powder Town. Forget about Bedrock. Just live where it's safe. I'm so tired of loss. I can't lose anyone else."

"Neither can I, Asher. That's why we *have* to do this."

"I misspoke: I can't lose you." He's staring at me now, as if

358

I'm the last bit of water in the wastes, the only thing that will keep him alive. He stands, and the house seems suddenly small. "Before, it was different," he goes on. "Before, if something bad happened, I could believe it was part of the gods' plan, something that was meant to be, even if I couldn't understand why. But now, if something happens to you, Delta, it will only be because of us —the people of the wastes, *me.*"

"Asher . . ."

He takes a step toward me. Another. We're only an arm's length apart. His eyes work over me, pausing on the scar that bisects my brow. He touches it with his thumb, featherlight. "I'm sorry I keep trying to hold you back. I want you safe, but I'm with you on this. I trust you." His lips brush my forehead, and they are unbelievably soft. He lingers there a moment, his thumb still by my temple, his breath warm on my skin. I want to step into his arms. I want to run.

I feel like I should say something, anything.

"I trust you, too," I whisper.

He pulls back, eyes locking with mine, and it dawns on me that we're not really talking about trust anymore. Not exclusively. *I trust you so much, and that's why everything is difficult,* he'd said on the wind wagon. I understand now; it is impossible for us not to get hurt. Life and death is the way of the wastes, love and loss. It's the cycle. We all lose eventually.

"Delta," he murmurs. That's it. Just my name. He takes my hand cautiously, threads his fingers through mine, and my stomach plummets like a stone in water.

"You could have anyone in the wastes," I say. And it's true.

359

He's beautiful. Caring. So much more than decent, which is all I can pass for on a good day.

"But I want only you."

My heart thrums wildly against my ribs. Like my lodestone always finding north, I let myself be drawn to him. He tilts his head to the side, lowers his mouth to mine. Our lips brush, and it's like I've found my heading. Like this was where I was always supposed to be.

He kisses me again, firmer this time, more deliberate. His lips are dry from days in the sun, but still somehow impossibly soft. He finds my hips and pulls me closer. When his hands slip beneath my shirt and roam up my spine, I don't fold into myself or try to become small. For the first time in my life, I want to be touched there. I want him to feel every inch of me.

"Is this okay?" he whispers when I shudder.

I nod frantically, not wanting him to stop. As his fingers trail my scars, I kiss his nose, his chin, his jaw. When I find the hollow of his throat, he groans, and I immediately want to make him do it again.

I fumble with the buttons of his jacket and push it open. Run my hands over his chest. We may be two halves of a whole, but he is foreign to me, uncharted land. My hands explore, memorizing the shape of him, creating a map in my mind. He captures my face, brings my lips back to his, and we stagger a bit, bumping the table.

Cleo snores from behind the curtain that separates the bed mats from the living area, and we freeze.

We stand there a moment, looking at each other, dazed by what has just happened.

"This plan still scares me," he whispers after a moment.

"It scares me too," I admit. "But I've been scared since I left Dead River. Sometimes I think I've been scared my whole life. I'm tired of it, Asher. I'm ready for a change."

"Let's not be scared together," he says. "After this is all over."

"Okay."

He kisses my forehead again, tugs me toward the bed mats.

We curl up together, his arm around my middle. It's like that night in Burning Ground, but I don't move away. Maybe there are worse things in life than needing someone. Maybe the needing is all that keeps us human.

✦ ✦ ✦

Reed sets out with the Reaper early the next morning. He regards me for a long beat before slipping through the gate, a hand on his chest in farewell. I touch my lodestone in return.

Maybe someday we'll understand why our father left, instead of helping. Maybe I'll have real answers instead of mere theories. But until then I will be grateful to have my pack growing rather than shrinking. It's like Zuly said, after all. Life and death is the way of things. Sometimes we lose. Sometimes we gain, and I hope I've gained well.

Construction on the wind wagons begins immediately. The Tender pulls a large group of her pillar to work on the job, and a flurry of activity fills the Powder Town clearing.

The *Gods Touched* is unloaded and the mag-rifles and ammo cases are stored in the defense barracks. Meanwhile, trees are felled from the foothills, sails are sewn, and rickshaws sacrifice wheels to the cause of building a fleet. Once proper construction begins, it's a sight to be seen — hundreds of women and a few dozen men laboring beneath the sun, sawing and nailing and knotting rope.

The Tender oversees everything, and I help on the Prime's orders; she wants me working on the brake systems, not harvesting sulfur. Asher, however, reports to Bronx the Chemist and is sent to work on the saltpeter beds. By the time we both make it to Cleo's in the evening, we're too tired to do anything but collapse onto our bed mats. We sleep beside each other, though, our limbs entangled. Sometimes I wake with his mouth nestled into the crook of my neck, and I lie there a moment, a smile on my lips.

✦ ✦ ✦

When Harlie emerges into the sunlight without a headache on the third day of construction, she wobbles up to one of the half-built wind wagons and immediately starts critiquing everything. I hear a few women grumble, but the Tender nods kindly and thanks her for her feedback.

"I appreciate your not leaving me behind," Harlie tells me.

"I wouldn't have left you behind," I insist, pride stung.

Harlie cocks a brow.

"Well, the old Delta might have. But not the new one."

"And who, exactly, is this new Delta? A gods touched? An actual *goddess?* I've heard what they're saying in the streets."

"They're saying what gives them hope."

"Maybe you're the great-great-great-something grand-daughter of General Amory," she says with a snort. "Sure sound like him with all that 'hope is most important' talk."

I brush sweat from my eyes, the rigging I'd been working on

forgotten. "Isn't it?" This way of thinking is all that's kept me from blurting the truth out to the construction line. The Prime insists that her people don't need to know the truth, that they came to her to be shielded from the darker parts of the wastes, and she will let them believe in whatever gods they choose—even me—if it helps them get by. If anyone among us is related to Amory, it's her.

"Nah, the truth is important," Harlie argues. "People should know who they're fighting for, why they're fighting, and how likely they are to succeed."

"Well, I'm not in charge here. If the Prime doesn't like what she's hearing in the streets, she'll put an end to it."

Harlie rolls her eyes, which means we're done talking about this but she in no way agrees with what I've said.

That afternoon, as she has every afternoon since we began building, the Prime stops by to check in with the Tender. After receiving updates, she lingers, helping a group of women tie knots and eventually climbing the rigging to assist another with the sail. Her willingness to work alongside her people—to be a part of their trials and triumphs—makes something stir in my chest. Pride? Hope? I only know that I am happy to be here, laboring with her, working toward something bigger than the two of us.

A horn is blown on the defense wall, and chatter spreads through the clearing. "The Reaper is back!" someone shouts. A moment later, the door raises to let the returning group pass through. The Reaper appears first, followed by three of her women, then Reed. His ram-skull mask is pushed back on his forehead, and a second dangles from his right hand. Horses trail behind, corpses slung over the saddles.

The Prime hurries down the mast and vaults over the side-board, running to the Reaper and kissing her firmly on the mouth. The women embrace, clapping each other on the back. I hear Luce say, "He did the deed himself. No hesitation. Killed the Second and the three Loyalists who accompanied him."

Reed glances at me, his expression pained. Even knowing he was doing the right thing, it couldn't have been easy, ending the lives of those Loyalist men, seeing the shock in their eyes when they realized they'd been betrayed.

The Prime calls for him, then me. "Meeting at Prime Hall. There are details to work out," she says, and she starts up the street, answering questions of the townsfolk who have gathered.

I wonder why they don't call *her* the Bringer of Life. She is a force, and Powder Town is lucky to have her.

✦ ✦ ✦

The plan is this: Reed will head for Bedrock at dawn.

Some of the story he tells the General will be true: I cornered him at Harlie's Hope, killed his bird, and held him captive.

The deaths of the other Loyalists ... we'll use that to our advantage.

Reed will say that the first group (the group we barely dodged when returning to Harlie's Hope) died in a dust storm, but not before sending Ember back with a request for aid. The second group — the one he just lured into a trap with the Reaper? Reed will claim that *I* killed them. I hid among the rocks, took them and their horses out one by one. But while I was busy doing that, Reed got his hand on a spare knife and managed to kill me.

Exhausted and weak after a moon in captivity, he will claim to have burned my body rather than tow it to Bedrock. But he'll bring with him a braid of my hair, my beloved jacket, and the ash of my bones, which will actually be the ashes of the Loyalists he killed.

"Will it work?" the Prime asks as we sit at the meeting. "Will he believe it?"

"He has no reason to doubt me," Reed says. "And I'll have Delta's jacket and ashes to prove the point. Delta's pack will remain safe from executions once I claim she's dead. He won't kill them when he needs workers."

"And you'll blow the powder when?" the Prime leads.

"The summer solstice, nearly a year from now."

Given the increase in recent storms, we've estimated that the sun's active cycle should kick off any day now, and according to what we learned in Eden, that cycle should last nine or ten moons. It will be over by midsummer, and the fleet should be ready by then too.

"I'll make the powder explosion look like an accident," Reed adds. "You'll attack any time after that, but before you're due to deliver his next shipment of powder."

The Prime nods. "And if you have complications with the 'accident'?"

"I'll send word with Ember. And if you don't hear from me at all by the solstice, it means I've been found out somehow, that I'm likely dead."

"What do we do in that case?" I ask.

"We'll attack anyway," the Prime says grimly. "If Reed is found out, we'll have to assume that the General has learned about our plan. I'll leave a security detail behind to protect Powder Town, and the fleet will head east, hopefully to confront him on the plains before he can attack us here."

There's more discussion about logistics—the blast barrels and offensive attacks, but Reed and I are dismissed.

"I'll see you in Bedrock at midsummer," Reed says to me on the steps of Prime Hall. Nearly a full year from now. The enormity of that wait hits me for the first time. I'm agreeing to leave my pack in the General's clutches until this plan can be executed. Bay will be a year old by the time I'm reunited with her.

"I won't see you in the morning?" I ask. "Before you leave?"

He shakes his head. "Better to head out early, before crowds gather. I don't like all those eyes."

"*You* don't like them? Have you seen the way they watch me? Have you heard what they're saying?"

"Yes, and I'm starting to feel left out. Shouldn't I be a god too? We're related, after all." He smirks.

"Very funny." I touch my lodestone through my shirt. We look out over Powder Town. Down in the clearing, three masts stand proud, the makings of a fleet. So much has to go right for this to work, and the stakes are too high for us to fail. I turn to Reed. "If you betray us, I will kill you myself," I tell him. "I will draw my blade across your neck, and I won't feel bad about it."

His face blanches. "Gods, Delta. And here I was, thinking you were starting to trust me."

"There are varying degrees of trust. I trust that you want to do the right thing. I pray that you will."

Reed swallows, looks away. "He called me a traitor before I killed him," he says, talking more to the horizon than me. "Did you know that? The General's Second. He said I was a traitor and a coward and disloyal to the gods, that I would rot . . . somewhere. I'm not sure where, exactly. I'd slit him open by then. But it's interesting, how each side thinks they are the valiant ones."

"Our side doesn't drug people."

"But this side still kills. They do what they think is necessary."

"What do you think is necessary, brother?"

He almost flinches at the term. He touches his lodestone, feeling it through his shirt. As he looks out over Powder Town, I take in the slope of his nose, his wide eyes, the shade of his hair. How is it that we can share so many features, when Indie and I, also half-siblings, never looked like blood?

"This," Reed says finally. "What we're doing, what the Prime is planning. This is necessary. Our father knew it, but he was too scared to see it through. So we'll see it through our-selves."

I shrug out of my jacket and pass it to him. "I want that back," I say before severing a braid of my hair and handing it over as well. "The hair, I'm not as attached to."

He chuckles. "If this goes well, you can have them both back, plus anything in Bedrock. If you want the General's star chain, I'll give it to you."

"I want him dead. That's all."

He nods silently, then offers me his palm. I take it, and we shake.

"Godspeed, sister," he says.

It's nice to be called that again, even if it reminds me of the one I lost.

CHAPTER FORTY

hree days after Reed heads for Bedrock, with Ember soaring overhead, the largest aurora I have ever seen paints the northern sky at dusk. What begins as shifting ribbons of green and blue stretching for the stars becomes a rippling wall of color. Like a curtain, hanging from the sky to the horizon, red in places, even yellow or purple. It shimmers, flexes, inverts.

Powder Town's residents gather in the foothills, their eyes turned to the sky, speechless. It is eerily quiet, but there is a tension in the air, the understanding that something is about to change.

There's a tug at my sleeve, and when I look down, a girl stands beside me. "What is it?" she asks, wide-eyed. It takes me a moment to place her — Rain, the child who didn't know what an execution was.

"The start of a very big storm," I tell her.

Her eyes gleam with excitement. "I always knew you were gods touched," Rain whispers.

A woman steps up behind her — the girl's mother. "What sort of storm?" she asks. Others are turning toward me now, drawn by these questions. "What have you seen?"

"A silent storm that will rage for many moons. Nine or ten."

A murmur spreads through the crowd.

"Will it bring dust?" someone calls out from the shadows.

"It might."

"How will our crops survive?" a panicked voice asks.

"And what about our trade with Bedrock—will it be safe to travel?"

"The wastes haven't seen a storm like this in over a hundred years," I say. "There's no telling what, exactly, it will bring. But it *will* pass, and when it is over"—my gaze flicks from the northern ribbons of light, east, toward Bedrock—"the General's rule will end too."

Now the crowd chatters wildly.

"Have you foreseen this, Bringer of Life?"

"How will we beat him?"

"Where is the Verdant? Shouldn't we go there now, before the worst weather?"

"Tell us, Green Goddess."

"Should we pray?"

"What do we do?"

"Tell us!"

A hand closes over my wrist—the Prime. "I must borrow your Green Goddess," she announces, "but all will become clear in time." She tugs me through the throng of people, down the hillside. "That's enough mingling," she says as we approach the Serpent River. "They're getting frenzied."

"Maybe if we told them I'm just a girl. Not a Green Goddess. Not gods touched, either."

She shakes her head, trains her good eye on me. "If you're just a girl, then I'm just a woman. A woman who let a deserter back into Powder Town, accepted her Old World weapons, and plotted how to take out the General with that untrustworthy deserter's help. I can't be a woman right now. I need to be the Prime. So you will be a god." She raises her chin, motions for her Reaper. Luce steps from the shadows, another two sentries on her heels. "See that Delta reaches her bed without interruption from citizens. And check with the Tender. I want the wind wagons tied down in case the storm brings gales."

✦ ✦ ✦

The following day, a new normal begins: construction beneath an ever-raging silent storm. Harlie and many of the other elderly hands helping with the wagons retire to bed, their hearts racing, their heads pounding, weakened by the storm we can't see.

Adjustments are made to the bow of the boats, allowing room for the Prime's blast barrels. They will be dissembled and loaded onto the wind wagons belowdecks, so as not to slow the sailing for the bulk of the trip, then reassembled as we close in on Bedrock. At that point we'll want the fleet to be slowing anyway.

Harlie, who is still in bed, looks over sketches of the design changes, nodding or grunting through her headaches, offering advice when she can manage. Those not weakened by the silent storm continue construction as the weather allows. Most days the skies are blue, and the only proof that the storm continues is a curtain of light visible in the northern sky. Other days the sun is blotted out with dust, and construction is ground to a halt as rubble spills over the foothills. Workers rush to cover the crops. Windows are shuttered tight. Everyone hunkers down and waits

370

and prays. The dust always clears, but the aurora continues to dance.

Traders aren't allowed in during the construction. Our work in the town's clearing is impossible to hide, and the Prime fears word of what we're building might make it back to the General. She orders traders to lower their rickshaws outside the perimeter wall, and all bartering happens on the wastes, the goods brought inside only after the men have cleared out. I see Clay during one of these trades and assure him that Bay will be safe again soon.

"Safe how? Are you planning something, Delta?"

I don't miss how he peers over my shoulder, trying to get a glimpse beyond Powder Town's wall. Clay may not be the brightest, but even he knows that this new arrangement is odd. "Just keep your head down," I tell him. "Keep doing what you're doing. It will all be right in time."

When Powder Town is due to deliver its first batch of powder since my return, the Prime sets out with her convoy, modified rifles and bows at the ready, goggles and scarves in place. I watch them roll out toward the boardwalks, wondering if I will see them again. What if a dust storm hits while they travel? What if they don't make it back? Will the Reaper rise to the position of Prime in that case? Will she still want to attack Bedrock? But my worry is needless because the Prime returns a few days later, her wagons loaded up with iron and water.

The days blur together, but the questions from citizens never fade. I am plagued by crowds that ask me when it will end—this silent storm that drags on. I give cryptic, poetic answers, the way I imagine a god would. Some townsfolk whisper when they see me. Others turn away, as if my eyes might set them aflame. Children run to me in the streets and tug at my sleeves, muttering praise, asking for blessings. By the time two moons have passed, I'm exhausted by the act. I don't know how much longer I can keep it up. Certainly not until midsummer.

"You'll do what you have to," Asher says after listening to another bout of my complaining. "You always have."

We're sitting on the roof of Prime Hall. We started meeting here a few days after Reed left for Bedrock, and we haven't stopped since. The streets are too crowded with townsfolk always shadowing me, and Cleo's isn't private enough to talk freely. Or to . . . not talk either.

But here on the roof, with only the stars for company, we can steal a few moments together. Between his work in the saltpeter beds and my time spent on wind wagon construction, these opportunities are few and precious.

Tonight there is no aurora—no ribbons or curtain of light. Just a quiet sky filled with stars. It's a small break in the string of storms, just as the documentation at Eden had described. It's happened only once since the active phase began and lasted only a day and a half. The Prime was off delivering another supply of powder to Bedrock, and the Reaper used the opportunity to run all her soldiers through training with the mag-rifles. Asher and I joined in target practice, relishing the sound of the weapons as they fired, operable in the tiny break between storms.

"I don't know," I say to Asher now. "The kids idolize me. They've got these big eyes, as round as the moon. They believe everything I tell them, and all I'm telling them is lies."

"No, you're not. The storm *will* pass. And then the General *will* fall."

"But I'm not who they think I am. I'm nobody."

He shakes his head, breathing out a quick laugh. "You are far from nobody, Delta. And not just to me," he adds before I can argue, "to everyone. The weapons you brought the Prime mean that her plan is more likely to succeed. The changes you made to Harlie's wagon allowed it to sail. The truth you found at Eden —the truth we found . . . It will reshape everything."

"You act like I did those things alone . . . Like I read the map without your brand and traveled without Harlie's wind wagon. Plus, I hate lying to the kids here. I wouldn't want Bay to think I'm some Green Goddess. I'd want her to know the truth: I'm just a girl with a brand that led to the biggest lie of all."

"We're frauds together then," he says. "Branded with false-hoods."

I crack a small smile.

"Although I feel like I'm the one with a bone-dry waterskin," he says. "You get revered as a god and I still have to turn over shit all day. Damn saltpeter beds."

I'm laughing into my palms when a flash of light erupts to the east. A yellowish cloud glows low on the horizon, flickering, fading. It's small—so tiny I may have missed it if I wasn't looking precisely in that direction—but I shoot to my feet, terrified.

It's too early. Far too early. I wait for the resounding blast to come a few heartbeats later, rolling through the night like distant thunder, but there's nothing. We're likely too far away to hear it.

"What was that?" Asher says, eyes fixed on the horizon.

"The powder," I say. "I think Reed just blew the black powder."

✦ ✦ ✦

"Could he have betrayed us?" asks Luce the Reaper.

Everyone has gathered in Prime Hall—me, Asher, the Trinity, the Prime. Tensions are high and tight, poised to snap.

"No," I say. "He wouldn't have done that. Something went wrong."

"Hold on. We don't even know if the flash of light you saw was the powder blowing," the Chemist points out. "It could have been something else."

The doors to Prime Hall fly open and Saph bursts through.

The Prime bolts to her feet.

"Apologies for the interruption," Saph says between gasps. "A falcon just flew over the wall and dropped this in the clearing." She tosses a leather pouch onto the table. The Prime and I share a glance before the woman upends the tiny bag. Two tiles topple out—one aged and worn, the other made of pale, fresh wood.

Everyone leans in for a closer look.

"That's Bedrock's symbol," the Prime says, pointing to the bird emblem on the older tile. "But what's this?"

On the newer tile is a crudely burned circle, with eight points of varying lengths branching off it.

"A star?" Asher offers.

But it's too sloppy to be a star, too haphazard. It looks more like a circle bursting apart, more like—

"It's an explosion," I say. "Reed sent this to warn us. He blew the powder—and that's what I saw flashing to the east."

"But why?" the Reaper asks.

The Prime tucks the tiles into the pouch and hands them to Saph. "Did the falcon wait for a reply?"

"She dropped the pouch, circled once, and then flew east."

"Thank you, Saph. You may return to your post."

Saph gives a curt nod and jogs off. The rest of us watch the door fall shut behind her.

"*Why* would Reed blow the powder early?" the Reaper asks again.

"Should we wait until the next trade to confirm the message?" the Chemist asks. "Or do we attack now?"

"We only have nine wind wagons ready," the Tender says. "Our goal was fifteen. And it's possible it's a trap. He could have sent that message to ensure that we sail into an ambush."

"An ambush in which the mag-rifles will be useless," Asher points out. "They won't function until the storm passes."

The Prime looks to me. "What do you think, Delta?"

I touch my lodestone through my shirt. "I'd like to believe he didn't betray us, but what I think doesn't really matter." Asher frowns. The Prime raises a brow. "If Reed betrayed us," I explain, "it means that the General now knows everything and will attack us within days. If Reed didn't betray us, something caused him to blow the powder early, and it must have been something *big*. Something that made him think this was our only chance and we'd be fools to waste it."

The Prime nods. "Exactly what I was thinking."

"But the mag-rifles," Asher repeats. "They're worthless if we go now."

"We have the blast barrels," the Prime says. "They will get us through the dam wall. And we have our archers, plus some modified rifles of our own. Delta's mag-rifles were always a bonus, not the crutch we planned to lean on."

"And they *might* work," I offer. "There wasn't an aurora tonight. No ribbons, no curtain. Nothing but stars. Like that short break in the storm when the Reaper oversaw the mag-rifle training. Reed probably noticed that break, too. He knew that if we left immediately, we'd have a window when the weapons would function. So he sent the falcon and blew the powder."

"We're going to hang everything on a maybe?" Asher says.

"The wastes are nothing but a giant maybe," I argue. "Maybe there will be enough water. Maybe a dust storm won't level my home. Maybe my pack won't die. We gamble daily, and we stay alive by finding the situations where the *maybes* lean closer to *will pan out* than *won't*. And this looks like it will work. This is as good as we're going to get."

The Prime presses her palms to the table. "Tender, wake your crew and ready the completed wagons immediately. I want the fleet moving at first light. Reaper, I know you've selected troops for the fifteen wagons, but as we'll have only nine, you need to whittle that number down. Choose carefully. Arm them with mag-rifles, but have them bring their preferred weapons of choice, too. And Chemist? Load our black powder and balls for the blast barrels. We sail at dawn."

THE VERDANT

CHAPTER FORTY-ONE

The sky is just beginning to lighten when a fleet of nine wind wagons rolls through Powder Town's main gate, one after the next, sails filled with wind, flags flapping. The wastes are bruised and purple in the early dawn. I stand at the bow of the foremost wagon, a hand on the side rail, breathing deeply.

I am dressed for battle, which isn't all that different from any day on the wastes. My scarf over my head, goggles pulled into place, and a leather jacket the Prime lent me to replace the one I sent to Bedrock with Reed, buttoned high beneath my chin. A mag-rifle is slung across my back, the shoulder strap cutting from one shoulder to my opposite hip. My bone blade is sheathed at my waist.

The Prime shouts orders from the tiller. We'll cut south of Burning Ground, avoiding the worst of the dangerous land. Then, staying well out of view of the Barrel, we'll swing north and approach Bedrock from the southeast.

To our left, the second wagon is creeping up alongside ours. Harlie shouts orders from its tiller, echoing those of the Prime. She probably shouldn't be captaining one of the vessels, not given how long the silent storms have waged and how weak they've rendered all of Powder Town's elderly. But she insisted. "They're *my* darn invention," she said that morning, cornering the Prime and the Reaper as the troops boarded the wagons. "I'm seeing them sail. I feel fine, besides. Nice break in the storms. Heart hasn't been racing since last night." How long this break will hold is another matter. When the Prime tested a mag-rifle this morning, it fired true. If the storm lull stretches a full day, we might get lucky.

Harlie's crew immediately goes to work adjusting the sails. I catch sight of Asher on the starboard side, gathering spare rope.

Behind our two wagons, the third is captained by Luce the Reaper, the fourth by Amari the Tender. Bronx the Chemist has stayed behind in Powder Town, the secret to making black powder safe in the recesses of her mind, a group of the Reaper's soldiers stationed to protect her and the town. The final five wagons are led by soldiers the Reaper selected, such as Saph, who brings up the rear.

There are about thirty of us per wagon, packed in tightly despite construction that scaled up the model we sailed to Eden. That puts our numbers just shy of three hundred. Bedrock is thousands strong, the Loyalist army at least fifteen hundred men. But we have blast barrels and mag-rifles and the element of surprise. They have only their modified rifles and the powder in their horns.

Still, the numbers make me shudder. We need everything to go right, or things will go very, very wrong. They might have already. Who knows why Reed blew the powder early—if he's safe, or even alive.

As Powder Town disappears behind us, the cheers from the town fade out as well. Cries of good luck to the Prime. Prayers that the Bringer of Life guides the fleet true. Teary farewells shouted to friends and family. Soon it is just our fleet beneath the beating sun and the expanse of waste that separates us from the battle of a lifetime.

✦ ✦ ✦

We make good time.

By midmorning we've safely bypassed Burning Ground and are just a few clicks north of Alkali Lake. We'll cut north shortly, riding the currents easy the rest of the way to Bedrock. But for now I'm at the side rail, a hand held up to shield my eyes, squinting at my childhood home in the distance.

The lake is smaller than I remember, shrunken and eaten like everything in the wastes. The banks are a dark ring around the lake itself, which is blue in its center, white with alkaline along the shallows. People must live here again — the bread I ate at Bedrock was tinged green, a sign that the soda is still harvested here — but even if they see us sailing past, we will reach Bedrock before word of our fleet can. The only thing that might hinder us is a trained Bedrock falcon with a pouch of tiles in its claws. The Reaper has sent her best archers into the crow's nest of each wagon — a small platform high up the mast that Harlie suggested adding during construction. From these lookouts, the archers scan the sky, ready to shoot down any such messenger that might soar past.

"It looks different, doesn't it?" Asher says behind me.

I startle, shocked. "Where did you come from?"

"Told Harlie to bring us close enough to your wagon so I could jump over. We'll be turning north soon. Wanted to say goodbye while I could."

"Don't do that. Saying goodbye means you think we won't make it through this."

"We might not."

"Asher."

He sighs, rubs his mouth. Over his shoulder I can see the Prime scowling at us. "The heart is unpredictable, especially in battle," she'd warned me just before we left Powder Town. "We can't risk temptation — the opportunity to put one person above the whole. This is why Luce does not sail with me. It is why Asher will not sail with you. I'm putting him on the second wagon, with Harlie. It is best for us all."

The Prime is already calling Harlie's wagon back, ordering Asher to return to his vessel. I hold up a finger, telling her just a moment.

"We should have spent every second together these last days," Asher says, taking my hands. "I should have demanded to change pillars, should have helped with construction. I didn't even ask. I accepted that all we'd get is stolen moments on the rooftop, and I never said what I should have. I think I've been afraid to, because if I say it, it will hurt that much more to lose you."

I nod, understanding.

The unknowns that lie ahead, the wind against my cheeks as we sail into battle — it makes everything sharp and clear. I can't predict the future, and I can't always protect the people who matter most. But keeping everyone at bay and locking up my heart and refusing to say what I feel won't diminish the hurt if the worst comes to pass. It will hurt anyway. It will always hurt to lose the people we love, so we might as well love them fiercely with whatever time we're given.

"I trust you, and that's why it's so hard," I say, echoing the sentiment he expressed on Harlie's wind wagon several moons ago. I shrug happily. "I trust you, I love you. They're one and the same."

"I trust you, I love you," he repeats, and lowers his face to mine. When our lips meet, the battle ahead of us feels distant, as if it will happen to different people in a different time, because this moment, now, is inescapable. The tug between us is magnetic.

"Stay strong, Delta," he says as he steps away. He whistles for Harlie, hops from our side rail to her deck once her wagon is close enough.

I can feel the tug still, his nearness calling to me. I may not believe in the gods or fate or promises foretold by the stars, but I believe in us. I believe in magnets, propelled apart, then drawn together. Like a lodestone finding north. Like the Gods' Star above the horizon. Constant, inevitable, and true.

But the thing about magnets is that they fail during silent storms. They can be turned around, forced apart. Magnets come together—or they don't. Those are the only two endings, and I'm scared to learn which is ours.

We turn northwest beneath a high sun. The fleet spreads out, forming a line that will advance on Bedrock, eventually attacking the entire eastern half of the dam. Far beyond the starboard bow, I can make out a needle on the horizon. East Tower. We'll reach the General's domain by afternoon.

The dam appears first, little more than a dark line on the horizon. As we close in on it, it takes shape, grows in height. We assemble our wagon's blast barrel. It has a rear wheel that we can push left or right on the wagon's deck, changing the aim of the projectile, but for now, the barrel points straight ahead, over the bow. Between the assembled blast barrels at the front of the vessels and the brakes being applied in the rear, the entire fleet has slowed.

"Falcon!" someone screams. It circles high above us, its wings catching sunlight. The sharpshooters unleash their arrows, but to no avail. Someone even fires a mag-rifle, until the Prime scolds them for giving away our position. The shot rings, echoing over the wastes, and the bird screeches at us before tearing north.

He'll know we're coming now.

But we're nearly there. The smudges atop the dam are taking shape. I can make out limbs. Dark Loyalist uniforms. Muffled shouting reaches us. I can't make out a single word they say, but they race atop the dam, scrambling to positions.

"Load!" the Prime yells as we glide into range.

Stone balls are shoved into the blast barrels. Flints are held at the ready.

"Steady . . ."

We roll onward.

"Steady . . ."

A swarm of arrows unfurl from Bedrock's dam, some aflame, others dark spindles against the sky. They arch up against the sun and rain back down, hitting the wastes well before us. We're safely out of range.

"Steady . . ." the Prime screams again.

We're almost close enough. Almost. A lurching movement atop the dam wall catches my eye—a giant arm swinging. "Catapults!" Someone yells in warning.

"Fire!" the Prime shouts.

"Fire!" I scream.

The word repeats across the decks. Fuses are lit. Powder crackles. The blast barrels buck at the front of each wagon, firing one stone ball after the next. The world screams with noise. I can't hear anything, not even my own pulse. Our projectiles hit the dam in succession, creating a shower of mud-packed rock.

Then the ground explodes between our wagon and Harlie's —the boulder from the Loyalist's catapult—and I'm thrown from my feet.

Rock and rubble rain down. I protect my head, stagger upright.

The Prime is screaming orders from the bow of the wagon, her lips forming the word *reload* even though my ears can't hear it yet. Dirt explodes around us, more boulders striking the earth.

"Reload!" I hear her yell, muffled and distant. The troops are already at work, shoving another stone into the blast barrel, pouring the powder.

A new batch of burning arrows rains down from the dam, still not able to reach us, but closer than before. If one of those arrows hits our powder supply . . .

"Fire!"

More blasts from the fleet. But not from our wagon. Our flint striker is splayed out on the deck, stunned, rubble from one of the catapult crashes having struck her.

385

I scramble forward and pluck the flint from her fingers. Strike it against the stone, aiming for the powder fuse. Sparks fly, miss. I strike again. The Prime gives the order to use the mag-rifles, and as our troops open fire, my ears ring endlessly. The world is so loud it's gone quiet. A spark hits true, and the powder line goes ablaze and travels into the barrel; then the weapon bucks. I clamp my hands over my ears. When I look up, a new section of the dam wall topples. Loyalists fall, screaming.

Our wagon banks to the left, the starboard side facing Bedrock, allowing our gunners better aim. We've nearly come to a halt.

"Reload!"

And we're at it again. Cramming in another ball, pouring more powder, aiming the blast barrel so we might strike true. In the madness, I've become the new flint striker. As I prepare to light the fuse line, a bullet clips the woman beside me. Blood sprays.

We're now so close to the dam wall that I can nearly make out the faces of the Loyalists along the rim. They're firing their modified rifles, using whatever powder they have left that wasn't destroyed in the explosion.

"Fire!"

I strike the flint. Another chain of blasts from our wagons.

This time, an entire section of the dam wall crumbles. Water streams into the wastes, crashing and churning. Filling ruts. Sweeping toward the Barrel by way of a channel that has long been dry. The outpouring of water slows quickly. The General must have diverted aqueducts as we approached. Maybe even closed off the upper dam entirely.

"Wagons one, three, and five, on foot!" the Prime screams, using the barrel of her mag-rifle to point at the gaping opening, where the last of the water trickles through. "Everyone else, reload! Go, go, go!"

I swing the mag-rifle around to my back and sprint for the side rail. As I vault over, I catch sight of Harlie. She's in the crow's nest of wagon two, screaming for her troop to reload their blast barrel, and when her eyes find mine, she smiles. She is glowing and triumphant, completely in her element.

I'm in freefall—mid-jump—when shadows flicker across the dirt. A new round of burning Loyalist arrows. They hit Harlie's wagon—one, two, three—and the explosion throws me sideways. I crash into the wastes, the wind knocked from my lungs. Gasping, ears ringing, disoriented, I stagger to my feet.

Harlie's wagon is flipped, broken in two, a gaping hole where the powder was stored, splintered wood burning everywhere.

CHAPTER FORTY-TWO

"Harlie!" I scream, stumbling toward the wreckage. "Asher?" I trip on a body in the dirt—no, a torso and head. The woman's face is charred and half burned off, her legs missing. I turn away, gag, then force myself forward, toward the burning shell of the wagon. The prow and a small section of the mainmast are the only parts still recognizable. "Asher!" It's just splintered wood. An inferno. An entire wagon reduced to a pyre.

He's gone.

He can't be, but he is.

I sink to my knees. Another wagon burns farther down the line. People jump from the vessel, escaping just before it explodes. I can smell burning flesh, singed hair.

Someone grabs my arm—the Prime.

"He's gone," I mutter. "Him and Harlie. Everyone on that wagon."

"Then make their deaths matter," the Prime grits out. "Make your anger into a fuel, or it will consume you."

Tugging me roughly behind her, we race toward Bedrock. Our troops are running for the dam, some of them dropping as they go, others reaching the breached section of wall and scrambling over the muddied rubble.

I follow the Prime, driven forward only by a deep-seated drive to *live*. Catapulted rocks hit behind us. Arrows strike around us. We sprint past bodies, the wastes running red. I look for Asher among the fallen and see him everywhere—torn apart, bleeding, eyes ghosted and wide.

He's gone, he's gone.

By sheer luck, we reach the dam wall. Through the settling dust I can make out the crop fields, hundreds of workers paused in a crouch, frozen with fear, or perhaps uncertain whether they should keep harvesting despite the chaos. Farther beyond, a section of the Backbone sports a gaping hole along its base— evidence of the explosion Reed set off last night. Several floors of residences are missing.

As we scramble over the dam wreckage, the Prime goes down, shouting. I expect the worst as I check her, but there's no blood, no bullet. It's her leg. She's misstepped, gotten her foot wedged between two rocks. She draws it out, cringing. When she tests the joint, drawing an invisible circle with her toes, she gasps.

"Go!" she shouts. "Find the General. End this."

"I can't leave you!"

She tucks low behind a boulder as a few bullets ping down on us. The Loyalist rifle shots are coming less frequently now, their powder supplies nearly depleted. "I can't run," she grits out, "but I can cover you. Now go, Delta, before our moment has passed." Sweat coats the Prime's dark brow, and there's a ferocity in her gaze, a drive to survive this moment, nothing more. I need to survive it, too.

I bolt to action. No second-guessing. No time for fear. I move, or I'm dead.

I clutch the mag-rifle to my chest and push to my feet, sprinting as fast as I can. Through the fields, finding the straightest path, my boots pounding the dirt. And then I see him among the workers —Asher, crouched low and taking aim, covering me along with the Prime. I nearly lose my footing at the sight of him. When I look again, he's not there. And of course he's not. I'm imagining things, my grief conjuring up ghosts.

I shake my head, force myself on.

The Prime's mag-rifle barks behind me. Over and over. Bullets ping near my feet and whiz past my shoulder. But whoever she is firing at never manages to strike true. Gasping, a stitch forming in my side, I duck beneath the Backbone's lowest overhangs, entering the storerooms and stables. To the left, destruction, the result of Reed's work. Sections of ceiling are propped up with haphazard stone and wood planks. To the right, stores of crops and water, wagons and horse stables. I find the nearest staircase and climb.

Memories come back, searing and sharp.

Corridors that are familiar.

Ghosts of moments I've already lived. Reed leading me to my room, my jacket clenched to my front as my shirt hung open in the back, my brand bared. Being led to the library, desperate for the Oracle to know how to read an unreadable map.

The halls are eerily quiet, every last Loyalist probably called to the dam wall when they saw our fleet coming.

I take another stairwell. Then another.

The General will be in his chambers, far removed from the fighting, letting others bleed for him as he hides.

When I'm nearly to the top, a shadow moves at the far end of the hall. I turn to retreat, only to see another shadow about to round a corner. Loyalists.

I duck into the nearest room, heart racing, willing the beaded curtain that serves as a door to stop swinging.

I freeze at the sound of crying.

I've stumbled into the nursery.

Bay is here. My eyes skirt over the cradles, searching even when I know I should hide.

"Please don't hurt them," a woman says. Two toddlers cling to her legs, their faces buried in her skirt. She thinks I'm the enemy. That the Powder Town forces are the ones to fear.

I shake my head, put a finger to my lips to signal silence. But she takes this the wrong way—that I will harm her if she's not quiet—and she breaks down sobbing.

Footsteps sound in the hall. There's another doorway behind the caretaker, a second room. Maybe I can hide there.

Too late, I register the sound of the beaded curtain clicking behind me. "Someone promised us that you were dead." The Loyalist wears a ram-skull mask obscuring his face—the General's Third. The last of his Four that remains, aside from Reed.

Another Loyalist ducks through the curtain. No mask. An

average solider. He moves toward the caretaker, blocking my way into the second room.

I back away from the cradles. Slowly. Until my hip hits the window ledge.

Glancing out, I can see the wreckage of battle. Our fleet is scattered beyond Bedrock's dam, half the wagons overturned, charred and burning. The others stand abandoned, Powder Town flags whipping on their masts, their crews now infiltrating the settlement through the opening blown into the dam. Aqueducts have splintered and fallen. Water spills into the wastes, flowing like blood over stone. The crop fields have descended into chaos, workers running for cover while the Reaper's troops clash with the Loyalists. The air smells like blood and fire.

"Are you gonna shoot her or not?" the Loyalist asks the Third.

"Not yet," the Third says, eyeing me through the slits in his mask. "The General may want to question her."

"I'll bring her to him," says a familiar voice. Reed, stepping through the curtains.

"You said she was dead," the Third grunts.

"She was. I burned her body."

"Then how is she here?"

Reed shrugs. "Perhaps she's gods touched after all—maybe even a god."

The Third's weapon remains on me, but he looks fearful now, as if I might turn him to ash by blinking.

"I'll take her to the General myself," Reed offers.

"No. Something's off."

Reed strides quickly across the room and grabs me by the

shoulders. His eyes are distant, and he barely looks at me as he brings his knee up, driving it into my gut. I buckle, cough, nearly hit the floor. Only Reed's grip keeps me from collapsing. When I straighten, he has a knife at my throat. I try to jerk away, but he plants the blade firmer, draws a drop of blood. Dread coils in my stomach. Have I trusted the wrong person, been betrayed again?

"I'm on your side," he says to the Third. "Let's go."

But the man's eyes are thin, suspicious. "Why would a god let you do that?"

"I'm only allowing it because I want to speak to the General," I say quickly. "Take me to him, and you will be rewarded."

"Go then," the Third says to Reed, motioning with his weapon. "Lead."

Reed shoves me into the hall, walking me in front of him now, my arms held behind my back. The Loyalists follow.

"I will slit your throat," I grit out. "I promised you."

"My throat or theirs. Your call." He presses something into my palm. The hilt of the blade he held at my neck moments earlier. I feel his hand on my back, lifting the strap of my mag-rifle.

I twist, dipping my neck to the side so he can lift the rifle strap over my head as I turn. Then I throw, the blade spiraling down the hallway. It buries into the chest of the General's Third, whose eyes go wide with shock. Reed fires twice, and both men fall. I jog to retrieve the blade. Turn back to Reed. "Just playing a part again?"

"Same as you were. That was good—your line about rewarding them." He nods at my stomach. "You okay? I tried to not have it land too hard, but it had to be convincing."

"I'll survive. What happened? You blew the powder early."

"The General sent scouts to Harlie's Hope to confirm my story. He couldn't find any evidence of a pyre—or a gunfight. I said a squall probably obscured things, but he was suspicious of me, said I should have brought the body back—or, at the very least, your head. There was talk of suspending me from the Four. Moving me to general gunner duties in the Barrel. I knew I had to act before it got away from me. There was a break in the silent storms last night, and I blew the powder while I still could. I was worried you might not understand my message."

"We pieced it together. Where's the General now?"

"His chambers. I left him guarded, but there's only three. We can take them out."

I nod, and he leads.

CHAPTER FORTY-THREE

We creep up the stairs like shadows—silent, steady. Peering around the corner, I can make out the Loyalists guarding the General's room. Eyes scanning the hall. Modified rifles held at the ready.

Reed grabs me above the elbow and totes me into view. The Loyalists' eyes twitch, first wide with surprise, then narrowing with doubt. Reed is shooting before they can act. They go down like cornstalks, cleared for replanting.

Reed jogs ahead to check them. Gives me an all-clear sign, then draws the beaded curtain aside, revealing a slice of the General's room.

We step through together.

A sitting area, remnants of lunch still on the table. A bed with a curtained canopy. A bathing area fed by a pipe that comes through the wall. The waterfall itself—channeled into this room when the General needs it. Running water for him, when his workers aren't even given a clean drink. Tapestries hang on the walls—some beaded, others woven. Propped up against one wall is a giant slab of metal, the Federation's winged bird symbol displayed proudly. On the far wall, a balcony extends into the sky.

"Where is he?" I whisper.

Reed shakes his head.

Something's not right. The room was guarded. He should be here.

That's when the metal panel falls, shoved forward into the room. It clips Reed's shoulder, and the General appears from behind it, roping an arm beneath Reed's neck as his mag-rifle goes clattering to the floor. Before the General can pull Reed firmly to his chest, my brother kicks the rifle to me.

I pick it up. Aim.

"Don't even think about it," the General snarls. He's hidden behind Reed, only half his face visible. There's no shot I can take, not without risking Reed's life in the process.

"Drop it," the General demands. "Drop it right now." He tightens his grip beneath Reed's neck, and Reed gags. The General holds a knife in his free hand, blade positioned at Reed's side, just above his hip. A simple thrust, and Reed's stomach will be pierced. A slice, and his entrails will slide from him, gutted like an animal.

"Delta, take the shot," Reed says. "Shoot through me."

The Prime's words echo back to me. *Make their deaths matter.* But this can't be what she meant. We've already sacrificed so many of our own. I can't bear to do it. Asher is already dead. Harlie, too. All the people on their wagon. Dozens more from the others. Maybe even workers in the fields.

But we're so close, and my finger twitches, knowing I should pull the trigger. What is one more death? A new life will replace Reed. Death and life—the cycle, just as Zuly promised. Reed's life for a new future. Kill Reed and kill the General with the same shot.

"You think I won't do it?" the General screams. "That I won't kill this scudding traitor? Drop it now or he's dead." He's still got one arm looped beneath Reed's neck, positioned so that his heart is behind Reed's shoulder.

Reed will be angry at me for not aiming for the General's head—for not taking them both out. But I take the only shot I can live with.

My bullet glances the meaty part of Reed's arm and buries into the General's chest. He roars, releasing Reed. My brother turns, trying to tackle him, but the General swipes with his blade, catching Reed in his already injured arm. They both collapse, Reed to his knees, the General against the wall.

I race to Reed. There is blood everywhere. His arm hangs limp, his shirt drenched. He slides his legs out from beneath him, rolls back to look at the ceiling, grimacing.

I twist back to the General, bring the rifle up again. Aim.

But before I can fire, an ear-piercing screech fills the room. Something rushes me from the balcony, a blur of dark feathers. I lose hold of the weapon as talons rake my face, and I drop to my knees. A wetness drips through my lashes.

I glance up, wincing through the pain.

The General is still braced against the wall, perhaps an arm's length from me, the falcon on his shoulder. He glares at me down the length of his blade. His leather robes are dark near the patch that reads GENERAL. There's a small hole in the material, the mag-rifle shot embedded in his skin below. The shot should be fatal, but maybe he got lucky. Maybe he'll live just long enough to take me with him.

"Why?" he asks. "Why you two?" His eyes dart to Reed.

"We're blood. The strongest of bonds." I blink rapidly. Have I lost an eye, like the Prime? I don't think so, but the pain is white-hot and my vision is wrong, obscured by red.

"I don't understand. Reed served me loyally for years, only to betray me . . . why? To claim Bedrock when the Verdant is all that will save us?" His breathing is labored, the words a trial to get out.

"You'll never understand. You wear those stars on your neck and think it makes you better than everyone else. It's not about being better. It's about being the same, being family in blood or spirit. Being willing to die for those people to secure a better future."

"Then you die for all the wrong reasons — fight for the wrong reasons." The General pushes off the wall, steps nearer. "You are weak. The water is fading. A ruler *has* to be ruthless, and I am marked as worthy. I wear the stars of our gods around my neck. I alone can save the wastes!"

"You are nobody. You will be forgotten, and no one will mourn you."

He takes another step, stopping right before me to slash his blade. Heat blooms across my cheek. I tuck my chin down instinctively, the nape of my neck exposed to him.

"And yet you kneel before me now."

I reach for my waist, painfully slowly, praying that my bowed head hides my hand from his view.

"Pledge your allegiance to me, Delta of Dead River, and I will forgive your sins. Pledge yourself to the cause, and when we find the Verdant, I will share it with your pack instead of slaughtering them."

My fingertips graze the tip of the knife handle.

"Submit to me, and call your troops off, or I will kill them myself." He grabs my chin, forces me to look at him as he says almost gleefully, "Bay first."

But by now the knife is mine. I yank it from my belt and thrust it up in one quick movement, burying the blade in the General's neck. His falcon flaps away in surprise, screeching. The General makes a guttural noise as he straightens and staggers away from me, the blade still embedded in his throat. He touches the hilt, panicked. His eyes graze my torso, as though he is trying to read my brand through my clothes.

"My map leads nowhere," I say. "Not without Asher's. But we read our brands together, and we sailed across the wastes to the remnants of the Old World, to the secret it holds."

"What ... secret?" he croaks out, the words broken by my blade.

"There is no Verdant. There are no gods. Everything you believe is a lie." I grab the hilt of my knife, twist, and pull it free. Blood gushes, coating the front of the General's leather robe and turning it deep black. He takes a single step toward me, eyes wide and haunted. Maybe he can't believe what I've told him. Maybe he's shocked by his own mortality. Maybe he's still waiting for the gods to save him when he collapses at my feet and doesn't move again.

His falcon screeches from the balcony rail, then streaks into the sky.

Reed grabs at my hand, his breath coming in uneven bursts. "You have … to blow … the horn," he grunts out, nodding to a curved instrument that hangs on the wall just inside the balcony. "One long. Two short. One … long."

I slice at Reed's shirt with my knife, cutting the sleeve off his injured arm. There's a gaping cut above his elbow, so deep I can see bone. "Oh, gods," I mutter.

"It's fine," he says, but his eyes roll, and I think he might be near passing out. "The horn … They'll surrender …"

I tear the discarded shirtsleeve, creating two long strips of cloth, and tie them both above the wound as tightly as I can manage.

"They'll surrender … to whoever … wears …" His head tips back, eyes falling shut.

"Reed? Reed!"

I press two fingers to his throat. The kick of life pumps back against my skin. He's just passed out.

I sprint to the window and grab the horn. Below, a portion of the crop fields are burning, and I wonder, briefly, if the General was right. If ruthlessness is needed to keep these wastes from imploding. If all we've done is destroy this paradise.

But crops can be regrown.

Powder Town's flags fly on the dam, and their gunshots echo through Bedrock. It's over. We've won, and the Prime will kill every last Loyalist if she has to. But if they surrender, if they stand down …

Maybe they don't deserve mercy, but maybe, as Asher said, they were just trying to survive, like the rest of us. Maybe, with limited privileges and a close watch, they too can do more than just survive.

I raise the horn to my mouth and produce the call as Reed instructed. The noise sails over Bedrock, and the General's falcon —circling above the fields—echoes my call with shrill cries.

I blow the horn again, repeating the call until the small, dark shapes of Loyalists below cease their fighting and turn toward the Backbone, raising their faces toward the General's chambers. There's shouting when they don't find him standing on the balcony. The air grows taut, the tension as sharp as the metallic scent that fills the air. They don't believe the surrender call.

They'll surrender to whoever wears . . .

I dart for the General, put a hand behind his head, and lift the star chain free. It is heavier than I imagined.

Returning to the balcony, I hoist it high, letting the chips glint in the sun. When I lower it over my head, the Loyalists drop their weapons and raise their hands, their surrender spreading across the fields like a storm.

And just like that, with all that remains of my ancestors resting against my heart, it's over.

CHAPTER FORTY-FOUR

I stagger away from the window, rip the chain off. I don't want it on me, don't want it anywhere *near* me.

"You're alive," a familiar voice says, and I freeze. This isn't real. I'm imaging him, my brain conjuring him into the world so that I don't have to be without him.

"Delta."

I turn.

It's Asher, his chest heaving with exhaustion, blood along his brow. He drops his mag-rifle and rushes to me, gathering me up, pulling my face to his. His lips taste like salt and sweat, and then they are in my hair, kissing my head, my temple, the side of my jaw. He inspects my face, muttering about falcon talons, telling me that it looks bad, but I'll be fine, that instead of a single scar through my brow, I'll now have several. The star chain dangles uselessly in my hand, chips clinking.

"You were gone," I say into his chest. "The wagon. It was burning."

"I jumped from the bow. Just before the explosion. Three of us made it off."

"Harlie?" I ask, looking up.

He shakes his head. She was in the crow's nest when the wagon was hit. I saw it happen. Still, my ribs ache, as if I'm witnessing her death a second time.

"I saw you running for Bedrock," he says, "and I followed. Helped the Prime cover you."

"It *was* you," I murmur. "I thought I imagined it."

His right ear is covered in blood. I notice that he tilts the other ear toward me, and I wonder if maybe he can't hear properly out of the injured one. I touch his face, make sure he's real. The General's stars knock between us.

"I don't like that chain," Asher says.

"Me either." I set it down beside the General's cooling body. "Here, quick. Help me with Reed."

Asher grabs him beneath the arms. I take his feet. We're approaching the curtain when the Reaper bursts through, breathless. Her nose is swollen—broken most likely—and her teeth are coated in red. "Delta, the Prime requires your immediate audience." Her gaze flicks to Reed. "Dead?"

"Unconscious. Needs a healer."

"I'll help bring him to the Tender," the Reaper says. "We're already seeing to the injured." She takes Reed's ankles from me. Asher gives me a reassuring nod, a silent promise that we'll see each other later. As soon as they have disappeared through the curtain, the beads part again and Kara the Prime enters.

Her dark skin is covered in a sheen of sweat, and if it weren't for a few traces of blood on her garments, I'd assume she'd simply been working in the sun, not fighting a battle. Her gait is uneven, her weight pressed through her uninjured foot.

"Delta of Dead River," she says heavily. "We need to discuss what happens next."

But I already know what happens. I retrieve the star chain and stand before the Prime, holding it out in offering. She frowns, pausing a moment, then eventually drops her chin. I lower the chain over her head, letting the chips fan across her chest, some rusted, others gleaming.

"You made this possible," the Prime says. "The chain could be yours."

"I don't want it. I don't know how to lead."

"I think you underestimate yourself."

I lick my lips and glance out over the balcony. Powder Town's forces are combing the fields, separating the injured from the dead. I can make out several water wagons, too, which I'm sure are filled with clean water for the ilked-up workers. Beyond the wall, crumbling where the blast barrels did damage, the wastes beckon. The horizon is a shimmering wall, rippling in the heat. A dark trail in the dry earth shows where the spilled water had begun snaking toward the Barrel. If we open the upper dam, just above the General's quarters, will that water reach the Serpent and in turn Dead River?

"You're considering going home," the Prime realizes aloud.

"No. I was thinking about home, but all the things that made it home are gone. I won't return there."

"Selfishly, I'm glad. We need you. The people believe in you."

"They believe in the gods, and that the gods have blessed me somehow, neither of which is true."

The Prime exhales. "You may not be gods touched, but you

have a godly power on your side, Delta. You have inspired my people, given the wastes hope. I'd like to offer you a place in my Trinity."

"Not much of a Trinity with four pillars."

"A Tetrad then," she amends. "You would be a trusted adviser. Delta the Goddess. A beacon of hope. A pillar of faith."

I frown. "You ask me to be the symbol of something that isn't real. Something I haven't believed in for years. It's deceitful."

"Hope is important. And the people will need hope now more than ever as we rebuild this haven, as it becomes our paradise."

She sounds just like Amory, and I can't decide if that is dangerous or necessary.

I glance at the General's body, the patch on his chest. He is so fair-skinned, I doubt he was a direct descendent of Amory. More likely Amory gave the patch to someone he trusted before passing, and it continued to be traded that way until leadership fell to the unworthy man at my feet.

"Just because someone dreamed something long ago," the Prime says, "does not mean that the dream isn't real. The gods are real to these people, Delta. They've given them a reason to keep going. We cannot take that away."

She's asking me to never speak of Amory again. To swallow the truth. To let the people believe that the Verdant has always been here, in Bedrock. That after years of prayer and servitude, the gods saw fit to deliver this paradise to the deserving people.

"The General said the waterfall was running dry," I tell the Prime. "I don't know how many years it has left, how long this Verdant will last."

"All the more reason for you to stay. Help me rebuild this city. Help me scout above the Backbone and survey the water supply. If it is dwindling, there must be a reason why. Be a part of something bigger than yourself, Delta. After all, isn't that what this has always been about? Returning to your pack. And not just to survive a new dawn together, but to live. Truly *live*."

She's right. This was always about saving my pack, securing a better future for Bay. And she might have it now. She could grow up in a world that is just, where hardships won't outweigh comforts. She will know safety. She will still know loss, because it is truly as Zuly said—the cycle, souls dying, others being born. But we are standing on the cusp of a future where those deaths might only be from illness or old age. Bad luck. No more starvation. No more raids. No more living just to survive.

I want this for her—for everyone on the wastes. I'm just afraid of having a title, as the Prime proposes. I'm afraid of letting people down.

But I won't be doing it alone.

"No, you won't," the Prime says, and I realize I've said the last bit out loud. "You'll have me, the rest of my Trinity, Bay, Asher, your pack, even that Loyalist you're attached to, if he makes it."

"We're blood," I remind her.

"Yes, the strongest of all bonds." She holds out a hand. "So what do you say, Goddess? Will you be my fourth pillar?"

It seems fitting in a way, the General and his Four falling so a new, more worthy ruler and tetrad can rise.

"On one condition," I say finally. "I don't want goddess or deity or anything divine in my title. I will stand for the people, for the truths *they* decide to believe. If they ask me about the gods, if they want to know why they truly abandoned us, I will not lie. But if they choose to keep their faith in the stars, I will not discourage them. Hope is important, but so is the truth. Amory never gave people a chance to choose."

The Prime considers this a moment. "Delta the Verity," she amends. "A protector of the truth. A champion of our history and beliefs."

"Deal." I clasp her forearm, she clasps mine, and we shake, forging a new future.

✦ ✦ ✦

The rest of the afternoon is a frenzy of activity. Clearing the fields and putting out fires and seeing to pyres for the deceased. The smell of smoke lingers. The Loyalists took the worse losses, but Powder Town wasn't without theirs. Harlie's broken body is found on the wastes, an arrow in her chest. The Tender said that she likely died quickly, her neck snapping in the fall from the crow's nest. She was found on her back, her face turned toward the sky.

I like to think that she was happy in those final moments before she fell. Her life's creation worked, and it brought about the demise of a monster. I hope she knew this.

The dam is repaired in a haphazard manner, if only to keep the Barrel from flooding. The upper dam will be opened soon, in order to bring water to all citizens, but too much excess water entering the wastes could choke the narrow channel, taking out the homes and businesses that have grown roots there. The Prime has a plan for water distribution, or so she claims, but for now the focus is on caring for the injured and helping the General's workers get clean from sleeping ilk. I'm there as carts with fresh water roll through the fields, and I can see disappointment glance their features. Already, they miss the drug.

I race through the roads, searching for my pack among the crowds and freezing when I find them. They're all here — everyone but Vee, who is probably still stationed in the Barrel as a spy. They look haggard — thinner than when I left, darker from the sun, and on the verge of collapse. Pewter somehow appears both older *and* younger, her shoulders hunched from the burden of her labors but her eyes still wide and childish. I pull her into a hug. I don't think I've ever cried in front of anyone in my pack, but I come undone. She's here, in my arms. I made it back to them. We're going to be okay.

"Something's wrong with the water," she tells me, seemingly oblivious to my tears.

I wipe them away. "It's clean. Keep drinking. You'll feel better in a few days."

"I want the regular stuff," she argues. "Why are you keeping it from us?"

"Pewter, please."

"You're not being loyal to the cause. You're going to condemn us!" She grabs the ladle I'm trying to force on her and throws it across a row of crops, then shouts to the others. "Don't drink what they give you. It's bad! Spoiled!"

"It's clean," I insist. "What you've all been drinking is the bad stuff. Drugged."

Pewter shoves me, but she's so weak she ends up clutching her wrist to her chest and fleeing into the fields. Saph catches her a few rows over, drapes a blanket over her shoulders, and walks her, sobbing, to a wagon where she can sit.

"It's good—clean," I repeat to my pack and the other workers still watching me. I retrieve the ladle and scoop a drink from the wagon, sampling it before them. "How often did you see the Loyalists drink the water they gave you?" Foreheads wrinkle with thought. "It will be hard for a few days, I won't deny that. But this will make you well."

Alder shoulders through the crowd, staggers up to me. Her brown hair, streaked with white, hangs in strings. She pauses before me, peering at my face. "Are you gods touched? You look familiar."

"No. There are no more gods touched among us. I am Delta the Verity, but you know me as Delta of Dead River."

A glimmer flashes in her eyes—recognition. "Delta," she says softly, and cups my cheeks. "Where have you been, child?"

"Everywhere on the wastes, it feels like. And all to get back here."

Alder kisses my forehead softly and walks to the wagon. Retrieves a fresh ladle of water. Drinks swiftly.

The crowd watches.

"Is it good?" someone asks.

Alder takes another sip. "It is plain, but yes. Delta the Verity drinks it, so it must be. She wields the truth."

The group rushes to join her.

✦ ✦ ✦

That evening, ribbons of light paint the northern horizon, a silent storm building. By tomorrow the mag-rifles will no longer work.

The Prime sends the Reaper to salvage whatever black powder remains from our wind wagons. Most of the Loyalists have stepped down willingly, ready to serve the Prime, and those who haven't are already locked up and detained. Still, she wants powder on hand, and she has confiscated all the modified rifles for the Reaper's troops. Saph is sent on horseback to Powder Town with a message to deliver several wagons of powder to Bedrock as soon as possible.

I'm exhausted from the day, which feels like it's been years long, but there is something I have to do before I rest. I head to the nursery.

The same caretaker who thought me a threat earlier now shows me to a sunken area of the room, where a baby lies on her back, playing with a wooden rattle.

There is no way this child is Bay. She's huge. The backs of her hands have dimples and her legs are chunky and plump. There is not one crease in her arm when she bends her elbow, but several. She is fat and healthy and so much bigger than the newborn I left behind. I hadn't realized she would change this much, so quickly. I wonder, briefly, if it's even her, but then she turns her face toward me and I'm looking into Indie's eyes. A lump forms in my throat.

"Hi, Bay," I say, crouching beside her.

Her face changes, uncertain, and she begins to cry. The caretaker lifts her, and she turns into the woman's chest, wailing.

She doesn't recognize me. She has no clue who I am. Of course she doesn't. She's so young, and the moons I've been gone have been a lifetime to her. The woman bounces the baby lightly in her arms until the crying turns to whimpering, then happy cooing.

"You've gotten so big," I tell her. She risks another glance my way, eyes wide. "I'm not leaving you again. We're joined. I'm the delta and you're the bay, remember? I lead to you." I reach out a pinkie, and Bay takes it cautiously, her tiny fingers wrapping around mine. They are still so small, yet so much larger than the last time she took my hand like this.

"Do you want to try again?" the woman asks, glancing at my arms. I nod, and she passes Bay to me. She squirms a little, whimpers lightly. But I bob her in my arms and sing the lullaby I sang when we traveled the wastes together days after her birth. She quiets, transfixed, her wide eyes staring up at me. When I finish singing, she smiles, and I feel something crack open in my heart —a crack that isn't damaging, but life-giving. Like something is emerging from a shell, being born.

Her little smile fills me with purpose, and I know that if she had smiled like this as a newborn—if she'd been able to—I never would have said half the things I did. I never would have said anything. I would have melted into a puddle in the dirt, turned useless by this small human. I didn't know it was possible to feel this way: to be willing to give anything for someone else, to love someone so deeply even when they know nothing about love. It's different from the way I love Asher, the way I loved my mother or my pack. It's a bit like how I loved Indie, but even that was different.

This is . . .

I suck my lip to keep from crying.

I understand, finally, why mothers put up with it all. Why they give so much of themselves.

I will do anything for Bay.

I will pull the stars from the sky.

I will give her the world.

And here we are, in the green paradise we've always dreamed of, her entire life unfurling before her, full of possibility.

CHAPTER FORTY-FIVE

The days pass.

I sit in countless meetings as part of the Tetrad. We discuss jobs, responsibilities, defense, agriculture, production, water. Relations with the Barrel. Relations with all settlements throughout the wastes. How to utilize the falcons for communication. How to train more falcons. How to extend that communication beyond simple tiles.

The Prime asks me to speak with the Oracle about it.

"Can anyone be taught how to read?" I ask her as I enter the library.

"Good to see you too, Delta of Dead River."

"It's Delta the Verity now."

"So I've heard." She nods at the chair beside her, inviting me in. "And yes. It is simply a matter of learning the Old World symbols, all twenty-six of them, each with their own unique sound. Some of these letters even have multiple sounds, depending on the letter they follow."

"It sounds confusing."

She smiles. "At first, perhaps. But once mastered, it is second nature. Here, look." She drags her twig through the tray of wet earth.

DELTA

"This is your name," she says.

"The *E* was on my brand." I stare at the strange string of letters that make up my entire existence. I take the stick from her and write *E D E N* in the dirt. "What does this say?"

"Eden." She frowns. "What does it mean?"

"Two *E*s," I say, ignoring her question. "But they make different sounds."

"Yes, *ee* or *eh*."

"And that letter that starts my name; it makes a *duh* sound."

"*D*," the Oracle says, nodding. "This is the start, Delta. With enough practice, you could be reading within a few moons. Writing, too."

I look at the *T* in my name, the *A*. I know their sounds, too, just from knowing how to pronounce my name. Flurries fill my chest.

This can be taught to anyone. To Bay, to all the children in the nursery, to the Prime and the Tetrad and every person in Bedrock. This isn't for the mythical gods touched. We could all do this. Record our histories. Communicate by written note. I fold the news away to report to the Prime later.

"Can you show me how to write *Bay*?" I ask the Oracle.

She draws the name in the dirt. It is even more beautiful than mine.

✦ ✦ ✦

From the ashes of conflict, Bedrock reshapes itself. The Prime renames it Verdant, and a set of new flags fly from the dam wall

—pale fabric marked by a symbol for the settlement: a drop of water positioned inside a teardrop-shaped leaf. Blue. Green. Life.

I visit Reed when I can (he's healing well), eat meals with Asher when schedules allow it (rarely), and spend the bulk of my time sitting in meetings with the Tetrad. Our talks become overwhelmingly focused on water. How long will the waterfall flow through the settlement? How much of it can we safely share with those beyond our walls? What is causing the supply to dwindle?

The Prime asks me to pull together a scouting party. I'm to travel above the Backbone, survey the state of the river that feeds the Verdant, and report back with my findings. When I mention that this task seems more fitting for the Tender or the Reaper, she bats a hand at me. "I need the truth of this world—what lies above the Backbone, what secrets the river holds. That is a job for the Verity."

I'm starting to wonder if I should have accepted the title of Goddess. At least then I would be firmly fixed to matters of religion.

"With that reasoning, you could have me heading up practically any task," I grumble.

"I trust you with this, Delta," she says, "and my Reaper is still far too busy here with security and training new troops."

I nod, accepting the mission. "Do you want to approve my team before we head out?"

"If you are confident in your choices, so am I."

"When should we leave?"

She sighs heavily. "I wish I could say that you could wait for the active period of this solar cycle to pass, but that will be many moons still, and we need answers now. Depart as soon as you're ready. I'll see to it that the Reaper arms your team with plenty of black powder and modified rifles. Until we meet again, Verity."

We shake hands in parting, and I make for Reed's chambers. When I arrive, the room is empty. After asking around, I hear that he's returned to the infirmary, and I break into a run, panicked.

Even ten days after the battle, the place still smells like blood and decay. I find where they're holding him and push through a sheer curtain, revealing his bed.

"Hey," he says, smiling, and I exhale heavily.

"You weren't in your room, and I panicked and—"

I freeze as he sits up and the blanket falls to reveal his injury. His arm has been severed below the shoulder, cauterized and bandaged. The last I saw him, he was healing well. He had two arms. The stitches kept pulling, and there was a bit more puss than the Tender had hoped for, but he'd been dismissed back to his room.

"Reed, I'm so sorry. I didn't know."

"It was just yesterday," he says.

"Still. No one told me. I should have come by."

"I'm here. Probably wouldn't be if you hadn't applied that tourniquet, so don't go beating yourself up."

I can't stop staring at his arm. How it's just . . . gone. "What happened?"

"The wound got infected. Skin changing strange colors. The Tender decided it was best to take my arm before it spread to my heart."

I swallow, taking in this information. "How long until you're out of here?"

"Any day now."

"Good. That's good. I'm running a scouting trip above the Backbone and I want you with me. If you feel up to it."

He frowns. "Don't you think I'll slow you down?"

"Kara the Prime is blind in one eye. Bronx the Chemist can't set foot comfortably in the sun. You have one arm." I shrug. "So long as you feel up to it, I don't see why I wouldn't want you."

He nods. "I'll let you know."

"Thanks, brother."

✦ ✦ ✦

The night before I'm set to leave, I find Asher in his room. He's standing at the window, gazing out over Verdant, his forearms resting on the sill.

"You're not packing," I say.

He glances over his shoulder, frowns. "You never asked me to come."

"I thought it went without saying."

He rolls his eyes. "You are the Verity now. I don't assume anything."

"If I'm the Verity, so are you. We're two halves of a whole, right? We both have the truth marked on our backs."

He smirks. "I'm not sure the Prime would agree with that, but I like the sentiment, Verity."

I groan. "Don't call me that. I can handle it when the others do, but not you." A pause. "Did you decide which pillar you'll serve here? It's not like there are saltpeter beds around."

"The Chemist would love me to move back to Powder Town to man them. I hear she left this morning, and I'm shocked that she didn't drag me with her."

I smirk. We all watched the Chemist ride off with a small detail at dawn. She's been running Powder Town and overseeing production since the battle, but the Prime had called for her a few days ago and she made the trip to Bedrock for some meetings. I gave her a message when she left—told her to send Clay to us the next time she sees him. He has a daughter to meet.

"The Chemist could request you any time," I tease. "Especially once we train more falcons."

Asher angles toward me. He touches the scar on my brow, the three newer ones from the General's falcon. "I thought it would be obvious," he says softly, "which pillar I want to serve." His lips brush mine, and he whispers, "I want nothing more than to please the Verity." He kisses my neck, nips my ear. "What can I do? Tell me, and I'll do it right now."

I push him away, laughing. "What did I say about that name?" He captures my wrists and we collapse onto the bed in a fit of playful wrestling that lengthens, slows.

Tomorrow I have to leave again, venture into the unknown. There's no guarantee that I'll see another year, or five, or fifty, because that's life—an uncertain path, a continuous cycle that leads to death and back again.

But I have this moment now, with Asher, and I'll steal an hour or two with Bay at dawn before we leave. I have a brother who will travel with me, and a pack that will wait for me to return, and a band of sisters not in blood, but in spirit, who I will follow anywhere. Women who inspire me to be more than I ever dreamed.

The ease with which we all fit together fills my heart.

I trust these people with my life. I trust them with my soul.

All this time, I realize, I was only trying to find them. They are my Verdant, my green place, my paradise among the desert.

The map always led to them.

ACKNOWLEDGMENTS

This book would not exist without my dear friend Jodi Meadows, who listened when I needed to brainstorm, provided suggestions when I was stuck, and cheered me on when I lost confidence. Jodi, I am deeply grateful.

Thanks also to my agent, Sara Crowe, and the team at Pippin Properties, as well as my editor, Kate O'Sullivan, and all the wonderful book champions at HMH who touched this story during its journey to publication. Matt Griffin and Virginia Allyn, thank you for the incredible cover art and stunning map, respectively.

To my writing friends (you know who you are), thanks for your support and camaraderie. This is a strange yet wonderful career, and it's a blessing to have friends to discuss all the highs and lows with.

I spent a lot of the brainstorming phase for this novel talking aloud, bouncing worldbuilding ideas off my husband as I obsessed over tiny details. Rob, thank you for tolerating me. Kids, thanks for "tolerating" when I had to work. (We can discuss what those quotation marks imply when you're a bit older.) You are *my* Verdant, my green place, my paradise among the desert. Mommy loves you, always and forever.

And last, to you, the reader: Thank you for spending some time with my words. You are the reason I have this job and that is never lost on me.